Y0-AGO-485

grace grows

grace grows

SHELLE SUMNERS

with songs by Lee Morgan

St. Martin's Griffin ✦ New York

This is a work of fiction. All of the characters, organizations, and events portrayed in this novel are either products of the author's imagination or are used fictitiously.

GRACE GROWS. Copyright © 2012 by Shelle Sumners. All rights reserved. Printed in the United States of America. For information, address St. Martin's Press, 175 Fifth Avenue, New York, N.Y. 10010.

Design by Anna Gorovoy

ISBN 978-1-62090-669-9

for my husband and daughter,
who take me to love school every day

HOW TYLER WILKIE WRECKED MY LIFE
and what I thought I'd do about it
an exploratory memoir

Because you're going about your life—you get up, brush your teeth, spill your coffee, go to work. Then one day everything changes. And how are you supposed to make sense of it all?

the first autumn

day zero: my unravelment begins
(unravelment: is that a word?)

The first time I met Tyler Wilkie, I was dressed like a call girl.

By pure, titillating coincidence, my strategy for work that day was cleavage. The big guns. Or, in my case, the medium, B-verging-on-C ones. Because yesterday, having dressed like a Mennonite librarian for our meeting with the textbook lobbyists from Texas, I'd sat there mute and limp while imagination was besieged by the powers of ignorance.

Forbes and Delilah Webber loved my blouse with the Peter Pan collar. Delilah called me "the sweetest little thing" and "precious." They promised to recommend our middle school *Teen Health* textbook for statewide adoption if we agreed to:

a) Remove all information regarding condoms.

and

b) Change the word *imagine* to *suppose*. *Imagine* being "too like the word *magic*—it might upset some people."

They also asked us to get them orchestra seats to *The Lion King*.

After the meeting, I begged my boss to refuse the Webbers. My traitorous coeditor Edward, who happens to be from Texas, capitulated and offered to do the edits, reminding me that we "don't mess with Texas" and its four-hundred-million-dollar book-buying budget.

We were meeting with the Webbers again today, to show them the changes. I didn't know what I could do to stop the anti-imagine machine. I had tried to come up with a plan all the sleepless night, and I had nothing. This ship was going to sink, but I decided that I, their "sweetest little thing," could at least try to look taller going down. I could project confidence and strength. Defiance. Sex. A tall, cruel, European dominatrix vibe.

It was so not me.

I donned the black pin-striped suit my mother gave me for Christmas two years ago, which I have worn exactly once. To a funeral. Only I hiked the skirt up a couple inches and wore my push-up bra. Found an ancient pair of stockings in the back of my drawer. Then I squeezed into the black, four-inch-stiletto-heeled, pointy-toed shoes I bought on sale at Lord & Taylor to go with the suit. I pulled my hair into a low, severe knot, and put on mascara and lipstick. Red.

I pulled on my raincoat and grabbed an umbrella, my laptop, and the twenty-pound green leather shoulder bag that contained All I Might Conceivably Need, which might include (but was not limited to):

keys
wallet
cell

agenda
lip balm
hairbrush
hair band
big hair clip
tissues
book (*Lolita*, it happened)
iPod
bottle of water
bag of raw cashews
70% dark chocolate bar
apple
black pen
red pencil
black Sharpie
red cardigan sweater
tacky vinyl zipper bag with photo of fuzzy kitten on it,
    stocked with:
        various-sized Band-Aids
        small tube of antibiotic ointment
        antihistamine and antidiarrheal tablets
        Tylenol
        Tylenol with caffeine
        Tylenol with codeine
        Advil
        nail file
        tampons
        water lily oil
        hand lotion
        travel-size Shower Fresh Secret

and:

        tea light and matches
        mini-flashlight

> tiny fold-up scissors with needle and black thread
> ginger tea bags
> earplugs
> pocket copy of Strunk and White's *The Elements of Style*, for grammatical emergencies (memorized, but sometimes a tired mind becomes uncertain)

Oh, and one more thing: the silver pocket angel Edward gave me, wedged deep into a rip in the lining of the bag.

Thus aggressively attired and equipped for any eventuality, I headed down the three flights of stairs to the lobby.

Big dogs, barking.

I came around the last bend in the stairwell and saw them—our across-the-hall-neighbor Sylvia's prize-winning giant schnauzers—tugging at a guy who sat at the bottom of the steps with their sparkly leashes wrapped around his hand. He heard me coming and moved to one side, murmuring "sorry," as I stepped carefully around him.

When I reached the door, God help me, I looked back. Might as well have gone ahead and turned to salt.

He was rubbing his face.

"Everything okay?" I chirped, willing him to say yes so I could go. The dogs shifted their Batman-like ears toward me.

"Uh, not really. She left me a note." He spoke with a slightly countryish kind of drawl that reminded me, unpleasantly, of the Webbers. "Blitzen and uh . . . Bismarck here have just been groomed for a show and I'm not supposed to get their feet wet."

Clearly Sylvia was even more insane than I had suspected. And the guy looked pathetically bleak.

"Hold on," I said, and went back upstairs. I grabbed a cheap umbrella from the pile of extras in our hall closet and a box of zipper bags from the kitchen, and rooted around in our junk drawer until I came up with an assortment of rubber bands and a roll of masking tape.

I tiptoed back downstairs (the shoes), sat next to the guy, and bagged one of Blitzen's meticulously pedicured paws while she tickled my neck with her beard.

Once I had just about successfully finished the first foot, I looked to see if the guy was watching and learning.

He lifted his eyes from my chest and said, "Oh hey, thanks!" He grabbed a bag and got busy on Bismarck.

It took the two of us about six minutes to double-bag all eight paws. Then I lurched back up en pointe, belted my raincoat firmly across my waist, and picked up my laptop bag. The guy stood too, handed me Big Green, and startled me with a smile that was blindingly sweet. I blinked and lost my grip on the strap, but he caught it and resettled the purse firmly on my shoulder.

"Thanks, you really saved me," he said.

I held out the umbrella. "Here, take this. I think the rain's just about stopped for now, but you might need it later."

He smiled *the smile* again and tucked the umbrella in the pocket of his army/navy outerwear.

"I'll bring it back to you," he said. "What's your apartment number?"

I waved a hand. "Don't worry about it."

He took up the dogs' leashes and pushed the door open for me. Blitzen and Bismarck pulled him toward the park and I tippy-toed double time in the other direction, toward the subway.

"Hey!" I heard him call out.

I turned around. He was at the other end of the block. He mouthed the words *thank you*.

I smiled and shrugged. No big deal.

day zero continues
and I encounter my doom, again

Damn. The Webbers canceled the meeting so they could go on a Hudson River breakfast cruise. They promised their approval over the phone, and I had dressed like one of Robert Palmer's "Addicted to Love" video girls for absolutely no reason.

Ed came out of his office and saw me limping down the hallway. The shoes were killing me. "Oh, the fashion fuck-you!" he said. "Too bad they canceled, it almost works."

"What's wrong with it?" I asked.

"You're about a foot too short. Not even a little intimidating."

"And?"

"Your blacks don't match. The suit is blue-black and the stockings are green-black."

"Hm."

"And I can see the lines of your granny panties."

"They're bikinis."

"And they shouldn't *be* there." He patted my shoulder. "Grace, stick to your strengths."

I was still mad several hours later when Edward and I went out for dinner at Herman's Piano Bar. It was our Tuesday thing. My friend Peg would join us when she wasn't working on a show, but now she was assistant stage manager of the new Broadway musical *Tie Me Up! Tie Me Down!*, with Antonio Banderas reprising his movie role. It was a big hit, so Peg wouldn't be with us at Herman's for a while.

I dragged a large fragment of greasy onion ring through the puddle of ranch dressing and ketchup on my plate. "So what is wrong with you Texas people, anyway?"

He looked at me darkly. "Are you associating me with those yahoos?"

"You're from Houston. So are they."

"And am I like them?"

No. He wasn't, at all. It gave me hope that there were other sane Texans. "Okay, I'll shut up," I said.

"Yes, I believe you will!" he pretty much shouted. The sour was kicking in.

I slid his glass away. "Eat more, drink less."

Edward barked his distinctive, walruslike bellow of a laugh, and the woman sitting on the other side of him turned around and shushed us. "We're trying to hear the singer!" she hissed.

Ed and I looked at each other. Who listens to the singer?

Apparently everyone. The room had actually gotten quiet; hardly anyone was talking.

The voice . . . how to describe it? *Piercingly soulful* might be a start. He was singing a ballad I'd never heard before, and the words—something about trying to find home—combined with the quality of his voice, put a knot in my stomach. But not necessarily in a bad way. More in a *Jesus Christ, who is that making me feel this way?* way.

I stood on the rungs of my barstool and balanced against Ed's shoulder so I could get a look at the singer. He was hunched over the keyboard, mouth on the microphone, eyes closed, moving his body the same sinuous way his voice was moving—all over the place, but never out of control.

He finished the song and people clapped. A lot. And said woo-hoo! And whistled. He looked out at us all, a little surprised, it seemed. People quieted down and he launched into another song.

Ed looked at me. "He's amazing."

"I know that guy!" I said, not quite believing it myself.

He wasn't wearing the knit cap, and he had a terrible haircut—too short and choppy—but it was definitely him.

The dog walker.

He finished his allotted second song and I watched him squeeze through the crowd. He stopped a few times to shake an offered hand or listen attentively to a comment, but finally made it to the end of the bar, several people down from me. The next performer was up and talking into the mic, so the bartender had to speak loudly while he was pulling the guy a beer.

Bartender: You wrote those songs, man?
Dog Walker: Yeah.
Bartender: Awesome. You have more?
Dog Walker: Lots more.

The bartender leaned in closer to say something else and I lost the thread. I waited till they finished talking and told Edward I'd be back in a minute.

On approach, I studied him more closely than I had this morning. He was pale, rather gawky, all Adam's apple and bad haircut. A kid, really.

I reached up and tapped him on the shoulder. He turned.

"Hi," I said.

"Hey!" he said. "It's you!"

He gave me that radiant smile and the gawk factor inexplicably transferred from him to me. Suddenly he was grace, and I wasn't.

"You're shorter than this morning," he said.

"Oh, yes." My face was getting warm. Annoying! "I had on those tall shoes."

"Yeah, they were pointy."

"Yes, I was trying to—well, I don't usually dress like that."

He nodded. "It looked hot, but painful."

"What's your name?" I asked.

"Tyler Wilkie." He definitely had a drawl. "What's yours?"

"Grace. Barnum."

He lit up. "Like the circus?"

"Exactly."

"Cool."

We looked at each other and it occurred to me that he was autumn-colored. Auburn hair. Hazel eyes. He tilted his head and the corner of his mouth turned up, and I became aware that it was time to go. Edward had a late date and would want to leave. And Steven, my boyfriend, was probably home from work by now.

"Nice to meet you again, Tyler. I liked your singing."

"Thank you, Grace," he said courteously.

I turned to leave, but he tugged on my sleeve. "Your eyes are this color."

I glanced down at my sweater. Yes, pretty close. Bluish gray.

"And your face is shaped like a heart," he added.

How charmingly random! "Oh, is it?"

"Yeah. I noticed it this morning." His finger traced the air, following the curve of my cheek.

"Well, I really have to go now."

He shoved his hands into his pockets. "Okay, Grace Barnum. See ya."

I huddled under Ed's arm as we headed down Columbus. The temperature must have dropped ten degrees since the morning.

"I don't feel good about the health book, Ed. What if we were teenagers in Texas?"

"I was."

"And how did you learn about condoms?"

Ed shrugged. "Word of mouth?"

"It just doesn't make any sense. They don't want people to have abortions, but they don't want them to learn how to prevent pregnancy!"

"Baby girl, it drives me right up the wall too."

"And *imagine*! I mean . . . *imagine*? How can we participate in this travesty?"

"I hear you."

"And Bill. What is it with him? He's so deadpan. Doesn't he *feel*?"

"He's just doing his job."

"It's disgusting."

"If you're not careful with Bill he'll transfer you to the New Jersey office. And I would miss you."

I sighed. "It doesn't feel good, Ed."

"Listen. It would be nice to try to save the children, but first we have to put the oxygen mask on ourselves."

"Huh?"

"You know, when you're on a plane and they give you those instructions—"

"Boy, you are really bugging me."

"It's just a fact, Grace. We can't fix everything."

His complacency was driving me crazy. But Edward grew up a gay black kid in Texas in the late seventies, and probably had a lifetime of sublimating injustices and sad things he couldn't change. You'd think I'd be that way, too, from some of the hard stuff in my childhood. But I grew up watching my mother forge platinum out of rust. It was going to take me a while to accept this *imagine* thing.

We said good-bye at the corner of Seventy-ninth and Columbus.

"Grace!"

I turned around. It was Tyler Wilkie, half a block behind me. I waited till he caught up.

"Hey," I said.

"Hey." He was wearing his fatigue jacket and knit cap, and had a canvas guitar case strapped to his back. "Are you headed home?"

I nodded.

"You shouldn't go alone," he said. "I'll walk you."

"Thank you, but that's really not necessary," I said.

"I'm going this way anyway."

I shrugged and started walking.

He caught up. I looked at him sideways. "You play the guitar, too?"

"Yeah. Mostly guitar. I play piano if they have one."

I could see our breath. I wound my wool scarf around my neck an extra rotation and pulled it up over my ears. "Are you from Texas?"

He laughed. "No!"

"Then where?"

"The Poconos. Monroe County. Why?"

"You just sound kind of . . . Southern, or countryish, or something."

"Maybe you're mixing up small-town Pennsylvania with Southern."

"Yeah, I guess so. And now you live in the city?"

"Yes, ma'am, for six whole days." I looked up at him, probably kind of sharply, and he smiled. "You're by far the nicest person I've met."

I laughed. "Six days? Are you serious?"

"Dead serious."

"Why'd you come?"

"To see if I can get people to listen to my music. Maybe get some paying gigs." He looked at me. "How long do you think I should give it?"

"Gosh, I have no idea. . . ." How old could he be? Nineteen? "Maybe you should go to college first."

"I tried that already."

"Oh? Where'd you go?"

"Community college. For a year. I didn't like it."

"Well . . . maybe it just wasn't the right school?"

He shook his head. "School's not for me. Not now, anyway."

The light changed as we came to the corner of Amsterdam and we crossed the street. I couldn't imagine taking such a gamble, moving to Manhattan with no education.

"Well, I hope it all works out," I said. "You're certainly very talented."

"Thank you."

"You'll probably need to give it some time."

"I been thinking five years, and then I'll know."

"Oh, yes." I felt somewhat more cheerful for him. "And you'll still be young, you can go back to school."

"I won't be that young," he laughed. "I'm twenty-eight."

Twenty-eight? He couldn't be my age, with that boy face. "I'm the same age," I said. "For some reason, I thought you were a lot younger."

"Really?" he said. "I figured we were about the same, or maybe I was older. When's your birthday?"

Turned out he was older. By two months.

We came to Broadway and before the walk signal came on he took my hand and pulled me into the crosswalk. Halfway across we had to dash to the corner to miss being tagged by a homicidal taxi driver. It didn't bode well for Tyler Wilkie surviving five more days, let alone five years.

My building was just a couple of blocks up. "I'll be fine from here. Thank you."

"Okay," he said, blowing into his cupped hands and pulling his collar up around his ears.

"Where do you live?" I asked.

"Forty-seventh, between Ninth and Tenth."

"You can get the train right there." I pointed to the subway entrance across the street.

"Oh yeah, thanks. Well, 'bye, Grace." He leaned down. To my embarrassment I reflexively leaned away, and the kiss he must have been aiming at my cheek landed on the tip of my nose. We both laughed.

"'Bye. Thank you." I headed across Seventy-ninth.

Halfway up the block I peeked back over my shoulder. He had bypassed the subway and was walking briskly down Broadway, head down, hands tucked under his arms.

Steven was on the couch, watching *The Matrix*. He probably had a rough day. He rewatched *The Matrix* the way I rewatched *Chocolat*. And how about that Carrie Ann Moss!

"How long have you been home?" I asked, shedding my coat.

"A couple hours."

Steven is a big, bearlike guy, six-four. Solid. Gentle, with kind blue eyes. I sometimes jokingly called him Even Steven.

I kissed him lightly on the cheek and went to bed. I didn't want to disturb him in the middle of the "I know kung fu!" scene; it was probably recalibrating his entire outlook on life.

On Friday morning I stepped out the door directly onto something bulky lying on the doormat. My umbrella, it turned out, with a single pink gerbera daisy rubber-banded to it and a folded piece of notebook paper tucked underneath. The spelling was appalling, but the words were nice.

Grace!
Here is your umbrela. You rock for letting me use it! It is great
to be treated like a human being by someone in this city. I got
another job besides dogwalking. Come on over to the cafe Sofiya
sometime and I'll slip you a cappechino!
  Love,
  Tyler Graham Wilkie
  Cell #5702439134

I folded the letter back up, dug *Lolita* out of Big Green, and tucked it between the pages.

lunch with Julia
and my subsequent urge for cloistration

Once a month on a Friday my mother comes to town to buy me lunch and direct my life. She hasn't lived in the city for twenty years, so she also uses our lunch meetings as an excuse to check out new restaurants. Yesterday I received e-mail instructions to meet her at a Malaysian place in midtown, close to my work.

I am a punctual person; I always arrive on time, if not a little early. But I will never arrive earlier than Julia Barnum.

When I joined her at the table there was already a milky Thai iced tea sweating at my place setting. She stood and enveloped me in the smell of freesia and expensive hair product. She works out daily and her embrace is wiry; she has beaten me at arm wrestling twice. We sat and unfolded our napkins.

"Has something bad happened?" She anxiously pushed coppery bangs out of her face.

"No!" I said. "Why do you always ask me that?"

"You always look a little tragic when I see you. I'm starting to think I should take it personally."

Best not to overdeny. I smiled and sipped my tea. "Everything's fine."

She perused the menu. "You need to cut your hair, don't you think?"

"Yes," I agreed.

"What looks good?" she asked.

"The ginger chicken?"

"Don't you want to try something spicy? Maybe the beef in chili sauce?"

"Okay, sounds good."

"Or how about something with tofu?"

"That will be fine."

She slapped down her menu. "Stop agreeing with me!"

My mom is a county prosecutor in Trenton, New Jersey. She is crafty and convincing and inexhaustibly determined to win, and no matter what I choose from the menu, she'll try to talk me into something else just for kicks.

"Sorry," I shrugged.

She rolled her eyes and ordered for us when the waiter came.

"So, how is Steven?" She pushed her hair back again, and her silver bracelets jingled. My mother is beautiful, fifty going on thirty, always flawlessly turned out, whether dressed to prosecute, or as today, to persecute (kidding!), in jeans and sweater and boots.

"He's good. Still going to Munich and D.C. a lot."

"Well, that doesn't sound too bad. Actually, kind of perfect, don't you think?"

For my mom, men were a troubling necessity. She resented her attraction to them but was practical about it. We needed their sperm and their willingness to wet-vac a flooded basement, and they wanted things from us that we could trade for those commodities.

She radiated approval, however, when we talked about Steven. She didn't care that he was divorced and almost ten years older than me, she just loved that he was a patent attorney for a major pharmaceutical corporation. I know I'm making her sound mercenary, but this is one of the ways I know my mother loves me, her excitement over my potentially secure future.

I told her something next that I thought would really thrill her.

"How are you putting that much of your paycheck into your 401K? What about your rent?"

"Steven pays the mortgage."

"But you pay half, yes?"

"I tried at first, but he tore up my checks. He says it's not fair because it's his place, and we're not married yet, and he doesn't need my help. So I pay the utilities and buy the groceries and bank the rest."

"But you are getting married, aren't you?"

"Maybe. We're going to evaluate when we've been living together for a year."

"When will that be? Spring?"

"April."

My mom shook her head.

"What's the problem?" I asked.

"I'm trying to decide." The food came, and she picked bits of green chili out of her beef curry with the tines of her fork and piled them on the edge of the dish. "On one hand, I think it's great you have the opportunity to save, in case things don't work out with him. But decent, secure housing is the foundation of a lasting relationship. If you help pay the mortgage, he will subconsciously value you more when it comes time to consider getting married."

As usual at our monthly luncheon I was developing heartburn, and I had yet to take a bite of my chili shrimp. "Does everything have to be so calculated?"

My mom set her fork down and leaned over her plate toward me. "Grace. Do you remember your childhood?"

"Yes."

"I don't know if you actually do. We struggled."

"I know."

"I'm just saying you should keep your eyes open and think ahead. If I had done that, things might not have been so bad for us."

"They weren't so bad, Mom."

She picked up her knife and fork and diced up a chunk of curried beef. "You're sweet."

"Mom, what's the big deal about marriage? You did it once and it sucked, right?"

"Not until the surprise ending. And you're going to be smarter about it than I was. Look at it as a business arrangement, Grace. Strategize."

She was loving me, in her way. And I felt sorry for the painful things that had hardened her. Still, I took a moment to do that thing I've done a million times since I was thirteen. I smiled and nodded at what she was saying. And silently, effusively thanked God or The Heavens or Whomever that I was not like her.

Saturday, and I was headed for the Cloisters. The gardens would be barren now, but I could be alone for a while and soak up the quiet.

Gaze at the reliquaries and tapestries and recharge my tranquility battery.

Steven had been to the Cloisters with me once and considered that to have filled his medieval monastery quota for life. He liked a bit of mindlessness on the weekend and wanted to stay home and play with his Wii. I kissed him, bundled up, and walked out the door just as Tyler Wilkie was letting Blitzen and Bismarck into Sylvia's apartment.

"Hey, Grace!"

"Hi." I smiled back.

He stood in the doorway, unleashing the hounds. "Where you going?"

"The Cloisters."

He tossed the leashes inside and pulled the door closed behind him. "What's that?"

"A museum. Medieval art." We started down the stairs together.

"That sounds cool. Can I come?"

I faltered on the first landing. Could I politely say no? "Well, sure . . . if you want. It's kind of a ways on the train, you might have other things you need to do this afternoon—"

"I'm free all day!" He waved his hands expansively. "Not counting the dogs."

He opened the door for me downstairs and when we got out on the sidewalk he pointed at Big Green. "Do you want me to carry that for you?"

I shifted the bag to my other shoulder. "Oh, no, I'm fine, thanks."

"It looks kinda heavy."

"It's just my wallet, cell phone, keys, a book."

"Looks like you got a lot more than that in there."

"Well, also emergency snacks, things like that."

We headed down into the subway. "Emergency snacks? You can buy something to eat just about everywhere in this city."

"I like to be prepared." I knew I might sound huffy and decided to explain. "One time I was on a train that was stuck between stations for three hours. I was glad to have a protein bar with me."

"Three hours, no shit?"

I slid my MetroCard through the reader and went through the turnstile. He was still on the other side digging around in his coat pockets, so I found my backup card and held it across to him.

"Hey, thanks, I'll pay you back."

I waved a casual hand and smiled. "My treat. Welcome to New York." I tucked the card away and we headed down the platform.

We stood there awhile. He was wearing the same thing as the first day we met, a fatigue jacket and jeans and Converse sneakers and a knit hat. I saw a plaid flannel shirt peeking through the turned-up coat collar. His throat looked vulnerable in the chill. He needed a warm scarf.

He saw me looking at him and smiled that insanely appealing smile. He had such a nice face, so good-natured. Warm eyes. I couldn't help smiling back.

"You look pretty," he said.

I flailed my hands and muttered something about my beat-up old shearling jacket.

"You had all that makeup on, last time I saw you. And your hair," he picked up a strand and rubbed it between his thumb and forefinger, "I didn't realize it was so long."

Okay, so the guy was a player. I could handle it. I'd been flirted with before.

"Yeah." I pulled a band out of my pocket and whipped my hair into a ponytail. "I need to cut it."

"I just cut my hair, right before I came here."

"Cut it yourself, did you?"

"Yeah. My friend Bogue said I couldn't come to New York City looking like a freaky redneck. We were drunk and he was showing me some pictures in GQ magazine, telling me I should try to look metrosexual."

It was impossible not to laugh. "How long was it?"

He held a flat hand about an inch below his shoulder.

"That's pretty long. What'd you cut it with?" I figured a steak knife.

"My sister's fingernail scissors. It took a fuckin' long time! Especially doing the back. And then I get here and see these long-haired men, all over the place. And nobody here gives a rat's ass what your hair looks like, anyway!"

Unless it looks like a rat's ass, I thought, remembering him hatless the other night at Herman's. I smiled.

"What?" he said.

"I'm just . . . so happy that you have that hat."

He told me a lot more about himself during the twenty-minute train ride to Inwood. His childhood best friend/fashion adviser, Bogue (rhymes with *Vogue*, appropriately enough), had come with him to the city. They'd found an apartment on Craigslist—a fifth-floor walk-up that was basically a twelve-by-sixteen room. They were sharing it with a female performance artist named Rash.

"Rash?" I asked. "As in a skin problem, or imprudent?"

"*Im* what?"

"Foolhardy. Impetuous."

"Oh, yeah, foolhardy . . ." he mused with a little smile. He nudged my leg with his. "You know a lot of big words. What are you, an English teacher?"

"Close. I edit textbooks and reference materials."

"No shit!" He laid an arm across the back of my seat. "So there's a gigantic brain hiding behind that lovely face."

I gave him what I hoped was a rather dry look.

"What?" he laughed.

"See, the words *gigantic brain* pretty much destroy your intended effect. I picture nineteen-fifties sci-fi, *The Woman with the Gigantic Brain*. That kind of thing."

"That is definitely not what I intended," he said, pressing his leg against mine.

"I have a boyfriend."

He withdrew his arm from behind me and leaned forward, elbows on knees, clasping his hands. He looked at me sideways. "I figured. Sorry."

"It's okay."

We were coming to our stop. He was probably regretting riding all the way up here with me now. "You don't have to come, if you don't want to. The downtown train should be here soon."

"Why wouldn't I? I want to hang with you and see the medieval art!" He seemed genuine, maybe even a little offended.

He looked duly impressed by the neo-medieval castle on the hill-top in Fort Tryon Park. Admission to the Cloisters was pay-what-you-can. I paid the full twenty dollars and saw Tyler give five dollars that he probably couldn't afford.

As we climbed the long flight of stairs to the entrance I felt a twinge of excitement. I was so used to coming here alone, but since this guy was here with me, I might as well show him some of the things I especially loved.

I led him straightaway to the Unicorn Tapestries—seven large, intricately woven wall hangings that had probably decorated some-one's castle bedroom. We started at *The Hunters Enter the Woods* and I took him through all of them slowly, outlining the story of the cap-ture and killing of the mythical unicorn.

He studied *The Unicorn in Captivity*. The gorgeous white beast is confined beneath a pomegranate tree inside a circular corral, sur-rounded by a millefleurs extravagance of dozens of varieties of color-ful flowers and plants.

"This is my favorite tapestry," I said. "He doesn't get killed. It's like the alternate ending. Although it looks similar, they think it's probably not a part of the rest of the series."

"He seems peaceful."

"Supposedly he represents a happily captured bridegroom. See how he's chained to the tree? That's the 'chain of love.'"

He looked more closely. "Are those drops of blood?"

"Pomegranate juice. See how the fruit above him on the tree is ripe and bursting open? The drops of juice may represent fertility."

"Awesome." He grinned.

He liked the guy stuff I showed him, especially the tomb effigy of the young knight lying beneath his sword and shield. But he also looked for a long time at the sweet, sad face of the grieving mother holding the body of Christ in the small Bohemian Pietà. He was turning out to be a very gratifying museum companion.

We went out to the Bonnefont Cloister and sat on a bench near the culinary herb bed, now dry and fallow. The sky was heavy, dove-colored.

"You should see this in the summer," I said.

"My parents have a garden," he said. "A big one, behind our house."

"What do they grow?"

"Vegetables, flowers. They're out there every spring, hoeing and planting."

I was impressed. "Do they live out in the country?"

"It's all country, pretty much, where I'm from."

"That must be nice," I said, "to garden together."

"Seems to be working for them, they've been married thirty years."

"Wow, that's quite an achievement. My parents split up when I was four."

He looked at me. "Who'd you end up living with?"

"My mom. I hardly ever saw my dad. Until I got older, that is."

"How come?"

I shrugged. "He was an artist, wanted to devote everything to that, I guess."

"What do you mean, like a painter?"

I nodded. "He's kind of famous in the art world. Dan Barnum?" I didn't really expect him to know the name. "The Cheesecake Series?"

He stared at me blankly.

"You know, the paintings of presidents eating dessert? The one of Reagan, with strawberry sauce running down his chin?"

"Oh, yeah!"

I could see he had no idea what I was talking about.

"So where did you and your mom live?" he asked.

"A tiny apartment in Queens, near the Steinway piano factory."

"Steinway. Cool."

"Right. Cool. My mom had no job skills. So she waitressed and finished college and went to law school."

"She's a lawyer?"

I nodded.

"Where?"

"New Jersey."

"So you visit her, sometimes?"

"I see her pretty often."

"What about your dad?"

"Once in a while we get together."

"That's good, he stayed in touch at least." Tyler nudged me with his elbow and smiled.

"Yeah, I guess." I looked at the sky. "I think it's going to snow."

We were silent, looking upward, and he started lightly drumming two fingers on his thigh and humming under his breath. He just zoned out, staring at the sky, making quiet music. As if nothing else existed.

He resurfaced, pulling a scrap of paper out of his jacket pocket. "Do you have a pen?"

I felt around in Big Green and handed him a Bic and watched him scrawl something on the paper, fold it up, and tuck it back in his pocket. He held up the pen. "Can I keep this?"

"Sure," I said. "Compliments of Spender-Davis Education."

"What's that, your work?"

"Yeah."

"Where is it?"

"Midtown. Avenue of the Americas."

"That's not too far from my new job. Come by sometime, eh?"

"Okay, I'll try."

He looked at me for a long moment, then softly sang a few words. About Christmas coming, and trees being cut down, and wishing he could skate away on a river.

Joni Mitchell. The saddest song, ever. I'd never been personally sung to before, let alone by someone with a voice like that. So I didn't say anything. I'm sure I looked a little dumbstruck.

"Where'd you meet your man?" he asked.

"An alumni picnic. We, uh, we went to the same school. Not at the same time."

"You live together?"

"Yes."

"How long?"

"Eight months."

"No kidding. That's solid."

Big flakes floated down on us and I caught one on my gloved palm.

He leaned over and breathed on it. We watched it melt.

book lady
Boo Radley
and warm vanilla

I brought Tyler home with me and found that Steven had gone out. I supposed it would be okay.

Tyler wandered around the living room looking at my books and Steven's records while I made tea. I set out cups, sugar, milk, sliced lemon, and cookies on the dining room table and invited him to sit while I went back into the kitchen for the teapot.

"You got any honey?" He helped himself to a handful of Pirou-lines.

"I think so." I came back to the kitchen doorway. "Would you like a sandwich? It's almost suppertime."

"Yes, please."

"Ham and cheese okay?"

"Awesome."

I sliced the ham thick and made him two sandwiches on the crusty sourdough that Steven had made in the bread machine the night before. I brought the honey, tea, sandwiches, and a big bag of Doritos and sat with him at the table.

"Do you have a kitchen in your apartment?" I asked.

"Kitchenette," he said, around a mouthful of food. "It's gross."

"Rash is not a good housekeeper?"

"It's gross since me and Bogue got there. She threatened to kick us out. Bogue is supposed to be cleaning it up today."

"Bogue and I."

He raised an eyebrow.

"It's not 'me and Bogue,' it's 'Bogue and I.'"

"Are you gonna eat those?" He pointed at the crusts I had just peeled off my own sandwich. I watched him devour them, along with everything else on his plate, three-quarters of the bag of chips, the remaining cookies, and two cups of Earl Grey.

"So, what will you do if things don't work out the way you're hoping?"

He shrugged. "I don't have a plan for that yet. I'm just thinking about the music."

The key turned in the lock and Steven came in, with snow in his hair and on his coat. He seemed surprised to see that I had a guest, a man he didn't know. Come to think of it, a man I didn't know. It did feel a little strange.

Tyler wiped his hands on his jeans and stood up.

"Steven, this is Tyler Wilkie. He walks Sylvia's dogs."

Steven came over and shook Tyler's hand. "Nice to meet you." He took off his coat and hung it on the back of one of the dining table chairs.

"We met a few days ago," I said. "Do you want a sandwich, honey?"

"Oh, really?" Steven said. "No thanks, I just had a burger." He pulled out a chair and sat down. Tyler sat, too, looking polite and subdued.

"Dog walking for Sylvia . . ." Steven mused. "Have you ever actually seen her?"

"No, we just talk on the phone," Tyler said. "I got the keys to her place from the agency."

"I've lived across the hall from her for almost three years now, and I've never seen her, either," Steven said.

"Weird," Tyler said.

I leaned toward him. "What does her apartment look like?"

"It's nice, I guess. I haven't paid that much attention."

I sat back and smiled at Steven. "She's our Boo Radley."

Tyler smiled vaguely.

"From *To Kill a Mockingbird*," I explained.

"Oh, yeah, I've never seen that movie."

"It was a book first!" I said. "A great one."

Steven patted my hand. "Grace has this thing about reading the book first."

"Yes, I do. In fact . . ." I got up and went to the bookshelves to find my copy. I held it out to Tyler. "You can keep it."

He took the book from me and looked at the cover.

"You're scaring him," Steven said. "Relax, Book Lady."

I didn't like that. One shouldn't joke about *To Kill a Mockingbird*. "I'm giving him a gift. A beautiful one, if he'll take it."

Tyler stood. Probably eager to get away from the crazy people. "I have to get going. There's an open-mic down at a bar in the Village, I want to try to get on the list."

Steven stood. "Are you a musician?"

Tyler pulled on his coat and slid the book in a pocket and buttoned it. "Yeah."

"Jazz, by any chance?"

"No, man, rock, soul, singer-songwriter stuff."

"Oh, yeah," Steven said politely. They shook hands again.

I followed Tyler to the door and opened it for him. He walked out into the hall, turned, and leaned in to speak to me conspiratorially. "Thanks for feeding me, Grace."

"No problem!"

He patted his coat pocket. "And for the gift."

Peg called. *Tie Me Up! Tie Me Down!* was in technical rehearsals at one of those big old theaters only a few blocks from the Spender-Davis building. Did I want to meet somewhere midafternoon for a quick coffee? I told her to meet me at Café Sofiya. Two birds and all that—I hadn't run into Tyler in several days and was curious as to how things were going for him.

Peg had been my landlady when I first came to the city after college. Well, not so much landlady. I had rented a room in her apartment. Peg was in her late thirties then, very bohemian. No makeup, long, curling brown hair, flowing peasant blouses with jeans and Birks. Kind of Stevie Nicks-ish, without the big platform boots. She was a practicing Pagan. The five years I lived with her, if she wasn't stage managing a show, she'd frequently disappear on the weekends upstate or to New Jersey to commune with Nature and her pantheistic Internet community.

Peg and I knew all of each other's stories. I would have still been living with her if I hadn't moved in with Steven.

When I got to Café Sofiya she was already at a table, huddled over a giant cup of coffee, a nubby, rainbow-hued muffler thick around her neck. The café was small and modern, empty except for a guy working on his laptop at the coffee counter. I threw my coat over a chair, kissed her, and sat down.

"What are you having?" I asked.

"Triple mochaccino. We've been setting light cues for two days, I needed a chemical cattle prod."

I looked around. "Is there a waiter?"

"Yeah." She craned around, searching behind the pastry case. "Back there somewhere."

I got up and went over to pretend-peruse the pastries in the refrigerated case and peered into the open door that led into a back room. Tyler came out with an armload of boxes and dumped them on the floor next to the cash register. He saw me and beamed.

"Hey!" He was wearing the compulsory waiter uniform—white dress shirt, black pants and shoes, black apron. He came around the counter and enfolded me in an emphatic hug. He smelled like vanilla and baking bread.

"Thank you for coming to see me!" His voice seemed so loud—as if he had natural, built-in amplification. I patted his back and gently disengaged.

"Grace, I got a steady gig! And this guy offered to manage me. Someone who saw me at an open mic told him about me and he came to see me and asked me to come to his office the next day and play for him."

"Wow, Tyler, that's great!" I said. "It happened so quickly!"

He grinned. "So come see me Monday nights." He pulled a chair up to our table and wrote the address on a napkin. The guy at the counter was watching us. "It's this bar on Bleecker."

"That's my neighborhood," Peg said. "And my night off."

"Cool. I play from nine thirty to twelve. Hey, what's your name?"

"I'm sorry," I said, "this is Peg."

He gave her his hand. "Hey, Peg. Grace, what's your favorite song?"

I hate surprise questions like that. Impossible to answer immediately. Options must be reviewed. Choices considered.

"Um . . . can I tell you later?"

"Yeah. Think about it and let me know."

"My favorite song is 'Take Me to the River,'" Peg said.

"Awesome, I know that song," Tyler said.

"So if I come see you, you'll play it for me?" Peg smiled.

"Definitely."

"Tyler," the guy at the counter with the laptop said.

"Right," Tyler said. "That's the boss."

He stood up, took a towel out of his apron, and flicked an imaginary crumb off our table. "See you Monday," he said, with that smile of his. And then he was off.

new faces, old songs, hungry girls, and the importance of apostrophizing

I met Peg at her apartment and we walked the few blocks to the bar on Bleecker. Except for some girls sitting next to the stage, the place was pretty empty. Edward and a blond man who looked like he might have been the model for Michelangelo's *David* were waiting for us in a booth.

The beautiful man's name was Boris. It disoriented me. With that name, he should be hulking, bald, have lots of nose hair, and deliver unmarked packages to remote warehouses in exchange for suitcases stuffed with cash. He should have a surprise bionic hand that could crush your windpipe in seconds. Unless you were Daniel Craig, in which case Boris was, eventually, toast.

"Hi, Boris," I said. "What do you do?"

"I'm a neuroscience research technician."

A likely story.

I went to the bar to get beers and felt hands on my shoulders. Warm, firm hands that made me want to sink onto a stool and fall into a cozy, drooling doze on the bar. I shook it off and turned around. Tyler.

"Oh, hey," I said.

"Did you think of your favorite song yet?" he asked.

"Oh, gosh, I'm still working on that. I have it narrowed down to eight possibilities."

"Can you just tell me a couple?"

"Well. . . ." This felt strangely private. A little embarrassing. "I like old songs." No need to tell him I almost minored in music of the sixties and seventies at Brown. Old music was my escape for most of my teen years, to an extent that many of my Grunge-loving friends just didn't get.

"Me, too! Like what?"

"Like, well, there's this song I used to hear on the classic-rock radio station my mom listened to. I have it on my iPod."

He nodded encouragingly.

"'Bell Bottom Blues.'"

He staggered back a step with a hand to his heart. "No shit! Derek and the Dominos. I love that song!"

"But I'm not sure that's my all-time favorite," I hastened to add.

He dug his cell out of his pocket, checked the time, and pulled me with him toward the front of the room. The stage was by the windows. "Why don't you just give me your whole list?"

"Well, maybe I'll write a few down."

I went to the booth and he went to the stage.

He started on the piano. After two amazing, original songs, Peg looked at me with wide eyes. "He is really talented. There should be more people here."

"Nobody knows about him," I said.

Then he sat on a stool with the guitar and, wearing a harmonica in a neck-brace thing, played a blues song I'd never heard before.

"Dang," Edward commented, "he sang that like an old black man."

"That you'd like to have sex with," Boris added.

"Yes," Edward said. "Although his hair is almost a deal breaker."

"That could be fixed," Boris said. "Reshaped."

"Be patient, he's growing it out," I said.

Then Tyler winked at me and said he was going to play something he'd just written called "This Sign."

The melody was playful and so were the words; it sounded like the soundtrack to a sunlit afternoon. I was charmed. So, I realized, were the six girls sitting at the tables by the stage. They were visibly into him, despite his choppy hair.

"Tell me again how you met him?" Peg asked.

"He walks my neighbor's dogs."

"Those girls look like they want to eat him," Edward said.

They did. And he looked very comfortable with that sort of attention.

On his break between sets Tyler spent some minutes chatting with the girls. Then he pulled two chairs up to the end of our table for himself and a big galoot of a guy, who turned out to be his infamous friend-slash-stylist, Bogue.

Bogue sat in the chair next to me. I had thought Tyler looked young, but Bogue looked as if he was about seventeen, like one of those beefy, sweet kids from high school who was on the football team *and* in the drama club. He even had a semi-buzz cut and a bit of an adolescent skin condition.

I offered him my hand. "Hi, I'm Grace Barnum."

"Oh yeah, Grace, I knew it was you. You look just like Ty said."

I darted a glance at Tyler, who was listening to Peg effuse about his playing. "What did he say I looked like?"

"Small. Sweet. Curvy. Soft eyes. Long dark hair. And I, uh, I think he also used the word 'edible.' Or words to that effect." Bogue turned pink, but he leaned toward me and plowed on ahead in a slightly slurred, seductive whisper. "And I have to say, I agree."

Bogue was quite the smooth, drunk operator. His face was now bright red. Adorable! Or maybe I was a little tipsy, too. I scooted closer and gave him a friendly peck on the cheek. He grinned.

"What are you doing, Bogue?" Tyler said. He and Peg were looking at us.

"Just following the biological imperative, man," Bogue said.

"Why don't you follow it right on out of here."

"Don't worry about it," Bogue said.

"You're gonna worry," Tyler said.

"When you do what?"

"You don't want me to show you."

"Come on, show us," Boris threw in.

A girl came and tapped Tyler on the shoulder. He stood up and moved away with her and while they talked he pulled out his cell and added a number.

"Oh, sure," Bogue said. "He can score a hookup, but I'd better not even try in the same space. New city, same old shit. I don't know why I still hang out with him."

"You two do seem kind of different."

He looked at me with interest. "How so?"

"Well, 'biological imperative.' I think Tyler would say the same thing differently."

"Yeah." Bogue grinned. "He'd call it 'the urge to fuck and run.' I'm way more educated. Not to mention classy. Do you want another beer?"

"No thanks," I said. "He's lucky to have you. This would be a hard city to come to alone."

"No shit. He probably wouldn't even have come if I hadn't dragged his ass here. I told him it was time to spread the musical love in a much wider radius than Pennsylvania, see if he could make something of it. I told him I'd learn what to do and be his manager even, but already he's found someone else. Asshole."

"So what do you do? Have you found a job yet?"

"I'm looking. I'm gonna get a beer, be right back."

Peg went to the ladies' room and Edward and Boris left to meet friends at a bar down the street.

Tyler finished with the girl and came and sat on Bogue's chair. "Her name is Jennifer. She offered to start a street team for me with those other girls."

"What's that?"

"I guess they'll hand out flyers for my gigs, try to get people to come. Hey, can you help me create a Facebook fan page? I don't have a computer."

"I guess I could try . . . I don't know much about it. Let's ask Peg if she—"

"Come on, we'll figure it out. When can I come over?"

"I—well, I need to check my schedule." I stood up. "Can we talk about it later? I have to get going."

He seemed genuinely disappointed. "Can't you stay?"

"Not this time, I'm sorry."

He moved back to let me out of the booth. "Next time, then. I might have something special for you, if you give me that list. Why don't you text it to me? I'll give you my number."

"I think I have your number, actually." I knew I did, buried in Big Green. Now bookmarking *The Age of Innocence*.

He got his cell out. "Okay, give me yours. I promise to only use it twice a day."

My stomach was starting to hurt.

"Grace?" He was waiting. I gave him the number.

A couple of mornings later I stepped outside my door to go to work and did an ungainly, windmilling slide across the floor, just catching myself on the banister before I ate honeycomb tile. Had Mr. Rojas just mopped, or what? I searched for the telltale shine and found that the instrument of my near wipeout was not gray mop water, but a lethal calling card—a slick little bit of lamination from Pocono Community College.

Tyler's picture on it stopped me cold. He was shaggy-haired, grinning, a dimple in one cheek. Cocky. Completely adorable. How could anyone be that photogenic in a college photo ID?

The card had apparently been paper-clipped to a scuffed piece of notebook paper I found nearby on the floor. I opened it up and sat on the stairs in an attempt to read his execrable handwriting. It was a poem. Or—of course!—the words to a song.

this sign

would you like to take a walk with me
hold hands see what we can see
come back and take a cup of tea with me

suns leavin would you like to stay
I didn't expect it to go this way
but theres all sorts of games that we can play if you stay

I wanna be with you rain or shine
theres nobody elses heart on my mind
and if I went lookin, lord, I'd never find this sign

theres nothin out there that we can do
but look at each other without a clue
and what if the others thinkin I love you?
well I do

The charming song he'd played Monday night. I read the words again a couple more times.

Maybe I could tutor him on apostrophe usage.

drinking at work: the dream and the reality

Ed and I had a meeting with Bill about the third-grade reading book we were developing. Have I mentioned that Bill is distractingly orange? Too much self-tanning lotion, maybe, or too much carrot juice. It kind of clashes with his blond brush cut. Also, by the way, Bill never smiles. Ever.

"So here are the issues," Bill said.

We were still settling into our seats. I pulled out a legal pad and uncapped my pen.

"We need to add someone old to one of the stories. Maybe in the one about the Latino kid who goes Rollerblading in the park. Make it his granny who takes him, instead of the teenage brother."

"Okay," I said slowly, "the thing is, that story is an excerpt from a Newbery Medal–winning book. The brother is important to the little boy in the plot. I don't know if the author—"

"He'll change it for our text. Tell him we can't use the story, otherwise."

"The author is a woman."

"Right. All the more reason she'll agree to change the brother to an old lady. Okay, next." He consulted his notes. "Get rid of the ice cream sundae in the story about the kid who loses her library book. Change it to fruit salad."

"Fruit salad." Ed wrote it down. "So, she knows she's going to get in trouble for losing her book, and she uses the last of her allowance to treat herself to *fruit salad*, before she tells her parents?"

"Yeah, it sucks," Bill said. "But we can't have foods with no nutritional value in the stories. Too many little fatties will be reading them."

Ed kneed me under the table.

Bill looked at his notes. "And one more thing. We're dead in the water with California if we don't have an equal number of male and female characters throughout the book."

"We do!" I said vehemently. I knew this for a fact. "Forty-nine of each!"

"Not true," Bill said. "You have to count the animal characters, too. Freddie the Fox and Malachi Mouse in that barn story bring it up to fifty-one males. So change one of them to Fanny the Fox or Mary Mouse. Well, maybe not Fanny. That's awkward. Felicia. There you go."

He stood up and slid his folder across the table to me. "Double-check my notes to make sure I covered everything." He left the conference room.

I looked at Ed, who smiled ruefully.

"Do we have to pick life apart like this?" I asked.

"We do, to ensure diversity."

"But we're making this book dumb and bland. It's *un*diverse, what we're doing!"

"Is that a word?"

"I just invented it." I gathered my stuff and stood up. "You know what, Ed? This meeting made me want to drink."

"I have a bottle of Bushmills in my desk. Let's make Irish coffees."

"Some of these stories aren't even that good. What is our priority, here?"

"Demographic balance. Grace, you know we have to follow the bias and sensitivity guidelines if we want to sell this book."

"What about literary quality?"

"That would be nice."

"Ed. You're becoming a Stepford editor."

"Oxygen, baby girl." He patted my shoulder. "Slip on the mask and breathe."

Tyler called me that afternoon.

"Hey, beautiful, how's it going?"

"Just great, thanks."

"Where are you?"

"Sitting at my desk at Spender-Davis Education."

"Oh, yeah. The job. So will you still help me do the Facebook page?"

Apparently he was helpless. And apparently I was a sucker for it.

"Well, I guess we can try to figure it out." I told him to come to my office Thursday night at seven.

He showed up at 7:22.

"Hey!" He hugged me with one arm and held up a fragrant paper bag and a plastic bag that clanked in a bottle-y way. "I brought supper."

I led him through the maze to my deluxe, corner, outer-wall cubicle.

"Hey, that's pretty." He liked my rosemary-bush Christmas tree.

"I have windows!" I said.

"I see that." He touched the grinning Green Man sun catcher hanging on the glass.

"That's Pan. Father Nature. Peg hung him there to keep me 'connected' while I'm up here in this artificial environment all day."

"She seems like a real friend."

I cleared many piles off my desk and got us plates and forks from the break room while he unwrapped our first course: mozzarella and prosciutto panini. The singular of which is panino, but not many people realize that. My stomach twanged.

"I got here just in time," he laughed. He pulled out a Swiss Army knife and opened a giant bottle of beer and placed it in front of me.

"Either you're way overestimating my capacity for alcohol, or you have evil intentions."

"It's the second one." He opened his own two-liter. "Why are we doing this here?"

"My computer here is better. Faster. Plus Steven is out of town, so I can stay late."

Instant flash of unease. I was here alone with him in this big, empty office, after dark on a cold December night. He had a knife in his pocket. And now he knew that no one would notice if I never made it home. I took a tiny sip of beer and studied him for any sign of a dark vibe. What I saw was a pale, scruffy, hungry young man with crumbs on his chin, looking at me with warm eyes. It felt like I had known him much longer than just a few weeks.

"Where'd he go?"

"Steven? London."

"For how long?"

"Four days, this time."

"Does he go away a lot?

"A fair amount."

"How come?"

"He's a patent attorney for a pharmaceutical company."

"I guess he makes a lot of money."

I shrugged. "Some, for sure."

"So, you gonna bring him to hear me play?"

"Not likely. He's a recovering alcoholic. He stays away from bars."

"Yeah, I'll probably end up having to do that one day." He grinned and I got a flash of the adorable college ID guy.

"By the way." I reached under my desk and groped around in Big Green till I found my wallet. I waved his ID at him. "Thanks a lot. I skated across my hall on this when I came out to go to work the other morning."

Tyler smiled. "No way! Sorry about that."

I pushed it across the desk.

"You can keep it, if you want." He took a giant bite of his second panino. "Do you want some of this?"

"No thanks." I nudged the ID closer to him. "You might need this."

"I don't think I'm going to. But could you keep it for me? Sometimes I lose things." He seemed completely earnest. But something about the way he was looking at me made my face feel warm.

"Oh, well, okay." I opened up my wallet. "It'll be right in here with this picture of my mom."

He leaned across the desk. "Hey, let me see."

I held up the photo.

"Your mom looks like one of those desperate housewife ladies."

I slid the pictures back in my wallet. "That's just the surface. My mom is powerful."

"Yeah, she looks like she could kick some serious ass, if she wanted to."

"Believe me, she wants to. And she does."

He laughed. "Okay, I think I'll steer clear of her."

He broke out a gigantic cheesecake brownie and we split it. I washed my half down with beer while I brought up Facebook on the computer. He pulled a chair around next to me.

We created his personal profile and then a musician profile page. Then I showed him the pages of several musicians and bands.

"So," I said, "we're going to need pictures of you. Do you have any?"

"I just got some taken, I can get Bogue to e-mail them. He's building me a website, with songs on it and everything."

"Oh, great, we can—" I did a double take. "Wait a minute, he is? Why isn't *he* doing this for you?"

Tyler shrugged.

"Maybe you should have brought him with you tonight."

He smiled. "No way."

I looked back at the monitor. The animated frog on my screensaver was doing a jaunty little dance. I tapped the keyboard to wake up the computer and closed Facebook. "To be continued, I guess, when we have the photos to upload."

He leaned back in his chair. "Okay. Thanks, Grace. I appreciate you being so sweet and helpful to me." The drawl was thicker than ever.

"Oh, no problem!" I said crisply, gathering up our empty plates, sweeping crumbs off the desk. I stood up, and found myself just about standing between his knees.

"Well," I said.

He was not getting the message that we were leaving. He sprawled in a casual slouch in his chair, looking up at me from under auburn lashes.

He patted his thigh. "Sit here."

"No."

"C'mon, Gracie." He grazed a finger down my forearm. "I promise you'll like it."

I kicked his chair.

He got up.

Coming down in the elevator he asked, "Are you mad at me?"

"Why would I be?" I said cheerfully.

He walked me to the subway at Fiftieth and Broadway.

"'Bye," I said. "If I don't see you, Merry Christmas."

"I thought you were coming Monday night."

"Well, probably not, it turns out. Lots of shopping still to do."

"But you have to be there! I've been working on your Christmas gift."

"You have?"

He smiled.

"Ty, what is it?"

"Come and find out."

arson becomes a subconscious possibility

It was my last day at work for more than a week. The next day was Christmas Eve, and Steven and I were going to New Jersey.

No one actually did any work. Edward had already gone to Houston, and the office was boring without him. We had cookies and eggnog in the break room and opened our Secret Santa gifts.

I was Secret Santa to a slightly gruff older woman in Production, named Carol. We hadn't worked together much, and all I knew about her was that her husband had recently died and she liked making crafts. Someone told me she had cats. So I spent way more than the twenty-dollar Secret Santa limit and gave her a needlepoint kit I got at the Met gift shop, based on *The Favorite Cat* lithograph by Currier.

She unwrapped it, smiled tremulously, and covered her face with her hands.

I put an arm around her shoulders. A couple of others gathered around us.

"It's just so *hard*," Carol said.

None of us knew what to say. I hoped just listening was helpful, somehow. Someone gave her a tissue. I patted her shoulder.

"Sorry," she said, wiping her eyes. "It's this fucking time of year."

Turned out Bill was my Secret Santa. He gave me a tin of Danish butter cookies and a Chia Pet in the shape of a cow. Obviously he did his Christmas shopping at Walgreens. I pondered the placid, bovine expression on my Chia and said thank you.

Before I left work Peg called to check in with me about going to Tyler's gig. I said that I would meet her there, but first I had to go with Steven to his office party.

When we hung up, I grabbed my personalized Spender-Davis notepad and jotted down a sampling of my favorite songs. It was a mix of old oldies, like Earth, Wind & Fire's "That's the Way of the World," and semi-oldies from high school days, like Blind Melon's "Change." I also special-mentioned Kate Bush's seminal album *The Kick Inside*, an incredible late-seventies record a friend turned me on to in college.

Steven's company had rented a midtown nightclub for their party, complete with lavish buffet and open bar. A jazz band. We sat with two of his fellow attorneys, Nico and Ron, and Ron's wife, Jody.

Nico was going through a breakup that sounded a lot like what had happened to Steven: He met his wife in law school, was married a few years, and then she fell in love with a guy she worked with in private practice. Nico was doing a pretty good job of functioning socially, but he had this base facial expression of haunted vulnerability, overlaid with quick flashes of anger and cynicism. He laughed too quickly and loudly. When he spilled his drink, Steven cleaned it up and Ron went to the bar to get him a cup of coffee.

"Poor guy," Jody whispered to me.

"Hey, man," I heard Steven say quietly while he was blotting Nico's shirt. "It gets better. Remember how I was when Katie left me? I thought my life was over. I could barely get out of bed, except to drink."

"I know, man," Nico said. "I'm drunk now!"

"Ron's bringing you some coffee." Steven squeezed his shoulder.

"Hang in there, man. Look at me. Look at this beautiful girl I get to go home with."

Nico peered at me across the table. "Yeah, man. Sweet." He raised a drunken power fist in tribute to me. "I hope I meet someone just like you one day, Grace."

"Oh, thanks, Nico."

I realized that I hadn't yet told Steven that I wasn't going directly home with him. Maybe I'd wait till later.

"You missed it," Peg whispered in my ear. "Ty played 'Take Me to the River.' It was incredible! A whole new interpretation."

Now he was singing a classic blues song, and he seemed so inward, so absorbed, I thought of Ray Charles. It was like he was locked inside a small personal universe where only sound and feeling existed. He had evolved beyond the need for sight.

At the break I watched Ty navigate the crowd; it seemed like everyone wanted to talk to him, to touch him. He saw me and came over and I handed him his Christmas present. He opened the bag and pawed through my carefully arranged tissue paper, finding the rust, cream, and caramel alpaca scarf I'd bought for him at a yarn store in Soho. It was made of the same colors he was.

"Hey, now I have two scarves!" He pointed across the room at a skinny blond street team girl with big boobs. "Keely knit me a red one. This is way nicer. Did you knit it?"

"Um. Not really. No."

He wrapped it around his neck and gave me a hug. "I love it. But all I have for you is a song."

"I'll take it!" Speaking of, I handed him my song list.

He silently read it. "Damn, girl, you've got good musical taste." He quirked a brow at me. "Who's Kate Bush?"

"Are you kidding?"

He shook his head.

"I don't even know how to answer that." I might have to come back to see him just one more time, to bring him a CD.

"Hey, I started reading that book."

"Oh yeah, how is it?"

"Pretty good, so far. I'm just up to where Atticus shoots the dog. Awesome! Reminds me of my dad, when we go hunting."

"Hunting?"

"Yeah, he's a crack shot."

"Do you . . . shoot things?"

"Yeah, I got an eleven-point buck, one time."

"A deer?"

He smiled. "Yeah. We ate it."

It was just too awful for further comment. "Well. Keep reading and let me know what you think."

"Okay. This is so pretty, Grace. Thank you." He folded the scarf up more carefully than he'd extracted it and put it back in the bag. "What are you doing for Christmas?"

"We'll be at my mom's in New Jersey. What about you?"

"Me and Bogue are driving home. 'Scuse me. Bogue and I."

I smiled appreciatively. "You have a car here?"

"Bogue does. He's only got about ten parking tickets, so far."

A burst of loud, raucous laughter erupted nearby, so he leaned in close. "I'm gonna go play for you now. I hope I get it right."

"Okay, Ty." I patted his arm. "No pressure."

"Merry Christmas, Grace." He was so serious. "Thanks for helping me so much, when you didn't even know me. I wish I had some mistletoe right now."

I laughed and pushed him toward the stage.

I wonder if Eric Clapton knows it's possible to play a rolling, hypnotic version of "Bell Bottom Blues" on the piano and mesmerize a hundred people. Ty started with the words "this is for Grace" and to my embarrassment and, okay, acute pleasure, he sang the song to me. Looking so tragic and intense with all the words about making him cry, and crawling across the floor to me, and begging me to take him back. Not to mention the part about dying in my arms. I'd bet anything he did some acting in high school. Peg's theatrical friends certainly ate it up.

"Are you his girlfriend?" Doris, who was Antonio Banderas's dresser, asked.

"No!" I laughed. "He's just being dramatic."

"He's really good," Doris said. "I'm going to bring some people to see him."

I should have gone home about then, but I stayed and drank two more glasses of wine. Which means, since I'm not a large person, that I sloshed as I serpentined back to the bar to order another.

After 3.5 glasses, I felt a little sick to my stomach. That happens when you are pre-ulcerous and you drink alcohol. Doris got me a glass of water.

Ty, having finished playing, offered to take me outside for some fresh air.

"Good idea," Peg said, bundling me into my coat before turning back to her show friends.

We walked a couple of blocks. Ty reeled me back in with a firm hand on my elbow whenever I veered off-course.

I was shivering. "I don't usually drink that much."

"I didn't think so," Ty said. "Hold on." He tugged my knitted hat down firmly. "You have to keep your ears covered." He unwound the scarf I had given him from around his neck and wrapped it around mine. He tied it under my chin and tucked the ends into my coat. He had the nicest face. I liked watching it while he did all that tucking and tying.

"Ty. Do you want to know what I'm thinking about?" I asked.

"More than just about anything, Grace."

"Those girls who sit by the stage when you play."

He hooked my arm through his and we started walking again.

"Oh, yeah. My street team."

"They want to kiss you."

"Do they?"

I snuck a peek at him. "Stop smiling."

"They're just girls who like my music."

"They're groupies. You have groupies, Ty! They want to shag you!"

I stopped in the middle of the sidewalk and leaned over with my hands on my knees.

He touched my back. "Are you gonna throw up?"

"Maybe. Give me a minute."

He rubbed my back in small, warm circles.

I peered up at him. "Why aren't you drunk? I saw you drinking at least as many drinks as me."

"I have a pretty high tolerance. And you're only slightly larger than Mini-Me."

"Well, anyway," I muttered to the sidewalk. "I am a terrible person."

"Why?"

Where to begin? "I said *shag*. That's a bad word in England."

"Grace, you're a beautiful person. One of the most beautiful, ever."

"Completely unfair, Ty. Singing that song to me. When I've been drinking! Stop laughing."

"Sorry."

Peg came toward us on the sidewalk, carrying Big Green. Thank God! I straightened slowly, clutching my stomach. Holding myself together.

"I have to go now," I said to Ty. I started unwinding his scarf to give back to him.

"Don't worry, babe. I'll get it later."

"But . . . I'm afraid you'll be cold!"

He laughed, a little. "I'll be okay."

I woke to knives in the eyeballs.

A tankard of coffee helped with the head pain. Unfortunately, it also sharpened my ability to recall. If only I'd drunk that last half-glass of wine and blacked out.

Cringing self-loathing.

What the hell was wrong with me? I had been completely inappropriate. I had never done anything this ridiculous. Clearly, I did not function rationally in the world of bars, drinking, music, and groupies. Ty and I—well, I liked him and all, but we really had very little to base our friendship on. It was like we were not even of the same species. In the animal kingdom, he'd be a lion and I'd be—I don't know—a duck.

While Steven drove that afternoon—thanks, Zipcar!—I tried to nap but spent most of the time obsessing about how I might quietly, gently segue out of this troubling friendship. But as we got deeper into New Jersey and closer to my mom's, I was able to put last night, and Ty, away.

In spite of all the ways she makes me crazy, my spirits always lift in anticipation of Christmas with Julia. She lives near Princeton, in a five-bedroom house that has a sunken living room with a stone fireplace and a huge, flat-screen TV. A granite-countered epicurean kitchen with stainless-steel appliances. A master bedroom suite with a sitting room, fireplace, and jetted bathtub. A swimming pool. She is so clearly overcompensating for our days in the bug-infested studio in Astoria.

Julia has four Christmas trees in the house. A white tree with all-blue lights and ornaments, which is actually kind of nice. Then there is the Santa ornament tree: total multicultural Santa overload. Saint Nick. Sinter Klaas. Pere Noel. Babbo Natale. Hoteiosho and Kaledu Senelis. Black Peter. Then there is the plastic fruit tree, which appeared circa 1989. It's just a lot of fake bananas and pineapples stuck to the branches, and a Carmen Miranda winged angel at the top. I think she was depressed the year she came up with it. The best tree every year is a real Douglas fir that she festoons with glass icicles and snowflakes, and then she perches about fifty species of fake birds all over it. The birds are pretty; they have real feathers.

My point is, for all that she constantly tries to direct me away from various doom scenarios, my mom is actually a closet optimist, and I know this because of how much she enjoys Christmas. Would someone in an Edvard Munch mental state, who has no small children, grandchildren, or even a boy child, have a working toy railroad set up in the foyer of her McMansion?

She met us at the door with hugs and eggnog.

"No whiskey in yours!" she said to Steven. She had clearly been imbibing for a while.

"Thanks, Julia." He winked at me over her shoulder.

A big, muscular guy stood up when we came into the living room. He was wearing jeans, a sweatshirt, and a holstered gun.

"José, this is my daughter Grace and her boyfriend Steven."

We shook hands. José was gorgeous, in that intentionally bald way. I looked at my mom and smiled.

"José is having dinner with us tonight."

"But first I have to go back to work for a while," he said. He had a very deep voice.

"José is a detective in Arson," Julia explained.

"Hey, that sounds interesting," Steven said.

José smiled. "I have a few stories."

While my mom and I were in the kitchen slicing cheese, defrosting the shrimp ring, and chopping spinach and water chestnuts for dip, we could hear Steven and José in the TV room talking about burn patterns, gas chromatography, accelerants, and insurance fraud.

"It's completely inappropriate. We work together on cases," Julia said.

"Yeah, but look at him."

She grinned. "He's thirty-five. Is that shocking?"

"I think it's great."

She waved a hand dismissively. "I'm just having fun."

"Why shouldn't you?"

She came to me and tucked my hair over my shoulders and held my face in her hands. I liked my mom when she was a little drunk. She could be unusually sweet.

"Are you happy, my darling?"

"Yes, Julia."

"Sometimes you look so serious. Don't be all work and no fun."

"I do fun things."

"I'm not talking about reading books. Does Steven take you out sometimes?"

"Sure, we go to dinner, and movies. And I go out with Peg and Edward."

I wanted to tell her about my interesting new friend, Tyler Wilkie, but something stopped me.

"Is there something you're not telling me?"

"No! Why?"

"I know that sad look in your eyes. You used to get it about your father. Has he done something to hurt you?"

I took her hands in mine to release her viselike grip on my shoulders. "Julia, he doesn't hurt me. I hardly ever see him. And when I do, he's nice."

"Hm," she grumbled.

My mom makes chili on Christmas Eve, and we stay up late to watch the midnight mass at the Vatican. Not that we're Catholic. Julia just likes it. And José is Catholic, so now she has even more reason. I made it through the first fifteen minutes of the mass and told them good night.

Steven was still awake when I got into bed.

"Hey, what do you think of José?" I asked.

"I think he could kick my ass."

"Yeah, he seems kind of tough."

Steven grinned. "I bet your mom really likes that about him."

"Ew. Shut up."

Steven laughed and turned on his bedside light. He handed me a flat, square turquoise box. "Merry Christmas, sweetheart."

"Oh." I smiled. "You don't want to give me this tomorrow?"

"No, it's officially Christmas."

It was a bracelet, from Tiffany. Three bangles, bound by a single link attached to a silver heart.

"Steven. It's so pretty. I love it."

He smiled, pleased with my response. I slid it onto my wrist and admired it. He turned out the light and I sank down under the covers with him.

He pulled up my nightgown and I tried to relax, but I kept thinking about my mother and José downstairs, watching the pope.

Atticus

On New Year's Eve my dad cooks. A few early-evening hours of visiting and playing catch-up, and then we go our separate ways.

Oh, he takes me somewhere for dinner around my birthday in September. He e-mails me almost daily and every few weeks or so invites me to do something with him. Usually I decline, though, because it starts to feel like too much. Something like love for him starts to creep in, and then I remember not being his priority when I was a kid. And my chest starts to hurt. So I have found that I have to measure how much time I spend with him. Keep it light.

When I was younger I was careful never to let Dan see that I thought anything about him or his life was cool. On top of the normal teenage disenchantment with my parents, I had an extra, thorny layer of pain. I was carrying around my own anger and some of my mom's, too. For most of my teen years I barely spoke to him, even when we were in the same room.

To his credit, he kept trying with me. He still tries.

Now I try, too.

Dan lives on the top two floors of an old garment factory he owns in SoHo. You use a key in the elevator and it takes you up to his lower floor and then you walk right out into his gigantic living space. It's furnished with weathered leather couches and his paintings, and it has big windows with an incredible view of New Jersey. One time I came off the elevator as David Bowie was getting on. He owns some of my dad's paintings.

"You're Grace, I believe," Mr. Bowie said.

I eventually closed my mouth. And then opened it again to say yes.

"Your father showed me your photograph."

"Oh," I said. Intelligent, reasonably verbal girl becomes idiot.

Tonight it was just the two of us.

I stepped inside the apartment and found twinkling white lights strung all across the ceiling. Maybe he was having a party later.

"Dan?" I called.

"Grace?" There was an alarming, glassy crash overhead. I ran up the iron spiral staircase in the middle of the room.

Dan was standing in the middle of the paint-splattered floor of his studio, grinning. My dad is short. Taller than me, but shorter than my mom. He has shaggy, silvery hair, and—for a man circling sixty—a disconcertingly young face.

"Are you all right?" I searched him for injury, surveyed the room for disaster.

"Oh, sure." Then I saw the remote he was holding. He pressed a button and this time we were treated to the shriek of shredding metal. Like I imagined the *Titanic* striking the iceberg might have sounded. I covered my ears till it was over.

He pressed the button again and it was crickets, in a summer, twilight meadow.

"I vote for that one," I said.

He pressed the button again. Strange, high, trilling noises, and then this juicy, mucky, sucking sound. "That's an elephant giving birth."

"May I go now?" I asked politely.

"Absolutely not. For the next one hundred and eighty minutes, you're mine."

Dan had a major gallery exhibition coming up in Atlanta. He showed me the paintings that went with the sound effects. For a while now he had been into abstract expressionism—splattery, spiky, *what's red, white, and black all over?* stuff. But these were gigantic, realistic paintings, of naked plastic doll parts. Disturbing. They made me think of a creepy Beatles album cover I saw one time.

"So, they're looking at the dolls, and they push a button next to the painting, and in their wireless headset they get a random sound?"

"Yes. Maybe a nice one, maybe not." He looked devilishly pleased.

"Dan. What does it *mean*?"

"My darling, what makes you think I am ever going to answer that question?"

"I don't think you know." Like that was going to make him tell me.

He laughed. "Maybe not."

We went downstairs and he made us a cup of tea, then we sat together on one of the couches and exchanged gifts. His was a bunch of Calvin Klein gray tees. They're all he wears, with khakis. He gave me a chic, black-leather belted coat to replace my worn old shearling, and an overly generous gift card to Shakespeare & Co. It was touching that he paid attention to what I needed and liked. And it made me squirm.

"Thanks, Dan," I said, trying not to bolt. "That sure will buy a lot of books."

"What's wrong?" he asked. "You still read, don't you?"

"Of course!"

He looked at me with his x-ray vision. I got up and wandered around the room and pointed at the sparkly, dangling ceiling lights. "Are you having a party later?"

"Oh, no, those are permanent."

"They're beautiful."

"Do you and Steven have plans to celebrate?"

"We're just going to watch the ball drop on TV."

"Don't take the subway home. I'll call for a car."

"I don't think it will be all that crazy yet, at nine o'clock."

He shook his head. "Don't take the subway."

Great. So something awful was going to happen in one of the stations. Or hopefully it would just be that a train was going to stall.

My dad is psychic.

About me.

He says he gets feelings about things all the time, but only tells me the really strong ones.

I happened to be visiting him for a month the summer I was thirteen and came home from Rollerblading to find a package of maxi pads sitting on my bed. Embarrassed, and despising him even more than usual, I shoved them in the back of my closet. Two days later, I got my first period.

When I was looking for a job in publishing he told me I was going to get a job in education. I scoffed, but a week later I got the call to interview at Spender-Davis. And one time last summer he called me at work and told me to get up and leave, right away. I didn't tell everyone because I knew no one would believe me. But Edward and I went out for lunch, just in case. When we came back the building was cordoned off and people were filing out. There had been a bomb threat.

The next day I e-mailed my dad and asked him: *Why is it just things to do with me? Why not world events, or your own life?*

I think it's my guilt, he wrote back, *in overdrive.*

I could smell curry. Dan cooks great Indian food.

"Can we eat soon? It smells so good."

He got up. "Come on."

Place settings were arranged on the kitchen island. I hopped up on one of the tall chairs and watched him spoon basmati rice and lamb curry onto a plate.

"Give me a lot," I said.

"There's raita and mango chutney in the fridge," Dan said. "Will you get them?"

I was rooting around in the refrigerator when I heard my cell ring.

"Excuse me." I went across to where I'd left Big Green and looked to see who was calling. TWILK. A 570 area code.

"Hello?"

"Damn, Gracie. *Damn.*"

"Ty?"

Silence.

"Are you okay?"

"I just finished the book." He sounded strangled. Was he crying?

"Are you okay?"

"No! Were you, when you finished reading this?"

"No." I smiled, delighted. "It wrecked me."

"In a good way?"

"Yes."

"Man, Atticus was awesome."

"Wasn't he?"

"He *tried*, you know? Even when everything sucked and there was no way he was gonna win. Damn, that pissed me off! What a bunch of fucking idiot people, in that town."

"I know! In that time."

"He was righteous. A righteous human being. And the stuff at the end, with Boo Radley!"

"Yes!"

"Let's try to be like Atticus, Grace."

"Okay, let's."

"Tell me what else that lady wrote."

"Sorry. That's it."

Long silence. "No fucking way."

"Yes. She wrote one genius book."

"Damn. Why?"

"No one knows. Maybe she scared herself with how good this one was. Or maybe she only had one story she wanted to tell."

"It's a mystery," he said.

"It is."

He blew his nose loudly. "Are you at your mom's still?"

"No, actually, I'm at my dad's. For dinner."

"Okay, I'll let you go. Sorry."

"No, it's all right. Where are you?"

"At my parents' house. Heading back to the city tomorrow night."

"Oh."

"While we've been home I got Bogue to help finish the Facebook page."

"Oh, that's great!" I was so happy to be off the web-geek hook. I peeked over my shoulder at Dan, who was sitting at the island, watching me, waiting patiently.

Tyler was quiet.

"Are you there?" I said.

"Damn, Gracie."

His response to the book was so completely gratifying. I knew exactly how he was feeling.

"I think I'll read it again," he said.

I laughed. "Okay, well, happy New Year, Ty. Be safe."

"'Kay, Grace. You, too."

I returned to the table.

"Who was that?" Dan asked.

I helped myself to a big spoonful of chutney. "A friend."

"Must be a good one."

"Huh?"

"Well, you changed, when you were talking on the phone. Your face. It was like you woke up."

"Have I been asleep, all this time?"

"Let's just say you've been typically enthused to see me."

"Dan—"

"Never mind, dear." He patted my hand. "What's your friend's name?"

"Tyler."

"Five Words."

I smiled. "Oh, come on."

Five Words is a game my dad made up when I was a sullen teenager, to force me to communicate. As clever parental manipulation goes, it bordered on the diabolical. With my thing for words, I could never resist. And there was cash involved, if I managed to make a small poem.

"You come on. Give me five words about Tyler."

I laughed and shrugged. Easy money. "Warm . . . smiling . . . shining . . . autumn . . ."

My dad leaned toward me as I reached for the last word.

". . . song."

"Ahh," my dad said, as though I had just painted a fascinatingly comprehensive verbal portrait. He got out his wallet and handed me a five. All the while piercing me with his extrasensory Dan Barnum eyes.

"I barely know the guy," I said as I tucked the bill into my pocket. "He's just . . . really nice. And I am glad to see you, Dan, please don't think I'm not."

"Susannah Grace Barnum." My dad smiled and patted my arm. "All is well." He passed the basket of fragrant bread to me. "Naan?"

sad, inevitable, winter wedgie

It's winter in New York, and you do what you have to. You hunker down, pay your holiday bills, and try not to freeze your ass off schlepping to work and home again. You drink lots of hot tea and put full-spectrum lightbulbs in all the lamps. You watch *What's Up, Doc?* three times in one weekend for some medicinal Madeline Kahn. You decide that now is the time to take that trip to Cancún. You go online and choose a vacation package, but no one else can go with you right now. You seriously consider going by yourself.

You vacuum out Big Green and restock all items. You set aside the Toni Morrison you are reading and pick up Janet Evanovich. You think about dyeing your hair blond. You think about going back to therapy. You hijack your boyfriend's Wii and play *Dance Dance Revolution: Hottest Party*, ignoring the downstairs neighbors' complaints, until you are sidelined by a pulled groin muscle.

You time your comings and goings to minimize the possibility of running into the dog walker. You only run into him a handful of times, and you keep the interactions friendly but brief. You let him leave messages on your cell and leave him a quick reply in return. This gentle weaning strategy goes on for four whole weeks, and seems to be working.

Then he leaves you a note on the doormat:

Hey Grace are you alive? I miss you. I wrote a new song. Check it out. I will play it for you if you come Monday.
TGW

calling

well the time has come for calling
and I know that your in town
I heard you cry the other day
and I think I'll try and tell you

I love you, do you love me
lets get together again

well I never could stop falling
and I know that your around
I saw you smile the other day
and I think I'll dial and tell you
I want you, do you want me
lets get together again

where did you go to, baby
who did you run to see
why in the world did you leave me, honey
aint you glad to see me again

now the time has come for calling
and your somewhere around
I caught your eye the other day

I was dumbstruck. Did he actually mean me, with the crying? When could he have heard that? Oh, I realized. Just about any January weekday morning, before work.

Why was he doing this? He had volumes of girls fawning over him. Did he really need another conquest? It was exasperating. There was no way I was going to go hear that song.

Then Peg called me. "Do you want to go hear Ty Monday night? You've missed a lot. He has a band now."

"Really?"

"Yeah, a drummer and a bass player. And the crowds have grown exponentially. I got there a little late last time and almost didn't get in."

"Wow."

"He keeps asking where you are. He thinks you're avoiding him."

"I left him a message. It's just been too cold to go out at night."

"I think his feelings are hurt."

This was crazy. "What's the big deal? We've only known each other for a couple of months!"

"Well, you know those artistic types. They're very sensitive."

I sighed. "I'll see if I can come for a while."

"I'll try to save you a seat."

I hung up. There were predictions of a massive winter storm late Sunday into Monday. I crossed my fingers.

Those people on the Weather Channel are liars. It barely snowed at all. So I went. When I arrived at the bar Ty was already playing with his band. The place was packed. Peg waved to me from the back of the room and I squeezed my way toward her, peering over my shoulder at Ty. I was hoping he'd register that I was there so I could leave soon.

The song finished and people clapped. Ty said into the microphone, "Hey, Grace."

I turned around and gave him a little wave.

"Aw, I embarrassed her," he said. Mass laughter. He began another song.

Peg was sitting with Bogue and a tall, emo-ish, black-haired girl who turned out to be Rash. She was pretty, in a wan, purple-lipped way.

"Rumor is there's a *New York Times* reporter here, doing a story on Ty," Peg said.

"Really?"

"Yeah, for a series on singer-songwriters in the city."

I ordered a glass of wine and asked Rash about herself. She was from Virginia, a psychology student at NYU, and a performance artist. She was working on a new piece, to be staged in front of the New York Stock Exchange. She was going to dress in a man's suit and run a half-marathon on a treadmill while reading aloud from the *Wall Street Journal*.

"How are you going to power the treadmill?" I asked.

"Generator. And my friend has a van to haul it in."

"There are a lot of police down there."

She shrugged. "If I just get five minutes of video, it's cool."

I asked about her experience of living with Bogue and Ty.

She leaned closer and spoke confidentially. "Bogue's a total slob. And he doesn't have a job yet. But he's rich, so I guess maybe he doesn't have to get one if he doesn't want to."

"He's rich?"

"Yeah, his dad owns grocery stores."

Who knew? "What about Ty?"

"He's a little better. He hangs up his wet towels. And makes his bed. Which is more than I can say for Bogue. And neither of them jerk off where I can hear them, unlike other guys I've roomed with."

"Maybe you should stick to female roommates."

"Nah, sometimes I need something heavy moved."

I excused myself to go to the bathroom. Two girls were huddled over the sink, laughing, fixing their hair and makeup. I recognized them as being on Ty's street team. The taller, prettier one had on thong undies that were displayed way over the top of her pants in back.

I went into the stall. They were dead silent the whole time I was peeing.

I came out and they made room at the sink.

"Grace, right?" Thong Girl asked.

"Right," I said.

"So are you and Ty hooking up, or what?"

I thought about not answering such appalling rudeness but it seemed better to squelch a stupid rumor. "No," I said. "He's just a friend."

"Yeah, it didn't seem like you were his type. No offense." She flipped her ice-blond hair over her shoulder.

I resisted the urge to grasp the edge of her tiny underpants and give her the mother of all wedgies.

Squeezing back through the crush of people at the bar, I ran into Ty's manager, Dave. We hadn't formally met, but he seemed to know me. He was a big, good-looking guy, mid-forties, dark hair and beard. Very white teeth. He smiled at me, so I thought up something pleasant to say.

"Ty sounds great!"

Dave leaned in close. "He's fucking brilliant. It's just a matter of time."

"Till what?" I asked politely.

"Till he makes us both a shitload of money. Enjoy him while you can, soon he's going to be very, very busy."

Why? Why did people make this annoying assumption?

"Oh. Well. Hopefully he won't change that much."

Dave smiled like he knew a clever secret. "Change is inevitable."

"Yes. Okay, I have to go now. 'Bye." I hated being rude, but I needed to get out of there.

I pushed through the drunken multitudes—had the door in sight—when Ty stepped into my path. He grabbed my shoulders, laughing, his eyes glowing from alcohol and the high of performing. His hair had grown out a lot and curled ruddily around his face, brushing his collar.

"Hey!" he said. "Sorry about making everyone look at you earlier."

"Yeah, that was kind of uncomfortable."

"Thanks for coming. I thought you didn't like me anymore."

"I've just been so busy. In fact, I'm sorry, but I have to go now."

"No, I'm gonna play that new song for you!"

"I'm so sorry, I'll have to hear it another time."

He tilted his head and gave me a long, unsmiling look that might have meant he knew what was up. Which was probably for the best.

"I'm sorry," I said again. "Good-bye."

He kissed me on the cheek, close to my ear. "'Bye, Gracie," he whispered.

spring

learning the Heimlich/hearing the song

When March comes I desperately grab on to it. It's only marginally warmer—the wind and sleet are biting and I know we could have a freak snowstorm in April—but still, I pack away my heavier clothes and start planning picnics.

Self-delusion. I'm good at it.

At work things had settled to avoidance and false camaraderie between me and Bill. *Healthy Teen* was at the printer. Now I was busy proofreading a fourth-grade Indiana history textbook.

I went to Peg's Vernal Equinox celebration. We had dinner, then lit candles and planted herb seeds in little clay pots. Peg talked about how this was a time of new beginnings, of new growth and fertility. She had us write our prayers for positive change in white crayon on hard-boiled eggs, then one at a time dip them in a bowl of dye made from grated beets.

My turn came. I nudged my egg around in the soupy redness and watched it turn pink.

Peg peeked over my shoulder. "Your egg is so bare. Couldn't you think of anything you'd like to see change?"

"I needed more time to think about it."

She sighed and scooped up my egg with a slotted spoon. "Hey, look!"

A tiny, improbable adornment was attached to my otherwise plain pink egg. A fragment of shredded beet in the shape of a perfect little heart.

"Hey, how did you do that?" I asked.

"I didn't."

"I mean, how did you make little tiny beet hearts?"

"I didn't! I just grated them to smithereens."

"Weird."

We contemplated the egg.

"It's a message, Grace," Peg said. "Pay attention."

Steven spent the first three weeks of March in London, working on the European patent application for a new drug for blepharitis. I enjoyed the time alone. I liked sleeping in the middle of the bed, spread out, a foot in each corner. I liked walking around naked without worrying about bottom wobble. I liked bringing home page proofs and spreading them out on the table and working while slurping down a half-gallon of takeout tom kha gai. Maybe I dribbled some on my shirt. Maybe I belched. Or worse. Maybe I got up and looked at myself in the bathroom mirror and observed that my hair, blindly piled up and banded in a knot on top of my head, made me look like the mayor of Whoville. Maybe all the mascara on one eye had completely disappeared and, on the other, had slid down almost to the corner of my mouth. Maybe, it turned out, *I* was the building's Boo Radley, not Sylvia. So what? Who was there to see it but me?

It bothered me how okay I was with Steven being away for so long.

But it's perfect! my inner deluder reassured me. Because he would always be traveling for work, and it would never make me miserable.

Ty had stopped calling weeks ago. I knew that Peg was still going to see him play on Monday nights. Edward went, too, sometimes. But neither of them talked about it much after I made it clear I wasn't interested. Sometimes Peg would glare at me during a conversational lull, as if she had something exciting she was just busting to tell me, and I would divert her with a quick dive into a new subject. But I could only hold her off for so long.

"What is your problem with Ty?" she blurted out during one late-night phone call. "What did he do?"

"Nothing!"

"Why won't you go see him play anymore?"

"You know what it is?" I said. "He's very flirtatious."

"So what?"

"Well, he's just relentless about it. It's tiresome."

"He's a horny young guy, he flirts with everyone. Can't you just ignore it? I think you may be missing out on a major sociological phenomenon."

"And that is?"

"Well, I know this sounds cheesy. But a 'star' being born."

"Golly."

"Seriously, Grace. There are more people there every week. It's like watching a religion grow. It's fascinating."

"It's not. It's painful."

Silence.

"I know that sounds weird," I said.

"Well, I guess you're worried about him, or something."

"Yeah, I guess."

"He's going to be fine, Grace. Just fine." Peg sounded a little deflated.

"You know me, always overthinking."

He was still walking the dogs. I knew the routine, could hear it from my comfy perch in the corner of my couch. He'd come up the stairs whistling every morning at seven thirty. Bismarck and Blitzen would hear him, too, and start woofing till he got the door open. The door closed, muffling his friendly greeting. The door opened. Doggy nails clicked on tile, followed by the shuffling commotion of two big dogs and one (probably) hungover man going down three flights of stairs. Sometimes I'd go to the window in time to catch sight of them ambling toward the park.

At eight, all the seven-thirty arrival sounds played in reverse. At 8:05, he'd have unleashed and watered the hounds and left the building. At 8:15 the coast would be well clear, and I'd leave for work.

Until one Tuesday morning in late March. Major deviation. He came up the stairs late, at 8:07, and slower than usual. No whistling. No jingling keys. There was, however, a knock on my door.

I sat frozen in my couch corner, willing him to go away.

It wasn't that I expected never to see him again, I just wanted more time in between the last time and the next time. More weeks. Months, even.

He knocked again. I crept to the door and peeked out the peephole. The top of his head was right there. He must have been leaning against the door.

"Grace?"

I stayed very quiet.

"Shit," he said, and moaned. Yep, hungover.

Finally, he shuffled away, down the stairs, without ever walking the dogs.

I couldn't give him more than a few minutes to clear out of the vicinity, or I was going to be late for work. I grabbed Big Green and headed out at 8:15, hoping he'd gone in a different direction.

But there he was, right in front of my building. Flat on his back, the bottoms of his black Converse high-tops peeking out among the feet of the five or six people huddled around him.

"Oh God!" I pushed through to him, knelt, and grabbed his shoulders. "Ty!"

He groaned.

"He just sat down on the ground and keeled over," said the guy with blond dreds who was squatting beside me.

"Tyler! Wake up!"

He obliged me by coming to, blinking at me, grimacing, and rolling onto his side in a fetal position. "*Shit*, Grace!"

"What happened?"

"It fucking hurts!"

"What hurts?"

"I'm fucking dying!"

"You'd better get him to a hospital," said an old lady carrying a Chihuahua and a Fairway bag.

"Right." I groped around in Big Green for my cell.

"Don't wait for an ambulance," the dreds guy said, getting up. "Get a cab to take you to St. Luke's-Roosevelt."

"Right! Good idea," I said. The guy was already at the curb, his arm in the air. A taxi pulled over.

"Ty." I pulled on his arms. "Get up. We're going to the hospital."

He was moaning, dead weight. I couldn't move him.

"Ty, please. You have to get up. Hold on to me."

The dreds guy, the cabdriver, and Salvatore, our street-corner Louis Vuitton handbag-and-used-books vendor, helped me get him in the backseat of the cab.

Ty leaned heavily against me, eyes closed, face tight with suffering.

"Hold on." I held his hand firmly and tried to sound confident. "We'll be there in a minute. You're going to be okay."

I think I made the wrong career choice. It seems like emergency room workers have way more fun. Every time anyone came through the swinging doors that led into the emergency inner sanctum, I could hear people laughing and whooping it up. Some guy was taking orders for a Starbucks run and wow! Are those people caffeinated. Meanwhile, my friend was lying curled up on his side across three of the vinyl waiting room chairs, pale, sweating, wincing with every breath. It was half an hour before a nurse invited us into the triage room.

He told her that the pain in his abdomen had started at around one a.m. and had grown steadily worse. It felt like being stabbed with needles. And he needed to throw up, but couldn't.

He had a fever. "Probably a virus," the nurse said. "Go back to the waiting room and finish getting him registered. We'll call you."

"Whatever it is, he passed out from the pain," I said. "Please, how soon can he see a doctor?"

She smiled like she hated me and all of my kind. "We'll try to get him seen as soon as we can."

As gently as possible, I helped him settle back onto his improvised chaise lounge.

"Ty," I said, "I'm going to get your ID and your insurance card out of your wallet, okay?"

His face was buried in his arm, his answer unintelligible.

I slid his wallet out of its niche in the back right pocket of his jeans. It was worn, brown leather, warm with his body heat.

"I'm looking in your wallet now, Ty." I did not want to look in his wallet.

Pennsylvania driver's license. Frayed Social Security card.

Photographs: A graduation portrait of a scowling, red-haired girl. Bogue, kneeling on a playing field in his football uniform.

A small stack of Ty's business cards, printed with a recent, brooding publicity photo on one side, his contact info on the other.

Paper-clipped other business cards. Among them Peg's, his manager Dave Silva's, and assorted club and record label people.

Seventeen dollars.

Three guitar picks.

"Ty," I asked, "where is your insurance card?"

He squirmed around on the plastic chairs, unable to get comfortable. He mumbled something.

"What?"

He put his arm over his face. "Don't make me talk right now."

"You don't have health insurance?"

"Grace, I'm dying, and you're yelling at me."

"I'm sorry." I stuffed everything but the license and Social Security card back into his wallet, hoping for his sake this was just a stomach bug. The admissions lady, looking grim, brought a clipboard over with a stack of papers for Ty to sign. Shortly after that we were called and I helped him walk slowly back to a curtained cubicle. A nurse handed me a hospital gown.

"Should he leave anything on?" I asked hopefully.

"Everything off," she ordered.

I pulled off his sneaks and helped him take off his flannel shirt and black T-shirt.

"Let's leave these on," I said, of his mismatched black and gray socks.

He was shivering, hugging himself, eyes bleak with pain. I had only seen him cheerful or happily drunk. The way he looked now made me feel afraid.

"Grace," he said, "I'm fucking freezing."

"Let's get the gown on."

He stood slowly and I noted that, actually, he wasn't as skinny as I'd thought. He had some biceps going on. And pecs. His nipples were the same pale pinkish terra-cotta color as his lips. I wasn't staring. Just some flash observations.

I slid the gown up his arms and went around behind to tie it at his neck. The skin on his back was creamy pale but felt hot where my knuckles brushed his nape. He shuddered and I saw goose bumps rise. I went back around front.

He pushed the gown aside and fumbled with the fancy brass buckle on the beat-up Western belt he always wore. His fingers were shivering, like the rest of him. I pushed his hands out of the way and took hold of the buckle to figure out how to disengage it.

His breath, a small, laughing exhalation, stirred the hair on top of my head. I didn't look up, much as I wanted to see that flash of humor in his eyes. I got the buckle undone and loosened the top button of his jeans. The hair trailing down his lower belly was the same reddish brown as the hair on his head. And apparently he was going commando. I stepped away to study a Heimlich maneuver poster while he took care of the rest.

I heard the jeans and heavy buckle hit the floor and the mattress creak.

"Fuck!" he said.

Ty finally settled on his left side, knees drawn up, eyes closed. I tucked the sheet and blanket around him and folded his jeans and shirts and stacked them neatly on a chair. Tucked the Converse away beneath the chair.

"I'm so cold." His teeth were actually chattering. "Come sit next to me."

I perched on the edge of the bed. He drew his thighs up firmly against my bum, hooked his left arm under my bent knees, and curled around me.

"Is this comfortable for you?" I asked.

He buried his face in my skirt.

"Ty, um, am I hurting you, sitting this close?"

The moist heat of his exhalations was seeping through the fabric, scalding my thigh. I was afraid there was going to be a big wet spot. I vaguely noted that his hair and skin tones looked great against my pink, beige, and brown paisley print. And my new mocha tights had runs in both knees, probably from when I knelt beside him on the concrete.

I didn't know what to do with my hands.

He shivered again and I pulled the blanket over his shoulders and placed my left arm around his back, carefully cradling him.

His hair had grown out a lot. It moved in rich, rusty waves. I went ahead and touched it, pushed my fingers through the thick softness.

Ty turned his head and came up for air, sighed, and slept, on and off. More than two hours passed, during which I barely moved. By the time the doctor came in, every muscle was burning and I was desperate to pee.

She was a pretty intern, about my age, Indian-American. I moved to the chair and listened to him retell the whole story he'd told the nurse in triage.

The doctor pressed gently on his lower belly. Ty recoiled and said, loudly, *shit, fuck, motherfucker, son of a bitch, son of a fucking bitch, get away from me, I hate you,* etc.

"Right," Dr. Pallava said. "We need to get a CT scan."

I waited in the hall outside Radiology. A nurse with a kind face came out and told me to go back to the ER and get his clothes. He had acute appendicitis and they were calling a surgeon.

"He's having surgery?"

"Yes, as soon as the doctor gets here. We want to get that appendix out before it ruptures."

I stared at her.

"Get his things and meet me at the fifth-floor nurse's station." She gave me a gentle shove in the right direction.

When I got to the fifth floor, they told me the surgeon couldn't get there till three o'clock.

"That's more than two hours!" I said to the nice nurse.

"We'll try to make him comfortable till then," she said.

"But what if his appendix bursts?"

She patted me on the arm. "We hope that won't happen."

She took me to his room. He was in the bed nearest the door. I couldn't see who was on the other side; the curtain was drawn. There was another nurse, an older man, putting an IV in his arm.

I piled all our stuff on the chair and sat on the bed and held his hand.

"I have a cute appendix," he said.

"You would."

"The doctor can't come take it out till three."

"I know. Let's call your parents, and Bogue."

"Yeah, get my phone, it's in my jeans."

I found the phone and brought it back to the bed.

The nurse finished inserting the IV and said, "I'll be right back."

"Hurry, man," Ty said to the nurse. To me he said, "He's going to give me morphine."

"Good." I wanted that desperate look in his eyes to go away.

He rested a weak hand on my shoulder. "Thank you for taking care of me."

Tears came, surprising me. One rolled down my face before I got myself together. I wiped it away fast. "Of course."

"I'll be all right, darlin'."

"Oh yes, I know."

He laid his head back and closed his eyes. His hand slipped down and came to rest momentarily with his palm lightly cupping the side of my left breast. He was dangerously ill and still trying to cop a feel.

The nurse came back in and inserted a syringe into the IV line.

"Ty," I said, "why did you come to walk the dogs? Why didn't you just go to the hospital?"

"I don't know. It *hurt*, Gracie. I came to you."

I laid my hand over his. I didn't know what to say.

His eyes opened wide, looked at me in surprise, and rolled back in his head.

"How's that? Better?" the nurse asked.

"Unnnnnhhhhh," Ty said blissfully.

"I'll take that as a yes," the nurse said.

Ty floated away. I stepped out in the hall to make calls. I scrolled through his phone book, found Bogue, and left him a message that Ty was going to be all right, but to come to St. Luke's-Roosevelt ASAP.

Then, looking for his parents, I scrolled through numbers for Cathy, Celia, Cindy, Denita, Felicia, Gina, Giselle, Gita, Hannah, and Hosafeena (yeesh, his spelling) before coming to ICE: Mom.

I was impressed that he was that organized. I'd been meaning to reprogram my In Case of Emergency numbers with the ICE prefix and just hadn't gotten around to it yet.

I hit Send. Four rings, and a woman answered cheerfully. "Hi, son!"

"Hello, Mrs. Wilkie?"

Hesitation. "Yes?"

My heart was pounding, I was so nervous about how sick he was, and how to tell her without scaring her.

"I—my name is Grace Barnum, I'm a friend of Tyler's."

"Is he all right?"

"Well, I think he's going to be, but he's going to have to have his appendix taken out this afternoon."

"Where is he?" Now she sounded steely.

"St. Luke's-Roosevelt Hospital, on Tenth Avenue and West Fifty-ninth."

"What time is his surgery?"

"Three o'clock."

"We're leaving now, but we can't get there by then."

"No, I know. I'll be here, and I'll call you and tell you how it's going."

"Thank you. What did you say your name was?"

"Grace Barnum."

"Grace, is Tyler able to speak with me?"

"Let me see. They gave him something for pain and he's been a little loopy."

I opened the door and peeked in at him. He was watching TV.

I went to the bed. "It's your mom."

He took the phone from me. "Hey, Mama! Yeah. Yeah. Yeah. Oh, great! Yeah. Okay, see ya. Oh, hey—when you come, can you bring me the shiny purple thing? From the front yard. I need it. You know, it sings? Yeah. It's purple. Okay. See if you can find it."

He gave me the phone and I stepped back out into the hall to speak further, but she had already hung up.

Just for kicks, I scrolled through his phone book and found Keely, after Jennifer. Good to know he was staying in touch, since she had knitted something for him. It showed gratitude. She was followed by Maria and Nancy. I wondered what they did for him?

I flipped the phone shut. Grace the Stalker. Not my finest moment.

The surgeon finally arrived. He was tall and blond and reminded me of a TV weatherman. He talked to Ty for a few minutes, described the surgical procedure. It would be laparoscopic, and didn't sound all that bad. I just wanted them to hurry.

The morphine seemed to have worn off some. He was in pain again and a lot more lucid. I gave him a careful hug.

"Will you be here when I come back?"

"Of course! I'll be right here, the whole time."

"Give me a kiss, Grace. It might be my last."

I leaned over again and pressed my lips against his for a few seconds.

"You're going to be all right," I said firmly.

They started rolling him out of the room.

"Ty?"

"Yeah?"

I didn't want to scare him, but I needed to know: "What's your favorite song?"

"'Maybe I'm Amazed.' I'll play it for you."

Tyler's first word after the operation was "OW!"

The surgeon came in and told us that the appendix came out just in time—it was gangrenous and "about one minute away from exploding."

I thanked him. While the nurse gave Ty a shot of Demerol, I called his mom and told her he was in recovery and doing fine.

"We just arrived," she said. They must have driven a hundred miles per hour from eastern Pennsylvania.

Moments later they were waiting at the door of his room watching me approach, a man and a woman in faded jeans and tees, probably in their mid-fifties. She was lovely in a Nordic way, tall, no makeup, her graying blond hair pulled back in a loose ponytail. He had a beard and graying brown hair, longer than hers.

I held out my hand. "Hello, I'm Grace Barnum."

Ty's mom pulled my hand until I was in her arms. She smelled like rosemary, perhaps from puttering in their garden. She kissed my cheek and let me go and smiled at me. "Grace Barnum, thank you."

"Oh, no problem!"

"I'm Jean, and this is Nathan." I shook his hand and he gave me a gruff hello.

"He's doing great," I said. "They're going to bring him up here in a few minutes."

"I'm gonna go have a cigarette," Nathan said. "Be right back."

He gave me the package he was carrying. It was the weight and shape of a basketball, wrapped in several plastic grocery bags.

"All right, hon, hurry back," Jean said. He ambled away, toward the elevators. I recognized the loping walk.

"He's not allowed to smoke in the car," Jean said.

"Oh."

"How long have you and Tyler known each other?"

"A few months. He walks my neighbor's dogs."

I could see she was having trouble connecting the dots. "He passed out in front of my building, and I was on my way to work. Some people helped me get him in a cab and I brought him here."

"You mean he was that sick and he went to walk the dogs?" Her eyes filled. "Oh, my poor boy."

"He's going to be fine. Really. Look, here he is."

They were rolling his gurney toward us. His mom leaned over him and took his face in her hands.

"I'm okay," he said groggily.

"You'd better be."

When Nathan came back from smoking, he kissed his son and unwrapped the mystery orb. It was a mirrored-glass Victorian gazing ball. He set it on Ty's bed.

Ty was nauseous, sore, more ill-humored than I've ever seen him, but the corners of his mouth turned up.

"We weren't sure what you were talking about, we figured it must be this," Nathan said.

"What the hell?" Ty said.

"You asked for it, son. You said it sings."

Ty looked disappointed. "Oh, yeah. Unless they give me some more morphine, I don't think I'll be able to hear it."

He looked over at me mournfully. "Gracie. Morphine is the shit."

reassigning the angel

At home, standing in the shower, I thought about the scariness of the day. About Ty, in terrible pain, and the wait for the surgeon. With the water pounding on me, I sat down and cried until I was exhausted. I ate some canned mushroom soup and went to bed with the phone next to me in case Steven called.

A couple of days later, Ty's mom rang to say that she and Nathan were going home and would I mind checking on Ty? He was going to rest at home for a few more days, and Bogue had finally gotten a job and wouldn't be around a lot.

I swung by after work. The front door to his Hell's Kitchen tenement was ajar, so I let myself in and crept up the stairs. I tapped on the apartment door.

"Come in, Fuck-face!"

It was, as expected, a single room, with a tiny, separate kitchenette. The walls and ceiling were painted dark blue, with not a lot of daylight making it in. There was a futon, a floor lamp, and an Ikea-type white dresser. Besides an electric piano and assorted milk crates crammed with clothes, CDs, harmonicas, and amplifier cables, that was it for furniture.

Ty was wearing a Metallica T-shirt and black boxers, lying on his back amid rumpled sheets on the open futon. He looked wan and depleted, but sat up on his elbows when he saw me.

"Oh, hey. I thought you were Bogue."

"Good to know," I said, taking off my coat and draping it over Big Green on the floor.

"He's supposed to be bringing me a pizza. It's been two hours."

"Why would he knock? Doesn't he live here?"

"Not anymore. He and Allison hooked up and got their own place, up on Fifty-second."

"Who's Allison?"

"Rash. She changed back to her real name."

"Oh. That's weird," I said. "Them as a couple."

"Yeah."

"Will you be able to afford this by yourself?"

"Bogue's gonna keep paying their part of the rent till the lease is up in August."

"What will you do then?"

He lay back down and stared at the ceiling. "Do I have to figure that out today?"

"Of course not! I just thought . . . maybe you had a plan."

"Did you come here to be a pain in the ass, Grace?"

Was he cranky! I opened the windows a few inches to give him some semi-fresh air. He had a lovely view of the brick wall next door.

"I came because your mom asked me to check on you."

"Well, don't do anything you don't want to." He turned on his side so his back was to me.

Sullen Tyler. This was interesting. I sat behind him on the edge of the futon. "What's the matter?"

"I'm sorry I took up so much of your day on Tuesday."

"Ty, don't be ridiculous."

"I knocked on your door for help and you didn't answer."

"What? I was—I must have been in the bathroom with the door closed. It's a thick door."

"Why would you close the bathroom door with your boyfriend gone?"

"I don't know! I just did."

"You heard me, Grace. You didn't want to see me."

"Ty, that's not true!" I have never felt more lying and evil.

He looked over his shoulder at me. "It's not?"

"It's not. I swear. Look at how—how surprised and upset I was to see you ill, on the ground!"

He turned over on his back and laid his hand on my leg, palm up. I set my hand in it.

After a long moment he said, "Don't do that to me again."

"Ty!" I protested. Apparently he had some of my Dad's x-ray vision. He would not be bullshitted. "Okay. I won't."

He sighed heavily and laid his arm over his eyes. I wanted to pat him, or brush his hair off his face, do something kind and reassuring. "How are you healing?" I asked.

"Pretty good." He pulled his shirt up and the top of his boxers down and showed me the three laparoscopic incisions, covered with surgical tape. One was in his belly button.

"Those don't look so bad," I said.

"They're sore."

"Well, don't try to do too much yet."

"I'm just lying here, babe."

"I brought you a book." I went and got it out of Big Green and gave it to him.

He read the title aloud. *"A Prayer for Owen Meany."* He eyed me suspiciously. "Is this going to make me cry?"

"Buckets."

"You're a sadist."

"It will make you laugh, first."

"Oh, great."

"Just trying to keep you entertained."

"You want me to tell you how I'd like to be entertained?"

"No."

He sat up and propped pillows against the wall. "All right," he grumbled. "Then hand me my guitar."

I got it for him out of its case on the floor, and went to the kitchenette to see if he had food. It looked like his mother had stocked up.

"Do you think Bogue is coming with your pizza?"

"I doubt it. He probably got called in to work and forgot."

"What's he doing?"

"Driving a limo. He has to grab it when they call him 'cause his old man is cutting him off."

"Oh, really?"

"Yeah, he had twelve hundred dollars in parking tickets and his dad told him to get his shit together or come home and manage a store."

"I'll make you something to eat. I don't know if you should be eating pizza yet, anyway."

"Okay."

I fixed him chicken and rice soup, and toast, and brought the plate to him.

He was playing guitar quietly. "Just lie it there," he said, nodding at the upside-down milk crate on the floor next to him.

"Lay." I sat cross-legged on the end of the futon.

"Huh?"

"*Lay* is a transitive verb. *Lie* is intransitive. You *lay* the plate down."

He smiled, still lightly strumming. "Okay, Brainiac. Lay. That should be easy for me to remember."

He showed me the lyrics of a new song he was working on, and played "Calling" for me, finally. It was so pretty. I loved it and said so. He seemed inordinately pleased; he actually got a little flush in his cheeks, which amazed me. With all the adulation he was receiving, why on earth did my opinion matter so much?

"Ty, eat," I said.

He set the guitar down. "I got the hospital bill," he said, slurping soup.

"How bad?"

"Twenty-four thousand."

"Those *bastards*."

"I hope they'll consider twenty dollars a month for the rest of my life sufficient."

I took one of his crackers and nibbled an edge. "You scared me, Ty."

"I promise, you will not have to deal with any more gangrene organs. Only fresh, strong, healthy, big ones. Or one, I should say."

"You just can't help yourself, can you?"

He laughed, then said "ouch" and got quiet, watching me wash his dishes and put them away. I picked up my raincoat.

"Don't go," he said.

"I have to." Steven had come home from London while I was at work.

Ty sighed. "That sucks."

"I'll call you tomorrow." I hated leaving him alone in his dark little flat.

In my coat pocket I had the tiny, silver guardian-angel medallion that Edward gave me; I had brought it for just this purpose. When I leaned over to pick up Big Green, I tucked it firmly into a crevice in the blue velvet lining of Ty's guitar case.

"Hey," Steven said when I came in the door. A kiss, and a big bear hug. After so much worry the past few days, it was a relief to lean into him.

"I missed you," he said. "Are you hungry?"

We went to our favorite burrito place a few blocks up. He told me about London, and I told him about the Indiana textbook I was working on. I told him about the movies I'd been to with Edward. I briefly sketched for him the story of Ty's appendectomy, keeping it light and humorous. I didn't tell him how wrenching it all was. I didn't need to.

"You must have been so scared for him," Steven said.

My eyes filled, maybe from post-traumatic stress, or maybe the right-now trauma I was feeling, telling Steven about it. Guilty butterflies. Which annoyed me. Why should I be feeling guilty?

"Grace, you are so caring." He took my hand. "Listen, why don't we take a trip Memorial Day weekend? A guy at work told me about this beautiful old B-and-B up near Woodstock."

"Oh . . . really?"

"Yeah, he said the room he stayed in had a canopy bed."

"A canopy? No way!" I am a sucker for canopied beds.

Steven nodded, looking particularly pleased with my reaction. That's when I knew that he planned to propose. He didn't give a crap about old furniture.

Late Sunday night, Ty called.

Sorry, I mouthed to Steven, who had just fallen asleep. I took my phone to the kitchen.

"What are you trying to do, woman, kill me?"

He'd been crying. I was coming to know the sound of it.

"You finished the book."

He'd spent the past hour pulling himself together and rereading the last twenty pages. He sounded changed. I remembered how deeply moved I'd been by the devoted friendship and sacrifice in the story.

"I promise, next time, something you will laugh at."

"I'm playing tomorrow night. Will you come?"

"Already? Shouldn't you rest a few more days?"

"Too much rest is bad for me, Grace. I've got to get up now."

"Okay, but no heavy lifting."

"Right. Will you come?"

"I don't think I can. Steven just got back."

"Oh, yeah. Well. I'll see you around, then."

"Okay, Ty."

Steven was sitting up in bed. "Who was that?"

"Ty," I said, and watched a tiny, uncharacteristic flash of irritation cross his face.

"It's kind of late, isn't it?"

"Yes, sorry. He just wanted to tell me something about a book. I'm not sure he pays all that much attention to the time."

"Hm," Steven said, punching his pillow and nestling into it. "I guess he keeps musician's hours."

There was no ignoring Tyler now. After going through the appendix episode with him, it felt like, well . . . like I'd been through something with him. Like we'd been through something together. He would call with an activity in mind, and I almost always said yes. We met a few times here and there—for hot dogs in the park on my lunch hour, a Saturday-afternoon Film Forum showing of *To Kill a Mockingbird*. What a softy—he cried more than I did.

He told me about every horrific injury he ever suffered in childhood. And there were some doozies. My reaction to each new story was surprisingly visceral. I got queasy. Light-headed. I had a couple of nightmares.

We were sitting on a bench at the Reservoir when he told me the worst one yet, about the time when he was twelve and he fractured his skull falling off the roof of his house.

"Okay, that's *it*!" I jumped to my feet.

He stood up. "What's wrong?"

"You could have died! What if you had a brain hemorrhage or something?"

He laughed. "I guess I wouldn't be standing here with you."

"I have to get back to work now." I race-walked toward Central Park West. He kept up with me.

"You're acting like you're mad at me."

"Ty! Ever since the hospital you have been telling me the most upsetting stories. The broken wrist. The near-drowning. The splinter in the eye. The nail in the foot. Need I even mention the incident with the *chainsaw*?"

He shrugged. "I was just a typical boy."

"Dear God." I laughed humorlessly. "That cannot be true." I continued briskly toward the park gate, done with him for the day. Maybe forever, I mused. Yes! Done with him forever. For my own good.

"I like telling you these stories."

"I know. Because you love torturing me."

I could tell, peripherally, that he was smiling. As usual, it made me want to smile, too. My sense of humor peeked out at me to see if it was okay to come back now. I ignored it and him, not ready to give in.

We reached the street. I raised my hand and a cab veered toward us.

"I like how much my stories bother you."

"Stop."

"I do."

"*Don't.*" I kept my eyes on the approaching car.

"Grace. . . ." And that was unnecessary, by the way, how close he was standing. Probably looking at my mouth.

He did that a lot.

One time over coffee I told him about the Webbers and the abstinence-only health textbook. I told him how worried I was about teens not being given real-life information and skills.

"That's retarded," he grumbled. Then he got all fired up. "What is their problem, anyway? Fucking is fun! Natural! It's good for you."

"Darn, if only you'd been there with me at the meeting with Delilah and Forbes."

That wasn't the only thing. I told him about *imagine*. You know it's something bad when it makes Tyler Wilkie become grave and quiet.

"Shit," he finally said. "Those people are really fucked up."

"I know."

"What are you doing, Grace?"

"What?"

"Why are you still working at that place?"

"Ty—"

"Doesn't it matter to you what you do with your life? With your mind and your heart and your hands?"

"Of course it matters! You're being simplistic."

"I like simplicity."

I got quiet.

He nudged my foot with his under the table. "Just be real, Grace. That's all I'm saying. Try to be real." He nudged me again. "Why are you crying?"

"I'm not."

"Yes you are."

"I'm getting my period."

He smiled. "You are so full of shit."

Except for minor excursions across the flirtation line, Ty was pretty cool to spend time with. Probably because he was having a hell of a social life. Really, the guy was just fine without me.

He got phone calls from girls all the time. He'd either look at who was calling and let them leave a message, or he'd answer, but keep the exchange brief. Monosyllabic even. He'd hang up and then not look at me right away. He'd jump right back into the thing we'd been talking about.

One time, walking up Sixth Avenue together, he did meet my eyes. I smiled teasingly. He smiled and looked away.

"One word, Tyler," I said. "As your friend."

"Go ahead."

"Prophylactics."

He studied the ground ahead of us. "That is not an area I need your advice on, Grace."

"I'm sorry," I said. I really, really was.

The week before Memorial Day, I e-mailed Julia and Dan to let them know that Steven and I were going up to Rhinebeck for the weekend.

Julia called me. "Something important is going to happen, don't you think?"

No point in denying it. "Probably so."

"Are you excited?"

"Yeah."

"What's the matter?"

I put some energy into it. "Nothing! I'm excited!" Anything, to cool her jets.

Dan IM'd me at work:

DanB: Have fun, but don't do anything you don't want to.

SueGBee: What do you mean?

DanB: I had a dream.

SueGBee: Oh crap. And?

 [three minutes of cliff-hanging]

SueGBee: Don't make me come over there.

DanB: Sorry. FedEx, downstairs. The dream: you were driving a car with bad brakes. You wanted to stop it, but you couldn't.

SueGBee: I don't like that. Would it kill you to dream something nice?

DanB: Sorry . . .

DanB: Are you there?

SueGBee: Sorry. Thinking. I guess that brake thing could maybe apply to a few things in my life.

DanB: Apply it then, my darling.

Friday morning I got my hair cut for the summer in breezy layers, chin-length, with bangs. I looked about twelve years old.

I went to work just for a couple of hours, to do some filing and show Edward my hair.

He touched it with faux-reverent fingers. "Shiny."

Edward was in holiday weekend mode already, too, jeans and a linen shirt. He and Boris were going to the Jersey shore.

"Be careful," I said, "you may run into my mom and José there."

"Lord no, not Julia Barnum."

"I'm serious. They're going to Ocean Grove. Staying in one of those little tent house things."

"Those are so cute! And you and Steven are going to Rhinebeck?"

"Yeah, he found this three-hundred-year-old farmhouse B-and-B. We're going to play golf."

"Golf." He made a face.

"He swears it's not boring. We'll do other things, too."

"And you still think you're going to come back with a ring on your finger?"

"Yes."

"And that's a good thing?"

I hated when Edward got all older brother on me.

"Don't give me that look," he said. "I'm just making sure."

"I know." I hugged him.

Steven picked me up at work in a Zipcar. A convertible!

He hadn't seen my new look yet. I got in beside him and buckled up. He touched my hair. "Where did it all go?"

"Locks of Love. Let someone else deal with all that. It won't even hold a curl."

"If you'd told me you were going to do this, I think I'd have asked you not to. But it looks real pretty."

"Oh . . . really? I just wanted a change. I thought it would feel good for summer."

"Yeah, it looks great."

"Sorry."

"Grace, it's not a big deal."

"Sometimes you have to just go ahead and make yourself do things you're chicken about, you know?"

He eased us into the flow of traffic on Sixth Avenue with a wry little smile on his face. "Tell me about it."

The place where we were staying was rustic and colonial, situated in the middle of a retired apple orchard. Exposed beams in the very old kitchen with hanging copper pots and bundles of herbs. A hand-made quilt, on our bed.

Breakfast on Saturday was pear pancakes with smoked bacon. After that we played golf. Me, for the first time. It was not good. Then we had an afternoon spa visit. It was good. I had a facial and a full-body massage, and went back to the inn jelly-kneed and very pliable.

Steven took me to a fancy French restaurant for dinner, where we were seated in a lovely little private alcove. After my lobster salad but before my filet de boeuf, he took a small box out of his pocket. I set down my wineglass.

"You know what this is." Steven's face was turning red. And his hands were shaking, trying to open the little case.

"Do you want me to do it?" I offered, although my own hands had just gone numb.

"Got it!" He showed me what was inside. It was stunning. Platinum, with not one, but *three* antique-cut diamonds.

"Oh my goodness," I said faintly. My heart was trying to stomp its way out of my chest.

Steven got up from his chair and knelt beside me, just like in the movies. "Grace, I love you and I want to spend the rest of my life with you. Will you marry me?"

"Okay." Even though I had known this was coming, I still didn't know what to do with it. My body was discombobulated, too. I felt like the top of my head was about to lift away from the rest of me and float up to the ceiling. Not having a paper bag handy, I cupped my hands, held them over my nose, and aggressively inhaled my own carbon dioxide.

"What are you doing?"

"A little light-headed. Just give me a minute."

The floaty feeling subsided. Steven handed me my glass of ice water and I gulped too much, too fast. Ouch.

"Better now?"

"Much," I lied.

He picked up my tingling hand and slid the ring onto my finger. It stopped on the second knuckle and refused to go farther. He pushed harder, but it was a stubborn ring.

"I think my finger's too fat," I giggled, though I am not generally a giggler.

"Nonsense. We'll just have to have the ring resized. I'll make an appointment for us at Fred Leighton as soon as we get back."

"I'm sorry," I said. "Otherwise, it's so perfect."

He leaned forward and kissed me. Steven was always so steady and kind. I sighed and set my arms over his shoulders and smiled ruefully.

"Are you okay?" he asked.

"Yes."

"Are you sure?"

"Yes," I said, definitively. "Very, very sure."

blue Fiji swimming head

I didn't see Ty for all of June. I think he went to Philly to play a few times and I was just so busy with work and spending time with my fiancé. But Ty called to remind me that July 13 was his birthday. Rather than commit to his East Village birthday party, which would be heinously drunken and loud, I talked him into letting me take him to dinner at a sidewalk café on Second Avenue. I made an 8:30 reservation but told him to be there at 7:45. I watched him amble down the street toward me at 8:14. I took him by the elbow and walked him away from the restaurant.

"Hey, isn't this the place?"

"Yeah, I told the waiter we're coming right back."

I situated him on the corner of Second and Thirty-fourth, slid a pair of Ray-Bans on him, and turned him westward. "Look."

"Oh, *man*! Awesome!" he said, squinting.

The sun was setting on the horizon, bold and round and orange, in perfect alignment with the street. A lot of people were around us looking/not looking at it.

"Manhattanhenge. It happens a couple times a year. Happy birthday!"

"Yeah. Happy birthday to me," he mused absently. I could see that there was a song starting to brew while his retinas were frying.

"Stop looking at the sun now," I said.

"Okay." He smiled happily at the big blue dot he was probably seeing instead of my face. We walked back to the café.

We reclaimed our table and ordered. Then we looked at each other. It had been a while, five weeks at least.

"Your hair's longer than mine now," I said.

"Yeah, you look like Scout."

"Edward said Ramona the Pest."

He shyly slid a CD across the table to me. It had a charming black-and-white picture of him on the cover, in profile, laughing. He had the nicest nose.

"My new demo. It has all your songs on it."

"*My* songs," I laughed. "Please."

He smiled.

I gave him his presents. A book: Kurt Vonnegut's *Slapstick*, and a CD: Kate Bush's *The Kick Inside*.

He examined the book suspiciously. "It better be fucking hilarious."

"It is! Look, even the title is funny."

"Did they make it into a movie?"

"Um . . . I think maybe they did?"

"'Cause maybe we can watch it when I finish."

I smiled. "I'll Google it."

He picked up the CD. "Hey, this was on your list!"

"Yeah, I can't wait for you to hear it."

Our food came and for a while we just ate and watched people go by. That was something I liked about doing things with Ty. He could talk, quite a lot. But companionable silence was easy, too.

I figured I should let him know I was getting married. All my other friends knew. I was inexplicably nervous about telling him, but now seemed like a good, mellow time.

"Hey, by the way," I said. "I'm getting married."

He had been watching a red-haired woman swish down the street, but his eyes came back to me and his chewing slowed. He looked at my hand, resting on the table. At the big shiny piece of metal and mineral I was wearing. He drank some beer and wiped his mouth with his napkin. He looked at me, hard.

"Well, congratulations," he said rather loudly.

"Um . . . thanks."

"Um . . . you're welcome."

"Ty . . . aren't you happy for me?"

"*No.*" He was actually glaring at me now. So much for mellow.

"*Shit*, Grace!" he said violently.

"What is your problem?" I spoke sharply, but really I felt like crying. "Why can't you just be nice?"

He laughed in a mean way and stood up and tossed his napkin on his plate. "Shut the fuck up."

He walked away.

"Happy birthday!" I yelled after him.

Julia's kitchen table was covered with Internet printouts and brochures. She handed me one of those telephone-directory-size bride's magazines and asked me to look at the pages she'd flagged.

The wedding gowns she liked were crisp, spare, ankle-length sheaths. They looked like big calla lilies. I flipped through a few more pages. "Ooh." I pointed at an A-line halter gown with a high, lacy ruffle around the neck.

"Oh, no," Julia said. "Too frilly. You don't want to cut yourself off at the neck like that."

I flipped through some more pages and stopped at a breathtaking silk organza Empire gown with bare shoulders.

Julia took a long look. "The thing is, you're short, so you don't want to wear anything too voluminous, skirt-wise. It will absolutely swallow you. You don't want to disappear on your wedding day, do you?"

"I guess not."

"That's why I bookmarked those dresses that have a close profile, not too much fabric, and show some chest."

My inner storybook princess felt sad. She liked the gowns with big, flowing skirts.

"But it's *your* wedding, of course, and you have to pick something *you* like." It was amazing how Julia's words could be generous and still sound slightly grudging. "Have you two decided on a date?"

"We were originally talking about December, but I think I'd rather wait until spring."

"Good, spring is better. It should give us plenty of time to get the details just right." She held up a brochure. "What do you think of an outdoor wedding at this winery upstate?"

"We had talked about getting married at that church where we volunteer."

"All right," Julia said slowly. "A church wedding, with an elegant reception somewhere else. The Four Seasons, possibly, or look at this." A magazine photo of a gorgeous room: tables, candles, flowering trees, mellow light. "These people rented this loft space and brought in everything. Those are dogwood branches!"

"Ooh." I took a closer look. I do like dogwood.

"Of course, you have to pick your color scheme. And make a guest list. And decide on attendants. And what the men will wear. And the menu. And invitations. And have you thought about your honeymoon?"

"Steven showed me a webpage for a resort on Fiji. The water there is really blue. And they have snorkeling and horseback riding and a library."

"A library? People on their honeymoon don't need a library."

"I thought it was nice. And Steven said we could even get married there, if we want."

My mom crossed her arms. "Do you want me going with you to Fiji? Because I *will* be at your wedding. And what about Steven's parents?"

"He said they would be okay with not being there."

"Well, I'm sure they were at his first wedding." She looked at me and quickly backpedaled. "I'm not saying they don't care."

"Mom, can we save some of this for later?"

"Well, of course, we're not going to do it all today."

"Thank you." I really did feel grateful. My head was swimming.

A couple of weeks later Ty called me about his music-industry showcase at Joe's Pub. He said lots of important people would be there, and it would be recorded. Could I please try to come? He sounded nervous.

Then, same day, he called again. His lease was running out and he'd found a new roommate to move in with, a drummer who had done some work for him. But he'd just found out he couldn't move in until August 3. Could he crash on our couch for a couple of nights?

I had to check with Steven, I said. I looked at the refrigerator calendar. Turned out, he would be in Munich that week.

Hmmm.

What might that be like—just me and Ty, roomies? We could order Chinese and watch Lifetime. Maybe play a few rounds of Sorry. I'd go to bed and wake up being spooned. Or wake to the sound of giggling women in my living room. Or a Tupperware party, hosted by Hugh Hefner.

I called him back. "Can you try one of your other musician friends?"

"Dude, their places are disgusting."

"What about Dave, your manager?"

"He lives way the fuck out on Long Island."

I asked him to try Peg and thought for sure that would be the solution. She was so soft where he was concerned.

Turned out Peg had cousins from Kentucky visiting that week.

"Well, what about Bogue and Allison?"

"And listen to them hump all night?"

"Wear earplugs!"

"Grace, come on. I swear I won't make a big mess. I'll be invisible."

Yeah, right.

I called Peg. She agreed to sleep over those two nights. It would be nice to have a break from her cousins, an elderly married couple who were visiting for two whole weeks. The first night, a Monday, she'd be with us at the showcase. The second night she'd come over after work.

"You'll have to sleep with me," I said, "hope you don't mind."

"As long as you shave your legs."

People were queuing up when Peg and I arrived at Joe's Pub, but we were special. On the guest list. We joined Bogue and Allison at a table near the stage. This was a bigger deal than I had realized. I looked around at the other special people there.

"Is that Billy Joel?" I asked Peg.

"Yes, and that's Alicia Keys."

"David Bowie and Iman are over there," Allison said.

I took a peek, confirmed the sighting, and shrank back behind Peg, though surely Mr. Bowie wouldn't recognize Dan Barnum's daughter, all grown up.

"Where's Ty?" I asked Bogue.

He shrugged. "Last I saw, in the men's room throwing up. I told him if he sucked tonight he could always go back to working at the funeral home and he told me to get the hell out of there."

My own stomach was beginning to hurt. What if he messed up? What if he embarrassed himself in front of all of these famous people? Would the band be able to cover for him if he made a mistake?

They let the plebeians in, including the street team girls, all so aggressively sexy with their heels and cleavage and heavy makeup. They commandeered several tables back by the bar. The whole club quickly filled up.

"I feel so nervous for Ty," Peg whispered.

"Me, too."

There was an opening act, a girl singer, but I barely remember her. Then Ty's band came onstage, along with a stand-up comic everyone seemed to know. He introduced Tyler. "The buzz about this guy is pretty huge," the comic said. "I've never heard him, I don't like music. I'm going to try to get out of here before he starts playing. Tyler Wilkie!" Big whoops and applause.

Ty came onstage looking a little sheepish and adorable in his wagon-wheel shirt and ripped jeans and scuffed boots. They put a spotlight on him and everyone hushed.

He started playing, then stopped.

My heart was in my throat.

He quietly thanked everyone for being there. Then he started over again, with a song that I hadn't heard before. You couldn't tell he was nervous at all.

I relaxed as he ran through his repertoire with even more creativity and spark than usual. He sank into it. He went into his zone. I wondered how it felt to him to look out and see those familiar faces, people he'd grown up listening to, now listening to him.

I felt like I could cry, imagining how he might be feeling. Peg looked watery, too. It made me feel even closer to her, that we both cared for him so much.

He moved to the piano and played the slow, sensual intro to something I knew, though I couldn't quite identify it.

"My friend Grace turned me on to this song," he said.

Then he started singing.

It was "Feel It," my absolute favorite song from that Kate Bush album, *The Kick Inside*. An extraordinarily sexy, lush, tender song about going home with someone after a party and, well, having a shag. I'd never, *ever* imagined a man singing it, in this quiet, deliciously bluesy way.

I was beginning to feel awfully warm. I looked around the room. The women were leaning toward him. Even the men were paying close attention.

At the last note, pin-drop silence. Then spontaneous combustion.

He'd burned up every woman in the place, and a few men, too. We were all ready to go home immediately and start feeling it.

Before starting the next song, he took a moment to drink most of a beer and hold the bottle to his face. "Excuse me, I'm feeling a little flushed."

The street team girls screamed.

He played for another half hour, but it was icing. I was pretty sure that, for whatever industry executives were there, the deal must be done by now.

When he finished and they brought up the lights, he stepped off the stage and was swarmed by people getting up from their tables to congratulate him. We were going to have to wait awhile.

I headed for the ladies' room, feeling so happy about Ty's performance. On the way, a woman tripped me. I recovered and turned around and she smiled and winked. "Sorry, Grace."

I had seen her at other gigs, but I didn't know her name.

I got back to the table and told Peg, Bogue, and Allison I was leaving.

"Why?" Peg asked.

"There's a psycho fan here who has it in for me. She tripped me on the way to the restroom."

"Oh. Well, maybe it was an accident."

"It wasn't."

"Well, you can't go. You haven't spoken to Ty yet."

I looked across the room. You couldn't even see him, the crowd around him was so thick.

"We'll talk to him later."

"This is his big night!" Peg said. "We should at least make sure he knows we're here."

Bogue and Allison had the good sense to leave, after a while. Peg and I stayed and watched the street team amazons slowly infiltrate the knot of people around Ty. There was no way I was going to try to compete with them for his attention; they were all a foot taller than me and probably packing heat. So we waited on the periphery for almost an hour before the place thinned out and I was able to make eye contact with him.

He came directly to me and slung a heavy arm across my shoulders. He reeked of booze. I grimaced at Peg and fanned the fumes he was emitting away from my face.

"Hey, I'm going home with you, right?" He was just barely holding on to all of his consonants.

"That's the rumor."

"Can we go now?"

Thank God.

We got a cab. He sat between Peg and me.

"So I think maybe I got a major-label record deal tonight."

Peg and I both sat forward and looked at him. He smiled like the cat that drank the whiskey-laced cream.

"When will you know for sure?" Peg asked.

"They want to meet with me this week."

"Ty, that is so great!" I said.

He squeezed me. "How'd you like the song? Is it your favorite?"

I de-suctioned his hand from my inner thigh and held it lightly in both of mine. "It is. How did you know?"

"I know you, babe."

strawberry

Ty was in the bathroom a long time. I knocked on the door.

No answer. I opened the door and peeked in. He was lying on the floor on his back with my nightgown draped over his face.

"Ty! You can't sleep here. Get up!"

He rolled over. Peg came in and we shook him till he slowly rose to his feet.

"Did he get sick?" Peg asked as we guided him to the couch.

"I don't think so."

"Maybe you'd better put a pan beside the couch. And a towel."

"Yeah, and maybe we should make him lie down on his stomach, so he doesn't aspirate his own vomit."

"Ew," Peg said.

"Think Jimi Hendrix," I said.

"Well, hadn't Jimi done heroin, or something like that?"

"Stop talking about me like I'm not here," Ty said.

"You're not all here," I said.

"Some of me is."

"Unfortunately, only the part that needs to go to Betty Ford."

He thought that was funny. He put his arms around me and rubbed his scratchy face in my neck. "I love you, Gracie. Love you forever."

I patted his shoulder. "Ohh-kay. I love you, too." I looked at Peg and rolled my eyes.

"Lie down, now." I gave him a push.

"You lie down with me." He succumbed to gravity, and so did I; he pulled me down with him on the couch. I squirmed like an up-ended beetle till Peg pried me loose and hauled me up. He grabbed at my skirt but I scurried out of reach. I yanked his boots off. Peg tossed the blanket over him.

"Night!" We hastened to the bedroom and shut the door.

"I can hear you laughing," he said loudly. "What's so funny?"

"Nothing!" Peg said. "Go to sleep."

"Jeez, what a romantic drunk," I said in a low voice.

"Oh, honey." Peg was rummaging around in her overnight bag for her toothbrush but stopped to smile sadly at me. "You know he meant it."

It was a searing one hundred and one degrees when I left work the next day. Naturally, the air-conditioning was out on my train. I sat in a puddle of my own moisture and crossed my fingers that a rolling blackout wouldn't trap us in sweltering darkness.

I held my breath through the urine-scented Eighty-sixth Street station till I reached the street, where I gulped lungfuls of refreshing car exhaust. I popped into the specialty bakery across from my building and bought a strawberry icebox pie.

I felt oddly cautious going into my own apartment. I tapped on the door and stuck my head in. "Hello?"

It was quiet and hot. Ty must have been gone for hours. I wondered how late he'd slept. What had he done while he was here by himself all morning? Probably made a large dent in the fridge.

I wondered, queasily, if he'd peeked in my medicine cabinet. Eek. Or maybe in my underwear drawer? Wince. Definitely needed to weed things out, there. Oh, who cares! Let him see my diaphragm and my ratty old bras.

I put the pie in the fridge, cranked the living room window unit up to high, and let the icy blast freeze-dry my sticky skin. Went to the bedroom and turned on that AC. Fixed a big glass of sugary iced tea and took a cool shower. Put on shorts and a tee, and made a salad to go with the leftover turkey meat loaf. Sat in front of the TV and watched *Jeopardy!* and had a nice dinner and a gigantic wedge of creamy pink-and-white pie.

I went to the bedroom and arranged a workspace on my bed. We were developing an encyclopedia of the Renaissance at Spender-Davis, and I was tasked with writing most of the shorter articles about important inventions of the era. The first was wallpaper, and I needed to finish the article tonight, having been distracted and useless all day. I piled all the pillows up into a comfy nest, arranged my pile of source materials nearby, and opened my laptop. Then, because I have a big problem with procrastination, I turned on the bedroom television. There were still fifteen minutes left of the 7:30 *King of Queens*. My mom would have shuddered. *Queens, ugh! Why is that funny?*

I heard the key in the lock; then Ty appeared in the bedroom doorway. "Hey."

"Hey." I muted the TV.

His hair was curly from the humidity and he was wearing baggy shorts, flip-flops, and a beat-up blue chamois shirt with the sleeves cut off. Some kind of pewter rune strung on black leather around his neck. He was carrying a messenger bag and his guitar in its canvas case on his back.

"Damn, it's hotter than a motherfucker out there."

"I know, it's awful."

He took the bag and the guitar off and set them against the bedroom wall.

The TV was playing a commercial for New York Lotto. "What are you watching?"

"*King of Queens*. It's almost over. Then I have to work."

"Okay." He stuck his hands in his pockets.

Could you loosen up a bit, Grace? Be hospitable! "It's a great episode," I said. "Hilarious!"

"Oh, yeah?" He brightened up. Came and sat on the end of the bed. He smelled nice, a mingling of warm man and some kind of citrusy cologne.

"Doug accidentally shoots himself in the scrotum with a staple gun."

Tyler did not smile.

"No, really, it's great! Here, it's back on."

He lounged across the end of the bed. It was fun to hear him cackling with me when Doug tries to tell the ER admissions lady about his predicament and ends up drawing her a diagram of the injured area.

At the next commercial Ty told me he had spent the day with Bogue moving his things to the new place. It was all piled in the guy's living room until tomorrow, when he'd be able to actually move into his room.

"Are you hungry?" I asked.

"Yeah."

We went to the kitchen, where I poured him some tea and showed him the meat loaf. "There's also salad and pie. Do you want me to fix it for you?"

"No, I'll do it. Thanks, Grace."

"Well," I said. "I have to work, I hope you don't mind. Feel free to watch TV or whatever."

"I might work on a song. Will it bother you if I play my guitar?"

"No, I'll close the door."

"Okay, let me know if I'm too loud."

I left the bedroom door ajar about a quarter-inch, so as not to be completely rude. Re-situated myself on the bed with the laptop and picked up a source printout to read.

Wallpaper. Okay. Not that much was being asked of me. A mere 250 words. So far, after "working" on it all day, I had twenty:

For the less affluent members of the gentry in Renaissance Europe, wall-paper was an affordable decorative alternative to woven tapestries.

I looked at the examples of early woodcut-printed wallpaper that I'd Googled. Nice enough colors. Maybe a little too much orange. How much would it suck to be upper-class but poor and see the Uni-corn Tapestries warming your neighbor's walls, while you just had some cheap paper saints and shrubs pasted on yours?

Ty was eating. I could hear the click of the fork on his plate. He was watching something on TV; it sounded like one of those celebrity ballroom-dancing shows. At the rate he was going, maybe he'd be do-ing that in about ten years. I had a good chuckle at the mental image.

Apparently Henry VIII messed up trade with Europe when he ditched the Catholic Church, and no one could get a decent arras tapestry anymore. Everyone resorted to wallpaper.

Kitchen sounds. Ty was loading the dishwasher. That was nice.

Then Oliver Cromwell took over and put the kibosh on anything fun or frivolous. No more wallpaper for anyone until the reign of Charles II.

Tuning his guitar. Quietly strumming.

I leaned my head back on the pillows and closed my eyes. Maybe I should just start fresh tomorrow at work. I would get laser-focused and crank those wallpaper words out so I could stay on schedule and move on to the flush toilet.

Now he was quietly singing. I set the laptop aside and stretched out on the bed to listen. I knew he didn't mind.

I see her come
and watch her go
Things she feels are things I'll never know
Was she ever here with me?
Was it ever real?
Will it ever be?

Hope gets high, sun sinks low
I'll sail away on a little angel breath she'll blow
Then a million miles from here
in a land of love
oh let me disappear where

she's just the world to me
just a girl who knows
I could be good I could be bad
I could be what she's never had
And I can be wrong but you can be sure
I could be anything for her

For her

I dream of love
I pray for time
Close my eyes and get me
a little piece of mind
In another time and place
in a sun so warm
I see it in her face, and

she's just the world to me
just a girl who knows
I could be good I could be bad
I could be what she's never had
And I can be wrong but you can be sure

I could be anything for her
Was it ever meant to be?
Was she ever here?
Will I ever see?

In between now and then
moves so slow while she's waiting to come in
Then the darkness comes my way
with a million little things I wanna say

cause she's just the world to me
just a girl who knows
I could be good I could be bad
I could be what she's never had
And I can be wrong but you can be sure
I could be anything for her

I wished desperately for earplugs.

I wished he would leave.

I needed to cry, badly.

I rolled over with my back to the door and pulled a pillow close and let scalding tears come and rack me.

I finally pulled myself together, got up, and opened the bedroom door a tiny bit. He was on the couch, his back to me, still playing. I slipped silently into the bathroom and locked the door. In the mirror my face was just awful. Mottled pink and white. Swollen lids. Red nose. A cool washcloth helped, a little.

I came out of the bathroom and crept quietly behind Ty to the kitchen, thankful he didn't notice me. A spiral notebook sat on the coffee table in front of him, from which he was singing words.

I got a glass down from the cabinet and stood at the sink filling it. Took a long drink. Turned off the faucet and noticed it had gotten quiet. I turned around and was startled half out of my skin.

"Oh—"

He was standing too close. "Have you been crying?"

I nodded.

He put his hands on my face and then his mouth was on mine and his tongue was in my mouth, deep, and I was backed into the corner where the countertops met. He was all up against me, solid, warm, immovable.

Just for a moment, I let myself feel him. Taste him. Strawberry.

I pulled my face away but he didn't step back. I lowered my head. I didn't want to look at him, or him to look at me.

His hand cradled the back of my neck.

"You can't do that," I said into his shirt.

"Gracie," he whispered. He kissed my hair.

"We can't be friends if you do that." My voice was shaking. "Please. Do you understand?"

"Okay," he said, after a moment. "Okay."

When I came out of the kitchen he was gone.

autumn, again

my bff, the Lizard King

For my birthday my dad took me to dinner at a popular Greek restaurant, where I indulged in a creamy risotto with lobster and sea urchin, blackberry-rose-champagne sorbet, and pastries. I would have to tell Julia about it. Of course, I'd leave out the Dan part.

I told him that my wedding was probably going to be in May, that Julia was helping me plan it, and that Steven and I would firm up the exact date soon.

"Would you ask your mother to call me?" Dan said.

I looked at him with raised brows.

"So I can help with the wedding."

"Oh, yes. Of course. Well, what do you mean, help?" I was sure there was no way Julia was going to confer with him about the flowers.

"Write a check."

"Oh. Well, you know, Steven and I plan to pay for the wedding."

"Isn't the bride's family supposed to pay for it?"

"Yes, in olden times."

"And I'm old-fashioned."

I almost choked on my baklava.

"Last time I saw Julia was at your graduation," Dan said. "What does she look like now?"

"She's stunning." I got out my wallet and handed him a picture.

He studied it for some time.

"What are you thinking?" I asked.

He shook his head.

"Dan. Five words."

He gave the photo back to me. His eyes were red. "She used to be soft."

She used to be soft. Oh, man. Five words used in a sentence was worth double the money. Triple, if they could make you laugh or cry.

I tucked the picture away; I was not going to puddle up about my parents right now. "She's very professional. And she is definitely tough."

"When I first knew her, there were no edges."

It was hard to imagine. "How did you and Mom meet?"

"Hasn't she ever told you?"

"Only vaguely."

"I taught a life-drawing class at the Art Students League. She was one of the models, fresh in town from Piscataway."

"Really? You mean nude modeling?"

He nodded. "She was gorgeous. Not embarrassed at all about her body."

"So you saw her naked before you even really knew her?"

"Yes, which was . . . awkward. I had to teach standing at the back of the class."

"Dan!"

"I became obsessed with her. I found out she waited tables, so I ate at that diner almost every day. She was taking acting classes down in the Village. I'd wait for her outside the school and go home with her. Luckily for me, her roommate was hardly ever there."

"That's interesting, but now we are on the threshold of Too Much Information."

My dad laughed and raised his hand for the check. "So come to my show, you and Steven."

"I don't know, Dan. I don't have the right clothes for those kinds of events."

"I don't care what you wear. Buy something, I'll give you my credit card."

"No."

"Well, why not? I'd like you to come."

"Is it a big deal?"

"Very."

I sighed. The last time I'd gone to one of my dad's things I'd lost my balance and accidentally stamped on Yoko Ono's tiny foot. Then I walked in on Liza Minnelli in a ladies' room stall. She was nice about it but hey, would it have killed her to turn the latch? My point is, I was a New York culturati disaster. But Dan asked so little of me, and continually offered me everything. Showing up for him and his paintings seemed the least I could do.

"Oh, all right," I said. Not all that graciously. "I'll come."

On a Saturday afternoon in late September, Steven and I were in a record store in Times Square. He was in the Jazz section, headphones on, quietly bopping. I slipped over to Rock and flipped through CDs. Oh, look—Aerosmith. I had a simultaneous thought about their song "Janie's Got a Gun" and Bill, at work.

We had tickets to a movie down the block and it was about time to head over. I started across the store to collect Steven and suddenly had to duck behind the near-life-size cardboard cutout of Hoobastank.

Tyler. In the Soul section. A girl with him. Tall, long blond hair, and tight jeans. Glued to his side. One hand cupping his ass.

I thought about the layout of the store. I had options, other ways I could go to get around them without being seen.

"Grace, we need to go!" Steven practically shouted at me from Jazz. "The movie starts in seven minutes."

Ty looked up at Steven and then slowly around at me.

He was sporting the Johnny Cash look. Black jeans, black Western shirt, cowboy boots. Chewing gum. He lifted his dark glasses to the top of his head and smiled. I surmised several things:

1) He was stoned. In an elegant, Jim Morrison kind of way.
2) He was sexually satisfied. Recently.
3) The girl with him (also smiling at me) was Thong Girl.

"Oh, hey," I said, coming out from behind Hoobastank.

"Hey, Grace," he drawled. "Long time."

"Yep. Long time." I knew I was smiling the way my mom so often does. Which is to say, not really. Just stretching my lips. I tried to relax them, but it just wasn't happening.

"This is Roberta." She nestled even tighter under his arm, her left breast crammed into his armpit. How unfortunate, I thought, that she had a name that suggested a female truck driver. Stocky. Mustachioed. Someone with anger issues.

"Yes," I said. "And you remember Steven."

"Oh yeah, hey, man." Tyler offered his hand.

"How's the music going?" Steven asked. "Grace says you should be famous."

"Almost there. I just signed a record deal."

"No kidding!"

Tyler grinned and lazily worked his gum. His bloodshot eyes shifted to me and narrowed slightly.

"Well, our movie's about to start. Good to see you!" I flapped a hand at them and grabbed Steven and dragged him through the store.

Outside, he stopped me. "What is going on?"

"You know I can't stand to miss the beginning of a movie."

"Wait a minute. Why were you so weird in there?"

"Was I weird?"

He gave me a look.

I scrambled for something plausible. "Well, I think he was high, don't you? You know it's just not productive, trying to talk to people when they're like that. Best to move on."

Steven looked dubious, but decided to buy it. He settled an arm around me as we walked. "Yeah. I guess that makes sense."

It was not, technically, untrue.

For so long I prided myself on being a truth-teller, no matter what. And now I was dissembling all over the place. Telling very smooth semi-truths.

This situation with Tyler Wilkie had turned me into a liar.

That week I brought my pointy shoes to work so Edward and I could go on a lunchtime jaunt to Saks. My dad's show was coming up in four days.

We narrowed it down to two tiny, mod, sixties-style mini-dresses. I favored a hot-pink satin, sleeveless shift. Not a lot of shape to the body, just a straight line down to midthigh, but I have good legs. Which I guess is the point of a dress like that. The other dress was girlier: black, strapless, with a floaty hemline and a big black bow across the breasts.

I slipped on the cruel shoes and tippy-toed out of the dressing room to model each of the dresses for Edward.

"So, which one?" I asked.

"It's a myth, you know, that all gay men have exquisite fashion sense."

"Now you tell me."

"But it happens to be true of me. The black dress. With opaque black tights."

"But won't I look a little somber, all in black? Don't you think the pink is more fun?"

"Grace, I'm reminded in this moment that you have breasts. Why not let the girls out for a little fresh air? Steven will love it."

I bought the dress and the tights and a strapless push-up bra and also some big, sparkly, opalescent crystal earrings. A few hundred dollars later, we went back to work.

I had to admit, I should make the effort to look like this more than once every couple of years.

I still had bangs but the rest of my hair had grown out enough to wear in an updo. I had on tons of mascara, pale pink lip gloss, and my breasts looked like a couple of softballs nestled together on a shelf and all bound up with a bow. Although why you'd tie softballs up with a bow, I don't know. The black tights and heels made me look leggy, almost tall. Just for this evening, I was a hottie.

Steven was coming with me for the first hour of my dad's event, and then the driver was taking him to the airport for his flight to Munich. I left the bathroom as he was coming out of the bedroom and we gently collided. He stepped back to look at me.

"Damn, I'm canceling my flight and coming home with you tonight." He set his hands on my waist and pulled me closer.

"No you're not," I sighed.

"I could tell them I'm sick."

"Yeah, right."

He sniffed the tops of my breasts. "Is that a new perfume?"

"No." I straightened his tie. "It's just that body lotion I always wear."

He could be so oblivious.

We left my wrap at the coat check, I snagged a glass of wine from a passing waiter, and we strolled around so Steven could check out the broken baby doll paintings and try the sound effects. Someone had given us a program that included an essay about my dad and a list of the various sounds we might hear.

We stopped at a painting and Steven slipped on the headphones and pressed the button. And made a pained face. He took off the headphones. "Yikes," he said, consulting the list. "That had to be grieving Pashtoun women ululating."

I put the headphones on and pressed the button, feeling lucky. "*You got some 'splainin' to do, Lucy!*" Desi Arnaz shouted self-righteously in my ear. I always hated when he did that. I hung the headset back on its wall hook in disgust.

"This is even more creepy than you described," Steven said as we perused the rest of the paintings in that room.

"I know. Creepy and sad."

"I can't believe how beautiful you look." He discreetly nuzzled me. "How can you do this to me right when I'm leaving?"

"Sorry." I smiled. "I'll wear the dress for you again sometime."

"Yes, you will. The night I get home." He checked his cell for the time. "I'm going to find the men's room, okay? Be right back."

I traded a passing waiter my empty wineglass for a full one and spotted my dad in the next room talking to three people. A chic Asian woman, an executive-type man in an expensive suit, and—

TYLER WILKIE.

WTF?

Though the rest of me seriously balked, my feet automatically moved toward them. My dad stopped whatever he'd been holding forth on to come and kiss me. "My God, you look like your mother thirty years ago," he whispered. Just what a girl loves to hear.

He brought me over and I shook hands with: the director of the San Francisco MOMA; Tori, who represented my dad's paintings in Japan and might be his current girlfriend; and Tyler Wilkie, whom Dan had heard was an incredible singer.

"We know each other, actually," I said.

"Oh?"

"We do," Ty said.

It was so disorienting, seeing him in this context. Then I had the bizarre realization that he was a New York celebrity guest. Like Parker Posey or Liev Schreiber, both of whom I'd spotted when I came in. Tyler was more dressed up than I'd ever seen him, in a rumpled dark blue velvet dinner jacket, albeit with jeans, a black shirt, and black biker boots.

While I was mentally evaluating his appearance I endured his flash examination. It started at the tips of my pointy shoes and swept up to the crown of my French-twisted hair, slowing almost imper-ceptibly at the unavoidable speed bumps—my bow-bound boobs, glossy lips, and the mini-chandeliers hanging from my ears. Our eyes met when he reached the top. I expected to see a teasing glint in his, but he looked away. Totally unreadable.

"How?" Dan asked.

"I beg your pardon?" I said.

"How do you know each other?"

"Grace is my best friend in New York," Ty said.

"Really!" Dan looked at us, brightly curious.

I would have liked to accuse Tyler of gross exaggeration, but my throat was too tight to speak.

"So that explains your question," Dan said to Ty.

That comment tipped me over into full-scale paranoia. *What ques-tion?* It appeared that my dad and Tyler Wilkie might be in some kind of cahoots. A bizarre combination that had the potential to send me back to therapy for years. I looked around the room and gauged the distance to all exits. Ah! Here came Steven.

"Oh great, she found you," he said, shaking hands with my father. "I have to go to JFK now and I hated to leave her alone."

"Thank you for coming," my dad said. "Did you get a look at the paintings?"

"I did. They're interesting."

My dad grinned. I wondered how many times he'd heard that one.

"Hello, Tyler," Steven said. "This is the second time we've seen you this week."

"Yes, it is. An unexpected pleasure." Ty shook hands, all charming, drawling friendship.

Steven turned to my dad. "Dan, can you make sure Grace gets out of here okay? Help her get a cab?"

"Hey, man, I'll take care of her," Ty said. "That way Dan doesn't have to leave his party."

Dan smiled at Ty as if he was his new favorite person. "Thanks, Tyler."

"Uh, okay. Thanks," Steven said. Looking not all that grateful.

Ty smiled ultra-sincerely. "No problem."

I could not believe my ears. "I cannot believe my ears," I said. I was standing in the middle of what had to be the three most upsetting men in the world. "I can get my own cab!"

Steven pulled me away a few feet and whispered. "Don't be mad. I don't want you standing outside by yourself trying to get home, dressed like this." I felt like I was wearing Day-Glo pasties with tassles.

"Steven. Look around. Plenty of women here are practically topless."

"Grace. For my sake. Will you let your friend get you a cab?"

"I guess. I'm going home soon, anyway. My stomach is starting to hurt."

"Okay, sweetheart. I'll call you when I get to Munich."

He kissed me and I watched him leave.

I supposed the expectation now was that I would turn around and politely return to my dad and Tyler for more chitchat. Instead, I slipped into the flow of people and moved smoothly into the next room of paintings. Just two more large rooms to shove through, and I'd be at the coat check.

There was an irritating clump of beautiful, entitled people creating a bottleneck at the next doorway. I knew the odds that I could successfully slip away and get my own freaking cab were very small, but I would not look back. I just needed to keep moving. I shook a mental fist. *Damn you, Debbie Harry and Julian Schnabel, move!*

"You know these paintings are about you."

I stopped pressing forward and pretended to study the nearest sadly beat-up old doll head. It had only one sleepy blue eye.

"Are not," I said, not bothering to look at him.

"I asked your dad."

Clever. Made me look. "What did he say?"

"He smiled."

I shook my head sadly at his naiveté and returned my gaze to the painting. "That doesn't mean *anything*. Was that the question he referred to?" I asked nonchalantly.

"Yeah."

Okay, so maybe no cahoots, just Tyler being intrusive.

The people pileup dispersed and the path to the coat check was now clear. He stayed right with me.

"How ya been?" he asked.

"Okay. You?"

"Good. Looks like I'll be going out to California in January to make my record."

I found the coat-check token in my bag and handed it to the attendant. I knew I really should look Ty in the face while we were on this subject, given the momentous nature of his achievement.

I did a half-turn to face him and raised my eyes. "I am so happy for you," I said. "I know how hard you've worked."

When had he become so strikingly good-looking? His pale skin and warm eyes shone in contrast with the dark blue velvet of his jacket. And he knew it. I expected him to dazzle me with *the smile*, but he just studied me thoughtfully.

"I mean it," I said.

He nodded. "Thank you."

The attendant handed him my wrap. I took it from him and gave the guy a few dollars.

We walked outside. He went to the curb and raised his hand. I let him.

A taxi pulled over and Ty opened the door for me. I had learned earlier that standing up, sitting down, and getting in and out of cars was dangerous in this dress. I tried to sit gracefully and sort of recline/slide my way into the backseat in such a way that I wouldn't find myself needing those Day-Glo pasties.

"Thanks," I said, and reached for the door handle, but he held on and leaned in. The streetlight was behind him and his face was in shadow.

"Would it be okay if I call you? I want to ask you about something." He sounded neutral, almost businesslike.

"All right," I said cautiously.

He straightened up and took out his wallet, and before I understood what he was doing he opened the front door, overpaid the driver, and told him my address.

"Ty!" I protested.

"'Bye, Grace." Now *the smile*, quick and friendly.

He shut my door firmly and walked into the gallery without looking back.

songs of love
or
concealing the bling

My dad IM'd me the next day.

> **DanB:** So it was Tyler Wilkie who called you on New Year's Eve, yes?
>
> **SueGBee:** Yes.
>
> **DanB:** I take it he saw you into a cab?
>
> **SueGBee:** Yes.
>
> **DanB:** Could you be a little more terse? How did you become best friends?
>
> **SueGBee:** I don't know why he said that. He must have been a little drunk.
>
> **DanB:** He didn't seem drunk.
>
> **SueGBee:** Hollow leg. Hey, it was nice to see Tori there with you. That's been going on awhile, huh?
>
> **DanB:** Two years.
>
> **SueGBee:** Wow, that must be a record. I guess you really like her.
>
> **DanB:** I love her.
>
> **SueGBee:** I've heard that a few dozen times before, Dan. You give your heart away so easily. And temporarily. LOL.
>
> **DanB:** That hurts.
>
> **SueGBee:** Sorry. I'm sorry.

DanB: You could try giving your heart away once, Susannah
　　Grace.

SueGBee: Okay, I have to go, Dan.

DanB: Okay. Peace.

I tried to immerse myself in work, which at the time consisted of
writing student ancillaries for a series of middle school textbooks on
ancient world history. In ordinary times I would have eaten this stuff
up; making up study questions about Egyptian political leaders during Graeco-Roman rule was my idea of a good time. I would have
become totally absorbed in creating exercises about the metaphorical
meaning of "Achilles' heel," or the importance of clay-pot-making
technologies in ancient South Asia.

But I was not having fun. I was troubled. Because Tyler never
called.

I was bundled up on the couch on a Saturday afternoon watching
a classic Meredith Baxter Birney movie on Lifetime (SPOILER: the
one where she kills her own kid and then kidnaps someone else's son
from a playground but he gets older and remembers who he is and
the police find out and she ends up throwing herself off a balcony)
when I heard someone come up the stairs, whistling. I flew to the
peephole.

It *was* Tyler, letting himself into Sylvia's. I heard his low murmurs
mingle with the sounds of doggy ecstasy. Now here he came, with Biz
and Blitz on their leashes. When he passed my door he looked right
at my peephole, rubbed the top of Blitz's head, and said, "You sure do
have big ears!"

I pulled on jeans and a tee and washed my face.

When he came back I waited till he was coming out of Sylvia's
and opened the door.

"Hey!" I said nicely.

"Oh, hey."

His hair had been cut a little but was still longish and wavy.

"How are you?" I asked.

"I'm good. How are you?"

"Good! Do you want to come in for coffee? I have banana bread." Steven had made it.

"I'm sorry, I'd like to, but I have to be somewhere in half an hour."

"Okay. Another time." He was about to say good-bye. "I'm surprised to see you—I didn't think you walked dogs anymore."

"Oh, yeah. Sylvia called the agency, said the dogs were pining for me and could I just come once in a while."

I laughed. "You're such a softy."

"Yeah." He grinned. "And she's paying me triple."

"Hey, you never called," I said. "To ask me about something."

"Oh, yeah." He took out his vibrating cell phone and looked at the screen. Slipped it back into his pocket.

"Well, what was it?"

"Nothing. Just a thought I had that night when I saw you. And then I decided against it."

"Well, can't you tell me what it was?"

He shook his head at my tenacity, or his foolishness, or something. "All it was, was it's my grandma's eightieth birthday coming up and my parents are throwing a big party for her back home, the weekend before Thanksgiving. I'm supposed to bring someone. I had this idea that it would surprise everyone if I brought a smart woman like you with me. Not what they would expect. And it would please my grandma."

He rubbed at something on the tile with the toe of his Converse, then smiled ruefully. "I'm sorry, Grace. I was totally thinking of how I might use you to make me look good. I thought better of it the next day. That's why I didn't call."

"Oh."

"I'm sorry, you must have been wondering all this time."

"Well, no. It's just . . . hearing you this morning reminded me."

"Anyway, I'm sorry. I gotta go now. It's great seeing you."

"Yes, you, too."

My curiosity was piqued. I was dying to see where Tyler grew up, see his parents again. I wanted to see their house, and their big garden, and where he played as a kid. Where he fell off the roof. I wanted to see if there was something in the water or air that had made him grow up to be so very different from other people, so . . . interesting.

He probably knew that I could go with him to his grandmother's party as his friend, and people would make their own assumptions about our relationship. I could do something like hold his arm a time or two to help the illusion.

And I had never been to the Poconos. And Steven would be in Munich the weekend before Thanksgiving. I could go on a short road trip and be back before he got home. And I wanted to help Ty. How unimpressive, indeed, if he took someone like Roberta. And I wouldn't even need to tell Steven that I'd gone anywhere . . . though why wouldn't I tell him? I would, of course. Eventually.

So on Monday afternoon I called him. And, apparently, woke him up.

"What are you doing, taking a nap?"

"Just trying to get my eight hours."

Of course. He'd gone to bed at seven a.m.

"Well, listen. I could go with you to your grandmother's party, if you want."

"Oh, man, Grace, are you sure?" Now he sounded a little more awake. "If you could, I'll owe you a big one. Not *the* big one, of course."

"Ha ha. Which leads me to ask, would we be staying overnight?"

"Yeah. You can stay in my old room. I'll sleep in the basement. I'm glad you called. I was just about to ask someone else. But she doesn't have a giant brain."

Probably giant other things, though. "Well, I'll double up on *Jeopardy!*, just to make sure I impress."

"Maybe you could mention a book you've read or something, that would be good, too."

On the Friday of the Poconos weekend, I went home at lunchtime, changed into a sweater, jeans, and boots, and threw a few things into my overnight bag. I had a long-sleeved blue knit dress, V-necked, a little clingy but not too tight, that I hardly ever wore. With heels it would do for the birthday dinner.

I rechecked Big Green to make sure I had my book (*East of Eden*), checked the time on my cell, and shrugged into my leather jacket.

My cell rang: TWILK. I grabbed my bags and locked the door. Ran down the stairs and stepped outside. Where was he?

Beep, beep. The window of the black BMW double-parked in front of my building rolled down. "Come on!" Ty yelled from the driver's seat.

I threw my bags in the backseat and got in.

"It's Bogue's car."

"Oh, yeah, I forgot he had it here."

He pulled into traffic. "Rents a parking spot for it and everything."

"I thought he might be coming, too. Isn't he kind of like family?"

"He's gone with Allison to Virginia to meet her parents. I guess they're getting serious."

"Oh. Wow."

Ty was wearing jeans, a gray waffle-knit henley, and a Yankees baseball cap. He looked in my general direction and smiled but I couldn't see his eyes because of his mirrored sunglasses.

"Um, should I drive?"

"Why?"

"Have you been smoking marijuana?"

"No!" he laughed. "Why?"

I pointed to the glasses.

He slipped them off and showed me his eyes. Warm and clear. "Okay?"

"Okay."

Once we got on I-80 he played me some of the recording from Joe's Pub. We talked about that night and all the famous people who were there. I asked if that had made him nervous.

"Like I might crap my pants," he said, with a disarming abandonment of personal dignity.

"I felt that way, too. I was so nervous for you."

"The good thing was, the light on me was so fucking bright, I couldn't see who all was out there till after I finished. I came offstage and got an eyeful and my knees buckled."

"I guess that explains the heavy drinking that ensued."

"Hell yeah. That, and I was thirsty. And I like a good buzz."

"Aren't you worried that you'll do something embarrassing if you drink too much?"

He thought about it for a moment. "Nah."

He ejected the Joe's Pub CD and popped in another one. As we drove through increasingly pastoral and mountainous terrain we were surrounded by the elegant voice of Bryan Ferry singing "More Than This."

"Isn't it funny," I said, "that we both like old music? I don't know that many people who do."

"Yeah, me, either."

"Why are so many songs about love?"

"What's more important than love? And what expresses love better than music?" He looked at me like I would be graded on my answer.

"Nothing?"

"I'm glad you understand. Hey, try to stump me," he said. "Name something old you really love and see if I know it."

"Okay, but I'll sing it. Just a few words."

"Okay. Don't make it too easy."

I sang snippets of Dire Straits, Gerry Rafferty, Elton John, Pink Floyd, and the Kinks, and he came back with the next line, every time. He was unbeatable. Then I totally stumped him with "Blue Eyes Crying in the Rain."

"Ha!" I said. "I guess you're not all that into country music."

"Are you kidding? I know my Willie."

"Who doesn't?"

He reached for me with vengeful, goosing fingers. I shrank against the door.

"Careful," I laughed, "you're going to lose a digit. And you need them. STOP!" We were veering into the next lane. "Would you put both hands on the wheel, please!"

The drive turned out to be surprisingly short, less than two hours door to door. We got off I-80, passed through Stroudsburg, and kept going until we had left the two-lane highway and were bumping along a gravel road deeper and deeper into wilderness. The banjo strains from *Deliverance* crept into my consciousness.

The house was a big old Victorian that might have been lovely, were it not so Pepto pink. With lavender trim.

"Hey, they painted the house," Ty said.

"What color was it before?"

"Orange."

A white delivery van and a large motorcycle were parked in front of a carriage house that leaned alarmingly. "Don't go in the garage, okay?" He unbuckled his seat belt. "We think it might fall down." He put his guitar on his back and picked up his duffel bag and my overnight bag and headed up the front walk.

I stopped to look at the motorcycle. It was impressive. A big, shiny, blue-and-chrome Harley, sporting a black leather saddlebag embossed with a skull and crossbones.

"Ty? Whose motorcycle is this?"

He came back to me and spoke in a low voice. "My dad's. Don't touch it, he dusts for fingerprints."

"Is he a Hell's Angel?" I whispered.

He smiled and whispered back, "No. He's in a Harley club."

I didn't see the difference. I'd Google it when I got home.

I followed him past our old friend the gazing ball, now crowning a verdigris-encrusted pedestal in a leaf-strewn flower bed. He stopped short of the porch steps and turned to me.

"Hey, I just realized . . ."

"What?"

"Well, that." He pointed at my engagement ring. "You'll have to take it off, eh? We don't want to freak everyone out."

"Oh." I looked at the ring. "Yeah." I worked the ring off and slid it deep into the pocket of my jeans.

a country herbal

The house was dark and quiet, with high, ornate tin ceilings. It smelled weird, like a mix of cooking chicken and some pungent herb.

"Hello?" Ty called out.

We walked through the downstairs, which was furnished in a mix of elegance and kitsch. Lovely old pieces like an antique mahogany dining room table inhabited the same space as a circa-1970 wood veneer china cabinet with faux-bamboo accents.

Ty whistled a loud tune as he led me upstairs to his former bedroom. Whatever it may have looked like in his childhood, it was now tidy and generic, with fresh yellow walls and a flowered quilt on the double bed. A faded Monet print was tacked up over the old desk, the surface of which was etched with, among other words and phrases, *Tyler Graham Wilkie*, *TGW*, and *bite me*.

"I was pissed at my dad," Ty said, tracing the words with a fingertip.

He opened the closet for my jacket and I saw that it was full of his history—sports trophies, stacks of albums, tapes and CDs, and an old record player.

I was struck with a sad, hollow feeling. Envy. How wonderful it must be to spend all your childhood in one place. I had no childhood home to revisit, unless you counted my dad's loft. But I had never felt very comfortable there. And my old stuff—my yearbooks, my cassette tapes, my Beanie Baby collection—who knew where it all was? My mom's attic, maybe.

"What's up?" Ty said.

"It's nice, your room."

"I haven't lived here in ten years."

"But it's still your room."

He nodded at the Monet print. "I think it's yours, now. Looks like my mom prettied it up for you."

"Where did you live, when you moved out?"

"In Bogue's family's pool house for a year, then in town, in different apartments and houses. Let's go get a beer."

We ran into his mom and dad in the hall, coming out of their bedroom.

"Grace Barnum!" Jean was pink-cheeked, pulling her blond hair into a ponytail. When she hugged me I saw that she'd missed a button on her blouse. Nathan nodded at me and shook Ty's hand. He and his wife both had red eyes and smelled like pot. Which explained half of the herbal/cooking chicken smell.

"We just got here and we're thirsty," Ty said.

"Oh, yeah, we're starving!" Jean said. "There's beer and other stuff in the fridge. Help yourselves. We'll eat supper about seven."

I glanced at Ty, who winked and whispered, "That's why I whistled. So they wouldn't come out of there chasing each other down the hall butt-naked."

We got beers and chips and went down to a musty-smelling basement decorated in early-American rec room, with an ancient TV, a foosball table, a brown plaid couch, and a red beanbag chair.

He flopped down on the couch and ripped open the Tostitos while I looked around at framed pictures of Ty engaged in various sports: baseball, football, track.

"You were very athletic, weren't you?"

He shrugged. "I did all right. My sister was the real athlete. She kicked ass in basketball."

There was a photo of her airborne, in the middle of a layup. She looked like a fierce Viking goddess, lean and muscled. "What's her name?"

"Rebecca."

"Who's older?"

"Me. By two minutes. But she was bigger and louder. They said she practically shoved me out."

My eyes were drawn to a picture of Ty dressed in the garb of a Hasidic Jew, with a big fake gray beard. His arms were in the air and his mouth was open.

"*Fiddler on the Roof*?"

"Yeah."

"Were you *Tevye*?"

"Yeah." He looked embarrassed. "They cast me 'cause I was a senior and I could sing. Couldn't act for shit."

"This is bound to come out in the media as your legend grows."

"Not if I destroy all the evidence first."

"There will be a lot of yearbooks to burn."

He shoved a chip in his mouth. "It's the videos showing up on YouTube that I'm really worried about."

I clapped my hands, excited. "I know the first thing I'm doing when I get home!"

I kicked the beanbag chair a couple of times to plump it up before sinking into it. I hadn't sat in a beanbag chair in a good ten years. I closed my eyes. "Okay, I'm going to be here awhile."

It got quiet. I opened one eye. He was reading the back of the chip bag.

"Is Rebecca coming for the party?" I asked.

"Yeah, she told my mom she wasn't going to. She hates family reunion shit. But I used a little reverse psychology on her."

"Oh? What'd you do?"

"Well, it's a simple formula. First I called and left a cryptic message on her phone about needing to talk about something."

"Uh-huh."

"And of course, being my sister, she called me right away. But I let her leave a message and didn't get back to her for a day or two, to let the mystery build."

"Oh, yeah."

"And then when she called again, I answered. I told her I didn't want to hurt her feelings but I thought it would be a good idea if she didn't come to the birthday party. Why? she says. Well, you know how bad you get on Gram's nerves, I said. It might ruin the whole thing for her if you showed up."

"And what did Rebecca say?"

"She told me to cut the reverse psychology crap and said she'd already decided to show up just to put a bee in the old woman's hat." He laughed. "She always catches on to my shit. She's way smarter than me."

"Unlike *me*!" I rose from the beanbag chair in wobbly, majestic outrage.

"Hey, what are you talking about?" Ty paused, hand in the chip bag, all careful, blank innocence.

I kicked the leg that was dangling off the edge of the sofa.

"Ow!" He sat up.

"You let me wonder for a whole month what the hell you wanted to talk to me about!"

"Well, you could've called and asked me what was up! I had to finally come walk the damn dogs to get you to bite."

"And then all that 'my grandma will be so impressed with a smart girl' crap."

"Now, that is absolute truth. I swear it."

"You are nefarious." I snatched the chip bag and retreated to the distant side of the foosball table.

"Use that word with my grandma, it's perfect. And if you want to correct my grammar, that's fine, too. You know I love it when you do that, Grace."

I ate a few chips while glaring at him and trying to decide how mad I really was. He got up and meandered over to the table. Tucked his hands in his pockets. And then casually pulled out my kryptonite: *the smile*.

I looked away. "Should I go home?" I wondered out loud.

"Hell no, woman!" He spun a handle on the table. "You should play foosball."

I beat him two out of three games before Jean called us for supper.

He stopped me at the bottom of the stairs. "Listen, I told my mom you and I are mostly just friends."

"Mostly?"

"I thought that sounded more believable. Anyway, what I'm saying is you don't have to put on too big of an act in front of her and my dad."

"Okay. What about your grandmother?"

"I definitely want you to lay it on some for her benefit."

"What do you mean, lay it on?"

He thought about it.

"I could hold your arm once in a while," I suggested. "Will that do?"

"Yeah, okay, but if you're too subtle she might miss it."

"Okay. I'll try to be obvious."

"Great! Thanks!" He grinned and shot up the stairs ahead of me, two at a time.

We ate in their dining room at the beautiful old table set with a lace cloth and a mix of what must have been family heirloom china and everyday dishes. Nathan pulled out a chair for me, saying, "Jean wants you to sit here." He returned to the kitchen, taking Ty with him.

My setting was pretty. The plate was old, with scratched gold paint around the rim and a wreath of rosebuds.

Ty came in and set two covered dishes on the table. "I sure hope you're hungry." He took the seat across from me.

Nathan brought in a platter of roasted chicken. Jean followed with a basket of rolls. They sat at the ends of the table and smiled at me. Even Nathan. Ty looked like he wanted to laugh.

"Well, Grace," Jean said, "it's a week early, but this is a meal of thanksgiving. To thank you for being there for Ty with the appendix."

"Oh." My face was getting hot. "It was just what any of his friends might have done."

"Well, I know you gave him a lot of comfort. Isn't that right, hon?"

"Yeah," Ty said. "A kiss before surgery from Bogue would have been kind of depressing."

"You might not have wanted to come out alive after that," Nathan observed.

"Anyway," Jean said. "You are a darling girl and we thank you."

A darling girl. I looked at my napkin. Smoothed it across my legs. Picked at a bit of loose thread peeking out from the hemmed edge.

"Gracie," Ty said softly. "It's all right."

Jean came and hugged me with one arm and made comforting

sounds while she blotted my face with her napkin. Nathan cleared his throat.

"Sometimes she leaks," Ty said.

While we ate roast chicken, rice with gravy, green beans, creamed corn, and buttered rolls, Ty told us about the coming months. He'd be going to Los Angeles after Christmas to make the record. Once singles had been decided on, there would be music videos to make. By summer he'd go on tour, playing colleges and festivals.

"Ty, can you believe this is all happening?" his mom asked.

"I guess I'm starting to," he said.

"I'm worried that you'll be lonely out in California," Jean said.

"I'll be okay. I make friends pretty quick."

"Maybe you could go out and visit him, Grace."

"Maybe," I said. *Except that I'm saving my vacation days for my honeymoon.*

"What do you do, again?" Nathan asked.

"I'm an editor at Spender-Davis Education."

"She writes schoolbooks telling teenagers not to have sex," Tyler said.

"We could have used one of those around here, I guess," Nathan said.

"He's talking about Rebecca," Ty said.

"She was a free spirit!" Jean said.

"Where does Rebecca live now?" I asked.

"Philly. She's in veterinary school," Nathan said.

"That's why this house is falling apart. They spend all their money paying for her education." Ty looked at his mom. "I was surprised to see you'd painted the place. And my room."

"Well, I've been painting the outside for a few months now, bit by bit. And we did a big wedding, so I had a little extra. I just wanted to freshen things up for company." She smiled at me.

"Ty tells me you're florists," I said. "That sounds like fun."

"It's a trade," Nathan said. "I guess we'd rather handle flowers than Roto-root someone's pipes."

"Ty, bring her by the shop tomorrow," Jean said. "You two can put together an arrangement for Gram's party."

I looked at him, thinking we'd share a silent laugh at the idea of him arranging flowers. But he just nodded and stuffed his mouth with buttered roll.

"'Kay," he said.

I was not allowed to help wash dishes. Jean gave us mugs of hot coffee and handed Ty a blanket and told us to get our coats and go outside and watch the moon rise.

We sat on a wicker love seat on the side porch. Ty tucked the blanket mostly around me.

"Don't you want some?" I held up an edge.

"Nah, I run pretty hot." He hadn't even bothered to zip his brown bomber jacket.

The moon was big and full, cresting the skeletal tops of the trees.

"If the moon weren't so bright you could see a lot of stars out here."

"Oh, I would have liked to see that," I said.

"Do you want to smoke a J? I can probably get one from my dad."

"Erm, no. Thank you. You go ahead."

"Getting stoned alone is boring."

"Sorry."

"Have you ever?"

"I tried it once and nothing happened."

"Yeah, same here, the first time. You gotta try it again."

I couldn't quite say yes.

He must have felt encouraged by my silence. "Be right back," he said. "Stay there."

"Right here," I said dryly.

He came back in two minutes with a Zippo, an ashtray, and a fatty. "My mom wanted me to tell you that they're not potheads. They only smoke once in a while."

"Okay."

"Same with me," he said. "It fucks up my voice."

"That's your business."

"Just don't judge me on it, okay?"

"Am I in any position to judge?"

"Good point," he said, lighting up.

He sucked the smoke in deep and held it, squinting, passing the joint to me. I took a tentative little draw. He waved a hand at me, encouraging me to inhale more deeply. Gak, it burned my throat and lungs! I choked and emitted plumes of smoke.

He patted my back and handed me my cup of coffee. After I drank some he offered me the joint again. I waved it away.

"Come on, one more. Not so much this time."

I inhaled lightly and handed it back. "That's all I want."

He took another drag and put the joint out in the ashtray. Then he leaned back and tugged on the edge of the blanket. "I'll take some of this now."

We settled in to moonwatch.

The moon was watching us back. She had a tender, cream-and-gray Lillian Gish face.

"My skin is vibrating," I said, after a while.

"See? Second time's a charm."

"The moon is so sad," I said.

"I know. She's lonely."

"She is a she, isn't she?"

"Yes, she is. Of course!"

"She needs a song. A moon song."

"A moon song!" Ty agreed.

"I'm going to make one up," I said.

"Okay."

"Dear little moon girl. Way up in your moon world. Where are your ears? Why don't you have any?"

The wicker sofa shook.

"Stop," I said. "This is serious."

"Although this man is laughing, moon lady, ears are very important. Can you even hear me?" I croaked plaintively through my singed vocal cords. *"Do I need to sign?"*

"Sign!" Ty echoed in a tiny little soprano Kate Bush-y voice.

"You live in the big dark sky and don't ever get to play basketball."

"Basketball!"

"If it will make you happy I'll read you a book."

"But not A Prayer for Owen Meany *because it will make you cry,"* interjected my boy-choir backup singer.

"I feel a little light-headed," I said.

"Let's go for a walk." Ty held out his hand and led me down the porch steps toward the trees.

"Can you feel my hand vibrating?" I asked.

"No. I think you're just feeling that way inside."

"I don't want to get lost."

"I know exactly where we're going."

"How far is it?"

"Just a ways. Stay a little behind me so you don't catch a branch in the face."

"At least it's not all that dark."

"Nah, it's bright as day."

"Are there . . . bears out here?"

"Do they shit in the woods?"

I pulled him to an abrupt halt. He laughed and tugged me back into motion. "Any bears we got out here would run from us. We're good. Just keep hold of my hand."

Like I was in a million years letting go.

"Your fingertips are so rough!" I said.

"You get calluses from guitar strings."

"Ouch."

He stopped. "What happened?"

"No, I mean, ouch, the calluses!"

He turned and marched on. "You scared me," he grumbled.

"Sorry."

We kept going and going. "Are we there yet?"

"Yeah," he said. "We're there. See that tree?"

It must have been huge once but now some of it lay on the ground and some stood ruined, a long-dead, blackened spear pointing at the sky.

"What happened?"

"Lightning strike. I saw it get hit from my bedroom window. I ran out here and watched it burn till the rain got so heavy it put the fire out."

"You ran out here in an electrical storm?"

"Well, I was thirteen. And I told you, Rebecca got most of the brains."

"You could have been killed! What did your parents say?"

"Didn't hear me go out. I sure never told them, I might have gotten a whipping."

"They *beat* you?"

"Only when I deserved it. Anyway, it was pretty spectacular, watching it burn."

I would have to think about the burning tree later. I was having a problem with the whipping concept. They had seemed so kind, but they were monsters! How would I look them in the eyes now, knowing they had done that to him? I cradled his hand gently in both of mine and drew a ragged breath into my sore lungs. I hardly felt high at all anymore.

"What's up?"

"I'm so sorry," I said. "I wish they hadn't done that to you."

"What, the whipping? Shit, Grace. Didn't your parents ever wallop you a time or two?"

"Never!"

He sighed. "They did it because they loved me. To knock some sense into me. Because I scared them and pissed them off. Believe me, I was all over the place."

That, I believed.

"I guess it sounds strange to you, but that is just part of raising kids in my family."

"What did they hit you with?"

He shrugged. "Belt. Yardstick. Extension cord. Fly swatter. Badmitten racket."

"Minton," I said.

"Huh?"

"Minton. Bad*minton*, not mitten."

"Well, a mitten wouldn't have hurt as much. Anyway, they hit me with whatever was nearby. But only if they could catch me."

"You ran?"

"Hell yeah! Till sometimes my mom was laughing too hard to try to get me anymore."

These people were nuts.

He put an arm around me and shook me gently. "Come on, sing to the moon some more."

"I don't feel like it."

"If you don't sing, I'm gonna."

"Go ahead."

He looked up at Lillian Gish, weeping over us, and started snapping his fingers.

"*Fly me to the moon*," he sang, in a loud, dead-on imitation of Frank Sinatra, "*and let me* . . . play?" he looked at me. "Is it play among the stars?"

"How would I know?"

"*Da da da da da da da da on Jupiter and Mars.*"

"Hey, those are the same words in that Willie Nelson song."

"Do you mind? I'm trying to sing."

"Sing 'Moon River.'"

"*Moooon RIV-er*," he obliged me instantly in the braying Sinatra voice.

"No." I grabbed the unzipped edges of his jacket. "Really sing it."

He held my cold wrists, smiling. "I don't know the words."

"Do you know the melody?"

"I think so." He started humming. He knew it.

We couldn't think of all the words but it didn't matter.

He sang the three sweetest words in that song slowly, soulfully, in his real voice. *My huckleberry friend.* I absorbed them and they sharpened all other sensations—the cold, crisp air, the silvery trees. I gazed up over his shoulder at the sweet-faced moon. What had I ever done in my life to deserve this wondrous little moment?

Ty squeezed my wrists lightly. "Grace. What are the rest of the words?"

I reluctantly left the moon and looked at him. My mind was perfectly empty. I wanted it to stay that way. "I have no idea."

"Okay. Let's go, Zombie Girl. Are you hungry?"

"Ravenous!"

"Another good word for Gram! Come on."

He led me to chocolate.

Barcalounging, bloat, and bouquets

Cheez Whiz. Yes, my mouth tasted like I had squirted it full of Cheez Whiz. It was possible that I had.

I mentally catalogued the feeding frenzy that followed our illicit drug use. I remembered eating (in roughly this order): half a giant Kit Kat, a ham and Swiss on rye, two kosher dills, an indeterminate number of Combos Nacho-Cheese-Filled Pretzels, and fourteen watermelon Jelly Bellies—each one carefully hand-sorted from all the other flavors by my drug supplier, who made sure that I did not accidentally eat a jalapeño.

I had excused myself to go to bed at around one a.m. and fallen asleep in my clothes, on top of the covers, propped up against the headboard. Trusting that gravity was my friend and would not let me die a vomitous Jimi Hendrix death.

I woke up queasy, flat on my back in the gray November morning light. All the pillows were on the floor. I sat up squinting and emitted a monstrous belch that made me feel like a new woman. I tiptoed to the door and peeked out into the hall. All still and quiet; maybe Jean and Nathan had gone to work. I grabbed my toothbrush and fresh clothes and crossed the hall to the upstairs bathroom.

I showered and pulled on jeans and a sweater and crept quietly down to the kitchen. Half a pot of still-warm coffee sat on the stove.

I ate a bowl of Rice Krispies, then munched on a banana while I snooped around the living room. It featured a gorgeous bay window and a fireplace with a carved mantel, but also a purple velour couch and a camel-colored Barcalounger. An old upright piano stood against one wall, and above it, a dead deer mounted on the wall. Well, just its head.

I went back into the kitchen and checked the time on the microwave. Nine o'clock. I listened at the basement door for sounds of life.

I went upstairs for my book and brought it down and stretched out on the Barcalounger. Read two pages and dozed off.

At about eleven, I crept down a few of the basement stairs to take a peek. Nothing to see but a bunch of bumps and lumps under the navy sleeping bag on the plaid couch. Oh, wait, there was a bit of foot visible.

"Ty!" I hissed. "Ty!"

His head popped up, squinting at me over the back of the couch. Einstein hair. "What's wrong?"

"Nothing! Are you going to get up? It's eleven."

"Oh . . . okay . . ." He lay down and went back to sleep.

"Ty!"

He stood up and weebled around in his boxer briefs, searching the floor for something. He must have been having a rather *stimulating* dream. I scrambled up the stairs and back to the Barcalounger and picked up my book.

Minutes later he staggered into the doorway wearing his jeans and henley from yesterday. Barefoot.

"Please go find a mirror," I said. "You have to get a look at your hair."

He smashed it down with both hands. "I'm going to take a shower."

He was back in thirty minutes, clean-shaven, hair damp and much smaller, wearing a T-shirt that said SUITS SUCK. He came and stood beside the Barcalounger. "Comfy?"

"Very."

"Did you have breakfast?"

I nodded.

"Are you feeling okay?"

"Yeah, are you?"

"Yeah."

I pointed to the deer head. "Is that the deer you shot?"

He studied it. "It is."

"Did you . . . feel bad about it?"

"No, I felt great. There were a lot of trees between me and him. I was with my dad and a bunch of other grown men and it was a big deal, me making that shot. But I guess I'm getting a twinge about it now, with you looking at me like that."

"Sorry. It's just, well, I guess I just can't imagine it."

He nodded and shrugged and wandered out of the room. He came back minutes later with a travel mug of coffee in one hand and our jackets in the other. "Let's go."

We listened to *Car Talk* on NPR for the twenty minutes it took to get to town. It felt good to be quiet; I was still processing the night before. How on earth had I ended up with him here in the Pennsylvania hinterlands, slightly asthmatic from inhaling marijuana, bloated from the ensuing salt and sugar orgy, with my expensive engagement ring hidden in a sock in my suitcase?

The Wilkies' flower shop, Best Buds, was in a strip mall on a main drag, nestled between a realtor and a karate studio. Bells on the door rang when we stepped inside.

In the front of the store there were gifts for sale: porcelain boxes and crystal wind chimes and other pretty little tchotchkes. Silk plants that looked close to real lined the front window, and a refrigerator housed fresh arrangements of orange, brown, and gold flowers that would look festive on a Thanksgiving table.

We walked behind the counter and into a back room that had plywood and vinyl worktables covered with floristry supplies and tools. A football game was playing on a small TV.

"Good morning!" Jean said. She was sweeping up bits of stems and greenery on the floor. She set the broom in a corner and put an arm around my shoulders. "Did you sleep all right?"

"Yes, thank you. I'm sorry about the mess we left in the kitchen."

"If you made a mess, I never saw it."

Ty must have cleaned up.

"Hey, Grace, c'mere."

"He's in there." Jean pointed at a big metal door on one wall, slightly ajar.

I peeked inside. It was a walk-in refrigerator, with flowers of all colors in metal buckets covering the floor and shelves.

"Come in," Ty said.

It was so cold. I stood beside him and wrapped my arms around my shoulders and closed my eyes, breathing in the clean, bracing scent of carnations.

"Hey, Mom."

"Yeah?" her voice was muffled.

"What color are the tablecloths?"

"Pink!"

"What do you think of these?" He tapped a bucket of flowers with the blunt toe of his boot. They were fuchsia-colored, with lots of frilly petals going all up the long stem.

"They're beautiful. I can't think of what they're called."

"Gladiola."

"Oh, right!" The plural of which would be gladioli, of course, but I kept that to myself.

He handed me a bucket to carry—yellow gladioli—and he brought out the fuchsia and a bucket of pale lavender-pink ones, as well. We set the buckets next to one of the worktables, and from somewhere he produced a tall, clear-glass vase and filled it halfway with water at a big, deep sink.

"We need about ten of each color," he said. I helped pick out the best-looking stems and watched him trim them with scissors and settle them one by one in the vase. He finished by tucking in long, spiky pieces of grass.

Jean came over for a look. "Well, this is gorgeous. Let's put it on the front table for people to see when they come in. Gram is gonna love it."

The bells on the door jingled. "Excuse me," Jean said, and went up front.

Ty adjusted a gladiola.

"You are full of surprises, aren't you?" I said.

"Just one after another. What are you wearing tonight?"

"A dress."

"What color?"

"Blue."

We carried the gladiola buckets back into the refrigerator and while we were in there he pointed to a bucket of small, pale yellow roses and asked, "Do you like those?"

"They're beautiful."

He pulled from the bucket a rose bud and an open rose and, from another bucket, a small cluster of breathtakingly blue hydrangea.

I followed him back to the worktable. "Are you making something for me?"

He set down the flowers and wrapped a length of elastic around my wrist and cut it. "Yep."

I laughed. "I feel like I'm going to the prom!"

"Did you?"

"Go to the prom? Yes. Did you?"

"I only went to a dance once, when I was fifteen."

"Who was your date?"

He pushed green wire through the base of the rose bud. "My cousin Elaine."

"Your cousin?"

"My mom arranged it. Only Bogue knew that my cousin drove over from her college in New Jersey. All my other friends were shocked that I could get a beautiful older girl to go out with me."

"Why didn't you ask a girl from school?"

"I did. She said no."

"She must have been an idiot."

Ty looked at me and smiled. "Why, thank you, Grace." He was wrapping green tape around the wires he'd inserted in the roses.

"What was it, did she have a boyfriend?"

"No. She wasn't into me. I stuttered. Especially around girls. It took me a whole red-faced minute to get out the words 'would you go to the prom with me.'"

I stared at him. "I've never heard you stutter."

"Yeah, it doesn't happen much anymore. Only if I'm tired or upset, and hardly even then." He was doing something now with the elastic band and the hydrangeas.

"How did you stop?"

"I started singing, instead of talking."

"You mean, when you were speaking to people?"

"Yeah, sometimes. They were gonna laugh at me anyway. And then I just did it in my mind, imagined singing what I was saying." He shrugged. "For some reason, it worked. Hold out your hand."

He had nestled the tiny yellow roses in among the hydrangea and some curling ivy leaves and tied it all with opalescent blue ribbon. It was delicate, contained, perfect. An exquisite, living bracelet. He slid it on my wrist.

"Ty. . . ." I looked up at him. Astonished.

Gram is crackers

It was dark out. I could hear Ty downstairs playing the piano. I looked at the clock. I had overnapped and now had ten minutes to get ready. I threw on the blue dress and some lip gloss and twisted my hair up.

Ty was waiting for me at the bottom of the stairs. He was wearing a boxy, ill-fitting blue suit.

"You look nice," he said.

"You, too." I am a terrible liar.

He looked sheepish. "Last time I wore this was for my granddad's funeral six years ago."

I felt the slick fabric of his sleeve. "More blackmail material."

"Yeah, good thing I trust you."

"Where are your parents?"

"They left a few minutes ago."

When we got to the car he opened my door for me. He went around and got in and handed me my lovely corsage, cold from the fridge. I slipped it on my wrist and admired it as we were pulling out of the drive. "It is so weird that you can do this," I said.

"I had to help out in the shop weekdays after school. I didn't get paid, but it was the best 'real' job I ever had."

"What did you do after you graduated?"

"Moved out of my parents' house. Went to work at the lumber-yard."

"That doesn't sound too exciting."

"Yeah. I went through a few other jobs, too."

"Like what?"

"Hospital orderly. I got fired from that one."

"How come?"

"I was bringing a patient down to surgery and forgot to lift the rails on the gurney. Too busy writing a song in my head. He kinda fell off while we were wheeling him down the hall."

"He *kinda* fell off?"

"I caught him, mostly. Then I worked at a funeral home. It's harder to hurt those people."

"What did you do there?"

"Whatever they needed me to."

"Do I want to know what that means?"

"I don't think so."

Things got quiet, except for his fingers drumming a beat on the steering wheel. He was writing a song. "Do you need some paper and a pen?" I asked.

"Yeah." He pulled the car over to the side of the road and I handed him the little spiral notebook I keep in Big Green.

He scribbled for a while and tore the page out. "I'm gonna play this for you later, see what you think."

Ten minutes later we were parking at the Holiday Inn.

"Anything I should know about your grandmother?" I asked.

"Like what?"

"Like whose mom is she?"

"My mom's mom."

"And her name is?"

"Rebecca Rachel Sinclair."

"And she's eighty?"

"Yeah, next week."

"And the idea here is to impress her with my giant brain."

"Exactly. I want you to know that I really appreciate you doing this, Grace."

"Oh, sure, no problem."

"I really think it'll give Gram some peace of mind. She's been worried about me."

"Of course, I'm happy to help."

"So, what are you gonna do to make her think you're with me?"

"With you. Um . . . well, I thought I'd start by standing beside you when you introduce me."

"And then what?"

"I'll hold your arm?"

He looked dubious.

"You know, in a proprietary way. Like I consider you mine. An ordinary friend wouldn't hold your arm like that, would she?"

"I guess not." He didn't sound too enthused.

"Well, what do you want me to do, hump your leg?"

He was delighted. "Grace, you never talk dirty!"

"I'm sorry, that was crude."

"Okay," he said. "Holding my arm is fine. And maybe look at me like you love me a time or two."

"Can you give me further direction about that?"

He sighed. "Just do the best you can."

As we got out of the car, a woman walked toward us across the parking lot. I watched her unsmiling approach and resisted the urge to shrink back in awe. She was gorgeous. Tall, straight-backed, wearing a cream-colored wrap dress and heels. Her stunning red hair fell in smooth waves down her back. No discernible makeup, with eyes that were light-amber colored. Except for the dragonfly tattoo on her right ankle, she looked like she could be the elegant, cutthroat CEO of a Fortune 500 company.

"Hey," Ty said.

"Hey, ugly."

"This is Grace."

She eyed me narrowly. As discreetly as possible, I shifted an inch or two closer to Ty.

He laughed and reached out and tugged roughly on her hair. "Cut it out, Beck."

She smiled. *The smile!* On a girl. She was suddenly lovely, far less intimidating. "I'm Rebecca. The good twin."

I tried not to wince when she shook my hand. Maybe she didn't know her own strength.

She threw an arm around Ty's shoulders. "So how about if I hear from you once in a while?"

"How about if I hear from you?"

"I'm not the one with the big fucking record deal. That I have to learn about from Mom."

"Okay. Sorry."

"I guess you've been busy." She slapped him roughly on the back and winked at me.

"How's school going?"

"Straight As." She looked at me. "What do you do, Grace?"

"I'm an editor."

"Of books?"

"Textbooks and reference, yes."

"No shit." She looked at Ty and smiled. I saw that she had a slightly chipped front tooth that somehow only made her look more interesting.

She looked at me. "Have you ever met our grandmother?"

I shook my head.

"Well, you're in for a real treat."

"Beck," Ty said.

"Well, why the hell would you bring someone here with you for that?"

"She can take it."

I looked at Ty. What could I take?

Jean came out of the party room to greet us. She looked so elegant, almost patrician in a flowered skirt and celadon twinset that matched her eyes. "Grace, you are so pretty! That blue is your color."

"Thank you."

"Gram's waiting to meet you."

Ty looked around. "Where's Dad?"

She gestured toward the darkened room across the lobby. "At the bar."

"Can we go get a drink first?" Ty asked.

"Hell no," Rebecca said. "If I talked to her sober, you can, too."

"Oh, you guys. Be nice to Gram," Jean said. "She's old."

She led us to Gram and on the way across the room I remembered why I was there. I took hold of his forearm with both hands. He looked down at me, surprised. I raised my eyebrows. *Remember?*

He smiled.

Gram was a stoop-shouldered, busty, big-boned woman in a wheelchair, with bright apricot hair and thick, cat-eye glasses that magnified her blue eyes. She looked like a *Far Side* character.

"Mama, look who's here," Jean said.

Ty leaned down and kissed her cheek.

"Well," she said. "You're alive, I guess."

"I guess so," he said.

"Have you been practicing your scales?"

"Yeah, Gram. A lot."

She looked me up and down. "Who's this?"

"This is Grace." He set a hand on top of mine and squeezed reassuringly.

"Hello, Mrs. Sinclair," I said.

"Grace," she said. "You're pretty, but short. And hanging on to my grandson like a barnacle."

"Grace is an editor in New York City, Gram."

She squinted at him. "What the hell does that mean?"

"She helps write schoolbooks."

"Schoolbooks!" She looked at me. "About what?"

"Well, uh, actually, I've just finished work on an encyclopedia."

"Encyclopedia!" Boy, for an old lady, she had a loud voice. And from her tone you'd think I'd said I was working on a new edition of *Mein Kampf*.

"I bought you and your sister a set of those World Books one time," she said accusingly. "Did you ever crack the cover of even one?"

"Sure I did."

"When?"

He thought about it. "In sixth grade, when I had to write a report about Cuba."

She snorted. "Goddamn waste of money."

"Now, Mama," Jean said, taking pity on us. "Ty, why don't you and Grace go get a soda? We'll have our dinner in about a half hour."

"Okay!" Ty pulled me toward the bar. I was sweating. Ty looked a little drained, too.

"Sorry about that," he said. "She's dying. It's made her kinda crazy and mean."

"Oh, I'm so sorry, what does she have? Cancer?"

"I don't know." He shook his head grimly. "Something that's taking way longer than it was supposed to."

"She has a lot of friends," I said, looking at the many people around us. "Young and old."

"She used to be nice."

Nathan was getting up from the bar as we approached. He was dressy from the waist up, in a pressed white shirt and bolo tie. From the waist down he wore newish jeans and biker boots.

"Good timing," he said to Ty. "I need you to help me carry in Gram's gift from the van."

"Do you mind waiting here a minute?" Ty asked me.

"Not at all."

They left and I sat on a barstool. The bartender brought me a glass of wine. I gulped most of it immediately and felt the warmth spread. Getting a little drunk seemed like a good idea. It would fortify me for the next cultural exchange.

A blond man came and sat next to me. He was good-looking, clean-cut, and his suit was nice. He ordered a whiskey.

"Hi." He smiled.

"Hello."

"You here for Rebecca Sinclair?"

"Yes, I am."

"I don't think we've met, are you a relative?"

"No, I'm here with Tyler Wilkie, her grandson."

"Oh, really?" He looked around. "Where is Ty?"

"He went outside with his dad to get her birthday present."

"Oh." He examined me rather warmly. "Are you and Ty . . . ?"

I wanted to be truthful but not undermine the plan to impress. "Together? Yes." I was here with him, after all.

"Hm." He drank his whiskey. "You don't seem like his type."

"What do you mean?"

"Well, you're a bit demure."

Demure?

"I'm Dennis Sinclair." He offered me his hand. "Did you come with him from New York?" he asked.

I nodded.

He smiled. "Culture shock, eh?"

"It's different," I allowed.

It turned out he was Ty's first cousin, brother of the heroic Elaine, Ty's prom date. He was doing his medical residency in Philly. I finished my wine and ordered another.

"Okay," Dennis said. "I have one burning question."

I smiled politely. "Go ahead."

"What is a woman like you doing with Ty? He was a bright kid in high school—awkward, but no dummy. He could have made something of himself. But he never went to college, he's had a string of nothing jobs, and spent the last ten years hanging out in bars."

I had the charitable thought that maybe he was only mean when he was drinking. "Well, he's a musician, you know."

"Yeah."

"And all that bar time is starting to pay off."

"Is it?" Dennis smiled.

I felt like punching his smirky face. "I guess you haven't heard, he just signed a major record deal. He's actually a huge success."

Ty appeared behind us, and Dennis changed personalities. He stood up and shook hands heartily. "Hey, man," Dennis said. "Good to see you."

"I think it's time to go in for dinner," Ty said.

"Okay, let's go!" I hopped off my stool, happy to get away.

"Your cousin is a jerk," I said to Ty when we reached the lobby.

"He's a shithead, I could've told you that." He drew me aside at the party room doorway. "Did he touch you?"

"Only with his roaming eyes. And he called you an under-achiever!"

Ty smiled.

"He has no idea how hard you've worked, or what you've accomplished."

"Should we go back in so you can kick his sorry ass?"

"Don't you care?"

"He can call me whatever he wants, the pissant. Come on."

We were seated at the equivalent of the children's table. Ty, Rebecca, Elaine and husband, Dennis, Elaine's twins, who actually were children—well, preteen girls—and Nathan. I did a double take when I saw him. There was an empty chair at the main table.

"Why aren't you sitting with Jean?" I leaned down and asked.

"The old lady puts me off my food," he muttered.

I sat between Ty and Elaine, who greeted me warmly. She was a beautiful woman. Very beautiful, with blond hair and sky-blue eyes and a great smile.

"Are you taking good care of Tyler?" she asked.

"I'm trying to!" I said.

"He's special," she said. "Always has been. His mom tells me good things are happening with his music. We all knew it was gonna go that way, if he'd just take it out of eastern PA."

The little girl cousins thought he was special, too, even in his bad suit. They smiled at him and giggled and paid very little attention to their chicken almandine.

I asked Elaine about the prom date.

"Oh, he was so cute. So gangly and awkward, with that sweet smile. He had a terrible problem with his speech. You wouldn't know it at all now."

She went on to tell me about her part-time work as a beauty pageant consultant. She traveled around the state giving beauty and image direction to future Miss Scrantons and Miss Delaware Water Gaps.

Rebecca was across the table, next to the tweens. It felt like she watched me through most of the meal. Nathan, too.

I listened to Elaine with one ear and to my left I heard Dennis treat Ty to a detailed narrative of his years in medical school. Then he started grilling Ty about his time in New York. He wanted details about the record deal. Then he asked if Ty still had lots of girls hanging around him. Groupies.

"There are women who come to hear me play," Ty allowed.

"Are you getting pussy, like, all the time?" Drunken Dennis asked.

Ty leaned toward Dennis and said something too quiet for me to hear. Dennis looked at me and barked an obnoxious laugh. "Sorry, man."

Jean dinged on her glass with a spoon and made a toast to her mother. A surprising number of other people followed, speaking of Rebecca Sinclair's lifetime of generosity and friendship.

Gram was encouraged to speak. "Well. I have never seen such a to-do over nothing. I don't know why a person can't get old without everyone commenting on it."

A birthday gift was then presented—a large, flat-screen TV— and birthday cake was served from the buffet table. At which time I excused myself to go powder my nose.

I came out of the stall to find Rebecca lounging on the ladies' room love seat, elegant, long legs crossed, pinning me with her hawklike eyes.

"Oh, hey," I said, trying not to break into a sweat. Trying to look unflustered as I washed and dried my hands.

"So," she said, "how long have you been fucking my brother?"

"I don't—I haven't—"

"Now Grace," she smiled, all gorgeous animosity, "don't bullshit me. My mom told me you're his girlfriend."

"She has misunderstood the situation!"

The brutal smile faded. "You're not sleeping with him?"

I shook my head.

"No shit." She studied me as if I was an intriguing new species of female. "Just haven't gotten around to it yet?"

"We're friends. That's all."

There was a tiny shooting star just above her collarbone. She saw me looking at it. "You have any tats?"

I shook my head.

She stood and opened the bathroom door for me. "You want one, while you're here? Something small and pretty? There's a guy in town who does the best hummingbirds I've ever seen. My treat."

"Thank you, maybe another time." Part of me would have liked to take her up on her generous offer, but I was going to leave this world the way I came in—a pale, unmarked page.

Ty was still stuck listening to Dennis. Elaine and family were gone. Nathan had drifted back to the bar.

"Hey, Beck, why don't you sit here next to me?" Dennis invited.

"Because then I'd have to talk to you. I'm going for coffee. You want some, Grace?"

"Please."

"Damn," Dennis said, watching her walk away. "She is the same big bitch she always was."

I saw Ty's jaw tighten and his fingers drum on his leg, only I don't think he was writing a song. Poor guy, he'd been listening to Dennis patiently for over an hour now.

"Well," Dennis said, in a *let's wrap this up, I have important things to do* tone, "it's good to hear you're making progress, Ty. We've all been worried that you weren't going to live up to your potential."

It was the last straw. I put an arm around Ty's shoulders and whispered loudly in his ear, "Take me home. Now. I want you."

He looked at me with one eyebrow faintly quirked. I brushed his hair back. Kissed him on the cheek. The brow went up another notch. He smiled and set an arm around me and gave me a squeeze.

"Seems like you guys are pretty serious," Dennis said.

"My God," I blurted, "you have no idea. I adore this man. Frankly, Dick, I worship him. I—"

"Dennis."

"Dennis. Sorry. I've had some wine, so I hope I don't say too much. I don't even know how to describe it." I smiled fondly at Ty, who was watching me with interest. "But I'll try. And I'll be frank with you, since you're family. Ty is a god in bed. Right now I can't wait to get him home. He has the biggest—"

"Grace," Ty said.

"—heart and most generous spirit and he really knows what he's doing and it's like our souls become one and, well, I don't want to be graphic, Dick, but things happen in multiples, if you know what I mean."

A cup of coffee appeared in front of me. Rebecca sat in Elaine's empty chair and grinned at me. "Well, drink up then, and get on out of here."

the fall

We said good night to Gram, who was sitting in her wheelchair with her purse in her lap. Ty kissed her cheek.

"This is the first time you've brought a girl to see me, Tyler," she said. "What does that mean?"

"It means she's special," Ty said.

"Well, it was so nice to meet you, Mrs. Sinclair," I said, eyeing the door.

"And I hope it means you're treating her well. Respectfully and thoughtfully."

"Yes, ma'am."

"And it's a two-way street, young lady. Come closer, I'm going to give you some important information. Tyler, leave us."

I looked at him desperately. He shrugged and left me alone with her.

She peered at me over the top of her glasses. "Do you know what matters most to a man? Besides access to your privates?"

"What?"

"Tender, loving kindness. Never fail to give it."

"Okay."

"Especially to that young man. *Especially* to him."

I think I gulped audibly. "All right."

She looked around the lobby. "Now where is Jean? I am going to miss *Law and Order*!"

I had to ask. "So, how did I do?"

"You certainly exceeded my expectations," Ty said.

"Do you think your grandmother was impressed?"

"Hell yeah. Probably not as much as Dennis."

"He's creepy."

"He's always been insecure."

We were driving on the country road that led to the even more rural road where their house was situated. It was inky dark out.

"I guess you noticed," Ty said. "My sister has a strong personality."

"She's beautiful. And scary. She offered to buy me a tattoo."

He looked at me. "No shit? Look, if she likes you, she'll kill for you. Maybe literally."

"Gosh." That was something to think about.

"At the very least, she will take names and majorly kick ass on your behalf. She punches really hard." This said in the wincing tone of one who knows.

Ty had the radio on, low. I could just make out the delicate notes of a sonata.

"Your grandma really loves you."

"She taught me to play piano. She used to be cool."

"Does Rebecca play?"

"She can, but doesn't."

"But you *have* to play."

He smiled. "You've got me all figured out, Gracie."

"I wish I had known my grandparents," I said. "The only one who was alive when I was born was my dad's mom, but she died when I was three. I got my first name from her, Susannah. I look like her."

"Yeah, you look kind of like your dad, in the eyes."

"Shut up."

"If he were pretty."

"That doesn't help."

"How come you don't like him?" he asked. We were pulling into the drive. No one else was home yet.

"I do. For the most part." He turned off the car. I unbuckled my seat belt and changed the subject. "Did you really work at a funeral home? What did they have you do?"

"Carry boxes. Answer the phones. Help embalm people."

"You did not."

"I swear it."

"How could you do that?"

He shrugged. "It was interesting."

"I guess I'm too afraid of death. Are you afraid?"

He was quiet for a while. "Well, I don't want it to hurt. And I don't want to be embalmed. And I don't want to get to that moment and realize I didn't experience some things I wished I had."

"Like what?"

"It's a pretty long list."

"Just tell me one thing."

"Well, I've never been out of the country, unless you count the Canadian side of Niagara Falls. I'd like to go see some things."

"You'll get to see the West Coast soon."

"That's true."

"How long will you be there?"

"I don't know, maybe a few months."

"Are you nervous?"

"I get a little freaked out sometimes. It's a whole new ride."

"You'll be all right, Ty. Just . . . take care of yourself, okay?"

"Okay, Grace. Thanks for coming here with me."

"It's been good to get out of my world for a while."

"When's the wedding?"

"April."

"Are you scared?"

He'd know if I lied. "Yes."

"Of what?"

"Forever."

"Then why are you doing it?"

"Well . . . you don't meet a guy like Steven every day."

"What's he like?"

"He's . . . good. A good person. Dependable."

"What did he think of you going out of town with me?"

"He doesn't know."

He looked at me. "You didn't tell him?"

"He's in Munich," I said.

He was still looking at me.

"I—I'll tell him about it later."

Ty nodded. Looked away.

I felt I had a burning need to tell him something. I struggled to clarify what it was. "Ty—you're leaving soon, and I don't know how long you'll be in California, or when I'll see you again. Maybe not for a long time. I just want to tell you . . . I want you to know that . . ."

He was so still, waiting for me to get on with it.

"Sorry." My eyes were starting to water. I wiped them. "I just want you to know how much I want everything to go well for you.

I . . . hope your life is *so* good. What you said to my dad, about my being your friend. I feel that way, too."

He looked at me for a long time, then opened his door and got out of the car.

I followed.

He kissed my cheek at the bottom of the stairs and went to the piano. I went up to check my messages. Steven called while I was at the party to tell me he would be home early from Munich, tomorrow night, rather than Tuesday. Time to get back to my real life.

When I got into bed Ty wasn't playing anymore. He must have gone down to the basement.

I turned off the bedside lamp. The curtains were open and I saw that Miss Gish had broken through, high in the sky. Her cool light slid across the bedcovers.

I wondered what he thought about while he lay in this bed, searching this darkness, a boy struggling to speak.

Sunday morning Jean made a late breakfast, fried ham and French toast. She and Nathan ate with us. Rebecca, Jean said, had gone out for a run.

"Grace, we've loved having you visit. Haven't we, hon?" Jean asked Nathan.

"Sure have." Nathan obligingly glanced up from his food.

"Think you might come again sometime?" she asked.

I couldn't see how, or why. Here I went with the dissembling. "That would be nice."

"You'll bring her, won't you, son?"

"Yes, ma'am."

I went upstairs to get my bags and took a last look at his room. When I came back Ty was noodling on the piano.

"Hey," he said. "Listen to this." He played a pretty tune, humming along.

"That's pretty."

"I don't have the words yet. What do you think it should be about?"

"Well, love, obviously." My eyes drifted up to the deer head. "Or taxidermy."

He laughed, that genuine, happy sound of his. "Come on, I want to show you one more thing before we go."

I followed him again into the woods. It was an overcast November day, chilly, the trees like Chinese calligraphy against the rice-paper sky. The leaves on the ground were mostly muted, but here and there I saw a mottled, bright canary or cabernet. We passed the remains of the burnt tree. It was far less ominous to my sober brain.

We walked for at least fifteen minutes, mostly in silence, till we came to a wire fence as tall as me. He climbed over. I stood there and looked at him.

"Come on." He pointed to a foothold. "Put your toes there."

I set my toes in the indicated spot and slung my other leg over the top of the fence. He grabbed me by the hips and hauled me over.

"Are we trespassing?" I asked.

"Yes indeed."

We went up a steep hill that made my legs tremble. By now I could hear running water. We got to the top and were standing on a cliff that overlooked a lovely, wide creek. He helped me down a succession of steep steps hewn into the rock face. We walked upstream, around a bend, and came finally to where the water roared.

I had never seen a real-life waterfall. It was probably a small one as they go, only a couple of stories high, maybe ten feet wide.

"I want to touch it," I said.

I climbed on top of a big rock to get as close as I could to the curtain of water. He stood below and held on tightly to my other hand while I reached for it. The water was in a mad, heavy rush. It battered and stung and slapped my fingers away.

"Ouch!" I laughed at the sting and looked down at him. We were enveloped in a fine mist. "Your hair is curling like crazy."

He smiled up at me with such generous, uncomplicated joy, with that light in his eyes that I knew so well. And something happened. The stubborn, stuck thing inside me finally dislodged and moved out of the way.

Looking at him, I saw with perfect clarity: *You are my heart.*

I understood, finally.

Then, now, and forever, he was *everything*. No one else was even close.

Oh, God. Oh, God. *This* was what love felt like. *This.*

I was terrified.

He saw it and his face changed. He said, "It's all right, baby. It's all right." He helped me climb down and held me a long time, making soothing sounds until I stopped crying.

"I want to go back," I finally said.

We went slowly. It took a while to get back up the cliff face. He would have kept an arm around me, but once we got over the fence I moved away.

The smell of woodsmoke. A cardinal, darting low across my path. His worried face, looking back at me every ten yards or so. His back, solid, strong, in red-and-black–checkerboard flannel, leading me through the trees.

At the burnt tree I stopped. "Wait."

He turned and came back and I grabbed his head and pulled him down. I opened my mouth on his. He made a rough sound and my feet left the ground. Then all of me was there, on the ground, on the leaves, and my jacket was open and my sweater and bra were shoved up to my neck and his mouth was hot on me and his hand was in my jeans—in my panties—and *oh, God!* I could not do this.

I set my hands on his chest.

"Stop!" I said, desperate not to make the most disastrous mistake of my life.

His head came up and I could see that he hated me. Understandably.

"Please."

He moved off me. Watched me pull down my sweater and zip my jeans. Reached into his own jeans and made an adjustment.

I stood up. He knelt there still, looking up at me.

I touched his hair, with both hands. I touched his face. I wanted to lie back down with him. I was shaking so badly I couldn't speak. I didn't have words, anyway. I grabbed his hand and pressed my mouth against it, in devotion. In sorrow and apology.

Then I ran.

ruin and resolution
or
the smell of cloves still makes me sad

Terrible silence in the car, all the way back to Manhattan.

When he dropped me off, I did not go into my building. I got into a cab and asked the driver to take me to the first hotel I could think of, the Waldorf. I had been there for afternoon tea a couple of times. Ordinarily, I would have lingered in the lobby, absorbing the gorgeous mosaic floor and the gigantic arrangement of lilies on the table by the elevators. Today, an EconoLodge would have served my purpose just as well. And been within my budget.

I got a room with a king-size bed. Stripped naked and retreated under the covers and cried until I passed out. Four hours later I woke to my ringing cell. I crawled out of bed and staggered around in the dark until I found Big Green, but I was too late. It was Peg.

I threw the cell on the bed, went to the bathroom, and drank three glasses of water. I was completely parched from my crying jag. And my stomach hurt. I was hungry. I turned on the bedside lamp, found the room-service menu, and ordered a seventeen-dollar bowl of lobster bisque and a ginger ale.

The cell rang again. I put on the complimentary white terry robe and waited for room service. The guy rolled the food in on a cart. I tipped him and sat on the edge of the bed and ambitiously buttered a roll. The cell rang. I tried the soup but only managed a few spoonfuls. The cell rang. I gave up on the soup.

I wheeled the cart out into the hall and got the extra pillows out of the closet. Drank some of the ginger ale and got back into bed. I built a pillow fort all around me for protection and looked to see who had called.

Peg. Steven. Julia. Steven.

I put the phone on vibrate and set it on the bedside table, then pulled pillows over me until only my nose and mouth were exposed. I fell asleep again and woke to the phone buzzing across the surface of the table. I looked at the number: Dan. I answered.

"Grace, are you okay?"

"Yes. I'm okay."

"Steven called me, he's very worried about you."

"Would you do me a favor? Would you call him and tell him you spoke with me and I'm all right, and I'll be in touch soon?"

Silence. I could feel him evaluating my vibe. "Why don't you come here? You'll have your room. We don't have to talk."

I would not cry with Dan, as much as I wanted to. As much as I needed to. "Thank you, I'm fine where I am at the moment."

"Listen: Whatever is going on right now, it's temporary. It's not what the rest of your life is about. You'll get through it, and be stronger than ever."

"Okay. Yes. Thank you." Damn! Crying. "Gotta go," I squeaked, and hung up.

I was crying, yes—who knew when that would ever stop? But I actually felt a little better. My dad was right, I could get through this. I knew I could. I just had to figure out the next step.

I didn't sleep much the rest of the night. At around three a.m. I took a long, hot bath. And found I really like the clove-scented soap they give you at the Waldorf. Then I started writing out a rough-draft plan for my life in small steps that would get me through the next few days. I could regroup and plan farther into the future over the weekend.

At nine a.m. Monday:
STEP ONE: Call in sick.

STEP TWO: Text Julia, reassuringly.

STEP THREE: Call Peg.

"Hey," I said.

"Where are you?"

"I'm at the Waldorf."

"What's going on?"

"Can I live with you?"

Long moment of absorption.

"Okay. I'll have to kick out the guy who's been renting the room. How soon do you need to move in?"

"Today."

"You'll have to sleep on an air mattress till the guy finds a new place to live. Or maybe you just need a few nights?"

"No. I need forever."

More absorption. "You probably don't want to go into it all on the phone."

"Can we talk when I get there? Later this morning?"

"I'll be here."

STEP FOUR: Go home and a) get my things and b) leave a good-bye note for Steven, who would be at work.

Yes, a note. Yes, I was being cowardly. I knew that I had to deal with him face-to-face. But that could be soon. It couldn't be now.

Everything was quiet when I let myself in.

Then Steven came out of the bedroom. I was so startled that my teeth crunched into my tongue.

"Hey," he said. "Sorry, I didn't mean to scare you."

Great. More watery eyes, this time from my throbbing, bleeding, swelling tongue.

"Where have you been?" he asked politely. He was in jeans and a sweatshirt. Not dressed for work.

"I, uh—at a hotel."

"Why?"

"Just, um—"

He looked at my hand. "Where's your ring?"

Oh, man. The ring. I knelt and unzipped my overnight bag and fumbled around till I found the sock. I dug down to the toe. He watched me extract the ring with an expression of bemused disbelief.

"Grace, what is going on?"

"Steven, I am so sorry," I whispered. "I'm sorry." I held the ring out to him on the palm of my hand. He stared at it.

"What are you doing?"

"We can't get married. I can't. Get married."

"Have I done something?"

"No, it's me. I—"

"Is it Tyler?"

I nodded.

His face turned white, then red. He leaned against the wall and moaned. "Goddammit. God*dammit*! I've been an idiot. Such a fucking idiot."

"Please, no—"

"Was he with you at the hotel?"

"No!"

"You lied to me about being friends with him."

"I didn't. I didn't mean to lie."

"I *hate* you for this."

I had never seen him like this. He was Even Steven.

"Yes, I—I understand. . . ." I gently set the ring on the table by the door. "I—I'm just going to get a few things, and I'll go."

He followed me to the bedroom and watched me get my suitcase out of the closet and set it on the bed. It was hard to unzip with shaking hands. I pulled the dresser drawers open one by one and tossed things into the suitcase.

"Is it because I've been gone so much?"

"No. It's me. My problem."

"How long have you been sleeping with him?"

"I haven't."

"You haven't slept with him?"

"No."

"So . . . we can work through this. People get crushes, it's not a big deal. Stop. Stop packing."

I went to the closet and hefted a chunk of my clothes, hangers and all, into the suitcase. Threw in some shoes and belts.

"I thought you were smarter than this, Grace. Do you think he's going to actually love you? Just you? Women offer themselves to him and he takes them up on it. A girl I work with fucked him. I heard her telling her friend about it in the lunchroom. A meaningless, drunken fuck after one of his 'gigs.' He uses women and discards them. Are you going to waste yourself like that? It's disgusting, if you think about it. The possibility of disease."

I sat on the edge of the bed.

"Are you listening to me?"

I nodded.

He sat beside me. "Maybe you need more time to think about it."

"No."

He pulled me to him and put his head on my shoulder. He held me too tightly, leaned too heavily. Then he cried. I actually felt afraid; he had me in such a grip that I couldn't move. I made myself breathe and stay calm. Bear his weight.

After a while he sat up. Not looking at me. He wiped his face on his sleeve.

I stood up and tried to close the suitcase. God knows what I had crammed in it. Steven helped me zip it shut. He carried it to the living room and I followed, snagging my laptop bag along the way.

I started to open the front door but he stepped in front of it. "Did you love me?"

"I . . . Steven, I respect you. So much. And . . . I do love you . . . as a friend and good person and . . . oh, Steven . . . I'm sorry."

He was looking at my mouth. "I didn't know I had kissed you for the last time. I didn't know."

"I didn't, either."

"One more time," he said, closing in.

It was the best kiss we'd ever shared. I would have liked to have told him so.

————————

STEP FIVE: Move in with Peg.

Peg came from one of those old New York families that used to have money. She was somehow distantly related to J. P. Morgan. She had bought her apartment in the West Village when she was right out of college in the mid-eighties, with down-payment money she'd inherited. It was a large, two-bedroom, fifth-floor walk-up. The bathroom alone was larger than many studio apartments, with an old iron skylight over the bathtub. To open it, you turned a crank thing with a long, hooked pole.

The comfort of being able to come back at a time like this was immeasurable.

She buzzed me in.

"Is the guy here?" I whispered.

"No, he's hardly ever here. He's in school at NYU and he has a job. Do you want some tea?"

"Yes, please."

"Have you eaten anything this morning?"

"Not yet."

She made me two slices of buttered toast and milky tea. She sat across from me at the table and watched me peel the crusts off with trembling fingers. "Want me to cut those off?"

"No, I've got it." I took a tiny bite of the toast and chewed. Washed it down my dry throat with a swig of lukewarm tea.

She waited patiently the full five minutes it took for me to eat the first piece of toast before she asked, "What happened? Did you sleep with Ty?"

I set my mug down. "Why would you ask me that? Have I ever behaved inappropriately with him?"

"Not that I know of."

"We almost did it on the ground in the woods."

"Almost?"

"It was close, but I stopped it."

"That must have been Herculean, for both of you. You guys have been heading there for a long time."

"I wasn't heading there!"

"Well, Ty certainly was."

"No, he wasn't! He didn't try anything during the whole trip. What happened—I started it."

"What were you doing out in the woods?"

"He took me there. To show me a waterfall. And I was looking at the water, and looking at him, and it was like something in my brain *moved*. And I realized that I love him." I pictured his face at my moment of clarity and the tenderness washed through me again. "I *love* him." My voice was starting to shake.

She moved over to the chair beside me and rubbed my arm gently. "That's okay, Grace. It's good."

"No, it's not. It's not."

"Why?"

"I got so scared! Terrified. And my heart was beating hard, and strangely, and I couldn't breathe, and my face and fingers were tingling."

"Sounds like a panic attack."

"It was the worst feeling I've ever had. He helped me, stayed with me till I calmed down, and when we were going back to the house I just—I *leapt* on him. And then we were on the ground, and I was half-naked, and about one minute away from total disaster I stopped it."

She handed me a paper napkin and I blew my nose. "Well, you did the right thing."

"I know."

She nodded. "It wouldn't have been clean for you. Honorable."

"I know."

"What about Steven?"

"It's over. I went to get my clothes and I was going to leave him a note because I am such a coward, but he was there and I told him. He was so angry and hurt. It was awful."

She set a warm hand on my shoulder. "We'll put the air mattress in my room, and you can sleep there until the guy finds another place and you can move into your old room."

I couldn't believe there was any water left in my body at this point, but still more ran down my face. "Peg, I love you."

She patted my hand. "You just need to chill out and settle down and take things very slowly for a while now."

I nodded. "I think you're right."

"And probably with Ty, too."

I grabbed another napkin."I won't be seeing him again."

"What do you mean?"

"Well, that's not something that's actually going to happen, me being with him in any way!"

"You're confusing me. You just told me that you love him."

"Well, who doesn't?"

"But he loves you. He told you so."

I stared at her.

"The night after Joe's Pub?" she clarified.

"He was drunk!"

"But it was true."

Why was she trying to make this difficult? "Even if it were, it just wouldn't work."

"Why not?"

God. Where to begin. I grabbed at a few of the innumerable issues whirling in the cyclone of my mind and tossed them at her, in no particular order of importance. "Peg, he's *late*. For everything. No . . . no grasp of time management! He doesn't *plan*. He grew up in a house that was orange and is now *pink and purple*. He shoots animals. Deer! I saw the dead deer that he killed. Its head is on their wall."

"Really?" She looked a little queasy.

"Yes! He's practically Ted Nugent."

"Ew. Did he use a crossbow?"

"I guess—no wait—I don't know! What difference does it make? He killed Bambi's father!"

"Okay. The deer thing requires a little adjustment."

"Also: He didn't go to college."

She shrugged. "Does he need to?"

"And he drinks. A lot. He smokes marijuana. His parents are potheads who gave him *whippins* when he was a child. His dad is a Hell's Angel. His sister is Xena. His grandmother is . . . well, she's just plain awful."

"Grace—you hear yourself, right?"

How could she still look so unperturbed? "Okay, how about this: He talked me into doing drugs."

Finally, she was appropriately taken aback. "What do you mean?"

"I smoked marijuana with him."

"Grace!" She looked amused.

"It's not funny."

"Well, it's interesting."

"Peg. Look at his life. The late nights in bars and clubs. You've seen all the girls, and you know he takes full advantage. He is on a wild ride right now, and loving it."

"Grace, I'm certain you mean more to him than those girls."

"Maybe. But come on! Artists and musicians are not people you can seriously hope to have a life with."

"So this is about your dad."

"No! It's about loving this man and knowing that I want so much more from him than he is going to be able to give. Peg, I have to stop this thing, whatever it is, now. I have to take care of myself."

I could see that she was finally hearing me, but it had been hard work. I slumped in my chair, exhausted.

"Okay. But I think that you should ask Ty what he wants. Just ask him. To be sure you're doing the right thing."

"I won't be seeing him again. He's disgusted with me about what happened. He didn't even say good-bye when he brought me home. And he's going away. Probably forever. Could I lie down on your bed for a while? I haven't slept much."

She came into her bedroom with me. I lay down and she covered me with a knitted afghan. She patted my back. "Everything is going to be all right, Grace."

"Yeah," I said tiredly. "This is all good, Peg. Because I don't want a boyfriend. Or a fiancé. Or a friend with benefits. I just want to be with me."

"Grace, I'm curious. Why do you think you got so scared, when you realized you love Ty? Why would love be scary?"

"I don't know. . . . Maybe just the impossibility of the whole thing."

"Hm. Do you want a little Reiki, to help you sleep?"

"Yes. Please."

She made some mysterious motions in the air and moved her hands in a light, warm hover around the top of my head, my face, over my heart.

I slept.

Big Green declares independence
me, too

Peg went to a friend's house in the country for Thanksgiving, just for the day. Besides having to come back on Friday for work, I think she didn't want to leave me alone for too long.

The guy who lived in my room was gone, too, to be with his family in Michigan.

Steven and I had planned to spend the day with his parents, out in Kew Gardens. It worked well for me that Julia and Dan thought I had holiday plans and didn't pressure me to be with them. They would never know I stayed home alone on the couch in my underwear, wrapped in a quilt, alternately sleeping and watching the same stories over and over on CNN.

Edward came with me on Saturday to get the rest of my belongings. Steven wasn't there but he had boxed everything up for me and stacked it all by the door.

Edward looked at the neat boxes. "That's more than any of my exes have ever done for me when we broke up. You sure about this?"

"Please be helpful."

I started to write a note to thank Steven, to wish him well, but what could I say that wouldn't sound hollow?

I left the key on the kitchen counter.

At work I had recently been assigned to help Edward project-manage a junior high textbook, U.S. history to 1877. I tried to focus and be productive, but those first couple of weeks were hard. I cried several times a day at the most innocuous triggers: no mayo on my sandwich from the deli; snagging my sweater on the rough edge of a binder; dropping my last, just-unwrapped tampon on the bathroom floor. Edward telling me that we were about to get a revised edition of the *Chicago Manual of Style* sent me home for the afternoon. I crawled onto my air mattress and buried myself under pillows. I had the current edition memorized. How dare they do this to me at a time like this, those *Chicago Manual* bastards!

Peg's guy roommate did find another place and was moving out December 20, but none too cheerfully. I tried to be friendly and smile at him when I saw him, but otherwise, I hid in Peg's room.

And it was Christmas in two weeks. I had no idea where to begin. There was no answer for it, I would have to try to do all my shopping online and hope for the best.

I was in terrible physical shape. My shaky stomach lasted a while, so I force-fed myself toast and crackers and matzoh ball soup. Buttered white rice. Ginger ale. Then I started to have a small appetite, but only for appalling non-foods. Count Chocula cereal. Gummy bears. I ate so many scorching Atomic Fireballs and stinging salt-and-vinegar chips in one twenty-four-hour period that the top layer of my tongue peeled away. In three weeks I lost seven pounds and was well on my way to developing rickets and scurvy.

And then, the unthinkable icing on the cake: I lost Big Green. I was coming home from a visit to the Cloisters and in a disastrous moment of mental fog I left it sitting on the train. As the doors were closing I realized what I had done. I stood on the Christopher Street station platform watching it ride away. My cell. My wallet. My lists. Everything Else I Might Conceivably Need was in that bag. It was my safety net, my portable contingency plan for so many possible New York City challenges. Now I would have to rebuild even that from scratch.

I had my second-ever full-blown panic attack. A young Indian-American man saw me hyperventilating and crying and led me to a bench. He gave me his unopened water bottle and sent another concerned stranger off to tell a nearby policeman about my runaway purse. He sat with me through the arrival and departure of three more trains, until I felt well enough to get myself home. When I thanked him and said good-bye, he asked if he could take me to lunch or dinner some time. In another life I might have said yes. He was cute.

"I'm not fit company," I said, and walked away. Pity party in full swing, but also exasperated with myself. I knew I needed to do something.

That night I wrote down the plan for Part I of the rest of my life. I would start by finding another job after the holidays, some kind of work that I could feel good about, that would put my strengths and passions to good use.

I would practice self-care. I would eat kale and go to yoga. Give my hair a hot-oil treatment once in a while. Buy a premium subscription to the *New York Times* online.

I would maybe try to increase the time I spent with Dan. He had been so helpful, with his advice during my night at the Waldorf.

I would get a much smaller bag than Big Green, and try to live life a little more bravely and spontaneously.

I went to bed and lay in the dark, feeling almost positive after weeks of despair. Then I remembered what had been in my wallet. Ty's college ID, with the ridiculously adorable photo.

"You were going to get rid of it anyway," I said out loud.

"Yeah right," I said back to myself.

I said something else to me, but I couldn't understand it because by then I was blubbering.

———

A couple of days after I lost Big Green, I had a meeting with Bill, Edward, and people from Production to review some of the proposed visuals for the U.S. history text. I handed Bill the folder of images we had amassed so far.

We had a gorgeous painting of Chief Agüeybaná greeting Juan Ponce de León on the shores of Florida. A 1612 map of Virginia, published by John Smith. The elegant first page of the original treaty of the Louisiana Purchase (people used to have such nice penmanship!). A photograph of Harriet Tubman. Bill flipped past them all, which meant we were in good shape.

At Thomas Jefferson, the famous 1805 painting by Rembrandt Peale, he stopped flipping.

"What is it, Bill?" I asked.

"Well, I'm just thinking. All this stuff is so dry. It's for eleven-year-olds, right?"

"Yes, sixth grade."

"So let's do something fun. Like, instead of this boring dead president picture, let's have one of a bowl of ice cream."

"I beg your pardon?"

"Well, didn't I read somewhere that Jefferson invented ice cream?"

"I don't think he invented it," Edward said. "He just brought a recipe for vanilla ice cream to America from France." He wrote something on his legal pad and nudged me under the table.

I read: *Close your mouth.*

"So let's give them something to look at that will actually interest them. All kids like ice cream."

"Bill," I said, "what about nutrition?"

Bill waved a hand. "This book is for Wisconsin. They're big on dairy there."

"I don't know . . ." I said. "I mean, Jefferson wrote the Declaration of Independence. I really think we ought to have an actual image of him."

"They see him all the time. He's on the quarter, for God's sake."

"The nickel," Ed said.

"Whatever," Bill said.

I gathered up my pad and pen and folders.

"Where ya going, Grace?" Bill asked.

"Would you please excuse me? I'm not feeling well."

"Sure, go ahead, Ed and I will finish up."

I went back to my cubicle and Googled "New York City nonprofit jobs." From there I went to Idealist.org and found several positions that seemed worth applying for—executive assistant and coordinator openings at organizations for the homeless and people with disabilities.

Then I read a posting that made my dormant life force spark and flare—briefly, but brightly. A city health organization was looking to hire people to do community sexuality education. They would even do the training. I sat up straight in my chair. I could do that! I would *like* to do that. It would be wonderful to do work that was helpful. It might even be a chance to clear out some of that *Healthy Teen* guilt I was carrying around.

I reread the listing carefully, then spent the next hour writing a letter to the director. An impassioned letter, about how I would love the opportunity to help ensure that people, especially youth, receive complete, accurate sexual health information.

I opened up my resumé and looked it over. I had done work-study as a receptionist at the campus health clinic at school. I could perhaps add that I had taken a couple of classes in gender and sexuality studies; otherwise, it was all publishing, ever since graduation. All I had ever been, wanted to be, was an editor. Not really the trajectory for becoming a community health educator. And I had to assume that there were hundreds, thousands, of more qualified people hitting Send right now. But I was doing something about my pathetic life, and that felt great. It was a start.

There was no getting around it: time for my monthly lunch with Julia.

I suggested a Christmassy place, the restaurant next to the ice-skating rink at Rockefeller Center. I was counting on her holiday spirit to help her process the bad news I was about to present.

No, I had not yet told her that the wedding was off. For which I felt a little guilty. Dan knew; he had drawn the basics out of me in e-mails and instant message conversations. If Julia ever found out that he knew something about me that she didn't, it would be a very bad scene.

She was waiting for me at a table that looked out on the ice. She saw me coming in and came around the table and grasped my shoulders. "My God, you look awful! Have you been sick? Why didn't you call me?"

"I'm fine. I've just had a little stomach trouble."

"Have you been to a doctor?"

"I'm getting better. Really." She was squeezing my arms, frowning. "Please, let's sit."

Julia was radiant in a red turtleneck sweater-dress, big silver hoop earrings, and stiletto-heeled boots.

"You look great, Mom."

She flushed with pleasure. "José gave me this dress. An early Christmas present."

"Wow, you two are really going strong."

"Well, we both see other people, you know. It's casual."

"And you're okay with that?"

She laughed uncomfortably. "I insisted on it."

The waiter came. She ordered a salad for herself and said to me, "And you're having a nice buttery, creamy pasta. An Alfredo," she said to the waiter. "With penne. And extra butter and cream." He went away and she continued with me. "Not that you want to eat like this too often, once you've gained a few pounds back."

"Of course not."

She pulled a folder out of her bag and started showing me wedding cake designs. It took me a while to work up the nerve.

"Mom, these all look *so* good."

"But what? Too many flowers? We could have them do one with no flowers and just this lacy pattern in the icing."

"Mom." I breathed deeply and exhaled.

She started to look worried. "What?"

"Steven and I are not getting married."

Grim, staring silence.

"What happened?"

"I can't do it."

"You're nervous. That's completely normal."

"I don't love him."

"You should go home and talk about your fears with him."

"I moved out."

"When?"

"About three weeks ago."

Not good, the look on her face. "Well, thanks for telling me."

"I'm sorry."

"I've been making calls, pricing menus. *I have talked to your father on the phone.*"

"I know that was difficult for you. Thank you."

"And what are we going to do with a three-thousand-dollar wedding dress?"

"Let's sell it on eBay."

She rubbed her temples. "Grace, are you sure you're not being naïve? Marriage is a *partnership* that demands mutual respect and commitment. Love is nice, but honestly, it's a luxury. And it can even be a hindrance."

"How a hindrance?"

"Well, how do you easily leave the marriage if it goes bad?"

"Julia, do you hear yourself?"

She didn't answer. Our food came. We stared at it.

"It would have been so good for you," she said mournfully.

"How can you say that?" People were looking at me. I lowered my voice. "Julia." She looked at me with weary, disappointed eyes. "With what happened between you and Dan, how can you say marriage is a good thing?"

"Is it all right if I imagine things being better for my daughter than they were for me? Would it be all right if I do that? Be an optimist for you?"

She was slightly teary. I hadn't seen that in years, if ever.

"I'm sorry," I said.

She found a tissue in her purse and blew her nose. "Where are you living?"

"With Peg."

"Well, at least you have a decent place to live. Do you need money?"

"No."

"How did Steven take this?"

"Badly."

We finished our meal in silence. It surprised me, but I was able to eat. And in spite of the penne, the Alfredo, the extra butter and cream, I actually felt much lighter than I'd felt coming in.

I got an interview for the health educator job!

The office was in an older building in the West Forties, about halfway down the block from Times Square. Top floor. The frosted glass on the door read *Safe and Sound Sexually.*

A young woman at the desk nearest the door greeted me and I told her I had an appointment with Lavelle Hendricks. She led me through a large room with a lot of desks to a small, private office.

Lavelle was maybe a few years older than me, with a flawless, caffe latte complexion, hair pulled back in a sleek bun, and big, direct eyes. We sat down on a worn denim sofa and she told me about SASS. Nonprofit community health education. They needed people to teach safe-sex workshops for the SASS-2 project, which stood for Safe and Sexy Seniors. Because of erectile dysfunction medications, testosterone supplementation, and women feeling more liberated about sex, old people were getting it on in record numbers, with a corresponding increase in HIV and other sexually transmitted infections.

I was thrown for a bit of a loop. "So . . . the job is teaching elderly people."

"Yes. Teaching them about physical and psychological aging changes and medications that affect them sexually, how they can increase their pleasure, solutions for erectile dysfunction, and HIV and STI prevention." She looked at my resumé. "We need people who are bilingual. Do you speak Spanish?"

I had some Spanish from high school and reading the ads on subway cars. Oh, and watching *Sábado Gigante* on Saturday nights, after the double feature of *Golden Girls*. But I was pretty committed to no one ever knowing about that. "I can understand it and read it fairly well. I wouldn't say that I am a strong speaker. But I could work on it."

She looked skeptical, but seemed to be very interested in my writing and editing skills. In a thinking-out-loud way, she said, "I suppose we might be able to send you out part of the time as an educator and have you do our in-house writing."

"Yes, of course! Whatever you'd like."

She looked at me a long time, mulling me over. I tried to look as bright and as exactly what she was looking for as possible. *I am not a person with gigantic relationship failures and a broken heart. I don't cry myself to sleep every night. I am smart and cheerful! I am normal and healthy! I have eaten more today than five Tootsie Roll Minis and a bowl of Top Ramen!*

"Tell me something about yourself, Grace. Something that's not on your resumé."

She had such a quietly compelling face.

"Well," I said. "I just ended my engagement."

"To be married?"

I nodded. "Know anyone who could use a Vera Wang wedding dress for cheap?"

She shook her head. "There's a shop downtown where you can donate it, and if they sell it the money goes to foster care programs."

I wrote down the name of the shop.

She asked me why I wanted to make such a drastic career change. I told her about *Healthy Teen*, how working on it felt like a moral compromise I didn't want to be asked to make again.

She nodded. Looked over my resumé again, poker-faced. Stood and offered me her hand.

I left with absolutely no clue how the interview went.

Bill called an end-of-week meeting about the U.S. history book. He'd read through the page proofs and, it seemed, found it lacking.

"This," he thumped the thick folder of pages, "is the dullest thing I've ever read."

"Oh, is it?" Ed said. "We hired the freelance writers you recommended."

"I know that. We need to go back to them and tell them to punch it up."

"Bill," I said. "Could you please explain what you mean by 'punch it up'?"

"Tell them to make it more . . . I don't know, sexy."

"Sixth-grade U.S. history. Sexy."

"Yeah. As in: more exciting?"

I gripped the edge of the conference room table. It was such a good thing that I didn't have super powers.

"I see," I said, with uncontrollably increasing volume, "and Bill, when those sixth graders get all excited from reading this sexy U.S. history, are we going to tell them they have to be abstinent? Or would it be all right if we mention the word CONDOM?"

Ed patted my shoulder. I shrugged his hand away.

"Well," Bill said, "I think we're all done."

"Oh, good," I said. "Because I was just about to HURL all over this big, shiny table!"

"Grace," Bill said, "you're really flipping out. Calm down."

"Okay, will do, Bill!"

"Grace," Ed said. He looked worried.

"Grace," Bill said, "you're really not happy here, are you?"

I laughed. Not happily. "Not really, Bill, no."

"So I'll expect your resignation on my desk in the morning." He got up and left the room.

I looked at Ed.

"Congratulations," he said bitterly. "Now who will drink-to-forget with me during the workday?"

gray

So I moved back into my former bedroom, the one I'd lived in right out of college when I was new to adulthood and autonomy and so certain about what I wanted to do with my life.

And when the call came to say that I got the job at SASS, it felt like I was being allowed all kinds of major do-over. Now if I could just manage not to mess it all up.

I was glad to vacate Peg's room, after living there with her for a month. She was seeing a guy, Jim, this cute hippie dentist she met in the vitamin aisle at Whole Foods, and they'd had no privacy. Now they were on a romantic trip upstate for a week to celebrate the winter solstice. I was planning to spend Christmas on the couch in my underwear watching CNN, but Peg made me promise to leave the apartment. I went to my mom's.

When giving Julia news, the timing is crucial. So, after she tossed back several eggnogs, and while we were watching the pope, I casually mentioned my impending job change. She had an anaphylactic reaction to the word *nonprofit*.

"I can't believe you're giving up your editing career!"

"I know."

"You've worked so hard for it!"

"I know, but it's over. I might do some writing for SASS."

"I think you're being naïve. Grace, I think you're making a huge mistake."

I got quiet. I was learning, you can't always make people understand you. And that had to somehow be okay.

Christmas Day, her behavior was unusual. Several times she randomly patted my shoulder. She tucked my hair behind my ear and smiled at me. That evening, when she was driving me to the train station, the Julia Barnum Christmas Miracle fully incarnated.

"Grace, that thing I said about you being naïve. I'm sorry. I'm such a cynic, you know. I think the new job is great. I do want you to care about your work." She reached over and squeezed my arm. "I'm going to give you some money. How much do you need?"

"I think I'm okay right now, Mom. Thank you."

"All right. You'll tell me if you need help, won't you?"

"Of course. You'll be the first."

It was my last week at Spender-Davis and I didn't have any work to do. I watched old *Kids in the Hall* on YouTube, cleaned out my files, and packed the little that I was taking with me in a box.

I emptied my desk drawers. Jeez, the crap that accumulates! Mangled paper clips. A United Way brass lapel pin, missing the back clasp. Open, leaking sugar packets. Red pencils with no remaining eraser. Sticky pennies. An earth-painted marble that was in the drawer when I moved in. I decided I might take it with me; it was kind of pretty. I tried to slip it in the pocket of my jeans but dropped it under the desk. I went after it.

Scuffed black boots darkened my doorway. I experienced instant, mindless recognition of a particular scratch across the toe of the left boot and became very still and quiet, crouching in my particle-board cave like a terrified bunny.

He came in and rapped on the desk. "You okay under there?"

I leaned out just enough to peek over the top. "What are you doing here? How did you get in?"

"The girl at the front knew me from seeing me play. She let me back."

"Why?"

"Would it kill you to say hello?"

I slid out from under the desk and sat awkwardly in my chair. I didn't know what to do with my hands. Or any other part of me. Everything felt suddenly alien. "Hello. . . . Why?"

"I'm taking you to lunch."

I stared at him. He stared at me. I blinked first. "I guess I could go for half an hour. Friday is my last day here and I'm packing."

"Okay. Meet me downstairs."

He left and I exhaled and laid my head on my arms on the desk. Tried to regroup. I grabbed my bag and jacket and on the way to the elevator stopped in the ladies' room.

I looked awful. No makeup. A red spot developing on my chin. Hair in two farm-girl braids. *Does it matter?* I asked myself. *No.* Still, as a courtesy to my lunch companion, I brushed and rebraided my hair.

I got off the elevator and spotted him laughing with the building security guys. Typical.

He saw me coming and smiled as if nothing weird or bad had ever happened between us. In spite of myself, I soaked him in. Black jeans, gray T-shirt, black leather coat. His hair that thick and waving auburn, and his eyes—brown and green and gold, and warming me again, after such a long, chilly absence. Up close I saw that he was wearing the pewter rune on the short leather cord around his neck. And he had a small cut from shaving, on the tender place under his jaw.

I wanted to hear him sing again.

He took me by the arm and we walked a couple of blocks to a falafel place on Fifty-third.

Ty ordered the deluxe falafel platter with extra sides of pita and babaganoush. I ordered rice.

He frowned. "That's all you're gonna eat? You want some chicken? A gyro?"

"Just rice, with butter," I said to the waiter. "And a Sprite."

He eyed me critically. "You look skinny."

"I've lost a little weight."

"Have you been sick?"

I nodded. "Stomach problems."

"Are you gonna try to gain it back? Your elbow felt knobby."

"Thanks. I'm working on it."

The waiter brought cans of Red Bull and Sprite, and glasses of ice.

"So, I'm going to L.A. on Sunday."

"Finally, huh?"

"Finally." He popped open my soda and poured it for me. "I paid off that appendectomy bill," he said casually.

I looked at him. "All of it?"

"Yeah." Now he poured caffeine into his glass. "And I got health insurance."

"Wow, Ty. That's really great."

The waiter brought our food. His took up three-quarters of the small table. I buttered my rice and added salt and nibbled a few bites. Mostly I watched him eat. He had always been a bit rude and voracious about it. He ate like he sang. Like he had touched me in the woods.

"Is your family well?" I asked. "Did you spend Christmas with them?"

"Yeah. They asked about you."

I nodded.

"I went to your apartment. But your name is off the directory. Peg said you don't live there anymore."

I shook my head.

"She said you're not getting married."

"No."

He waited for me to say more. I ate some rice.

"Where are you going to work now?"

Best to be nonspecific. "For a nonprofit. Doing community HIV education."

"All right! Way to go, Grace! You're finally putting yourself to good use."

I beamed back at him. I couldn't help it. It was ridiculous, how satisfying his approval felt.

The waiter came and took away the plates. Asked if we wanted to try the baklava. Gave Ty the check. Good, we were wrapping things up.

"I have something for you." Ty reached into a pocket and brought out a small box, tied with a bow.

I took it slowly. "What's this for?"

"Christmas. And I missed your birthday, didn't I, in September?"

"I—I don't have anything for you."

"Don't worry about it."

I untied the bow and lifted the lid.

Earrings: delicate, silver, with dangling, pale rose-colored teardrop crystals. Exquisite.

"They're white gold," Ty said. "And pink diamonds."

He was watching me closely. It took a moment to think of what to say, and it came out too bluntly. "You shouldn't have done this."

He shifted impatiently in his chair and crossed his arms. "Why shouldn't I?"

I put the lid back on carefully. "They're too much."

"Actually, they're not. I have a lot of money now." His tone became ironic. "I'm incorporated."

"Well, that's awesome," I tried to joke. "Now you won't have to mooch your marijuana off your mom and dad."

He laughed, a little, but mostly he looked angry. And hurt.

"Sorry," I said. "I was—that was a joke." I set the box on the table in front of him.

"No." He pushed it back across to me. "Goddammit, Grace. Keep them."

"It's better if I don't."

"Why is it better?" He put his hands together on top of the table and cracked his knuckles unbelievably loudly. "Just so I know," he said calmly but pointedly, "how long are you gonna keep running from me?"

Okay. My heart was pounding. *Ask . . .*

"Ty. Why are you doing this?"

"The earrings? I wanted to give you something."

"Why?"

He looked at me, a long, silent time.

"What will happen, if I stop running from you?" I asked.

Still no words. Then he looked away.

I almost felt guilty for putting him on the spot. I knew that he didn't mean to be hurtful; he was all about fun. I stood up and put on my jacket and tried to sound calm and normal. End this pleasantly. "Thank you for lunch. I hope you have a great time in L.A."

I walked out, fast, but he caught up with me at the light. I jaywalked, faster, across Sixth Avenue. He was still with me.

We came to the big fountains outside Spender-Davis. I stopped and turned and he was right there, too close. I lost my balance but he caught me. I pushed away from him. "Please! Why won't you just leave me alone? I don't know what you *want* from me!"

I hated myself. Hated the furious, hurt look in his eyes.

"I w-w—" He stopped. Closed his eyes.

He inhaled and tried again. "I w-wa—"

I stood there appalled, frozen, thinking, *Don't try to help him, you'll make it worse.*

He stopped trying to answer and just looked at me and it was incredible, how much he looked like his fierce-eyed Valkyrie sister. He walked away, jaw and fists clenched.

I don't remember walking through the revolving doors into the building or following Edward onto the elevator.

"Oh, Edward." I covered my face and sobbed, sinking bonelessly against the wall. I couldn't say any more. There was nothing else to say.

For the next couple of days I spent most of my time in the living room armchair by the window, watching the winter sky. It was gray. Everything was.

Ed offered to stay with me but I sent him away, promising to answer when he called. Which turned out to be every two hours.

At one a.m. the first night I answered and said, "Ed. Go to sleep."

"Why don't I sleep over there?"

"No, thank you."

"Are you still in the chair?"

I didn't answer.

"I think I should call your mom, or Peg."

"No."

"Did you eat anything?"

"Yes," I lied.

"What?"

It took me a minute. "Cap'n Crunch."

"You're lying. I know when you lie, Grace, you're terrible at it."

"Ed, I love you."

"Just tell me you're not going to die."

"It kind of feels like I might. Please. I just need to be still for a while."

"Fine. I'm bringing breakfast at seven."

At 6:45 he rang downstairs, rousing me from my fetal curl in the armchair. I shuffled over and buzzed him in. Opened the door.

Ed came up the stairs looking tired and worried, carrying a bag of chocolate croissants and a package of plus-size Depends. "I'm sorry, but I just can't bear to see that flame-stitch upholstery messed up."

I smiled.

Ed brightened considerably.

bird's-eye view

I loved my new job.

I was sent out to learn community sex ed with a woman named Lakshmi Sharma. She was a few years older than me, originally from Delhi, but had been living in the States for almost twenty years. A little heavyset, pretty, with big brown eyes, thick, short black hair, and perhaps the driest, most unsmiling sense of humor I'd ever encountered. The kind where at first you think the person hates you, until she unexpectedly pats you on the back.

Although I was going to be working with seniors, Lakshmi made sure I learned how to teach everything.

"This," she said, holding up a box of emergency contraceptive pills, "is a big one. It keeps you from conceiving if you take it right after you've had sex. Saved my sister's ass a time or two when she was uncareful. I had a student who was date-raped, and she used it."

One day before we left the office she handed me a piece of gum and told me to chew it. Then she fed me a spoonful of peanut butter. As I chewed them together, the peanut butter disintegrated the gum into a nauseating blob of slime in my mouth. I gagged and hawked it into the trash can under my desk.

"That's what happens when you use vegetable oil as lubricant with a condom. It breaks down the latex. Do that demonstration with a group of kids, and believe me, they don't forget."

Another day she had a group of giggling, blindfolded eighth graders race each other putting condoms on bananas. She timed them with the stopwatch on her iPhone. At the end of class she served them banana muffins.

And then it was my first time teaching seniors. We went to a community center in the Bronx where the people spoke only Spanish. Lakshmi was fluent. I was sincerely trying.

During a break, a woman approached me. She spoke quickly, quietly, but I understood that she had contracted genital herpes a year ago and was too embarrassed to go to the doctor. In my clunky Spanish, I urged her to go to the doctor right away and tried to give her some basic information about how to avoid painful outbreaks. Then she muttered something about Crisco.

I leaned closer. "Mande?"

She told me again. I recoiled.

"Oh, no, no! Eso no es bien! Crisco! No, no." Boy, now she had me worried and she was really stretching the limits of my Español. "Pienso que . . . usted quiere mantener las lesiones limpias y secas así que se puedan curar y dejar de existir. . . . Si ponga Crisco en las lesiones usted las tendrían para siempre tiempo."

The woman looked frightened. Lakshmi, standing nearby, spoke to her in rapid Spanish. The woman smiled with relief at Lakshmi, looked askance at me, and went back to her seat.

"What?" I asked Lakshmi.

"You were doing good when you told her to go to the doctor, don't eat crap, get a lot of rest, and don't get sunburned. It went downhill when you said if she puts Crisco on the lesions she'll have them forever."

"Forever! I meant *longer.*"

"Yeah. I think she'll be all right."

At the end of the session, after handing out goody bags of condoms and lube and packing up our materials, I said, "Look, I probably shouldn't teach Spanish-speaking people."

"Maybe not by yourself, yet," Lakshmi said. "Repeat after me, *rr-r*oja."

"Roja."

"*Rrr*io."

"Rio."

She scowled. She wanted me to roll my Rs, but I am physically incapable. My tongue just lies there like it's sunbathing on the beach in Cozumel.

Lakshmi patted my back. "Work on it."

The next couple of weeks we went to retirement communities in the outer boroughs. I hadn't actually spent that much time around seniors. I never knew any of my grandparents. My life experiences were so limited! Old people and small children were complete mysteries to me. It turned out that the old people I taught were generally extremely nice to be with. They told great stories. They asked good questions. They laughed, a lot.

After I completed the training and started doing workshops on my own and became more confident, my appetite came back full force. By March I had regained the seven pounds lost, *plus* an additional seven. All in my ass. I didn't care. I wasn't on the market.

The first day of spring was gorgeous, a bright promise that winter really was ending. Peg had brought in the mail and left mine, as usual, on the kitchen table. On top was a postcard from the Hollywood Wax Museum. I flipped it over. Tiny, packed handwriting.

Hey. They let me out for a meal and fresh air and I came here. Someone said they had a good statue of David Haselhoff. True! But Sammy Davis jr totally sucked! Its warm here and people are nice. I think you would like it. They gave me a place to live in that has a fireplace and a <u>cleaning lady</u>. She brought me homade tomalies! Bogue came out to visit for four days and she almost quit coz he is such a slob!!! Gotta go sing for my supper now. Take care. TGW

I sat at the table and absentmindedly picked up a pencil and started making corrections. I mean, why so many exclamation marks? And Has*s*elhoff. Davis, *Jr*. It's. Hom*em*ade. Ta*m*ali*e*s.

Coz—where to even begin?

Peg came in and stood at my elbow for a moment before I realized she was there. I peeked up at her. She looked rather incredulous.

I set down the pencil. "This looks bad, doesn't it?"

"Um, yeah. Slightly nuts."

"Ha! Reflex, I guess. I just—honestly, I'm kind of bemused. I've never seen so many bizarre misspellings—"

"Step away from the postcard, Grace."

"Okay, yeah. . . . Okay."

I turned down five dates. One from a guy I sometimes saw at the Strand bookstore on Saturdays. The other four were from Felix, the Puerto Rican kid who bagged my groceries. I'd heard through the neighborhood grapevine that he was a sociopathic computer genius. He'd gotten into big FBI trouble for hacking into major retail websites but was only sentenced to community service and psychiatric rehabilitation because he was a minor.

Our exchanges at the register went something like this.

Felix: Hello, my love. (He is bagging my purchases. He kisses, and then bags, my box of tampons.)

Me: Hello, Felix. Don't do that.

Felix: When are you going to let me show you a good time?

Me: I'm not.

Felix: Come on, baby, why?

Me: Because you're fifteen and I'm twenty-nine? As a starting point.

Felix: You know that only makes me like you more.

Me: It's never going to happen.

Then he would abandon his workstation to follow me out of the store and down the block, sweet-talking me and threatening to hack into my e-mail.

I needed to find another grocery. But this was so close. And the only one in the neighborhood that did double coupons.

On a Sunday night in late June, Peg and I ran down to the drug-store on the corner for snacks. We had created our own little film series and committed to watching all the films of Ingmar Bergman. Tonight we would screen the epic *Fanny and Alexander*.

There were too many microwave popcorn options. The angel on Peg's shoulder delicately pressed us to buy the kind with no oil added. My tiny red fiend stamped his cloven hooves! He wanted lots of movie theater butter, and was willing to get ugly about it.

Then a distinctive voice intruded. Peg and I abruptly forgot about popcorn and turned to the ceiling-mounted television.

A music video. A close-up of Ty's face, photographed in sepia tones.

I knew the song he was lip-synching. He'd played it on the piano under the deer head for me that Sunday morning last November. Only now it was so much *more*, almost an eighties-style power ballad. And there were words. I heard them in a blur. I couldn't hold on to most of them, but they made my stomach feel awful.

Now he was no longer in close-up but sitting in a booth in a seedy diner, alone, staring at his untouched food, singing about missing someone's smell. Now walking down a deserted country road, bare-foot, in ragged jeans and beat-up T-shirt, carrying a guitar. Sad. Yearning. Soulful.

Now a girl, ethereally lovely, with long, wavy, blond hair, barefoot and wearing a skimpy little calico slip-dress, slowly comes to him, meeting him in the middle of the dusty road. She is crying. She touches his face. The guitar falls to the ground in slo-mo and the beau-tiful girl is enfolded in his arms and they stand there on the road, entwined. The camera pulls away, way above them, bird's-eye view, and keeps going, farther out, till they are just a tiny, satellite-picture speck at the last note of the song. The title caption, in the lower left corner of the screen:

Tyler Wilkie

"Something Sacred"

Album: Innocence and Experience

"Well," Peg said. "How about that."

"Yeah . . . wow."

"His song is in the Top Ten."

I looked at her. "How do you know that?"

She shrugged. "I saw it online. He's going on tour in the fall with some other bands."

Peg bought the Matinee Idol Double Butter. We walked home silently. And while she popped the corn, I went into my room, sat at the computer, and Googled "Tyler Wilkie Something Sacred lyrics."

Oh, look, he had an official website, with a lyrics page.

our final stand
a mountain breeze
you kissed my hand
and left me on my knees
so long ago
I still can see
how you were mine
it's in my memory

I need you tonight
don't think I'll make it
I need you tonight
wanna hold you naked
I need you tonight
we got something sacred
oh why?

longest night
lost again
I find your eyes
and they won't let me in
I miss your smell
and our history
back in your spell
and all your mystery

I wonder why
I feel the same
and if you cry
when someone speaks my name
you took so long
for my heart to find
it's all but gone
leaving it behind

I was shaking.

How could he?

How could he use our excruciating, private moment for commercial purposes?

I laid my head on the desk and wept. Suddenly it was all so clear: the moment in the woods hadn't done to him what it had to me. It hadn't shredded his guts and left a permanent, smoking hole in the middle of his chest. It was just another sad, beautiful moment from his life and it was fair game for public consumption.

I should demand a share of the royalties.

I heaved a final, shuddering sigh and sat up and blew my nose.

Somehow I made it through the movie, although I couldn't say what actually happens. There was a blond lady, and two kids. A mean, bad husband, toward the end of the story. I think there might have been a ghost.

After the movie I said good night to Peg. Got into bed with my laptop. Checked my e-mails. Then, for masochistic kicks, went to www.tylerwilkie.com.

The website had the same Ansel Adams feel of the "Something Sacred" music video. Sepia and black-and-white photography, set among rough-hewn backgrounds and locations, with falling-down shacks and wildflower fields and boiling, dark, about-to-burst cloudy skies. And this beautiful man standing in the foreground, gazing back at me, dark-eyed and direct. Or in pensive, close-up profile, eyes closed. Hair blowing across his face. They had made him look so lovely, so carelessly masculine. They had plenty to work with, of course.

I watched the "Something Sacred" video again and wondered if he might be dating that stunning girl in real life. She appeared to be really crying, and they seemed so in love, so relieved to find each other at the end.

I clicked on the *Music* link and heard other songs from his album, among them "Her," the lovely song he'd played in my living room while I'd been trying to write about wallpaper. At the end of "Her" I took a moment to lower the laptop lid and regroup. I should not keep looking at/listening to these things. They hurt. But I needed to know what was happening to him.

There was a Tyler Wilkie fan forum. With over *five thousand* members. How had all of this developed so quickly?

I clicked on the "Talk About Tyler" forum and skimmed the day's discussion topics:

Pics of Tyler live at the Knitting Factory LA
I met Tyler last night!
sexy Pics of TW
lyrics to . . .
Ty on Jay Leno
Live and Unreleased Recordings
are we sure he isn't gay?
TW on tour?
You Tube Interview!
My friend hooked up with Tyler Wilkie

I clicked on that last one. The thread went something like this:

RMluvsTy: Hey! I'm a newbie here. Two nights ago my bff met Tyler Wilkie at a bar on Melrose, in W. Hollywood. She said he was pretty wasted. He bought her a drink and then they went out to her car.

TyTyTy10: Damn! Lucky girl! What happened?

RMluvsTy: Um, "heavy petting."

Mesha3: what does that mean?

TyTyTy10: It means she blew him.

Mesha3: ewww.

RMluvsTy: They talked and stuff, too.

WilkWoman: We're not supposed to talk about his
      personal life on this forum. It's disrespectful.
      TyTyTy, you've been warned before.

TyTyTy10: What? I didn't start this one. It's not my fault
      he's a man-ho!

TLTy2: He's a man, yes, and SINGLE. And plenty of girls
      are making themselves available. He's not a ho!

RMluvsTy: My friend said he was nice.

Mesha3: he is nice, i met him at the garlic festival. he
      signed my CD and ticket and my shirt and my mom
      took my picture with him.

TyTyTy10: Nice and horny. Heh! RM, what about his, uh,
      "dimensions". Did your friend say anything?

RMluvsTy: She said he was HUGE. But honestly, she
      hasn't seen that many, so he might just be average.

WilkWoman: WHERE IS THE MODERATOR!

I tried some of the picture threads. How could I not? There
were some beauty shots from Ty's website and lots of cell-phone
shots of him playing live in clubs and at a music festival in Chicago. For a moment I felt happy for him; he'd gotten to see another
new city.

I watched the Jay Leno clip. No big interview, just small talk with
Jay about the new album, and then Ty playing with his band. I knew
it would probably happen, but how strange to see him becoming
national. This was the problem with only watching CNN and TV
Land. You miss things.

There was a link to a video on YouTube of him singing drunkenly,
tunelessly, with the house band at yet another bar. I could never have
imagined him singing badly, but there it was.

Against my better judgment, I finished with the *are we sure he
isn't gay?* topic. It consisted of only two entries:

Me&MrW: Are we sure he isn't gay? He's so darned pretty!

Smokinhot: LOL. I just took a poll of the 18-25 female population of Los Angeles County, and a large number of them confirmed that Tyler is into women. And I do mean INTO. Regularly.

You know? WHERE WAS THE FREAKING MODERATOR?

The guy at the Strand, whose name was Todd, asked me out again and I accepted, having decided that a careful, emotionally uncomplicated sex life might be a reasonable option after all. He was in grad school at NYU, attractive, blond and blue-eyed, with an athletic build. Other people had "friends with benefits." Why shouldn't I?

The week before our date I traded my cotton granny panties for thong underwear. I walked around in them for several days feeling like I was flossing my ass, but I threw out all the old undies, determined to get used to it.

We went to dinner at an Italian place and then to a movie in Bryant Park. *Annie Hall*, one of my all-time favorites.

Edward and Boris were at the park, too. I missed seeing Edward daily and went over before the movie to tell him so. We agreed to get together sometime the next week. On the way back to our blanket I stopped at an ice cream vendor. To my severely uncomfortable surprise, Steven joined me in the line. I hadn't seen him since the day of our breakup.

"Hey," he said. Like it was no big deal.

"Hi," I said.

"You look good," he said, glancing at my size-larger behind.

"Thank you."

"How's it going?"

"Okay. How are you?"

"I'm good." He surveyed the people around us. "Are you here with someone?"

"A friend, yes."

"Me, too."

The line advanced. The five-dollar bill clenched in my fist was growing damp. Soon I would have my raspberry Mega Missile and be on my way.

"So, I saw Tyler's music video."

"Yeah, me, too." Finally, my turn to buy! I got my change from the guy and turned to Steven. "Well, good to see you."

He followed me out of the ice cream line. "Are you with him?"

Maybe he had a right to know how things had turned out; no telling what he'd been imagining. "No. I never have been."

"So . . . was it the right thing after all, leaving me?"

What was he, a masochist? "Well . . . yes. Not that you did anything wrong, but it was the right thing."

"Okay. Fair enough."

My Mega Missile was melting. "So, 'bye. Take care."

"Yeah, you, too."

I walked away from him feeling not guilt, as expected, but perplexity. He was perfectly nice, a good guy and all, but why had I ever tried to convince myself I was in love with him?

I got back to our blanket just in time for the lobster scene in *Annie Hall*. The one where they're at the beach house with live lobsters crawling all over the kitchen floor, and one disappears, and Alvy says, "It's behind the refrigerator! It will turn up in our bed at night!" Ordinarily that line makes me do a spit take. But this time my laugh was more of a limp, reflex chuckle than genuinely from the belly.

Not long after that I let Todd kiss me, which was not unpleasant. After the movie he asked me to come home with him for a drink but I said maybe next time, finding myself not quite ready for full benefits.

Sigh.

autumn,
schmautumn

whisper

The weather in New York City is never more sublime than in the first two weeks of September. Cloudless blue skies, warm sun, cool breeze. A few leaves have fallen already. The rest are still green, but beginning to whisper good-bye.

The air seems more oxygenated, and you remember to breathe deeply, gratefully. Beauty and clarity coexist with sorrow and remembrance. You can't stop the PowerPoint presentation that, on autoplay, starts up now and again in your mind: the images of violent destruction, of faces filled with shock and fear and despair. You remember the care and tenderness with which people, strangers, treated each other for a long time after witnessing together unspeakable cruelty. You know that, unfortunately, you will never be able to completely forget any of it. You accept that, and try to focus on life as it is now. You keep moving forward.

voracious reversion to virgin
try saying *that* a few times

My thirtieth birthday fell on a Monday, Peg's night off. I accepted her invitation to dinner at an Ethiopian restaurant a few blocks from our apartment.

I had two glasses of wine and got a little maudlin.

Peg handed me a tissue. "Why are you sad, sweetie?"

"I'm not!" I blew my nose. "I'm actually happy. I feel like things are finally starting to make sense. I love my job."

"Grace, that is fantastic."

"And also, I know how to say *no*. If my life ever feels like a speeding freight train again, I have the power to stop it. To redirect."

"Yes."

"And not that I have this perfected or anything, but I've realized that I have to try not to make choices based on fear. Or what I think I'm *supposed* to do."

"That's a tough one."

"Yeah. I'm just shooting for seventy-five percent completion, with that."

"Wow. Grace grows."

"I know, right? It only took me thirty years."

The evening was a little chilly for the sundress and sandals I was wearing. Just in case, I had brought along my birthday present from my dad: a scarlet, butter-soft, silk-and-cashmere pashmina. I wrapped it around my shoulders and walked arm in arm with Peg and told her once again, for about the millionth time, how I treasure her. When I do that she always smiles and pats my hand like a no-nonsense, indulgent auntie, but of course she enjoys being told she is loved.

We came to the drugstore and she stopped. "While we're here, do you want to pick up some more Double Butter?"

"What movie are we watching?"

"*The Seventh Seal*. The one where the guy plays chess with Death?"

"Double, yeah. I wonder if they have Triple?"

Through the glass I saw three men coming out of the store and stumbled over my own feet trying to get out of the way quickly. I grabbed Peg's arm and pulled her till we were well out from under the fluorescent-lighted awning.

She was confused. "What are you—"

"Please!" I hid behind her.

The men emerged, all lanky, long-haired musician types in jeans, boots, leather jackets. One of them Tyler Wilkie. They headed down the street away from us.

"Oh!" Peg exclaimed involuntarily. Loudly.

He looked back over his shoulder. I could have strangled her.

He said something to his friends and they all turned and walked back to us.

"Hey, Peg!" He gave her a hug, which she returned enthusiastically.

"Hey." He leaned down and kissed my cheek with cool lips. I developed instant tunnel vision. I could still see him quite sharply, but all the peripherals became fuzzy. "Did you get my postcard?"

"Yes, thank you."

He introduced his blurry-faced friends. One of them was his drummer, the guy he'd once lived with for a few months. We shook hands all around.

"Today is Grace's birthday." Peg said. "We've just been to dinner."

"Oh, yeah," Ty said. "Happy birthday."

"Thank you."

"I guess now we've both hit the big three-oh. It's not so bad, is it?" He was smiling, but his eyes were still and dark. Impossible to read.

"So far, so good! Well, nice to meet you," I said to his friends. I looked at Peg. "We'd better get going, we don't want to be late."

"Oh, yeah," Peg said.

"Is there a party?" Ty said.

"Just a small get-together."

Note the deterioration. Two minutes in the presence of Tyler Wilkie, and I had once again become The Liar. I held out my hand. "Good to see you, Ty."

His warm hand briefly enveloped mine. I felt a strong urge to cry. I smiled brightly at his friends and moved several feet closer to home and waited for Peg to say a quick good-bye.

"Hey," Ty said. "I'm playing at Roseland next Sunday night, do you want to come? I'll put you on the list. There's a party after."

"I'll come!" Peg said.

He looked over at me.

"Sunday . . ." I frowned with concentration and faux-contemplated the date. "Oh, I can't, I'm already doing something that night."

"Do you have a date with Todd?" Peg asked. "Because maybe he'd want to go hear Ty play." She looked at Ty like *would that be all right?* Then she looked at me. And I swear, her eyes glinted with an evil light.

He shrugged. "Bring whoever you want."

"It's not—I don't have a date. I just can't come."

"'Kay," he said cheerfully, turning away with his friends. "See ya."

I waited till Peg and I got to our stoop.

"By the way," I asked. "are you possessed?"

"What? What did I do?" All innocence.

I tried to take advantage of the nice weather by walking home from work every day. The SASS office was near Times Square, so I had about a forty-minute walk home to the West Village.

It was a couple of days after the drugstore incident. I had already bagged some apples, and was testing the firmness of a late-season melon at my regular produce mart on the corner of Christopher and Seventh, when I heard a voice over my shoulder.

"Hey there."

I lost my grip on the melon and essentially bowled down the produce guy's entire pyramid of navel oranges. They rolled everywhere. Quite a few got smashed by cars.

"I'm so sorry!" I said to the guy, and the three of us started picking up the oranges that hadn't rolled into the street.

"Sorry, man," Tyler said. "I'll pay for them." To me he said, "You sure are jumpy."

I was busy rebuilding the pyramid, so I ignored him. He handed me the last undamaged fruit and gave the vendor some money. In the fading daylight, I got a better look at him than I had the other night. He was wearing one of his Western shirts, half-untucked. The scuffed boots, the low-rise jeans. Everything was more or less the same, but different, somehow. He was more man than boy. Even his shoulders seemed broader. And his eyes were canny. A little cold.

"What are you doing tomorrow night?" he asked.

"Tomorrow night. . . ." My mind was still pinwheeling. I had no idea what was happening ten minutes from now, much less tomorrow night.

"I'd like to take you to dinner for your birthday."

A pack of passing girls slowed on the sidewalk and came to a full stop. He glanced over at them and they collectively rippled and gasped, like someone had goosed all of them at once with an invisible stick. He looked back at me, waiting for my answer.

I scrambled for a convincing obstacle.

He leaned closer. "Come on, Grace," he said in a drawling undertone, "I know you're not gonna humiliate me in front of these girls." His eyes had warmed. He was once again the hapless, sweet-faced dog-walking boy for whom I would do almost anything.

"All right," I muttered ungraciously. "But not too late. I have an early workshop on Friday."

"Great." He smiled, but only with his mouth. The eyes had cooled again.

Why are you doing this? I wanted to ask. It was so clear that he didn't expect to enjoy it any more than I did.

I turned away to pay for my apples and one of the girls nervously approached him. He spoke kindly to her and then the others came to him, too, blushing, staring up at him with dazed eyes, asking him to write his name on their shirts and wanting to photograph him with their cell phones.

I took my change and walked away.

I wasn't teaching Thursday and a couple of people were out sick, including Lavelle, so I was able to slip away from work a little early and race home to get ready. I reasoned that because I didn't go out to dinner with people all that often, I might as well try to look nice. And while I had no intention of trying to compete with the aggressive girls who were continually throwing themselves at him, my pride insisted that I at least doll up a little bit. Maybe it would be good for him to get a reminder of what a grown-up, non-ho, everyday-attractive type of woman looks like.

I didn't want him to think I considered this a *date* date, so I didn't get too dressed up. Just jeans, and boots that gave me a little height, and a cranberry-red top that showed a tiny amount of cleavage. Silver hoops. A little mascara and lip gloss, nothing dramatic. I was representing all dignified women, and strove for appropriate understatement.

He rang the buzzer at 8:07. Practically on time. Impressive. I grabbed my bag and jacket and took a deep breath and went down.

He was sitting on the stoop. Wearing the perpetual jeans and boots, with a faded denim shirt and a gorgeous, expensive-looking, fringed suede jacket that brought out the autumn red and gold lights in his hair.

He stood when I came down the steps. "Hey."

"Why didn't you tell me we were dining on the frontier tonight? Let me run back up and get my coonskin cap."

Back in the day, that kind of thing would have made him laugh. Tonight he smiled coolly and took off down the sidewalk. I had to jog a little to catch up.

We walked to an Asian restaurant over on MacDougal. On the way we stopped at a guitar store on Bleecker so he could buy strings. Everyone who worked there knew him, of course. And a lot of people on the street either said hi or simply stared at him as we passed. With some of them, it probably wasn't even because he was becoming famous and recognizable. He was just beautiful. Me, I was the invisible woman, tagging along.

At the restaurant, Ty asked for a booth in the back. The waiter brought us menus and hot tea and a bowl of those crunchy fried noodles. I didn't have a big appetite; I was actually feeling a little headachy and funky. I ordered a bowl of egg drop soup. Ty ordered moo shu pork, General Tso's chicken, fried wontons, and three egg rolls.

We gave the menus to the waiter and shared a moment of uncomfortable silence.

"So," he said, with tears in his eyes. "My grandma died."

"Oh, Ty! I'm so sorry. When?"

"About a month ago. Not even from what she was supposed to die from. She had a stroke."

"Did you get to see her?"

He shook his head. "I was in L.A. They didn't call me about it till she'd been in the hospital for a while and it was starting to look like the end. I got on a plane, but it was too late."

"I'm so sorry."

"They said she wouldn't have known me anyway, she was unconscious."

"Maybe, you know, she wasn't even there anymore, in her body. Maybe she'd moved on to, um, whatever is next."

"Yeah, probably."

It hurt, seeing him like this. "I'm so glad I got to meet her."

"You met her too late. She used to be so great."

The waiter brought the egg rolls and wontons, and Ty dug right in. It seemed that not even grief could challenge his appetite.

"How is your mom about it?"

"She's okay. Peaceful. Rebecca cried for days and is still messed up."

I must have looked surprised.

"Beck acts all tough, but she's fierce about loving."

I picked up one of his fried wontons and nibbled it to try to take the edge off my headache.

"I'm glad to see you're not so skinny anymore," he said.

"Oh, yeah. Thanks." I set down the wonton.

He asked about my family. I gave him the brief sketch. Dan was taking the baby paintings to London. My mom was still fighting crime in New Jersey.

And Peg?

Still stage-managing *Tie Me Up! Tie Me Down!* Only, Antonio Banderas had left and John Stamos had taken over the role. And she was elected high priestess of her coven for the coming year.

The rest of our food came. I took one look at the blob of semi-cooked egg floating in broth and pushed the bowl aside.

"What's wrong with your soup?" Ty asked.

"I guess I'm just not in the mood for it, after all."

He spooned some plain brown rice onto a plate and set it in front of me.

"Thanks," I said dryly. I watched him overfill a moo shu pancake, roll it up, and cram it in his mouth. Voracious as ever. "I saw your video."

"Oh, yeah," he laughed. "Weird, huh?"

"It's pretty."

"Yeah. Bizarre. I had to watch it a few hundred times just to try to comprehend that that was me."

"Who is the girl?"

"This chick named Ralitsa. She's a model, just got off the plane from Bulgaria the week before. She knew about ten words of English. Her asshole manager boyfriend sat on the side of the road shouting at her the whole time, supposedly translating for the director."

"I thought maybe you were seeing her in real life."

"Huh?"

"The way she was crying and holding on to you at the end. It seemed so real."

He shook his head. "That was starvation. She was about to pass out. After the first take I asked her if she was okay, and she told me the manager boyfriend hadn't let her eat anything since lunch the day before because she was getting fat. So I asked for a ten-minute break and took her to the craft services table and stared the asshole down while she ate a bagel."

"Ty, that is heroic!"

He gave me a big, happy smile and shoveled in another forkful of General Tso's chicken. "Her acting really deteriorated after she ate. The director was annoyed with me."

"You did the right thing."

"That song sounds ridiculous now, they jacked everything up so much on it. It was just a quiet little tune, you know? I feel like they kinda fucked it up."

Don't get me started about the song.

"I told Dave, the next album gets made in New York, not L.A. It's so weird there. I figure maybe here I can stay clearer about how I want things to sound."

"That makes sense." Like I knew anything about recording an album. And I couldn't even look at the title of the song without my throat closing up. But I couldn't bear how disappointed he sounded. "Ty, I think the song sounds great. It's beautiful. So moving."

"Really? You were moved?"

"Oh, yes, definitely." He was watching me so closely. I turned my eyes to reading a sugar packet, before he saw in them all the ridiculous, embarrassing things that must never be seen.

"Aren't you gonna eat anything?" he asked, after a while.

I picked up a fork and made myself swallow some of the rice. I mostly just looked at him surreptitiously, until he caught me at it.

"What?" he asked, dousing an egg roll with soy sauce.

"You have big muscles." It came out sounding strangely accusatory.

"Huh? Oh, yeah." He looked down at his biceps, straining the denim fabric of his shirt. "Push-ups."

Annoyance flared. "I guess that helps."

"With?"

"Your social life."

"It doesn't hurt."

"I'm sure it doesn't." Somebody stop me.

"Well, I won't deny it." He set his fork down and wiped his mouth with his napkin. "But you can believe I'm not stupid about it."

"Sorry," I said. "Not my concern."

He shoved his plate aside. "Why do you think you know so much about my sex life?"

I spoke before thinking. "You know about this thing called the Internet, right?"

"Let's talk about *your* life," he said shortly, tossing his crumpled napkin on his plate. "Who are you doing now?"

I tried to lighten the tone. "I don't do anyone. I've reverted to virgin status."

"You lie," he said.

"I never lie," I lied.

He poured a cup of tea and sugared it up and slowly sipped it while he watched me toy with and choke down a few more bites of rice, although I did not want to eat at all and my head was pounding.

Obviously, being with him for even a meal was so bad for me that it was making me literally sick.

We left the restaurant, went down to Bleecker, and headed west.

"Come see my apartment," Ty said.

"No." I was feeling too ill to even make up a nice excuse.

"Come on, just for a minute. It's right there."

I was horrified. He lived only a few blocks away! No wonder I'd run into him twice already.

"Come on," he said.

God, I wanted my bed. "All right, only for a couple of minutes, then I have to go."

It was in a doorman building, a one-bedroom that he was in the process of buying. I walked in and down a few steps into the sunken living room.

"It's nice," I said, looking at a baby grand and a big white couch.

"But you need some more furniture." I shivered and wrapped my arms around my shoulders. "And you should turn the heat on, it's freezing in here!"

He gave me a funny look and tossed his jacket on the couch. He showed me the small but adequate bathroom. It had old, mauve-porcelain fixtures that were kind of pretty. There was nothing in the bedroom but a rumpled bed, a straight-backed chair, an amplifier, piles of cables, and four guitars. The kitchen was a small galley, but it had new stainless-steel appliances and, most wonderfully, a stackable washer and dryer.

"Well, congratulations, this place is great." I headed for the door. He got there first and blocked my exit.

"Wait a minute," he said. "Why are you in such a damned hurry?"

"I just have to go!"

"Okay. I'll let you go. But first you have to answer a question."

I rubbed my temples to try to ease some of the ache. "What is it?"

He came close and said in a low voice, "Have you been Googling me, Grace?"

I shivered. My nipples tightened like I was wading in the ocean on New Year's Day. I crossed my arms to hide them.

He put his arms around me. "Have you?"

I was feeling so ill and confused. But Ty was holding me. And he was *warm*. I nestled tightly against him and pressed my face into the opening of his shirt, to try to absorb some of his heat.

"That's it. Come on, darlin', look at me." He rubbed my back. "Let's just be real with each other, for once."

"Ty," I moaned. I looked up at him.

His eyes darkened. They went to my mouth and he leaned down.

"I don't think you should kiss me," I said. "I think I'm sick."

He felt my forehead. "Grace, you're burning up!"

"I am?" No wonder I felt so dazed.

"Yeah. Let's take care of you." He half-carried me to the bedroom. "Here, lay down."

"Lie," I said, getting into the bed. "It's lie down."

"Uh-huh." He pulled off my boots and covered me with the down comforter. He left the room and came back with a lovely crystal bowl that he set beside me on the bed.

"What is that?"

"In case you need to puke. Just lean over and do it. You don't have to get up."

"*If* I need to vomit, I'm not doing it in that! It looks like it was a gift from the president."

"It was. Of the record company. Go ahead, it's washable."

I was so cold, and my knees and elbows ached like someone was pounding them with a hammer. I burrowed under his comforter and asked for more covers. He left the room and came back with a crocheted afghan I recognized from his parents' house. He laid it over me and sat beside me and made a joke about how apparently even the idea of kissing him made me sick.

"Stop talking now," I said, through chattering teeth.

He felt my face and neck and arms. "You're really hot."

"That line may work with your average fourteen-year-old," I groaned. "Could you please call Peg and tell her to come get me? Tell her to come in a cab, and ask him to wait."

He went to make the call. I curled into the tightest possible ball of misery.

fever

Why was everything so quiet? Where was he? And how long did it take to make a simple phone call? It seemed like Peg should have been here by now to get me. I had no idea what time it was. Maybe she wasn't home from the show yet.

I drifted off. I came back to awareness, somewhat, at the touch of his hand on my face. Warm.

"Open your mouth," he said.

I opened my eyes. He was unwrapping a new digital thermometer.

I shook my head. I didn't want to open my mouth. Some of my small store of heat might escape.

"Or we can do this another way."

I opened.

He waited patiently, sitting beside me, until the thermometer beeped.

"Damn!" he said, reading it.

He went away and after a while came back and made me sit up. He pressed a glass to my lips. "Drink."

My sense of taste was messed up, but I think it was Sprite. Icy Sprite. I turned my head away and tried to hunker back down under the covers, but he pulled me upright again. "Grace. Drink!"

I swallowed some. And some more. And shivered uncontrollably.

"Damn. Something very bad has got a hold of you."

"Uuunnnhhh," I agreed miserably.

He went away with the glass. I drifted. He came back and next thing, he was pulling the covers off of me.

"Wha—"

He swabbed my face with a shockingly cold, wet washcloth. I shrieked and shoved his hand away. He pushed my shirt up and ran the cloth over my stomach.

"Stop! You're hurting me! Go away!" I pulled the covers back over me, burrowing deep.

"Grace, let me do this."

"No!" I was completely buried now under miles of king-size down comforter. "Leave me alone!" I shouted from deep within my comforter cave. "Did you call Peg to come get me? Please call her again!"

He went away again and when he came back he dragged me, cave and all, to the side of the bed. Then he took the comforter away completely and tossed it against the wall.

I started to cry. "Why are you torturing me?"

He was unbuttoning my blouse. "Baby, I'm not. We have to get your temperature down a couple of points, or I'm gonna have to take you to the ER."

"Just. Call. PEG!" I wept, winding my fingers tightly into the belt loops of my jeans. He pried my fingers loose and stripped the jeans off me.

I was now down to my push-up bra, knee socks, and underwear. Thong. I asked this illness, whatever it was, to just go ahead and kill me.

He reached for me. I tried to push him away. He carried me to the bathroom and half-lowered/half-dropped me into the bathtub.

I was momentarily, completely immobilized by the shock of the cold water. He sat on the edge of the bathtub and scooped the torture liquid up over my arms and chest and even my head.

"Stop, stop, stop," I wept miserably.

He wouldn't. I grabbed a bottle of Pert and managed to thump him hard in the ribs with it before he took it away.

"Okay, okay." He ended the freezing onslaught. I tried to stand up, but he held me down in the water. I clung to his shoulders and pressed every part of me I could against him, just trying to get warm.

"Get me out of here," I said.

"Not yet."

"It's too cold!"

"Grace, the water is lukewarm. Not even cold."

"Ty, that can't be true!"

He made me sit there for eons. My butt got numb. I fell into a light coma and woke up drooling on the leg of his jeans. Then, just for kicks, he scooped a few more handfuls of freezingness over me before he decided I'd had enough.

He helped me stand up and handed me a towel. He pointed out the folded T-shirt on the edge of the vanity and went away. I shut the door behind him and punched the lock on the doorknob.

I unsteadily peeled off the soaked panties and bra and socks. I was so weak and achy that I had to sit on the edge of the bathtub to dry myself. I pulled the big black T-shirt over my head. *Not all who wander are lost*, it said, in white letters.

I wrapped the towel around my wet hair and opened the door. He was waiting for me in the hall. I let him lead me back to the bed and cover me up and take my temperature again. I knew the fever had gone down, because I was no longer shivering.

"One hundred and one point five!" he announced triumphantly.

He pulled the covers back and got into bed, fully clothed. Not touching me, just lying on his back beside me.

"Aren't you afraid you're going to catch this?" I whispered.

"I'll take my chances."

"Why wouldn't you call Peg?"

He rolled onto his side and looked at me. "Because *I'm* here. Why shouldn't I take care of you?" His eyes were fierce.

"Thank you," I said. "For taking care of me. . . . I wish . . ."

"What?"

"That song," I said. "'Something Sacred.'"

He nodded, barely.

Tears came. They were hot, rolling down my face. "Ty, how could you? That was private, what happened between us."

He sat up on his elbow. "It's still private! No one knows if it's true, or about someone real. Maybe I just made up a story, for all anyone knows."

My whole body was shaking, I was crying so hard. "It hurts me when I hear it."

"I'm sorry." He smoothed my tangled hair, blotted my face with the edge of the sheet. "Baby, don't, please. I'm sorry."

"Let's stop talking," I said. "I feel so sick."

I slept for a while and at 1:30 a.m. woke up with the worst sore throat of my life. And the fever, high again. He helped me pull on my jeans, commando, and took me to Beth Israel Hospital. Turned out the triage nurse was a big fan. Ty unleashed the killer smile and the homey drawl and she was all aflutter. After midnight in a Manhattan emergency room, I only had to wait forty-five minutes to see a doctor.

They scraped my throat with a long Q-tip. Or maybe a white-hot piece of metal wire. Yes, probably that. "*Owwww*," I wept.

Turned out to be strep. I was given a shot of antibiotic.

"Now give her something for the pain," Ty said to the doctor. She looked at him, looked at me, and ordered another injection.

Ty was given a bag with more medications for me to take home. By three thirty I was out of the jeans and back in his bed, drinking a big glass of Sprite and really not feeling so bad at all. Not even sleepy.

There was no lamp in his bedroom yet, just the glaring overhead light. He saw that it was bothering me and turned it off, and in the dim illumination from the bathroom I watched him take off his shirt and jeans. He was just wearing his black boxer briefs now, and dear God, his body. Those push-ups were definitely working.

"I bet you're glad you didn't kiss me, now that you know I have strep."

"I bet I'm not." He got under the covers beside me.

"Shut up."

"You."

I knew that I still had fever, because although it didn't hurt, my skin felt so terribly sensitive. Even between my legs. Especially there.

I turned on my side and scooted over till I was all up against him. I took his hand and put it on me.

"Grace," he said. Maybe thinking he shouldn't take advantage of me in my sick, altered state.

I kissed his chest. He slid an arm under my shoulders and ran the other hand up under the T-shirt and all over me—my breasts, belly, hips, thighs, bottom. I shuddered; it was almost too much. He felt my skin rise up in violent goose bumps, and when he touched me again between my legs, it was feather-light.

I came, so quickly.

"Again?" he whispered, a few minutes later.

I nodded.

He shoved the covers off me and knelt between my legs. He put his mouth on me and burned away the remaining fever.

Sometime in what seemed like early morning, he said my name and felt my face and gave me my antibiotic with a glass of apple juice.

"How does your throat feel?" he asked. "Do you want a pain-killer?"

I shook my head. It only hurt a little, now.

I went back to sleep.

I woke up alone in the apartment. I sat up slowly, a little dizzy. Got out of bed carefully and shuffled out to the living room. I found my purse and cell and called work. I also left a message for Peg that I was with a friend for the weekend and not to worry.

Just getting up and doing that much exhausted me. I went back to bed.

It was dark in the bedroom when I woke again.

"Hey," he said. "How are you?"

"Better." I felt so shy.

"Are you hungry?"

I nodded.

He brought me soup. And ice cream.

When I woke Saturday morning he was asleep beside me.

I got up quietly and took a shower. It felt great to wash away all that sweaty sickness. I scrubbed my teeth with toothpaste on a washcloth, and combed out my wet hair. I wrapped up in a towel and went back to the bedroom.

He was awake, watching me. I sat on the edge of the bed beside him.

"How are you feeling?" he asked.

"Not too bad."

"That medicine took care of things pretty quick."

"Quickly," I said.

He smiled.

"I love you," I said. "I've loved you for so long. I've never loved anyone as much as I love you."

He nodded, like it was not a revelation. Like *Yes, of course. I know you do.*

He opened the towel and looked at me. He drew me down beneath him and touched my face with trembling fingers. His mouth was hot in the hollow at the base of my neck, on my breasts.

"I'm not going to stop," he said, already pushing into me.

"*Don't.*" Dear God, the relief. I wrapped my arms and legs around him.

When he was all the way in, he groaned and stayed still for a while. Then he took my face in his hands, looked into my eyes, and pounded the hell out of me. I had to put a hand up and brace myself to stop inching toward the headboard.

It was rough, and brief, and not about me. And that was just fine.

We made up for lost time.

We had more sex in the next twenty-four hours than I'd ever had in an entire month. We slept and ate, too, but only for brief intervals before we were at it again. At first, in between, I pulled on one of his T-shirts a time or two, but soon gave up. Clothing became a frustrating waste of time.

Somewhere in there I came back from the bathroom and found him sitting on the end of the bed holding his wallet. I sat beside him and he handed me a folded piece of paper that turned out to be test results from a clinic in Los Angeles. He was HIV-negative. Negative for other things, too.

"Oh," I said. "Great! When did you do this?"

"Seven weeks ago." He pointed to the date.

"And you always used condoms since then?"

"I haven't been with anyone since well before then."

I'm sure I looked mighty surprised.

"And I always used condoms before, anyway. When I needed to. Which *wasn't* that often."

"Even all those times you'd been partying? Are you sure?"

He scowled. "Don't believe all the shit you read about me, okay, Grace?"

"Okay." I tried not to sound dubious.

"I do have some restraint."

"Okay." I looked again at the paper. "Well, why did you get tested?"

"'Cause I knew I was coming home and I was gonna do whatever it took to get inside you. I figured that might mean documentation."

I wanted to laugh. But should I be offended? This was a brain-bender.

"Well, you didn't need it, apparently." I felt a little sheepish. "But congratulations. Mission accomplished!"

He laughed and then I did, too, and he pulled me onto his lap and we somehow ended up on the bedroom floor. I woke there later sprawled across him, my cheek stuck with sweat and drool to his chest.

He was awake, stroking my hair. I took a peek up at him. He smiled.

"I can hear your heart," I said. "You're alive!"

"I am. For fuckin' sure."

We did it so much that we ran out of condoms. And then we did it again, one more time.

I got in the tub at midnight, to soak my pleasantly exhausted body. He came and got in behind me, with lots of sloshing overflow. I lay back against him and sighed. His hand crept down my belly.

"Don't even think about it."

"Sorry," he laughed, cradling me, scooping warm water over my breasts.

I dozed and dreamed.

Kittens! There were so many of them! It was my job to contain them. I had to make sure they didn't get up this flight of endless, very steep stairs. I sat down on a step and gently shoved them all back, tried to block them with my legs and feet, but one tiny little calico devil leapt and attached, with splayed, needle-sharp claws, onto my dress.

"Ouch!" I squeaked.

He climbed over my shoulder before I could grab him. I turned and saw him scamper up the steps. He was so fast! Now more kittens slipped past me.

Ty's musing voice, far away, intruded on the kitty chaos. "I guess I shouldn't have come inside you those times. That was pretty stupid."

"Mm," I said, surfacing just long enough to be polite. Then I went back to the dream stairs, where I was *very* upset. Extremely anxious.

There was just no way I was going to be able to stop the kittens. There were too many, and they were so fast! That little calico, leading the pack, was so far up the stairs now I almost couldn't see him.

I shook a fist at the little guy and then felt like a jerk. He was a kitten, for heaven's sake. And why was I supposed to stop him, anyway?

Oh, wait . . . this was a *dream*. Not real! I could stop worrying. Phew!

plans b and c
and the Walrus, laughing

Sunday morning, lying in bed, I heard words and music from the living room:

Did you think I would ever
work up the nerve
and touch you
and touch you like I did
Did you think I would ever
ever return
and hold you
and hold you again
Tell me to turn up this flame that I feel
Tell me you burn up cause I'm touching you still
Did you think I would ever
turn on your light
and love you
I love you tonight
Tell me you're feeling the way that I do
Tell me, I'm reeling cause you're touching me too
Did you think you would ever
turn on my light

and love me
You love me tonight

"Are you coming tonight?" he asked.

We were sitting on his couch eating giant bowls of cereal. I looked at him blankly.

"Roseland, remember? Day after tomorrow I'm leaving."

My spoon faltered between the bowl and my mouth. "Where are you going?"

"Atlanta first, then all over."

I still did not understand.

"I'm going on tour. Colleges and festivals and nightclubs. We start in Atlanta, and end in St. Louis next spring."

"Oh."

"You should see the tour bus," he said. "I have my own room. Everyone else sleeps in a bunk bed."

He was leaving.

We looked at each other for a long time. He blinked and looked away. Then he looked at me again and grinned, excitement and shadow in his eyes.

I stood up.

"Do you—" he said.

"What?"

He pointed at my bowl. "Do you want some more cereal?"

"No thanks." I headed for the kitchen. "I think I'd better go home."

"I'll walk you."

A gray, mid-September Sunday morning. Chilly, as if winter was close already. And then we ran into Roberta, coming toward us on Grove Street. Blond, beautiful, boobalicious Roberta, in her tight jeans and high heels. She gave him a Big Hug. She aimed her lips at his mouth, but he turned his face just in time and she left a wet spot on his cheek. He rubbed it away, glancing at me. Probably doing some mental scrambling.

"I'm coming tonight," Roberta cooed. "I can't wait!"

She said hello to me, too.

"Hello. Oh, hey," I said politely to both of them. "Why don't I let you two catch up? Sorry to rush away, but I've got to get on home."

"Okay!" Roberta said.

"No." Ty grasped my arm. "I need to talk to you about something." He smiled kindly at Roberta, said see ya later, and hustled me on down the sidewalk.

"Sorry," I said, "I just thought you might like to visit with your friend."

He looked askance at that but said nothing.

At my building he walked into the vestibule with me and pulled me to him. He kissed my neck, my cheek. My mouth.

"I'll see you tonight, right? You're on the list. We play about ten thirty. You can hang out backstage. It'll be great to look off and see you there."

"Okay." I pressed my face into his shirt.

"And don't even think about bringing Todd," he added.

I nodded, breathing in his warm, wonderful smell.

"Todd. That's a stupid name."

I nodded.

"Everything okay?"

"Mm-hmm." I wanted to stay right here, just like this, until I keeled over dead at age ninety-nine. It felt so good to not think, to just be with him, close and quiet. I knew that thinking would inevitably start when I went upstairs, and I vaguely dreaded it.

He kissed me again, gently disengaged, and went out the door. Then he leaned back in.

"Grace."

"Hm?"

"I'll do 'Bell Bottom Blues.' And 'Feel It.'"

"Okay." I smiled.

He kissed the tip of my nose. "'Bye."

I went upstairs. Peg wasn't home. Of course she wasn't; there would be a matinee this afternoon.

I sat on the end of my bed, staring at the celadon wall, running through the blur of events of the past three days. I got quite warm all over again at some of the mental pictures. I lay back on the bed and touched myself through my jeans. I was a little tender, but I didn't mind. It felt like I had a very nice secret. I curled up on my side and hugged a pillow.

I thought about the ferocity of the first time we were together, yesterday morning. And the slow, sleepy tenderness of this morning.

And then I felt a knot in my gut. What had I done? I made my living teaching people not to do what I had just done. Unprotected sex. *Twice.*

I talked myself down pretty quickly about the possibility of sexually transmitted infection, having seen his test results. And maybe he really did always use a condom. Maybe he really only forgot to be careful with me, in the heat of the horny moment. Anyway, how could I get mad at him about it? I had blown it off as much as he had.

But.

I got my agenda out of my bag and searched the calendar for the first day of my last period. I remembered it well. I'd been at lunch with Julia at a Portuguese restaurant in Park Slope, eating fava beans with spicy chorizo. Just mentally noting the Hannibal Lecter-like glaze that came over her eyes as she described the ruthless legal vengeance she'd wrought on an unlicensed drunk driver, when I felt the first warm trickle and excused myself to go to the bathroom.

I counted the days up to today. Fifteen.

My hands tingled. I closed the agenda and lay down on my bed and willed myself to stay calm. I breathed slowly and lay there until I was clearheaded enough to figure out my plan. Then I got up, grabbed my wallet, and went to the drugstore.

I can give the spiel about emergency contraception in my sleep. It's a little white tablet, available at most pharmacies over the counter, for about forty dollars. It's up to ninety percent effective, but you need to try to take it within seventy-two hours of having unprotected sex.

This was my first time buying it for myself.

I knew that the odds that I was pregnant, even having had unprotected sex twice, were relatively small. I also knew that emergency contraception would not end an existing pregnancy, if I had conceived. It would only prevent conception if it hadn't already happened, by thickening up my cervical mucus and making it hard for any little swimmers to get through to the egg. Ideally, I should have taken it yesterday. But it still might work if I took it today.

My chest hurt. In my perfect dream life, I would make a baby with Tyler Wilkie. I loved him. I imagined the delight of loving a child with him. But that child's father was my dream Ty, who would never have said it was stupid that he had come inside me. Who would not own my heart and body so intensely for several days and then abruptly and easily leave for half a year.

I wanted to joyfully, hopefully let the possibility of the dream baby just *be*. But knowing that I would continue alone, and now more profoundly than ever, I swallowed the tablet. With tears dripping off my chin.

I did not go to Roseland.

I did not want to talk to him or see him again before he left. When I knew he would be onstage Sunday night, I left him a message. "Hey, it turns out I needed to stay home tonight. Just not feeling great. Probably the antibiotic. Have a great tour, okay? Be safe."

I didn't sleep much. He called and left a message at about two in the morning. It sounded like he was at a party.

"Gracie." Fumbling sounds, then laughing. He was at least a little drunk. "Hey. Sorry. I dropped the phone. Hey." He lowered his voice. "What are you wearing? Just kidding. I know this is a message. . . . Grace. Susannah Grace. Barnum. You taste like . . . warm . . . candy. Can I come over? If you're still awake and you get this, call me."

Monday afternoon Lakshmi had an emergency dental appointment, so I taught her group of thirteen-year-olds up in the Bronx. I timed their giggling, blindfolded, put-the-condom-on-the-banana races with a stopwatch and wondered if they could tell just by looking at me what a hypocrite I was.

After class, on my way to the subway, I checked messages.

"Hey, I know you're at work." He sounded brusque and preoccupied. People were talking in the background. "Can we get together tonight? I leave really early in the morning. Call me."

It would have been so easy. He was on speed dial. But I was caught in a descending spiral of heartbreak and my fingers would not cooperate.

He left a final message after midnight.

"I leave in a few hours. The bus pulls out at four. I wanted to see you. *Shit*, Gracie, why are you doing this?"

I didn't trust how my voice might sound if I talked to him, but I couldn't let him go like this. I sent him a text.

I wanted to say: *I love you. I will miss you.*

But I said this:

Have a great tour, Ty. Be safe.
xo Grace

As usual, I had a plan. I would call and talk to him briefly, cheerfully, in a couple of weeks, as soon as I got my life back on track and felt okay again about the reality of how things were between us.

But there's this thing that John Lennon said about making plans, and you'd think by now I'd have realized the truth of it.

Life happened, instead.

my angel returns

The third time I went out to teach at the Ethel J. Merman Retirement Village in Flushing, Queens, we had a party, complete with little penis- and vulva-shaped cakes ordered by the workshop organizer, my most ardent elderly admirer, Mr. Shapiro. He was only about a half-inch taller than me and had dense thickets of hair growing out of his nose and ears. He had taken to calling me Gracie a long time ago and liked to be shocking.

"Gracie, when will you come back and teach us about anal sex?" We were in the common room where I'd taught the class, standing by the punch bowl. He had a thin pink mustache from nibbling his cupcake.

"I already told you all you're going to get from me on that subject. Put on a condom and use lots of lube. Go slowly. If anyone says *stop*, stop."

"Telling is great, but I think I need a demonstration."

"You have Internet here, don't you?" I asked, looking over at the computer center.

"They suspended my privileges."

"Well," I said, patting his back. I had devoured my chocolate willy with brown buttercream icing and was ready to go. "Good-bye, Mr. Shapiro. Good-bye, everyone!"

All who were ambulatory gathered around to hug me. Mr. Shapiro, who had waited till last, took my hands and asked, "Are you absolutely sure there's no possibility of cunnilingus?"

"None whatsoever. Maybe Mrs. Benson? I've seen her looking at you."

He waved a hand. "I've had her."

His hug was emphatic. Boob-squishing. I gasped and pulled away, reflexively crossing my arms beneath my breasts.

"What'd I do? I'm sorry!"

"No! Nothing, Mr. Shapiro."

"Did I hurt you?"

"I'm fine."

When I got home I gingerly touched myself. My breasts were unbelievably tender, like my usual PMS soreness times ten. That sudden, large dose of progestin in the contraceptive had likely knocked things out of whack.

I went to bed early that night, exhausted. Woke the next morning to a message from Ty. He'd left it at 1:47 a.m.

"Hey, Grace. We just left Austin, Texas. It's a pretty great place, from what I hear. I didn't actually see much of it. I wish I knew why you won't talk to me. I guess you're mad about something. I thought we were finally getting somewhere, before I left. Anyway . . . I probably won't call you again. You call me. . . . Call me."

God, I loved hearing his voice. I replayed the message four times and saved it. However, I was just a wee bit freaked out about the sore boob thing. Rather than call, I texted him.

Got your msg. Will call soon. xo Grace

Over the next few days smells started to bother me. I avoided the subway.

Sunday morning I woke to the aroma of frying bacon, which meant Peg's boyfriend Jim had spent the night and was cooking for us. He was into meat for breakfast. Usually, I was too. Today, it was like something dead was being cooked.

Oh . . . yeah.

I lay there trying to stifle the rising nausea, but ended up bursting from my room and pounding on the bathroom door. Peg opened almost immediately, got out of my way, and held my hair while I retched.

And retched.

Retch-o-rama.

Until retching became a violent exercise in futility. And then I retched a tiny bit more, just to dot the i.

I collapsed over the toilet and laughed.

Then I cried.

Then I laughed.

Then I cried.

Peg looked worried. "Why don't you go back to bed," she said. "I'll send Jim out for some ginger ale. And an antipsychotic."

"Peg," I said, "I'm pregnant."

She touched my arm, wide eyed. "Are you sure?"

I nodded.

"On purpose?"

I shook my head.

"Does the guy know?"

I shook my head.

"What are you going to do?"

"I'm going to have a *baby*." I burst into a storm of weeping and laughing.

Jim knocked on the door. "Everyone okay in there?"

"We're fine!" Peg said.

"Breakfast is ready."

"Be there in a minute!" She squeezed my shoulder. "Is it Todd's?"

I shook my head and laughed and cried even harder. I lay down on the floor.

"Oh, Goddess. You finally scratched the mother of all itches."

I nodded.

She wet a washcloth and blotted my face. Over the next few minutes I calmed down considerably.

"How are you feeling now? Still sick?"

"Not as much." I sat up slowly.

"Maybe you should wait awhile to eat."

"God, yes."

"When are you going to tell him?"

"Pretty soon. He's busy, you know. On the road."

"So what?"

"Don't worry, I'll tell him."

She helped me stand up and hugged me, a long time. Smiling.

Three weeks later I had my first OB appointment.

It was a mellowly lit, Upper East Side, multi-physician practice, with comfy chairs and abstract art on the walls in the waiting room. Lots of paperwork.

When I opened my wallet and pulled out my insurance card, the pocket angel fell out with it, bouncing off my knee and onto the carpet.

Mystified, I leaned over and picked up the little pewter medallion. Then I figured it out. Ty must have found it in his guitar case at some point over the past year and a half and passed it back to me during the ER-strep episode.

I tossed the angel into my open purse and ruthlessly pushed down the emotion that threatened to bubble up. I was not going to go there.

My doctor was a pretty, youngish woman with an old-fashioned name: Myra Goldstein. Her hands were warm and gentle.

"Listen," Dr. Goldstein said, rolling a microphone thingy around in a slick of KY jelly on my still-normal-looking tummy. There was an amplified sound like tiny fingers drumming steadily on a table-top.

"Oh!" I said.

She smiled. "I think there's somebody in there."

She calculated that the baby would be born in early June. She gave me a prescription for prenatal vitamins and, noting the lines I'd left blank on the forms, tactfully asked who would be supporting me at the baby's birth.

"My roommate, maybe," I said. "And my mom."

She made a note about that in my chart. "At twenty weeks we'll do an ultrasound. You can schedule it at reception before you leave today."

I was tired and often a little sick to my stomach. It helped if I didn't let myself get too hungry.

My bras got too small. My nipples, previously a pale pink, turned light brown, and my breasts looked like roadmaps, the veins became so prominent.

I longed for Ty, the way you long for your best friend when you want to show them something interesting. I wished he could see what was happening to my body. I tamped down the powerful urge to call him; I didn't want to do it when I was feeling at all irrational or in a state of heightened emotion. Which was pretty much all the time.

In November Peg took the weekend off from the show and we took the train to Boston. Edward and Boris were getting married.

It was a small wedding, lovely and uncomplicated, at a historic Unitarian church. I watched Ed and Boris together and marveled that two lifelong-commitment types had found each other in New York City, of all places.

I missed Ty, so much. I wished things could be different between us.

I touched my belly, aware that it wasn't just me sitting there in my particular bit of space. There were two of us.

I had never cried at a wedding before. But there was a reading, "On Love," from Kahlil Gibran's *The Prophet*, that for some reason gave me a little pang of tearful anxiety. Peg handed me a tissue.

On our way to the reception line, she hooked her arm through mine. "Why don't you call Ty already?"

"I don't know what to say to him."

"Just tell him he's going to be a dad."

"Peg, it's not that simple."

"Why not?"

"I don't know. I'm scared, I guess."

"Scared of what?"

"It's hard to explain. And telling him won't change anything. He'll still be on his tour, and I'll still be where I am."

"Regardless of all that, he needs to be told. He has a responsibility."

"I know! Let me figure it out, okay? I'll call him when I start to show."

"Promise me."

"All right."

When we came home I did what I said I would never do again. Looked at his Internet fan forum. I wanted to try to get a sense of what was going on with him on tour, before calling him.

The gist of the gossip was that he was doing great shows, but not partying as much as he did during his time in L.A.

Was he unwell? I wanted to call him, to ask. I refrained.

Thanksgiving. Peg and Jim went to spend it at his mother's house in Westchester. I spent the day with my dad and Tori. She brought sushi but I stuck with the turkey; raw fish was risky for pregnant women.

On my way home that night in a cab, Ty called. My fingers itched to open the phone, but I let him go to voice mail. After I'd had my bath and settled in bed, I listened. He sounded kind of glum.

"Hey, it's me. I know I said I wasn't gonna call again. I guess I lied. Happy Thanksgiving. Who did you spend it with? We ate at this big fancy house in Taos. This guy who's an investor in the record company. You wouldn't believe the view of the mountains from his living room.

"Anyway, I wrote a song, it might be my best ever. I started it this summer right before I came home and I just finished it. Pretty sure you're gonna hate it. Especially when other people hear it." His tone became defiant. "Which they probably *will*. Because this is what I *do*."

I rolled my eyes. Great. Whatever.

"So I mailed it to you. Just a demo. When I get back you can yell at me about it or give me a titty twister or something. Okay, well. Happy Thanksgiving. See ya."

Crap. I wanted to talk to him. He was with strangers on Thanksgiving. But it just didn't seem like the right day to blurt the big news.

An envelope came by FedEx the next day. There was a CD, on which Ty had scrawled "A Breath Away" in black Sharpie. There was a sheet of lyrics that I quickly refolded without reading. I shoved everything back in the mailer and put it in the bottom drawer of my desk.

I'd check it out eventually, when I felt a little less vulnerable.

December came, and the nausea went away. Overnight, it seemed, a firm bump appeared where I used to have a normal, slightly chubby little belly.

"Oh, hey," I said, running my hand over the bump. "I guess this means you're really, really in there. Hey! Hello, little tiny human. Hello . . . my child."

My child.

expectations

I had seen Ty's tour schedule online and knew that he had the evening off. No show. So I reasoned that I might reach him by phone then.

I came home that night from work, ate a bowl of Peg's homemade minestrone, and took a warm bath. Sat on the couch in my night-gown and robe, and watched a little *Andy Griffith* on TV Land. Andy would have been a great dad for my baby.

At the end of the episode I muted the TV and speed-dialed number four. Got a recording: number not in service.

Well. That was that. I tried.

He probably changed his cell phone service. I could call his parents and ask them how to get in touch with him. I could call them at their flower shop, if I couldn't get their home number from directory assistance. I resolved to do that tomorrow afternoon from work.

Tomorrow came. Peg called me, late morning, and caught me on my way out to teach a workshop. "Have you heard the news?"

I always hate when people start a conversation that way. "No," I said cautiously.

"About Ty."

"What is it?"

"Get on CNN.com and look at the entertainment page."

"Peg, just tell me!"

"He's a Grammy nominee! Two times! Best Male Pop Vocal Per-formance and Best Pop Vocal Album! Are you there?"

"Yes."

"We have to call him!"

"I . . . I tried to call him last night. His number isn't working."

"So can we get it from his manager or something? What about his parents?"

"I was going to call them today."

"Oh, great!" She was quiet a moment. "So, I'll let you talk to him first, obviously, and then I'll give him a call in another day or so to congratulate him."

"Okay."

"All right. Well. I'll get that number from you tonight."

Jean was as friendly as ever, told me that Ty had changed cell providers a while back, and gave me his new number. She said she hoped to see me again sometime.

"Oh, you probably will," I said.

I hung up and, before I could psych myself out, dialed Ty.

He answered.

"Hello, it's Grace."

Long pause. "Grace. . . . Hey."

My brain seized up at the sound of his voice. And from everything I wanted to say.

"Are you there?" he asked.

"Sorry, yes."

He was silent.

"I'm sorry. That I didn't call. Before now." My speech was hitching like a car with hair-trigger brakes. "Are you well?"

"I'm good, yeah. Are you?"

"I—yes, I am."

Quiet.

"Congratulations. On your nominations."

"Thank you."

"I hope you win."

He laughed a little. "We'll see."

"Well. Take care."

"Okay, you, too. Hey—are you still at Peg's?"

"Uh-huh. Where are you?"

"Minneapolis."

"Oh, Minnesota."

"Yep."

"Those are Native American names, don't you think?"

"Uh . . . probably."

"Well, 'bye, Ty."

"Okay, Gracie. 'Bye."

I hung up.

Peg was going to kill me.

I bought a couple of large sweatshirts and wore them the whole two days I spent at my mom's for Christmas. It worked; she just thought I was getting fat.

"Well, this is better than how thin you were," she said, examining me when I first arrived. "But be careful, hon. You're looking a little *swollen*."

She made me fat-free eggnog and nodded approvingly when I refused the shot of whiskey. "Right, empty calories."

By now José had moved in, so he was there with us for all the festivities. Out of earshot of my mother, who had washboard abs, he tried to say encouraging things like "men like women with a little belly" and "this is better, last Christmas you looked like you were dying."

My mom must have snuck out and done some supplemental shopping after I went to bed early on Christmas Eve. Because my gifts the next morning included an Abercizer, a balance ball, stretch bands, and the book *YOU: On a Diet*, by Dr. Mehmet Oz.

"Thanks, Mom," I said dryly.

"You just don't want to let this get away from you. Get to work now and you'll be back in shape in a couple of months."

"Right, okay. I really appreciate this." I wasn't lying, I did plan to use it all. Next summer.

I was doubtful that the sweatshirt ploy would work with my dad, but I tried it. Upon my arrival New Year's Eve, he took one look at me and said, "When are you due?"

"June. How can you tell?"

"Your face is more full. And the quality of the light around you has changed. Like you're in soft-focus. I noticed it at Thanksgiving, but I wasn't sure what it meant. A couple weeks ago, I dreamed you were in a rock quarry, looking for just the right piece of stone to sculpt. You found it but had to smuggle it out under your shirt."

"Of course, a rock quarry. The common dream metaphor for pregnancy."

"And is the father who I think it is?"

"Yes. Mayor Bloomberg."

"How is he taking it?"

"He's out of town. I'll probably tell him in the next few weeks."

My dad looked at me.

"It's really not a big deal," I said. "I'm doing fine."

"Really?"

I nodded.

My dad held up five fingers.

I sighed. "I'm a little scared."

"That's four words."

"Freaked out, then."

He put an arm around me and led me to the kitchen island. "Did I see that he got a Grammy nomination?"

"Yes."

"When do they do that show?"

"February."

"So he'll be back in town next month?"

I shook my head. "The awards are in Los Angeles this year."

My dad was unusually quiet while we ate the meal he'd made for me, an awesome onion and goat cheese pie with asparagus. There was chocolate mousse for dessert.

"What's up, Dan?"

"I want you to be happy."

"I am. I will be. Please don't worry about me."

"You know I'm here for you."

I set down my spoon and blotted my eyes.

"I have to go to Japan in late April with the doll paintings. But you have my number. Use it."

"I will."

"Does your mother know?"

I shook my head.

"I want you to tell her before I go out of the country."

"Yes, I will. Thank you."

"For what, my dear?"

"For telling me what to do. It feels so good not to have to figure everything out myself."

"Okay, one more instruction, then. By the time I come back, before June, you will bring Tyler here for dinner."

"If he's around, all right." The very idea gave me butterflies, but okay. I'd try.

After we ate he showed me a new painting. Or maybe it was a sculpture? It was on a big canvas, but very sculptural. He had built up a thick, uneven layer of stuff on the canvas and painted it the colors of a patch of dry ground. Embedded in the surface were bits of wood, dead grass, stones, feathers, bird's nest, and, most amazingly, a tiny bird skeleton. It would have looked like something real that you might walk right over in a wooded area, except that he had covered it all with a glaze that elegantly heightened the drab colors and rough textures. I could picture it gracing the wall of some millionaire's monochromatically taupe penthouse living room.

"I like it," I said. "It feels poignant. It's about death, right? The circle of life?"

He smiled sympathetically. "Nice try."

Middle of January, I went for my ultrasound.

I lay on a table and pulled up my sweater and Dr. Goldstein squirted warm gel on my belly. She pressed and slid the probe thing all around my navel and lower abdomen, looking at the TV monitor. I couldn't see the screen, so I watched her face.

She looked so serious, so absorbed. She changed the position of the probe several times before looking at me and smiling.

"It's not twins, is it?" My voice sounded rusty.

"No, just one healthy baby. Do you want to see?"

I nodded.

She turned the monitor toward me. The picture was grainy and shifting. As she moved the probe around on my belly, limbs and body parts appeared and morphed away into other body parts. She showed me the spine, the feet, the beating heart. The skull. I could see the shape of a face. A perfectly formed arm, hand moving toward the mouth.

"Is it—"

"Sucking its thumb, yes." She smiled. "Do you want to know what it is?"

Of course! How else could I make a plan? "Yes, please."

She pointed to a rather nebulous region on the monitor. "That is a little penis and testicles."

Oh, yes! I saw it! "A *boy*," I breathed.

"A boy," she said. "Congratulations."

"A boy."

Dr. Goldstein smiled and patted my hand. "I have three of them. You'll be all right."

She printed ultrasound snapshots for me. I left the imaging center and walked to a coffee shop. Ordered a decaf latte and spread the astonishing pictures out on the table.

A boy. In spite of the fifty percent odds, I actually hadn't imagined the possibility. What on earth was I going to do with a son? It had always just been my mom and me. I had no idea what would be required of me, in terms of raising a male child. I didn't know where to begin, to make a plan.

"So, okay," I said to The Bump. "You're a boy. I'm going to have to ask around. Do some reading. I mean, how different can it be? Yes, eventually you're going to want to do boy things. Maybe. Or maybe you'll like girl things? Sometimes people turn out to be sort of a mix of boy and girl. Which is totally cool. Oh God, I'm an idiot, trying to figure this all out now! You see what you're in for? You will be the test child. I'm sorry. You're just going to have to bear with me."

That afternoon when I got back to work I asked Lavelle if I could speak to her privately in her office.

We sat on her couch together.

"Well, I don't know if you may have noticed," I said, "but I'm pregnant."

"I was wondering."

"And you know I'm not married."

She nodded and shrugged.

"The father is someone I care about very much, and a good person, but he's not around at the moment. I—I don't know what's going to happen, with that. For now, it's just me."

"Grace, I hope you're not worried about what people here will think. You know none of us will judge you."

"No, I know. I'm a little embarrassed . . . it's kind of ironic because, well, this happened because of a lapse in contraceptive judgment."

Lavelle smiled a little.

"We were in the moment, I guess, and got careless. It's probably a good thing that I'm not teaching contraception to young women, I would feel like such a poor example."

Now Lavelle was frowning. "Grace, I'm going to speak frankly."

"Okay."

"I don't know anyone who tries harder for perfection than you. You are so hard on yourself, and sometimes on others. Maybe this is a message for you to ease up a little. Sometimes we can't completely control everything, much as we might like to try. There are always going to be surprises."

"Tell me about it. I'm having a boy, Lavelle! And I know *nothing* about boys."

She patted my knee. "See what I mean? Just throw away the rule book right now."

On a bitterly cold February night, Peg and I ordered calzones and settled on the couch in front of the TV.

Every time the camera panned the Grammy audience we searched for Ty. Finally we caught a glimpse of him, wearing a stylish approximation of a black tuxedo. No tie. He looked so handsome, but also a little surprised to be there. And Jean was with him! I loved him for bringing his mother. She was all primped and made-up, and wearing an expensive-looking, sparkly peach-colored dress. With her Grace Kelly looks, she outshined most of the women I saw seated around her.

The show was long. People I had never heard of played, and I was not persuaded to add most of them to my iPod. I nodded off at least once, but Peg shook me every time they showed Ty in the audience.

He did not win the awards he was nominated for. They showed his face in those moments, on a split screen with all the other nominees. He looked a little disappointed and kind of relieved, I thought. But what did I know? Maybe he was completely crushed. Peg and I certainly were.

"Who are these voters?" I demanded to know. "Do they have water on the brain? Can they *hear*?"

"It doesn't matter," Peg said. "We know he's the best."

The next day she e-mailed me the link to a YouTube video of Ty in concert in Dallas. It was long, seven minutes or so, of him doing an old Otis Redding song, "I've Been Loving You Too Long." He started at the piano and then got up with the microphone and walked into the audience. They enveloped him, touching his arms, his hair, his back. It was an incredible vocal and emotional performance. The people around him seemed ecstatic. Transported.

Look at this, Grace, Peg's e-mail said. *He's entrancing those people. I just realized. Taking them out of themselves. Ty is sort of like a medicine man. A shaman.*

P.S. have you called him?

A shaman. I sort of knew what that was. Like a witch doctor or something. I Googled it. Definition: *a person with special magical powers who can mediate between the visible and the spirit world.* Hmm. I didn't know about the mediation part, but listening to him sing definitely could take you away from reality for a while.

Your father is a shaman, I said internally to The Bump, who was by now becoming too large and rambunctious to conceal under baggy clothes. *But you're still going to have to clean your room and take out the garbage one day.*

Intellectually, I knew I needed to get myself together, finally, and tell him, but I just wasn't quite ready. So the universe conspired to remind me of him constantly. As if my burgeoning belly wasn't enough.

I was on my way to Ed and Boris's for veggie sushi one evening and—oh, hey!—there was Ty. On posters advertising his CD. Plastered all over the construction wall surrounding the high-rise going up near their apartment in Chelsea. I had to stop and regroup before I went in the building; there is nothing like one hundred or so Tyler Wilkies brooding at you all the way down a city block to put you off your futomaki.

Then: Ty on the *JumboTron*. In freaking Times Square. Lip-synching one of his gut-wrenching songs. I just step out of the office for a minute, hoping for a bagel and maybe a glimpse of the Naked Cowboy. And I'm presented with *this*. At least I couldn't hear the words.

In the next month or so, I suddenly became exponentially more pregnant. The small person borrowing space inside me started bouncing around, making his presence known. A morning came when I saw myself in the bathroom mirror, naked, swollen, and began to finally, truly understand that I was going to have to woman up and call Ty immediately. This was awful, what I had done. How could I have let myself become so paralyzed?

The very same day Peg came home after her Sunday matinee in a state of distress.

"Grace," she said, "I have to show you something."

She led me to the laptop in her bedroom and opened up one of those garish, *TMZ*-like sites that proliferate like mold on the Internet. She scrolled down to a photo. It was Ty, with Roberta, sitting in a booth at a club. He was smiling at the camera. She was cuddled up close to him, arms around his neck, lips pressed to his cheek.

The caption:

TYLER WILKIE ENGAGED

The blurb said that model and makeup artist Roberta Smilyak had been traveling with pop singer Tyler Wilkie on the Midwest leg of his concert tour. A longtime friend of the couple confirmed that they were "very serious" and "making wedding plans."

Peg took my hand.

"How did you find this?" I asked.

"I get Google Alerts about Ty. I thought it would be fun, keeping up with him. Grace, I bet that website is lying," she said. "Or exaggerating."

"Yes, probably. The part about marrying her, anyway."

"So what are you going to do?"

"I'm going to call him."

"When?"

"Now."

I sat cross-legged on my bed with my cell. Reminded myself to breathe. For strength and courage, I had the ultrasound photos spread out across my comforter.

I dialed Ty's number. His voice mail picked up.

It wasn't the smartest or bravest decision I ever made, but listening to his greeting, I rationalized that it would be perfectly fine for him to find out the basics this way, in a brief, easy message. When he called me back, I could go into more detail, answer his inevitable questions, apologize profusely, and we could start to figure everything out. Together. I would no longer be alone with this. God, why had I waited—

The beep.

"Um—hey. Hey, Ty! It's Grace. I need to tell you something. I, um . . . remember that weekend we spent together, before you left? Back in September? Well, something happened. We, uh, we made a, uh, baby."

I was starting to cry. Crap. Pull it together!

"A baby. We're going to have a baby. A baby boy. You and me. I hope he'll look like you . . . I hope so. Well, that's all. You have my number. Talk to you soon, Ty. I hope you're okay. I'll talk to you soon. 'Bye."

I threw the phone on the bed and lay down and hugged a pillow. My heart was pounding. I picked the phone up again and checked it, to make sure it wasn't on mute or vibrate. I cranked it all the way up to eleven, as they say, and settled in for a sleepless night.

The first two days, I was certain I was going to hear from him any minute. He was, of course, traveling and very busy. Probably waiting for a quiet, private moment to call me back.

By the third day, I told myself that I must have really surprised him with my message, and he was just taking a little extra time to absorb the news and regain his equilibrium.

The fifth day, I stayed home from work, in bed.

On day six, I had the hopeful thought that something terrible must have befallen him, and Peg, though Google-Alerted about it, had decided not to tell me so as not to upset me and endanger the health of the baby.

That night I got up when I heard Peg come in from the show. She was standing at the kitchen sink, filling the teakettle. She turned off the water when she saw me. "What's the matter?"

"I called Ty on Sunday. Right after you showed me the website."

"Yes, I thought so! What did he say?"

"I left him a message. Told him everything."

"Oh, honey, you did?"

I nodded. "He hasn't called me back. Oh, Peg—"

Her arms were so strong, so immediate. She held both of us up, me and The Bump.

the chapter where, understandably, certain people get very upset with me

And just when I thought things were as bad as they could get—

Julia called. Insisting we meet for lunch. Tomorrow. She probably wanted to find out if I'd worked off that spare tire I'd been developing. The thought of what she was in for made me giggle. Kind of hysterically.

It was early for lunch at that Japanese place in Chelsea we liked. I peered around the dim, empty dining room. She wasn't here yet. It was hard to savor under the circumstances, but for once I beat her!

A gracious Asian lady led me to a table along the back wall. The room was toasty warm, but I debated whether or not to leave my coat on. Like it was going to make a difference, at this point. I took it off and smoothed my stretchy black sweater. The lady brought me a glass of water, no ice, and I gulped it down.

The bells on the door jingled. Here she came, making her way toward me, sleek and chic. Smiling. Happy to see me.

I smiled as genuinely as I could and stood up.

She slowed to a stop ten feet away. Her mouth fell open.

"Hi, Mom."

"Are you kidding me?" she said. "Are you *kidding* me?"

I clasped my hands over my belly in a futile effort to minimize the shocking visual. "So what do you want to be called?" My voice was cheerful, if a little tremulous. "Grandma? Grandmama?"

She didn't move or respond, just stared. Julia Barnum, struck dumb.

To try to jar her loose, I went for a laugh. "Mammaw?"

"Who is the father?" Her voice was deep and scary, like when I was ten and wore her mother's sapphire ring to school without permission and lost it.

"Could we sit down, please?"

She came over and tossed her four-hundred-dollar handbag under the table, jerked a chair out, and sat. Painful, bloody retribution brewing in her eyes.

"Grace, who is he?" she demanded.

"You don't know him."

"When will I meet him?"

"I don't know."

Her nostrils were flaring. Our server approached, got a look at Julia, and backed away.

"And why is that?"

"He is . . . not involved, at the moment."

"Did you consider an abortion?"

I shook my head.

"When are you due?"

"June eighth."

She looked at me for a long time. Really looked at me. Pulled a tissue out of her coat pocket and blew her nose. Then she laughed! "Well. I think I might actually be glad about this. I get to be a granny!"

"Oh, Mom." The floodgates opened. I covered my face with my hands. She pulled a chair up next to me and held me and said comforting things while I soaked the shoulder of her tailored jacket.

"It's all going to be all right, my darling," she said soothingly, as my tears slowed. "All will be well. But you are going to tell me who the father is. And you are going to tell me how this happened."

It was hard not to roll my eyes and give her the clinical version, just for kicks.

"Okay," I said. "His name is Tyler Wilkie. He's a singer. He has a song on the radio, you may have heard it."

She stared at me. "Of course I have heard it, what do you think, I live in a cave? I have his whole CD on my iPod!"

She handed me a paper napkin and I blew my nose. "Well, this is interesting." She settled back and crossed her arms. She sounded like an evil genius plotting world domination. "We will make him pay. Pay big, to support his child."

"Mom! Look at me. This is not your business. If you do anything—"

"Don't worry, I won't do anything you don't authorize. How on earth do you know him?"

I told her the whole two-and-a-half-year saga. The story of my life pulled inside out by this sweet, beautiful, amazing, talented, irresponsible child-man. I left out the part about Roberta. Julia was already dangerously close to rampage.

"Well. It sounds like you care for him. Maybe he's not a total creep."

"He's not!" My voice wobbled. "I—I used to think he might be my best friend."

She handed me a fresh napkin. "Then why isn't he involved? Does he know?"

"He's on tour. I haven't seen him in almost six months."

"But you did tell him?"

"Yes."

"And what did he say?"

"Mom, this is my business."

"Grace, what did he say?"

"He didn't say anything. I left him a message, and he never called me back."

"You left him a *message*? That he was going to be a father?"

It didn't sound great.

"When did you call him?" Julia asked.

"A week ago. Eight days."

"*Eight days* ago? Why did you wait so long to tell him?"

"I don't know! I was waiting for it to feel right, and time got away from me."

"Call him again. Something happened, maybe he lost his phone."

"Even if he did, he could still check messages from another phone."

"No. Something happened. You have to try again."

"Julia," I said evenly. "Thank you, but I am handling this."

She sat back in her chair, arms crossed. Deceptively quiet. I thought she was just strategizing and regrouping.

"Does your father know that you're pregnant?"

Oh, boy. "Yes. But only very recently."

She struggled with this, visibly.

"Only because he lives closer. And I knew I was going to be seeing you for lunch and you'd be in the loop very soon."

I think this helped.

"Mom, stop hating him," I ventured. "I have."

"Don't tell me what to do!" She twisted around looking for the server and spotted her, watching us furtively from behind a nearby potted tree. "Menus!" Julia barked, sending the poor woman scurrying.

At around seven months I had only gained twenty of the recommended twenty-five pounds. It's not like I was Shamu, but everything was swollen. My face. My fingers. My ankles. And I knew from catching a glimpse of myself in a restaurant window that I waddled.

It was a briskly windy, chilly Thursday. A few days after my lunch with Julia. After work I'd stopped in Gristedes for a few grocery items and was now on my way back home. I was at the intersection of Seventh and Christopher, waiting for the Walk signal.

The light changed and by the time I got halfway across the street I realized that Ty was standing on the corner directly in front of me.

I almost dropped everything.

He took his sunglasses off and stared at me and my stalling approach.

His hair was longer. And his beautiful face! What it did to my heart. But there were raw things happening on it. Shock. Concern. Anger.

When I reached him, I said, "Oh, you're back early." *Stupid*.

He took the grocery bags from me.

He was, apparently, speechless. At my building he just stood there looking at me, watching me fumble with the keys. My damned, unsteady hands! I finally got the door open.

He followed me up, carrying the bags. I now got winded by the third-floor landing, so I paused to catch my breath.

"Sorry," I said, gasping. Our son chose that moment to knee me in a kidney and I winced and grabbed my back and said *ow!* Tyler simply watched me like he had never seen a pregnant woman before and the very idea confused the hell out of him.

If he would just *say* something!

He followed me into the apartment. Peg was at a rehearsal, thank God.

He tossed the bags on the kitchen table and paced around. I unpacked the groceries, watching him cautiously. Wondering what to do next. What to say? It was hard to understand what was happening. Why was he here? Had he gotten my message?

I went into the living room and sat on the couch and watched him do agitated laps. He seemed so freaked out; it occurred to me that he might be afraid to try to speak.

Finally he stopped in front of me and crouched down, pale and intense. He had not shaved in a couple of days. He looked tired. How I wanted to touch him. He was so close, I could have.

He uttered one sharp word.

"*When?*"

"June eighth is the due date."

He ran his eyes over me once more, lingering on my ginormous midsection. He stood up, abruptly, and left.

The next day after work he was skulking in my lobby. He followed me outside. Took my elbow and steered me around a puddle on the sidewalk.

"Are you going to say anything?" I asked.

"I am trying to figure out how to forgive you for this."

"Well," I said, voice shaking, "I didn't do it all by myself."

He pulled me to a stop in front of Planet Hollywood. The flow of people on the sidewalk instantly diverted around us. "*Do what?*"

"We both decided to have unprotected sex, not just me!"

"I know that! What the hell are you talking about?"

"What are *you* talking about?"

He took off his dark glasses. "I'm talking about you not telling me I have a child about to be born. Jesus Christ! What the fuck is that?"

"I did tell you! I left you a message!"

He rubbed his face with both hands and glared at me a little less vehemently. "I never got any message. When did you leave it?"

"Almost two weeks ago."

He shook his head. "I lost my phone in Albuquerque. Need to get a new one."

"What? You were in Albuquerque almost a month ago." According to his website.

"Exactly."

"How can you go that long without a phone? It's—it's irresponsible!"

"I kept meaning to go get one, and then I'd forget. No one was fucking calling me that I wanted to talk to, anyway." Again, with the pointed glare.

"Well, what if your family was trying to reach you, or something?"

"Yeah, Grace, what if. And why the hell did you wait until two fucking weeks ago to finally call and tell me about this?"

"I—I was nervous."

"Of what? Of me?"

I nodded.

"Damn, girl." He smiled, but it was bleak. "Did you *ever* know who I was?"

This felt very bad.

He just looked at me for a long time. "Okay," he finally said. "So what happens now?"

"I don't know. My mom is trying to talk me into moving in with her, in New Jersey."

Another long silence.

"It's not a terrible idea, I could save up for my own place. And maybe you'll want to come out to my mom's and—and see him, sometimes. . . ."

His face changed. "It's a boy?"

I nodded.

"Shit," he said. He walked in a circle. And another. People walking past us eyed him warily and gave him extra room.

"*Shit!*" He leaned against the building, dazed.

cahoots

The weather took a wonderful, balmy turn that weekend. I had the windows open in my bedroom and was boxing up old books and papers, trying to clear space for my impending small roommate and all his accoutrements. He must have been energized, too, by the fresh air I was absorbing.

"Hey, what are you doing in there?" I said to The Bump, pausing to pat my belly. "Rearranging the furniture?"

The downstairs buzzer rang. I ignored it and continued packing.

Again with the buzzing. I stood there holding *Bleak House*, debating whether or not to go to the intercom. Maybe it was a delivery for Peg?

I opened the screen on one of my windows and leaned out to take a peek. Jean and Rebecca Wilkie were standing on the stoop. Rebecca was looking right at me.

Holy crap.

I buzzed them in. Listened to their long trek up the stairs. Opened the door when they got to our landing.

"Hello," I said.

"Grace!" Jean came right in. We shared an awkward hug. She touched my belly and kissed my cheek. "Oh, honey," she said, tears in her eyes. She seemed disappointed in me, but also excited. I latched on to that.

Rebecca stayed near the door, glaring at me, arms crossed tightly.

"I know it seems bad that I waited so long to tell him," I said to her. "But you don't understand."

"What kind of person do you think my brother is?"

Jean laid a hand on her arm. "Beck."

"We didn't plan this," I said. "I wasn't sure he would want it, with everything else going on in his life."

Jean shook her head. "Oh, honey, you don't know him at all."

"You don't deserve him," Rebecca added. Jean grimaced at her.

"You don't know what it's like," I said.

"Tell us." Jean pulled me over to sit with her on the couch.

"We . . . we were . . ." Oh, how embarrassing. It was hard to look at them. "We were . . . together. And not very careful. And after, he said he should have been. More careful." I snuck a peek at them. Jean was pink-cheeked. Rebecca, narrow-eyed but listening.

"And then he was gone, for six months. And whenever I thought about calling and telling him, I remembered him saying that he should have been more careful. I thought he might not be happy about the baby. I couldn't bear to hear that in his voice. You don't understand how much power he has to hurt me! More than anyone."

I had held it together, so far. Then Rebecca, anger apparently deflated, dropped down in the armchair across from us. She rubbed her face and cracked her knuckles just like Ty, and I quietly lost it—shoulders shaking and tears streaming down my face.

Jean patted my back and blotted my face with a tissue from her pocket.

"Ty told us you left him the message after he lost his phone," she said, after I'd calmed down some. "You must have been so upset that he wasn't calling you back."

"I was. It was terrible."

"He wasn't calling me back, either," Rebecca said. "I still may kick his ass about that."

"Sometimes he's a little oblivious," Jean said. "He's so busy writing songs, he forgets to do important things."

"Like get a new freaking phone," Rebecca said. "Or learn how to check messages remotely."

"I know," I said.

"Ty says it's a boy," Rebecca said almost kindly.

I nodded.

"My first grandbaby!" Jean clapped her hands lightly.

Her delight was infectious. "I have ultrasound pictures, do you want to see them?"

Of course they did. And they were appropriately amazed by the delicate perfection of his tiny skull, spine, arm, and hand.

"I wish Nathan could see these," Jean said.

"Maybe I could run down the street and make copies for you to take to him."

"Better yet, why don't you come with us to the hotel and show him the originals?"

"Why are you at a hotel?"

"Ty's staying there, he sublet his apartment till summer. Come with us and we can all go to dinner."

There was just no way I was ready for that. I didn't think Ty was, either. "I don't think I can do that tonight. Thank you."

I glanced at Rebecca. She smiled sharply at me and stood up. "Let's give her some space, Mom."

I stood with them and belatedly tried to play hostess, offering to make tea before they left. They declined.

We went to the office-supply store and I made copies of the ultrasound for Jean to show Nathan. I realized on my way back upstairs that Ty would see them tonight, too. What would he think? Would he be as astounded and humbled by them as I had been? I wished I could see his face when he saw them. I had to sit down on the steps for a moment and grieve. Parents were supposed to see their baby's ultrasound pictures together.

I spent Sunday mentally retracing my steps, trying to figure out how I had made such a sad mess of things. It seemed to boil down very simply to a) loving understandably but unwisely, and b) making several hundred snowballing bad choices.

It helped to go to work Monday and focus on others. I taught a half-day workshop on contraception and STI prevention at a girls' prep school on the Upper East Side. The whole time I was explaining the various methods of birth control, they were staring at my belly. I barely restrained myself from pointing at The Bump and saying *See? This is what happens.*

I stopped at a deli on the way home from the subway and picked up a Philly cheese steak for supper. Hauled myself up the stairs to the apartment and stopped on the fourth-floor landing.

Guitar. Someone playing. A song I knew.

I climbed up the last flight and let myself in. Ty was sitting on the couch, strumming. He paused and looked over his shoulder at me.

"Hey," he said.

There was a suitcase by the armchair, next to his guitar case.

"My apartment is sublet till August. I'm gonna sleep here." He nodded at the couch. "Peg gave me a key."

He went back to strumming.

I went to the kitchen and threw my stuff on the table. Walked to the window and looked down at the people crossing Hudson Street in the dusk. Went back to the kitchen door and watched the guitar-playing muscles in his back move under his plaid shirt. Crossed the kitchen to the window again. Oh, yeah. I was hungry.

I got the cheese steak out and set it on a plate. I went to the door. "Are you hungry? I have a cheese steak."

"No thanks." He didn't even glance back at me this time.

I sat at the kitchen table and ate half the sandwich. Drank a glass of milk.

Ty was running through all the heartbreaking songs in his repertoire. I thought about how I was going to have to stop at the drugstore tomorrow for earplugs.

I went to my bedroom and closed the door. Wadded up tissues and stuck them in my ears. I stripped down to my undergarments and stretched out on my back across the bed; it always felt good at first, but I could only stay this way for about thirty seconds before it became uncomfortable and I'd have to roll on my side.

There was a sharp rap on the door and Ty stuck his head in. I sat up on my elbows, startled.

"Sorry." He pulled the door shut.

Great. What a picture that must have been, me beached on the bed in my granny panties and thick-strapped support bra, wide-eyed, with big wads of tissue coming out of my ears. I got up and put on my robe. Discarded the tissues. Opened the door and went down the hall.

He was back on the couch with the guitar.

"What?" I said, from a few feet away.

"Hm? Oh, nothing." He smiled vaguely and kept playing.

I took a bath and tried to go to sleep, but now he had the TV on. So I lay awake and stewed about this new circumstance.

Yes, I had made a big, big mistake not telling him and had a lot to atone for. But Peg knew how hurt I was that Ty was involved with Roberta. That our intensely intimate weekend together had turned out to be, for him, nothing special. I was one of the multitudes. And now she was forcing me to live, *while pregnant with his child*, in close, constant proximity with him.

High dudgeon. That's what you'd call my state of mind by the time Peg came home around midnight. Ty was stretched out on the couch watching Jay Leno. I slipped past him and cornered Peg in the kitchen. She was making her bedtime cup of tea.

"Peg, how could you do this to me?" I whispered.

She set down the box of Sleepytime and looked at me. "I'm doing this *for* you."

"What does that mean?"

"You two have things to work out."

"Maybe so, but we don't have to *live* together to do it!"

"Don't be angry, hon. Just let the right thing happen, for once. There's a baby involved."

"Oh, is there?" My voice got loud. "I had no idea!"

They were both asleep when I left for work the next morning. I called Julia as soon as I hit the street and caught her in her car, just arriving at the courthouse.

"Can you come get me tonight? I'm ready to move in with you."

"Oh," Julia said. "No, I can't. I've just had the house painted. Inside. We need to give it a couple of weeks to air out. You don't want to inhale paint fumes."

"Julia! You said I could move in anytime. You didn't say anything about painting!"

"Didn't I? Listen, I've gotta run, let's talk later." I heard her car door shut and the lock beep. "Have to take a deposition."

I thought about going to Dan's for the next two weeks, but it would be such a hassle to move my things twice. I didn't want to live out of a suitcase. And my train to work from Peg's was so much more convenient.

By midday my ire at Peg had melted and I felt embarrassed about the way I'd behaved. I called her.

"Peg, I'm sorry."

She sighed. "I know. It's okay."

"I called my mom to see if I could move in with her today, but it will have to wait at least another week, maybe two."

"Why do you want to leave, anyway?"

"It's not the most comfortable situation."

"It will give you and Ty a chance to figure some things out."

"Maybe so."

"And Grace, you're a New York girl. Do you really want to give that up? Your OB is here. You don't want to commute to give birth."

"No. But, Peg, if I'm going to stay in the city I've got so much to figure out. I think if Ty pays child support I might be able to afford my own place. I just don't know if I'm up to trying to find an apartment and moving while I'm this pregnant."

"Of course not. You shouldn't try to do that right now."

"Okay. But I want you to know, I realize that The Bump and I can't live with you forever."

"Who says?"

"Peg, he'll grow into a little boy and need space. He may make noise and break things."

"Let's just wait till he's here and see how things unfold. Maybe I'll like living with a little boy."

"Peg, I don't deserve you."

"It's okay, Grace. You've been overwrought lately. It's understandable."

"Lately!"

"Well, all right, for a couple of years, at least. And the intensity does seem to have ratcheted up a notch or twelve since you got pregnant."

"Maybe we need to just take a deep breath. All of us. Especially me."

"Yes, please," Peg said. "Take a deep, deep breath."

She was right. I didn't want to leave the city. I resolved to try, as hard as I could, to just be nice. No matter what. To everyone.

Even, if absolutely necessary, Roberta.

———

I texted Julia and told her that I would stay at Peg's for the foreseeable future, at least until after the baby was born. She called me immediately and said that she thought that was a good idea. Saturday she would bring me the crib she'd found.

Since it was Monday night and Peg was off, she cooked dinner for us. I decided to try to look pretty. I put on a pink top with a scoop neck that displayed some impressive cleavage. My hair had gotten long again, and though I usually ponytailed it, tonight I brushed it and left it down.

Ty was already seated at the table. Peg was dishing vegetable lasagna onto our plates. She double-glanced at me and smiled.

Ty stood up and pulled out my chair.

"Thank you." I looked at him surreptitiously while I served salad. He had cut his hair. Probably himself, with Peg's kitchen shears. It wasn't exactly short, but it curled just below his ears now, rather than at his shoulders.

"I like your hair," I said.

He looked at me with those enigmatic eyes.

"Did you cut it?"

"Yeah."

"It looks nice."

"It does." Peg reached over to tug at the back of his hair. "You might need a little evening-up in the back. You could do that for him, couldn't you, Grace?"

I'm certain I must have grimaced. Who in their right mind would want me near their hair with a pair of scissors? Then I remembered my resolve to be agreeable. "Oh, sure! Probably."

I thought I saw a flash of humor on Ty's face before he bent low over his plate and hoovered up his lasagna and salad.

Peg asked Ty questions about life on the road. She asked me questions about what it's like to be pregnant, though I'd already shared with her plenty on that subject. She was clearly trying to help us make up for lost time.

I asked her what it was like to be the most curious woman on earth. She served us giant helpings of homemade tiramisu.

"I'm doing cleanup!" I announced cheerfully.

"Me, too," Ty said.

"Great!" Peg said. She added something about needing to make a call and abruptly disappeared.

I knew I should tie on an apron, to keep my blouse clean over my protruding belly, but I didn't want to look like the Michelin Man. I'd take my chances. I carried the lasagna pan to the sink carefully, holding it well away from my midsection.

Ty piled all the rest of the dishes up and carried them to the sink one-handed, no problem, bicep bulging. He filled the sink with warm, soapy water and started scrubbing the lasagna pan.

I picked up a dishtowel and stood beside him. He was wearing a tight gray T-shirt and jeans and smelled wonderful in that just-showered, clean man way. I wanted desperately to insinuate myself under his arm, to get as close as I could, to press my face against his shoulder; to just *breathe* him.

Then to be naked with him.

One time a month or so ago, a fellow pregnant lady had stopped me in the parenting section of a bookstore and asked me if the horniness was taking over my life. I understood in theory what she was talking about and smiled as if I could relate so as not to make her feel like a freak, but it had felt akin to reading that Inuit people survive for months at a time by eating only raw whale blubber. Fascinating, in a queasy, human-interest way, but for me it just didn't apply. I was too busy reading up on motherhood and making plans.

Now, thrust suddenly into close proximity with my impregnator, it seemed I was atingle with randy hormones! Maybe I would do some Googling on the subject tomorrow. The *New York Times* Science Page archives might have something.

I dried the last dish and Ty took the towel from me and said, "I'll finish up, wipe the table and stuff."

"Okay, thank you." *For smelling like God.*

I went to my room and sat on my bed. Checked the clock. Eight-thirty.

I went back out to the living room. He was just coming in from the kitchen. Peg's door was closed.

"Would you mind if I watch a little TV?" I asked.

"That's fine," he said.

I turned on TV Land and tucked into a corner of the couch. The second episode of *Andy Griffith* was just starting. It was one I'd seen a million times, in which Barney has been left in charge of running things in Andy's absence and he instructs his three hapless temporary "deputies."

"The minute it looks like there's gonna be trouble," Barney shrieked, "we got to NIP IT! Nip it in the bud!"

I always laugh at that line. But it's not a completely unsound theory.

Ty, sitting in the other corner of the couch, laughed, too. It was a relief to see that his anger at me hadn't killed all of his joy.

When the episode ended he reached for the remote and turned off the TV. We were quiet in the dim lamplight.

"I got a new phone," he said. He pulled it out of his pocket and showed me.

"Oh, that's good."

"I heard your message. And about a hundred messages my mom and sister left during those weeks. They're pissed off at me for letting it go so long. Guess I'll try not to let that happen again."

I nodded.

"I saw the pictures," he said.

I looked at him. He was looking at his phone, opening and closing the little hinged door on the cable slot.

"You did?" I sat up. "Did you see his—his arm, and hand?"

He nodded.

"And his face, could you see his face?"

He nodded.

"And the shape of his skull, and his spine? What—what did you think?" I asked tremulously.

He raised shining eyes. "I thought—fucking *awesome*."

I hiccupped a laugh and talked through tears, blotting my face on my sleeve. "You should see—sometimes I can see the shape of his foot, or hand, pressing through my skin. And he gets really active at night, right when I'm trying to go to sleep!"

Ty smiled, looking at my belly. I wanted to move closer, so he could feel it.

"I'm sorry," I said. "I'm *very* sorry. I would have told you earlier, but I thought . . . I was worried about how you'd react."

He shook his head and looked away.

I wondered, *What are the odds that you will ever like or trust me again someday?*

"Why did you come back early?" I asked. "Didn't you have a couple more weeks of your tour?"

It was a moment before he answered. "I got a cold and needed to go on vocal rest. It was just a few final gigs that got canceled."

"Well, I'm glad you're back safe. Are you feeling better?"

"Yeah."

I stood up. "Good night."

"Okay if I play for half an hour? Will that bother you?"

"No, that's fine."

He smiled. "I can get you some toilet paper for your ears."

"It was tissue. It doesn't work."

"I'll try to be quiet."

Ty didn't say anything when I mentioned that my mom would be coming on the weekend to bring a crib. He just nodded. But when Julia came on Saturday he was conspicuously absent.

"I'm downstairs," she called.

I got down to the street to find her double-parked and unloading the crib in pieces from the back of her SUV.

I kissed her cheek and picked up one side of the crib to carry upstairs. It was bulky, but not heavy. "This is pretty," I said, running my hand over the honey-colored wood.

"I was going to buy you a new crib, but my assistant's son just outgrew this one."

"It's perfect."

"You're not carrying anything." She looked over my shoulder at the front door. "Is there . . . um . . . anyone else here who can help me?"

I shook my head. "Peg's at the matinee."

She frowned. "All right, then. I'll do it."

"It's not heavy. I can help. I'll just be a little slow."

"Grace!" she said. "I forbid it!"

I turned toward the stoop and there was Ty. Beautiful, as usual, in jeans, Converse, and an untucked plaid cowboy shirt with the sleeves rolled up. Expressionless and enigmatic in his Ray-Bans. Chewing gum.

"Oh, hey!" I said.

He took the side of the crib out of my hands.

"Mom?" She was digging around in the backseat for the bag of hardware. She backed out and turned around.

"This is Ty. Ty, this is my mom, Julia Barnum." She started to smile and then stifled it. I could see she was experiencing reflexive fan-fluster mixed, probably, with an urge to get out her shotgun and drive us down to the justice of the peace.

Ty pushed his glasses to the top of his head, offered his hand, and gave her *the smile*.

It was freakish to watch my steely mom become discombobulated, but I certainly understood. It was the first time I'd seen him genuinely smile since he'd been back. It made my knees weak, too. It made me want to cry.

"Well, Tyler," Julia said. "What a situation! Congratulations."

I knew she actually meant it in a nice way. But it sounded like *Way to go, Sir Fucks-a-lot.*

The smile faded. "Thanks."

I tried to subtly communicate with my piercing gaze that she should stop talking now, but she misunderstood my expression.

"Grace!" She squeezed my shoulders. "Don't cry, baby."

I shrugged her arm off. "I'm not!"

"Everything will be all right now, won't it?" She looked at Ty. I wished I could let him know somehow that she sounded vaguely threatening even when ordering a vanilla shake at the Burger King drive-thru.

A corner of his lip turned up, but it was a far cry from the genuine sweetness he'd offered a moment earlier. "Sure it will," he said dryly, hefting most of the pieces of the crib.

In the time it took me to haul myself up the stairs once, they carried up all the bed pieces and leaned them against the wall in my bedroom.

There was also a large box of baby items that Ty carried up that included a bathtub and a big, firm, crescent-shaped pillow. Julia called it a Boppy. She said it was good for support under my arms when nursing the baby, or to prop the baby up against, to help him learn to sit up. I glanced at Ty. He was looking at the Boppy and at me. I wondered if he was feeling the bizarre reality of all of this as much as I was.

We sat together for a few cringe-inducing minutes of informative conversation in the living room. Julia asked Ty how his career was going, and I learned that he was about to start recording a new album. She asked about his family, what they thought about the baby. He described them, in a perfectly neutral voice, as "very excited." Then he stood up, shook Julia's hand again, and excused himself to go to a meeting.

We listened to his footsteps fade down the stairs.

I looked at Julia. "You knew he was staying here, didn't you?"

"Well, yes." She looked uncomfortable. Shifty-eyed. "Peg told me."

"You and Peg have been talking?"

"We've been in touch a time or two, yes."

"So, how are the paint fumes?" I asked.

"Hm? Oh! Better. Still kind of strong, though."

the father

I left work after lunch for my now semi-monthly checkup with Dr. Goldstein. I got off the elevator on her floor and came upon two women whom I recognized from the doctor's office, a young nurse and the woman who took my copay and scheduled my appointments. They were whispering furiously, but beat it down the hall when they saw me coming.

I checked in with the receptionist. "Hello, Miss Barnum!" Her greeting was extra energetic. "You have someone waiting for you," she twinkled.

I followed her pointing finger. Ty was slouched in a chair in the far corner, boot on knee, absorbed in a copy of *Fit Pregnancy*.

"How did you know I would be here today?"

He barely looked up. "You wrote it on the calendar on the fridge."

I took a peek at what he was reading: "You're Not Eating for Two! Healthy Nutrition for You and Your Baby."

I studied him discreetly. Why was he reading that? Why not something about how to find a maternity bra that fits? Why not a comparison of the best nipple creams? Or what to do about hemorrhoids? Did he want me to see him reading that? What was he saying? I'm fat?

He looked at me. "What."

I shrugged. "Nothing."

I sat on the chair in the examination room. Ty leaned against the exam table, still reading the magazine. My God, look at him. Beat-up cowboy boots. Low-slung jeans. Tight black tee. Bomber jacket. Baseball cap. Chewing gum.

Ignoring me, for the rest of our lives.

Dr. Goldstein came in and he rolled up the magazine and shoved it in his back pocket.

"Hello, Grace." She smiled at me and looked at Ty expectantly, with that extra underlying buzz. Either she too was a fan, or the office staff had filled her in.

"Hello, Dr. Goldstein." I gestured, openhanded, to Ty. "This is . . ." What should I call him? I had no idea. "This is my . . . um, my friend. Tyler."

Dr. Goldstein smiled politely and shook Ty's hand.

"I'm the father," he said.

"Yes, I assumed so," Dr. Goldstein said. Wow, they were doing really well at this. Didn't need me at all.

I got on the table and we carried on with the examination. He had only seen my bare belly from the bedroom doorway when he walked in on me the other night. Now he was getting the fluorescent-lit close-up, stretch marks and veins and all. He was typically unreadable. Perhaps shuddering internally.

The doctor found the heartbeat with her little microphone and he stepped closer to the table, listening with an absorbed expression. He smiled. At the doctor.

She asked us to meet her in her office. He helped me sit up and step down from the table. We went down the hall and sat in chairs across from her desk.

"Are you planning to attend the birth?" she asked Ty.

I didn't want him put on the spot about that. "My mother and roommate will be with me," I reminded her, to take off some of the pressure.

"I will be there," Ty said.

"Well, then, you two might like to do a childbirth class. They have them at the hospital." She handed Ty the schedule.

I reached over to take it from him. I tugged. He wouldn't let go. He folded up the sheet and tucked it into his pocket.

When we got outside I asked him for the class schedule.

"I'll give it to you after I look at it," he said.

"You don't need to look at it. It's taken care of. I've already read a book on Lamaze and watched a video. I know how to do the breathing."

A hot-dog vendor came toward us, pushing his cart. Ty pulled me over to a nearby stoop.

"I want us to do the class," he said forcefully. "This is my child's birth. I'm going to be there. I need to know what to do."

"Well. All right," I said, extra reasonably. "You're right. I . . . well, why don't you tell me when the class is, and I'll check my calendar."

He laughed. Unpleasantly. "You are so full of shit, Grace."

"Oh, am I?" My ever-flickering flame of hormonal temper flared and roared. *"Am I?* Who asked you to come today, anyway? Who asked you to come back at all? Don't you have a celebrity obligation somewhere? Groupies to do?" I marched toward the corner. "You just push yourself in wherever and don't think about what other people want."

He grabbed my arm and stepped in front of me. "Why should I think about what you want? You do that enough for both of us. It's all you think about. I totally get it, Grace. I have for a long time. You are better than me, and I am *not* what you want."

I was stunned. "I don't—that's not—"

"I think that you probably love me," he said. "But I know that I've never been good enough for you."

I tried to pull away. His hand tightened.

"But this"—a sharp glance at my belly—"changes everything. And no matter how crazy and irrational you get, I am *here*."

"You're hurting me!"

He let go of me and stepped back. My bag had fallen to the ground. He picked it up.

I headed for Lexington, rubbing my arm.

He caught up. "I'm sorry."

I was crying, hard. I couldn't help it.

"I'm sorry. Gracie. I was too rough."

It was unbearable, to think that he believed that about me. What an awful snob I must have seemed. I stopped and turned to him. "It's not true, Ty! I swear it's not. I do love you. I'm not better than you."

We were at the corner. The hot-dog vendor tapped him on the shoulder and handed him a pile of napkins for me.

"Okay," Ty said soothingly. "Okay."

I blew my nose. He smoothed the backs of his fingers over the red marks on my arm. I knew he didn't believe me. He was probably just worried I'd miscarry if I didn't calm down.

There was a guy across the street, staring at us. Holding a black thing at his waist. He saw me see him and started up the street.

"Ty," I said, "I think that man just took our picture."

Ty turned sharply and watched the man retreat.

"Great," he muttered.

He got me a cab.

Ty wasn't there when I got home from work. I ate supper by myself, took a bath, and watched a double Andy and Opie. Then double features of *Sanford and Son, M*A*S*H*, and *Designing Women*. Then I turned off the TV and sat quietly contemplating Ty's neat pile of belongings over in the corner by the armchair. Sometimes, when I was the only one home, I looked at his things. I didn't touch. Except one time, I picked up the shirt he had just worn, to smell it. I saw that he was reading a book, one that I haven't read. Cormac McCarthy. I got wet.

I told myself I was sleepy and went to bed. I heard Peg come in and do her post-show thing. Tea. Lighting lavender incense. A few minutes of puttering. A quiet phone conversation with Jim. Around one fifteen she went into her room and closed the door.

The Bump had hiccups. Sometimes if I changed my position he settled down. I turned onto my other side, which necessitated a precise repositioning of my support pillows, under the belly, between the knees.

Today, at the doctor, Ty had seemed so grimly determined to be responsible. So now, maybe he was with Roberta, trying to make up for lost time. He'd been here pretty much constantly the past couple of weeks. What a bummer it must be. Your twenty-four-seven sex party with the Amazon lady mud wrestler is all messed up because you feel obligated to take care of your short, round, pain-in-the-ass former friend whom you accidentally impregnated. What a great big bucket of cold water!

It made total sense. Roberta was so much more his type, exciting and beautiful. Why would Ty want an interspecies relationship with me? He was still a lion and I was still a duck.

I imagined Dan asking me for five words right about now. Pregnant. Pregnant. Fat. Alone. Pregnant.

I couldn't stop the negative loop I was in. I felt trapped. In this body. In this life. In this unchanging love for him. In how badly I wanted him . . . *needed* him.

Ty came home around one thirty. He took a shower. Brushed his teeth. Turned off the bathroom light.

Quiet.

I listened to the muffled traffic on Seventh Avenue for half an hour. Then I got out of bed and padded to the bedroom door. I skipped my robe and slippers. It was dark out there and he was, by now, asleep.

I went slowly, silently, stepping around the squeaky floorboard in the hall.

He was on the couch. Still. Peaceful. Lying on his stomach, one arm bent under his head. His beautiful, strong, naked back. I knew how smooth and warm it felt.

Was that a tattoo? I didn't remember it. A spiky, dark smudge, across his shoulder blade. Maybe a bruise? I crept closer. Hard to tell in the dim illumination from the street.

I wanted him so badly it was making my skin itch. Or maybe I was just developing a fresh patch of stretch marks. Whatever. I retreated carefully to the hallway and looked at him again. Just looked at him. Lying there. Breathing quietly. I was trembling. Why did he have this insane power over me?

"You. Are. Evil." I said it in the barest of whispers.

"So are you."

I jumped sharply and whacked my funny bone on the wall.

He rose up from the couch like a shadowy incubus in boxer briefs and came to me. I was cradling my throbbing elbow.

"Did you hit it?" he asked quietly. He was standing very close. I couldn't see his face. The light from the window behind him limned the edges of his hair like glowing filament.

"Uh-huh."

He lifted my arm and leaned down and kissed the back of it. While he was down there he tugged down the spaghetti strap of my stretchy nightgown and sucked my nipple and half of my breast into his mouth.

"Oh my *God*." My knees buckled. "*Oh!*"

He slid a steadying arm around me and drew me down the hall to my room. He shut the door firmly behind us and pulled my nightgown off over my head.

"Do you know what I'm going to do to you?" He ran a hot, liquid hand over my breasts and belly and cupped me between my legs.

I made some sort of unintelligible sound and sat on the bed.

He leaned down and told me, in my ear. Using appalling language. *Pussy*, and *lick*, and *suck*, and other rhyming, juicy, onomatopoeic words.

I came, the first time, before I ever lay down.

He was gentle, patient, and helpful when I needed to rearrange pillows or adjust my position, but also unremitting in moving us toward the objective. Clearly, not fucking was not going to be an option. I was so grateful.

Afterward he turned on the bedside lamp and uncovered me and stared at my body. I tried not to look away.

"Damn!" he said. "I had no idea."

"About what?"

"That the sight of you pregnant could make me so fucking hard. I've had blue balls for two weeks now."

It was apparently true. He was more than ready to go again. I was thrilled, having buried early-on any hope that he might still find me desirable.

I touched him, slid my hand underneath and cradled him in my palm. "Roberta would probably not be okay with me doing this."

He looked genuinely perplexed. "Huh?"

I tried to smile, to sound light and casual. "Well, she *is* your fiancée. I'm just the mother of your child."

He sat up. "Where do you get this shit? I don't have a fiancée!"

"She was with you all through the Midwest! I read about it and saw a picture!"

"She just showed up at some of those gigs. One time she said she drove eleven hours and brought a carload of people. What am I gonna do, tell her to fuck off? I bought her a drink."

"The article said you were engaged. And in the picture, you were all over each other."

"The article was bullshit. And s*he* was all over *me*."

The photo was seared in my memory, so I quickly reexamined it. It was true. His arm wasn't even around her.

"Couldn't you tell her to stop?"

He shrugged. "It wasn't out of hand. Why embarrass her in front of her friends?"

Jeez, why did he have to be so freaking *nice*? "Well, I'm sure there were others," I said sullenly.

"No. There weren't."

"Are we talking about the same thing?"

"I wasn't with anyone. But myself. A *lot*."

"When?"

"On the tour."

I stared at him. "The whole time?"

He nodded.

This just did not compute. "Wha? Were you sick?"

He gave me a very, very dry look.

"Well, then," I said slowly, lying back down. Trying to grasp the implications. "Well."

He was still looking at me.

"Then I guess you probably don't have any other babies gestating out there."

He lay down beside me and slid an arm around my belly. "As it happens, only this one."

The Bump did a flip. Ty raised his head.

"Did you feel that?" I held his hand in the right place and watched it rise over the shoving pressure of a little knee or elbow.

He laughed. "Damn, he's strong!"

"Tell me about it!"

His hand and eyes moved over me and his face changed. "I'm going to go down on you again."

"Okay!" Anything to be agreeable.

I piled up the pillows and shifted slightly to one hip to ease the pressure on my spine. And so I could breathe more easily. And so I could watch what he did to me. He was an artist at this, too.

By the way, it *was* a tattoo, on his shoulder blade. He got it in New Mexico. A little Kokopelli, playing his magical flute. In the middle of an orgasm I surged forward and touched it. I swear, I heard music.

family matters

Ty moved into my bedroom. We didn't talk about it.

My sleep improved drastically. I got tired early and went to bed knowing that Ty would eventually join me. Less than thirty seconds after my head hit the pillow I was out. Until he got in bed later and put his hands on me. Not that we had wild sex, or even all the time, and when we did it was very slow and easy. A strong, post-orgasm Braxton Hicks contraction had freaked us both out sufficiently to put heavy brakes on our lust.

He invited me to come with him to a movie premiere and a performance he was doing at a charity benefit. I declined, just too presently pregnant and historically camera-shy, but they were fun to hear about.

I got an e-mail at work from Boris with the title *You Are Outed!* He included a link to *Eye on the Apple*, a prominent New York celebrity gossip blog. I clicked on it and there we were, the top story, including that photographer's stealth photo of us. Me in my unglamorous sweater and sundress and leggings, the April wind flattening the yellow dotted-Swiss fabric tight over my big, round belly. Blowing my nose. Ty leaning over me urgently, saying something.

I read that sources had confirmed that the long-observed friendship between Grammy-nominated recording artist Tyler Wilkie and Grace Barnum, the low-profile daughter of Pop Art painter Dan Barnum, had blossomed into impending coparenthood. That Tyler had cut his tour short and had been back in the city for several weeks now, according to his watchers.

His watchers. I shuddered.

When I got home I sat on the couch next to Ty with the laptop and showed him the blog. He read it and looked at the picture tight-lipped.

"I'm sorry," he said. "I guess it could be worse. Like Princess Diana or something."

"It's not your fault. I just thought you'd want to know."

"So show me that message board."

Was he kidding? "You've never seen it?"

He shrugged. "You know I don't spend a lot of time on the computer."

It was true. He didn't spend any, that I knew of.

I showed him the fan forum, which had grown. The gallery had page after page of pictures people had posted of themselves with Ty.

"You've met a lot of people," I said, as he scrolled through them.

"Yeah. I remember some of them."

"Like who?"

"This chick asked me to sign her boob with a Sharpie."

"A Sharpie! Indelible ink, seeping into her breast tissue?"

"Yeah," he said dryly. "That's what I was thinking."

"Did you do it?"

"Of course."

I scowled. He smiled.

I clicked on the message board. The top threads read

He's Having a BABY
Grace Barnum
Ty missing various clothing
New Album?

"Hold it right there." I tried to take the laptop from him. He held on. "Give me the computer! I want to see what they're saying about me."

"So do I." He clicked on the *Grace Barnum* thread.

TysGal85: i know her from when he played a lot downtown. she always came with this hippie looking woman and sat off to the side or in the back. she always looked stuck up and a little board. the one time i saw her laugh was when he said something to her from the stage. some kind of joke. if she was there he usually went to her table between sets.

"Stuck-up!" I said. "Do I look stuck-up?"

Ty smiled in a way that made me want to pinch him, hard. "And I wasn't bored! I was *very* interested!"

Ty scrolled down and we read the next post.

ShowMeSomeLove: I read about her dad on wikipedia . . . man, having your dad bail on you that young, that's got to fuck you up!

I could feel Ty not looking at me.

MrsWilkie: Yeah my dad did that, and I'm a real case. [not]
ShowMeSomeLove: She'd better be pretty, at least! I can't tell in that pregnant picture. She's covering her face. I google-imaged her and nothing else came up.
TysGal85: not suprised you didn't find anything I think she's kind of a hermet. is she pretty. yeah kind of. i think she could try harder.

"Okay, let's shut it down," Ty said.

"I am calm." I was impressed with myself; I only wanted to destroy TysGal85 a little. Perhaps because her embarrassing inability to spell *bored*, *surprised*, and *hermit*, or to correctly capitalize and punctuate a sentence were going to hobble her in life almost as effectively as if I found where she lived and kneecapped her with a croquet mallet.

I had just finished reading *The Shining*. I don't recommend it in your third trimester.

Ty clicked on the *Ty missing various clothing* link. There were pictures of him onstage at gigs barefoot. With no shirt. There was one backstage shot of him semi-mooning the camera.

"That's dignified," I said.

"You get hot, under the lights. And I guess I might have had a coupla beers."

"You think?"

I went to fix us supper and peeked in occasionally to watch him reading the message board. He turned pink a time or two. Laughed. Scowled. "That's fucking bullshit," he muttered.

I called him to come eat.

He got up and put the laptop away. "Life just gets weirder and weirder, Gracie."

It was after supper, and we were watching *Andy Griffith*. One of the best. The one about Aunt Bee wanting to enter her terrible home-made pickles in the county fair. Andy and Barney call them "kerosene cucumbers."

I love Aunt Bee. One time after particularly great sex with Ty I rapturously quoted her: "I haven't had an experience like that since I was baptized!"

He liked that.

Anyway. We were watching.

"Can you take the afternoon off a week from Thursday?" Ty asked, at the commercial.

"Maybe. Why?"

"I'm making us an appointment at City Hall. Maybe you'd better take the whole day, in case there's blood work first. I'll call and find out."

Blood work. It shocked and hurt me, that he could even think it. "Ty! You're the father!"

He switched off the TV with the remote. "I swear, for a woman with a gigantic brain you can be as dumb as a bucket of hair. I am not talking about a paternity test. I'm talking about getting married."

I recoiled. Like he'd not only thrust a big silver cross at me, but also a braid of garlic *and* a pointy wooden stake. "Have you lost your *mind*?"

"Obviously," he said dryly.

I got up and went around to the back of the couch. "I-I just don't think that getting married is necessary."

"I do."

"It would be a terrible mistake. We would grow to hate and resent each other."

"See," he said in that same dry tone, "I thought it might make things better."

"Better for whom?"

He sighed. "Grace. You can put down the Boppy."

I looked down at myself. I was clutching the baby pillow to my chest as if it was an inflatable flotation device and my plane was about to go down over Lake Michigan.

He shook his head. "We can talk about it later, I guess." He picked up the remote and turned the TV back on.

When he came to bed I pretended to be asleep, afraid he'd bring up the subject again. I tried to understand why I was so freaked out. I loved him. Not only could I imagine spending the rest of my life with him, I wanted to. But the way the offer had come about made me feel sad. Was he just making it out of obligation, or responsibility? For whom was he doing it? The baby? Did he really want to make such a drastic change to his life? Had he really thought about it?

I went to see my dad. He was leaving for Tokyo the next day.

He made grilled cheese sandwiches and we sat on his rooftop patio and ate them while we watched rain clouds roll in from uptown.

"Dan, why did you and Julia get married?"

"You, of course."

"Damn," I moaned. "I knew it."

"What's the problem?"

"You got married because she was pregnant. And look what happened."

"Listen, I don't regret marrying your mother. And I certainly don't regret you."

"I know, but your marriage was disastrous, wasn't it? No offense."

"Are you getting married, Grace?"

"The idea has been mentioned."

He was thoughtful. "You and Ty are probably different. I think you really love each other."

"Didn't you and Julia love each other?"

"In some ways, yes. What has your mom told you about us?"

"Um, almost nothing?"

"Seriously?"

"Here are the talking points: You met in the city. She was an actress. She got married too young and should have gone to college and had a career first, though of course she's glad she had me. It just didn't work out. You cared about me, but needed to be alone so you could focus on your art."

"Do you remember me at all from when you were little?"

"You carried me to bed when I was sleepy. You drew pictures of anything I asked you to."

"And then I was gone."

I nodded.

"So," he sighed. "Time to fill in the blanks."

"Yes."

He didn't look happy about whatever it was he was going to tell me.

"Even five words would be helpful, Dan."

"I wasn't faithful." He looked at me. "I guess maybe you've heard about that."

"Yeah, I think I read something about it somewhere."

"Grace, I'm sorry. I went to Paris for three months to study. You and your mother were there with me for a while, but she was homesick and we were not getting along. I was in a lot of turmoil. My mother had died the year before, right after I turned thirty. My paintings weren't selling. I was grieving and afraid. Angry. Drinking too much, and sometimes raging. So Julia went home early and took you with her. After that, I made it all so much worse. I did hurtful, stupid things."

He sighed. "Someone told Julia about it all and she left me. I came back to New York to an empty apartment. I didn't mean to end it. Not permanently. I wanted to pull myself together and try again, but she was done." He looked at me. "You know she does not suffer fools."

"Not even a little bit," I said.

"And then she won custody of you. There were wild stories about me, and the judge was this conservative old bastard who severely limited how often I was allowed to see you. Any extra time with you was at Julia's discretion. If I had to travel for work and miss one of our days, I was not allowed to reschedule. I lost my chance and couldn't see you until the next month. It was infuriating." He looked at me. "What did you think was going on?"

"Once, when I hadn't seen you in a long time, I asked Julia if you were dead. She said 'To me he is.' I learned to not talk about you so she wouldn't get upset."

"I'm sorry. I don't think it was just about our marriage. Did she tell you about her dad?"

"She told me he died in a train accident and she never knew him."

"He died when she was two. He worked at the Hoboken station. He was a big risk-taker, very grandiose. They figured out later that he was probably bipolar, and in a manic phase. Apparently he took a dare from a coworker to lie down on the tracks when a train was coming and see who would stay there the longest. They were both killed."

"*God.*"

"Then, when she was a teenager, her mother died suddenly. A heart attack."

I nodded.

"So she was already on her own, by the time we met."

My poor mom. She had kept so much hurt so close. So private. "So . . . why did Mom let me see you so much when I got older?"

"I never stopped asking for more time with you. I called, sent letters. I offered more money than just the child support. She ignored me for years. Then one day, she got in touch. She said she was worried about you. You seemed quiet and sad, and she thought she might have made a mistake. She asked if you could come for a long visit with me. That summer you were almost thirteen. Remember?"

"Of course. I wasn't very nice to you."

Dan shrugged. "I figured at that age you would have hated me even if I'd been with you all along."

"I didn't hate you. Julia tried so hard to deemphasize you all those years and then when I spent more time with you I adored you. It was very confusing. I was scared you would leave again."

He handed me a napkin and rubbed my shoulder.

"Dan, what's weird is, she still believes in marriage like it's the Holy Grail. For me, at least."

"Maybe she dreams of a perfect love for you."

I laughed and blew my nose. "If so, I guess love with a few dents in it may have to do."

"I'm the last person who should advise you about marriage, Grace. Obviously I wasn't so good at it. All I can say for certain is, whether you get married or not—let your son be with his father as much as possible. It matters, for both of them."

I invited Julia to come on a Saturday, when Ty was at the recording studio and Peg would be gone to the matinee. I prepared all of Julia's lunch-at-home favorites, tuna salad made with apples and pickles and walnuts. Salt and vinegar chips. A big, icy glass of diet root beer.

"You're spoiling me!" she said, sitting down at the table. "Why?"

Typical Julia. Right to the point.

"Because I love you, Mom."

She smiled.

"And also . . . I want to have a talk with you. About marriage."

"Grace, are you thinking about getting married?"

"Well, yes . . . it is being discussed."

She clapped her hands, grinning. All but said "yippee."

"Mom, why does that make you so happy?"

"Well, a committed life with someone can be wonderful. And now you have the absolute right guy, no question."

"How do you know he's the right guy?"

"Well, look at how much he cares for you!"

The only time she had seen Ty in person had been while moving the crib upstairs and he had been pretty cool and impersonal. "Mom, what are you talking about?"

She started to say something and then clammed up. Sat back in her seat and stared at her sandwich. Picked it up and took a bite. It was like I was watching a film and suddenly there were a few crucial frames missing.

"Mmm, this is great tuna salad!"

"Julia!"

"Hm?" She crunched into her dill spear.

"What did you mean, he cares for me? How do you know?"

"Oh, well, you can just see it." She held her glass of diet root beer up to the light and peered through it as if she was trying to guess the vintage. "What brand is this? Barq's?"

"A&W."

"Yum!"

I could see why that acting career hadn't worked out for her.

Obviously, no one could actually give me something firm to go on. I was going to have to make this decision all by myself.

Susannah Grace, 2.0

I made a list.

Marrying Ty Pros and Cons

Pro (selfish, in random order)
Whenever I want, I will get to: Look at him. Smell him.
   Touch him. Be touched by him. Talk to him. Hear him.
   Have him. Hold him. Sleep beside him.

the eyes

the smile

we laugh at the same things

the music

help with the baby

I love his mom

Icing:

jar opening/heavy lifting/flower arranging

Pro (unselfish)
my boy will have his dad

we will be a family

Con (to varying degrees)
the penchant for partying

his scary sister

scary fans/the "watchers"

the twinge of anxiety I sometimes get when I'm especially
   loving him (what is that?)

I took a cab that afternoon to find him at the studio, which was in a renovated toy factory in Brooklyn. A knot of girls were sitting outside on the steps. I asked the driver to let me out halfway up the block and wait.

As I approached, the girls got up and came toward me. I wondered if I should turn around and go back to the cab—fast—but they were almost upon me.

"Grace?" one of them said as the four of them surrounded me. They looked like they ought to be home studying for finals.

They were blocking my way and staring like they'd never seen anything like me. "You're kind of small. And prettier than we thought," the same girl said.

Another girl stepped closer and reverently touched my belly.

"We hate you, kind of," the first girl said cheerfully. "But we like you, too! Don't take it personally."

"Okay, I won't!" I gave them a broad smile and squeezed past.

Inside the building everything was clean and bright and minimalist in that Scandinavian way, with shining blond wood floors and black leather-and-chrome furniture. The receptionist smiled when I introduced myself. She called someone and asked them to tell Ty I was there, and then directed me to the elevator.

He was waiting for me in the third-floor hallway. "What's the matter?" he asked, before I stepped off the elevator.

"Nothing. I just want to talk to you for a minute."

He looked at my belly. "Is everything okay?"

"Yes!" I laughed. "Would you relax?"

He smiled, a little. His shoulders settled.

I looked around. There were framed records and album covers lining the hallway walls, each with its own small ceiling spotlight.

He took my arm and led me down the hall to the room where he was recording. He introduced me to the engineers and musicians. Two of them, the drummer and bass player, had been on tour with him. I felt like he must have said good things because they greeted me kindly, as if they already knew me. One of them suggested that Ty and I come out to their house on Long Island to meet his wife and kids and have a cookout. I eagerly agreed, so relieved to feel approval from Ty's friends.

Ty took me into an office with a big desk and a leather couch, where we sat.

"Hey, don't you have one of those?" I asked, pointing at the shiny, framed CDs on the wall above the couch.

"Yeah."

"Is it really made of platinum?"

"Nah, plastic, I think."

"Where is it?"

"Hanging next to the deer head."

I winced. He smiled.

How to begin? "I—I've been thinking about what you said the other night. And, well, okay. I think it's a great idea. Let's do it!"

He stared at me. Perhaps not clear on what I was saying.

"Let's get . . ." I found I couldn't quite say the m-word. ". . . hitched."

He leaned back into the corner of the couch, eyes narrowed at me.

"Ty, do you want to?"

He sat forward slowly, elbows on knees, hands clasped. He looked at the floor for a long time. Scratched his neck. He looked at me and shrugged. "I think it's worth a try."

You'd think he was talking about experimenting with a new brand of shaving gel.

"Okay," he said briskly, standing up. "Listen, I have to go back in now, they're waiting on me to cut a track."

"Okay." I struggled to rise from the low couch. He took my arms and hauled me up. "So, should we, um, should we call City Hall and make an appointment?"

"We have one," he said. "Next Thursday at three forty-five."

"Oh . . . all right. Okay. I think that will be fine. I'll just check with my mom, and Peg."

"I found out we don't need blood tests." He ushered me into the hall. "But we have to go down to the municipal building at least twenty-four hours before to get the license."

His friends were going back into the recording room.

"Hey, I'm coming," he called to them. He gave me a quick kiss on the cheek and a wave as the elevator doors closed.

The girls outside were gone. I walked down the sidewalk slowly, my mind churning.

WTF, with the appointment? Had he been that sure of himself? Of me? What did it all mean? Would I ever understand this man?

The cabdriver was waiting, as requested. He was a solicitous Middle Eastern fellow who helped me into the car. Unfortunately, his kindness sent me right over the fine, overwrought emotional edge along which I'd been sidling.

"Are you all right, lady?" he asked, over the front seat.

"I don't know!" I said between boo-hoos. "I just asked someone to ma-harry me. Or I accepted his proposal. Or something."

"And he will marry you, yes?" He was looking at my belly, worried.

"Yes. But he's not excited about it. It's not very romantic!" I wept harder, though I knew I was being ridiculous.

"But he is doing the right thing," the driver said serenely. *He* was perfectly satisfied. "I take you to your home now, yes?"

We agreed to meet on Monday during my lunch break to get the license. I took a cab down to the municipal building on Centre Street, and to the City Clerk's office. I was a little early.

A guy at the counter gave me the license application, on a clipboard. I sat in one of the waiting area chairs and started filling out my information. It was pretty quick and straightforward. Name. Birthplace. Social Security. Marital history. I had to swear there were no legal impediments to the marriage.

Then I came to this part that said

> *You are advised to carefully consider whether to change your surname or not. The various options are listed on the back of the application. Whatever your choice of surname it will be final. Although you may amend other mistakes in your marriage record a surname choice is not considered a mistake and therefore cannot be amended.*

I turned the application over and read the various options. We could be Grace Barnum and Tyler Wilkie. We could be Tyler and

Grace Barnum-Wilkie. Or Wilkie-Barnum. Grace and Tyler Barnum. Tyler and Grace Wilkie.

I tapped the pen rapidly on the clipboard, until a woman a couple of seats over asked me to please stop.

Wilkie was Ty's professional name. He wasn't going to change it, add Barnum and a hyphen, or anything. This decision was about who I was going to be.

Barnum. It was an interesting name. My father's name. My mother's name. Which made me wonder, why had she kept his crazy circus name, when she could have returned to being Julia Dalton? Probably because it was my name. Grace Barnum. Which led me to think about The Bump. What would we name him? We hadn't even talked about it, and he would be out here with us soon.

I stared at the page for minutes, batting it all back and forth in my head. Then I decided: Let's just simplify and all be Wilkies. In for a penny, in for a pound.

I neatly penned *Susannah Grace Wilkie* on the line.

I signed my name—my *maiden* name—at the bottom of the page and dated it. Susannah Grace Barnum. I would be her for only three more days, but I didn't feel all that sad about letting her go. She was kind of a mess.

Ty came breezing in and the room brightened.

"Hey, sorry." He dropped into the chair next to me.

"You're not late, I was early." I handed him the clipboard. He took off his baseball cap, shoved his hair back, cracked his knuckles, and set pen on paper. I watched him scrawl his way through the form and just hoped the clerk would be able to read it.

He slowed way down when he came to the surname part. He read the admonishment to choose your name carefully and looked at what I'd written. Turned the page over and read the various options. Turned it back over and looked again at what I'd written. Then he wrote *Tyler Graham Wilkie* on his line, next to mine. He looked at me and winked.

I smiled.

We said good-bye downstairs when I got into a cab. He was going to his parents' for the next few days, so I wouldn't see him again until we met back here on Thursday afternoon.

When I got back to work, I told Lavelle I was getting married and asked for Tuesday, Thursday, and Friday off. It wasn't a problem; with my pregnancy now so advanced, other educators had taken over my teaching schedule. She was excited for me.

"What about the honeymoon?" she asked.

"I think we already had it. About eight months ago. I'll be here Monday."

Peg went with me Tuesday to look for something to wear. We found a knee-length, sleeveless dress of the palest blue lace, with a silk band that ran under the breasts and tied in back. I actually looked kind of pretty, in an overripe, about-to-burst way. I found a pair of silver sandals that gave me some height.

That night I called Ty in a panic. "What about wedding rings?"

"I have one for you."

Yikes. He was way ahead of me on this wedding stuff.

"Okay, well, what about you?" I asked. "Do you want to wear one?"

"Of course I do."

Of course he did. Good to know. "Okay. What do you want it to look like?"

"Nothing fancy."

"Gold? White gold? Maybe it should match the one you're giving me?"

"Yeah. Make it white gold."

He had a white gold wedding ring for me.

"Okay, Ty." I felt excited and shy, all of a sudden.

"Okay. Are you all right?"

"Yes. Are you?"

"Heck, yeah!" he said, with a lot of his old cheer. God, I loved him.

"I'll—I'll be glad to, um, see you on Thursday."

"Okay, Gracie. Me, too."

"Well, 'bye."

"'Bye, darlin'."

Wednesday I slipped out of the office and walked over to the diamond district to look for Ty's ring. In a store on Forty-seventh I bought a plain, white-gold band. I also got him a wedding present, a watch that cost me the equivalent of a month's pay. I'd never seen him wear one. Maybe that was the problem all this time. Though I had noticed that since he'd come back from the tour he'd hardly been late for anything.

Julia was at the apartment when I got home. She was spending the night.

Before Peg left for work, I heard her on the phone in her room, telling someone that all was well and we would be there.

"Who was that?" I asked when she came out into the living room.

"Ty."

I must have looked mulish, because she quickly added, "He said he tried to call you but your phone is off. Don't worry about calling him, he's going to dinner with friends. He'll see you tomorrow."

"Great," I muttered. Imagining the bachelor party. Lots of b-words flashed through my mind. Boobs. Beer. BJs? It was, theoretically, his last chance to be nasty with a complete stranger.

Julia was extremely solicitous, obviously afraid I was going to bolt. She massaged my scalp. Patted my hand. Rubbed my feet. She ordered takeout for us, and we sat on the couch and ate pasta e fagioli and watched a story on the health channel about a woman having a ninety-five-pound tumor surgically removed. Then I went to bed.

At almost midnight, my cell rang.

"Hey," he said. "I guess I woke you. Sorry."

"No, it's okay. How was dinner?"

"All right. It was me and Bogue and Dennis and some other guys."

"Dennis the mean cousin?"

"Yeah. He's still an idiot."

"Why was he invited?"

"Bogue asked my mom what relatives he should invite."

"So how was the food?"

"Not bad, Hooters has an awesome steak sandwich."

I knew it. They were probably off to the Hustler Club next for a few lap dances. "Well, that sounds great. Party on!"

He was laughing. Fine.

"I'm home now," he said. "I'll see you tomorrow. Three fifteen, right?"

"Yes. Right."

"Hey, Gracie?"

"Hm?"

"What are you wearing?"

"I'm naked, of course. Except for these stiletto heels. They keep getting caught in the sheets."

"Awesome."

leap

Early morning I lay in bed a long time, trying not to think.

It was impossible. I was getting married. To this guy I had only known for a few short years. Shouldn't you know someone for, like, twenty years before you married them?

And my father was going to miss my wedding.

I called Dan in Tokyo. "Hey," I said when he answered. "Supposedly I'm getting married today."

"I know. Your mother e-mailed me."

"I'm sorry, it's been so rushed . . ."

"I understand."

"But maybe you'd like to be here. Not to, you know, give me away or anything dumb like that. Just be here."

"Well, I would, of course. But don't worry about me. It sounds like you've got it all arranged, and I know you want to do it before the baby comes. You and Tyler and I can have a celebration when I get back."

"Okay."

"Get someone to take pictures."

"Okay."

"Be brave."

"Okay, Dan," I squeaked. "I—I love you."

"Yes. I love you, too."

After that I tried to sleep some more. It was useless. I sat up in bed and talked quietly to The Bump.

"Hey, in there. How's it going? I can't wait to see you. Your dad and I are getting married today. I think you are going to like him, a lot. He's strong. He has warm hands. And he's fun! You'll see. It will be cool to have him for a dad. People will think you're cool. Oh. Is that a good thing? How do I make sure you have friends who like you for you? I'm going to figure that out. You don't need to worry about that right now. I'll talk to your dad. Sometimes he thinks of things I haven't thought of. We'll both work on it. You'll be fine. *We'll* be fine."

All beautified, I looked like a very pregnant high school sophomore.

My dress worked as my something new and my something blue. For the something old and borrowed Peg had loaned me a pair of diamond-drop earrings that had belonged to her great-grandmother. They looked like something Mrs. John Jacob Astor might have worn to dinner on the *Titanic*.

I did not like, by the way, that I was thinking about the *Titanic*.

Julia and Edward had curled my hair, leaving me with long corkscrews down the sides of my face, like a Brontë. Not that they'd let me anywhere near the parsonage in this condition.

Julia had protested that my hair was too curly, while Ed just smiled patiently and gave me a look. Their paths hadn't crossed often, but he and Julia were too much alike in certain ways to get along very well.

"It will settle down," I told them sadly. I knew my hair.

Ed had brushed the curls into long waves and pulled some of it back with a silver clip. Peg had helped me into my dress, and since reaching or even seeing my feet was problematic, Julia knelt and buckled my sandals.

"You look *gorgeous*," she said.

"Thank you," I quavered, adoring not just Julia, but each of them in turn. "I love you."

Ed went off to meet Boris, while Peg and Julia escorted me downtown.

What a crowd greeted us at City Hall!

Ty's family. All of them were dressed up—Jean in elegant, pink faux-Chanel and Beck in a silky floral sundress. Even Nathan was wearing a suit.

Bogue and Allison—who, now blond and delicately pretty, couldn't be called emo anymore.

Dave, Ty's manager.

Edward and Boris, impeccably attired.

And Ty. Gone was the hideous blue suit he had worn to his grandmother's birthday party. He was wearing a vintage charcoal suit and vest that made him look like a romantic Victorian poet. He was so beautiful I had to look away.

Jean kissed my cheek and handed me a ravishing bouquet of ivory and peach roses. "Ty chose the flowers for you," she whispered.

I glanced over at him again, feeling shy and weird. It was like we were going to our prom and the most beautiful boy in school was, inexplicably, my date. He was standing with my mom. Listening to her, but looking at me. He came over to me and everyone moved away to the other end of the hall to give us a moment.

I looked up at him. He seemed so calm.

"Ready, babe?"

"Ready to rock!" I replied heartily. His lips twitched. "If I can remember to breathe," I added.

He laid a warm, firm hand on my shoulder and I felt all the crazy, kinetic energy in me just *settle*. He rubbed my collarbone lightly with his thumb. "This dress is pretty. It matches your eyes."

I looked up at him, at his autumn eyes, so uncharacteristically serious. I smiled and smoothed the lace over The Bump.

"How's he doing?"

"Asleep right now. I think I might get through my wedding without a kick in the ribs."

A clerk came into the hall and called out, "Barnum and Wilkie!"

"You just might." Ty set a hand on my lower back and guided me toward the wedding chapel. "I'm feeling pretty sweet-natured today."

Our officiant was a lady named Mrs. Garcia, who had red hair, penciled-on eyebrows, and on the lapel of her jacket, a gold cloisonné pin in the shape of a dragonfly. She took one look at me and asked if I'd like someone to bring me a chair.

I was bewildered and a little embarrassed. Yes, I was trembling, and yes, my darned heels were pitching me uncomfortably forward, given the front load I was carrying. But did I look like I was going to fall down?

Ty put a firm arm around me. "I've got her."

I looked up at him and saw such kindness and patience.

"Perfect," Mrs. Garcia beamed.

The ceremony was over in two minutes, and was generally very dignified except for the surge of audience participation at the end. There was no long preamble. No sermon. Just do you take this woman? And this man? Peg and Bogue handed us the rings. I almost dropped Ty's. Mrs. Garcia told us we were husband and wife.

Ty's hands were warm on my face, his kiss even warmer. And embarrassingly long, for heaven's sake, with all those people watching. I dropped my bouquet, because I had to grab his arms for balance. Beck stepped forward with a camera and immortalized the moment. Then someone, Nathan I believe, wolf-whistled, and there was laughter and applause.

Bogue yelled for us to get a freaking room.

We took cabs uptown. We had reserved the back room at a French restaurant in midtown that I've been going to for years. Not a big deal, but a pretty place, with simple, good food. We all sat at one big table and the waiters poured champagne. Ty told people to have anything they wanted.

I ordered something small and bland. Ty looked at my plate of pommes de terre and frowned.

"It's all I want, really," I assured him. "You know how I am with too much excitement. Plus," I patted the top of my belly, "I don't have a lot of room for food in here anymore."

"How about if we come back one day after he's moved out and nothing big is happening and you can stuff yourself?"

"Deal."

I watched my mother and Jean chat. It looked like they were connecting. "Look at our moms," I said to Ty.

He watched them for a while. "What do you think they're talking about?"

"My mom's instructing her on how to file for bankruptcy, should she ever need to. Or telling her what she ought to eat next time, and how to order it in French. It's making your mom a little tense and she's wishing she could slip off to the ladies' room and smoke a J."

Ty laughed. "Damn, you're probably right."

"I'm genetically very intuitive. My dad is psychic, did I ever tell you?"

"No way, really? I guess that makes sense."

"How so?"

"The baby paintings. That's some way deep shit going on, there."

"Speaking of babies, he dreamed I was pregnant before I told him."

Ty looked at me. "Hard to pull the wool over his eyes, eh?"

"Impossible."

"What does he say about you and me?"

I shrugged and went for a casual bite of potato. "He thinks we really love each other."

Ty nodded slowly. Thoughtfully. "Hmmm."

I looked at him and he gave me the kryptonite smile, which caused me to lose control of my small motor skills and drop my fork on the floor. He picked it up for me.

After dinner the waiters wheeled in an outrageous two-tier wedding cake.

"One layer is lemon pound cake and one is chocolate," Julia told us. "White chocolate icing. You can eat the butterflies!"

We got up to cut the cake. I pointed at the clever, lacy, butter-cream hydrangea. "You know what that reminds me of? That corsage you made for me."

"Oh, yeah." Ty touched the hydrangea and licked blue icing off his finger.

"Ty!"

"Baby, we're about to eat it."

"It's so pretty."

Ty picked up the knife. "It's like field-dressing a deer, you just gotta be willing to mess up that perfect exterior."

"That is the grossest analogy I've ever heard."

I set my hand on his and together we wrecked the cake.

Over coffee Julia told us that she had ordered the cake from a very expensive gourmet bakery and that Dan didn't know it yet, but he was paying for it. She still had his credit card number on file for the wedding that never was.

"Julia!" I was appalled.

She flipped a hand at me. "He'll thank me. It lets him be here for you."

I looked at Ty. One corner of his mouth turned up dryly.

"Maybe you're right," I grumbled.

"I know I am." She turned away to say something to José.

"Argh," I said to Ty. He squeezed my shoulder.

Ed tapped his spoon on his champagne glass and stood.

"Grace and Tyler, there's a wedding gift from us waiting for you back at Peg's. It's a DustBuster. Not really! It's something far more useful. You'll just have to wait and see. Meanwhile, we have another gift for you. A reading."

Boris handed Edward a book. He opened it and I saw the lettering on the spine. *The Prophet*.

Oh God.

He proceeded with "On Love," the reading from their wedding

that had inexplicably disturbed me. I wished I could put my fingers in my ears and lalala, but that was not an option.

There was all this stuff about love shaking your roots. Threshing you to make you naked. Grinding you. Kneading you. Baking you. And also, FYI, you can't direct the course of love.

Fair enough.

It was during a passage toward the end that the familiar unhappy twinge began. There was something about being like a running brook. Something about tenderness, and being wounded, and bleeding willingly.

My eyes were watering. I looked around. So were Jean's and Nathan's. Allison blew her nose. Ty set a hand on my leg under the table.

Ed finished the reading and he and Boris came around to us. Ed handed Ty the book and he and Boris gave us hugs.

"Congratulations to you, baby girl," Ed said in my ear. "Be strong together. Be good to each other."

Beck snapped away with the camera. Then she came over and hugged me, quite firmly.

"Take care of my brother, eh?" She gave me her sharper version of Ty's sweet smile and graciously left the words *or else* unspoken. Which I really appreciated.

Then Peg came over and knelt by my chair. "I need to tell you something."

"Please, no."

"No, it's good! I'm going to California."

"You are? When?"

"Now." She pointed to a suitcase tucked in a nearby corner.

"What the hell are you talking about?"

"I'm going to stage-manage the San Francisco production of the show for a few months."

I had known she was looking to move on; the show had been running for three years now. Antonio Banderas had left long ago and they had gone through a succession of replacements. Now it was Tony Danza. She was pretty burnt out.

"Who's going to play Ricky out there?" I asked.

"Javier Bardem, apparently he sings."

"*Oh*. That's what I'm talking about."

She smiled. "Yeah."

"I bet he smells good. You'll tell me, won't you?"

"The minute I get a whiff."

I smiled. But she was *leaving*. "What about Jim?"

"He'll come out to visit. It's not forever, I'll be back."

"I don't want you to go, Peg. What about when the baby's born?"

"You don't need me for that now."

"Well, why do you have to go tonight?"

"They want me to start Monday. This gives me a few days to settle in. And it gives you and Ty some privacy, now, and after the baby comes."

She was so good at big-picture clarity. I hugged her. Held her a long time. "I love you, Peg."

"I know. Take pictures of the baby and e-mail them to me, okay?"

My back was killing me. And it was taking a long time to get out of the restaurant with all the good-byes and well-wishing.

Bogue asked me where we were going for our wedding night.

"Home."

He frowned. "What is he, too cheap to take you to a hotel?"

"He offered. But at this point in the pregnancy I just want to sleep in my own bed."

I had my hand on the door. We were almost out, but Mr. Personality stopped yet again, for a few friendly words with José.

Typical manly small talk, till Ty heard that José was a cop in New Jersey. He looked sharply at José and, suddenly, spoke in tongues. "NJFOP?"

"Yeah, man." José grinned.

"No shit?"

"No, man."

Ty laughed and the two of them engaged in one of those complicated buddy-buddy, shoulder-bumping secret handshake things that men are genetically programmed to do. Then they went into a huddle.

I looked at Julia, wondering if she was as mystified as I was.

She smiled tightly and tapped José on the shoulder. "Hey, let's let these two get on with their wedding night!"

"Oh yeah." José kissed me and offered his hand in the normal way to Ty. "Congratulations, man."

I wanted to take the subway home. Ty balked.

"Come on, it's only a few stops."

"What if the train gets stuck in the tunnel and you go into labor?"

"That's not going to happen. I'm not due for four more weeks."

A man gave me his seat. Ty looked so cute, straphanging in his wedding clothes. I couldn't stop looking at him. He winked at me. He knew how cute he was.

The woman next to me got off at Thirty-fourth and Ty sat down.

"Where did you get my ring?" I asked. It was lovely and old-fashioned. White gold, carved with a wandering vine.

"It was Gram's. She used to say it would be for me one day, to give to my wife."

"Oh . . . Ty. I love it."

"You're not going to cry, are you?"

"Of course not!" I said stoutly.

He put an arm around me and kissed my shoulder. We were quiet till we got off at Christopher.

a breath away

Ty was in boxers and a T-shirt. I changed into the cute little nightie I'd bought at the maternity store, covered up by my plaid flannel robe.

We plopped down on the couch and turned on TV Land, just in time for the second episode of *Andy Griffith*. It was the one where

Opie meets this horrible, spoiled boy and starts imitating his awful behavior.

At the second commercial, Ty made an offhanded comment about Andy just needing to give Opie a few licks with his belt. Alarm surged through me. I muted the TV, laid a protective arm across my middle, and turned to him. "I hope you know, this child will not be spanked."

He looked rather askance at me and smiled like, *We'll see.*

"I mean it, Ty."

"Okay," he said. "But what if he drinks motor oil? Cuts the heads off all your mums? Calls you a dumb-ass dickhead? Smokes weed in the garage with his buddies at age ten? What if he sets the house on fire?"

With each listed offense I felt increasingly challenged. Ty almost had me rethinking corporal punishment, and the miscreant was still in utero!

"Did you do all that?"

"And much, much more." He looked frighteningly self-satisfied.

"Well. I will just have to hope that he has more of my genes than yours."

"Like I said, I guess we'll see," he said ominously.

We opened some of our gifts.

From Julia, we had a gorgeous, ornate, completely impractical silver pitcher.

"We'll use this when we have the Queen over for dinner," I said.

"Or we could put flowers in it."

It was depressing, how much prettier his mind sometimes was. "I would have thought of that. In a few minutes."

Beck gave us a Shark. A freakishly high-powered mini-vacuum, guaranteed to suck up nails, wood chips, gravel, and broken glass.

"What is she thinking?" I asked Ty.

He shrugged again. "She takes no prisoners. Even when cleaning house."

The box from Ed and Boris contained an expensive juicer and a lifetime Museum of Sex dual membership.

"There's a Museum of Sex?" Ty was wide-eyed, studying the bro-chure.

"Down on Fifth at Twenty-seventh."

"How did I not know about it?"

"That is one of life's true mysteries."

"When do you want to go?"

"Before the baby's big enough that we have to explain the exhibits."

"I have something for you." I went to our room and got the small gift-wrapped box.

He took it from me slowly. "I'm sorry. I have something for you, too, but it's at my parents'."

"You gave me this!" I touched the wedding ring. I couldn't imag-ine anything better.

He unwrapped the box and opened it. "Hey, look at this!"

"It's stainless steel and has automatic movement so it never needs batteries. It's the official time keeper for the Indy 500!"

"No kidding! Did you go all the way to Indianapolis to get it?"

"Ha ha."

He took the watch out of the box and slipped it on his wrist. "It's excellent! Thank you."

"Now you'll always be on time for everything."

"Absolutely."

He was smiling. I touched his face. "You know what time it is right now, don't you?"

He didn't even have to look at the watch. "Yes, I do."

It was trying to rain. We lay in bed and watched the sky above the building across the street occasionally illuminate. The lightning was actually striking somewhere in the wilds of New Jersey, judging by the low rumble of the thunder.

"Sing something to me," I said sleepily. Greedily, having already enjoyed one of the major pros of being married to Tyler Wilkie.

"What do you want to hear?"

"Something romantic. Something . . . old."

"You sing something to me."

"No, you."

He shook my shoulder gently. "Come on! Why does everyone always expect me to do all the singing?"

"You are the professional. Please, this is why I married you."

"So I'd sing to you in bed?"

"Certainly."

"I feel so cheap. And I like it!"

"It really is a win-win."

He sang, quietly. First a little ditty about the dangers of eating too many beans. Then a rude song about breasts. He finished up with "Mairzy Doats," right up against my belly.

"He can hear this, don't you think?" he asked.

"Yes, I think so."

He stayed down there and sang "Rock a Bye Baby" and "Amazing Grace." He came back up beside me and grinned.

I wound an auburn curl around my finger. "Hey, what was that with José—that NJ thing? Do you know him from somewhere?"

"Yeah!" He shook his head and laughed. "Only I just figured it out tonight. I came offstage in fuckin' Little Rock, and Dave hands me his phone, says it's my mom. First she reams me out about not returning her calls. Then she tells me she got this strange text on her cell. No name, just the initials NJFOP. And the text said 'Grace needs Tyler. ASAP.'"

I sat up in bed and looked at him. He set a steadying hand on my leg and continued.

"I flew home the next morning and headed over here to see what was up. That was when I saw you on the street and came up here with you. When I left I called and canceled the last four shows."

I stared at him. "You mean . . . when you cut the tour short, you . . . you weren't really sick?"

He shrugged. "It was useful as an excuse, so they wouldn't sue me."

"Oh. . . ."

He sat up. "What's the matter?"

I kissed him all over his face. Big, wet, teary kisses.

"What?" he laughed.

"You just gave me my wedding gift."

"I did?"

"You came home for me! Early!"

"Well, early, yeah, I'll take the points for that. But you already knew I was coming back to you."

I stared at him. Drawing a very large blank.

"You listened to the song, didn't you?"

The song. Huh? Then I pictured the FedEx envelope buried in my desk drawer. "Oh. . . . Well. Not yet."

He did not look happy.

"You said it would upset me! And I was very easily upset!"

"Oh, for fuck's sake. I was kidding!"

"I'm sorry!"

"Well, at least I know now why you still weren't talking to me. I kinda figured you might, after you heard the song."

"I will listen to it. I will."

He lay back down. "Whatever."

I snuggled close and kissed his shoulder, his hand, his chest.

He shook his head. "Man, if I'd known it would be this impressive, I'd have told you the minute I got here."

"No you wouldn't. You were mad at me."

"Well, what the fuck? That's how I find out we're having a baby?"

"I'm sorry. I was so afraid you'd be upset, or wouldn't care."

"Gracie." He sat up again, glowering. He reached over and turned on the bedside lamp. "You're the one who kept cutting me off all the time! Before I left for L.A.—"

"Ty! I didn't cut you off, at lunch that day I asked you what you wanted and you couldn't answer. You couldn't even look at me."

"Because I hadn't thought that far ahead yet. All I knew was I wanted to be near you. I wanted you to stop putting me off. And then I came back from L.A. with some clarity and we finally got close, but then suddenly you wouldn't return my calls."

"Because you were leaving! I didn't understand how you could be with me like we were, and then leave like nothing happened."

"It wasn't like that. I had a contract. I had to go do my job."

"You were excited to leave."

"Come on babe, of course I was! But I tried to talk to you before I left. And after I left. I wanted to ask you to meet me on the road whenever you could."

"You did?"

"Yeah, but I wasn't gonna leave a message about it for you to ignore. And then when you finally did call me when I was in Minneapolis, you said good-bye before I could even begin to ask. It was real clear you weren't into me."

"No, I was!"

"I thought there might be another guy. I knew I had my work cut out, but I was still coming back to try with you."

"Ty. I didn't know."

"Listen to me, Grace. You are the only girl I've ever been unable to forget. The only one who mattered. You've been messing up my sleep ever since you got down on the floor with me in your dressy clothes and bagged those dogs' feet. To help a stranger. I left knowing I was gonna have to find out who you were."

I sat up on my knees. "Your sleep got messed up? Is that all? You smiled at me that morning and wrecked my entire life."

"You put me in a permanent state of sexual frustration."

"You did that to me. And you gave me an ulcer. *Twice*."

"You made me keep coming back to walk those fucking dogs way past when I needed to financially."

"You made me abandon my stupid textbook career."

He thought a long moment and looked at me triumphantly. "You made me stutter."

I kissed him all over his face again. Gently. "You got some good songs out of it."

"My best songs."

"So far."

He got quiet. He went away, though his body was still with me. He pointed at my desk. "Can you hand me that pad and pen?"

I got them for him and he started scrawling.

"Do you need help?" I asked. "I could probably come up with

rhyming words. But not for orange. Did you know that there is no word that rhymes with orange?"

He looked at me, momentarily intrigued, then turned his attention back to the notepad. "Let me finish this," he said shortly.

Yikes. I crept out of bed and went to the bathroom.

When I came back into the room, he was no longer writing words. Now he was staring at the wall. Tapping fingers on the bed. Composing.

He surfaced long enough to say, "Bring me the guitar, would you?"

I went and got it from its stand in the corner. Then stood there before him naked and invisible, watching him strum and jot notes. I went back around the bed and got under the covers. Arranged my pillows. Stuck in earplugs. Might as well grab this opportunity for a nap. I knew him. He wouldn't be writing a song forever.

The wee, dark hours.

I was hopelessly awake. The Bump was doing his calisthenics.

Ty was awake behind me; I could tell by his breathing.

"How did José get your mom's number?" I asked.

"Your mom called Peg and got my mom and dad's names and everything else she knew about them. Then José and your mom tracked down my mom's cell number and he texted her from the New Jersey Fraternal Order of Police."

I remembered Julia telling me that Ty really cared for me. She must have been talking about how he came home immediately in response to José's text message. Then she clammed up when she remembered I wasn't supposed to know they'd contacted him. Oh, Mom. Always engineering life for my benefit.

I turned over and settled against Ty. Rested The Bump on him.

"I'm sorry," I said. "For every stupid thing I ever did. I love you. I *love* you."

"Okay." He rubbed my hip sleepily. "Okay, baby. Me, too."

The next day he went to the studio for a few hours. I dug out the FedEx envelope, made a cup of tea, put on the CD, and sat down

with the lyrics to "A Breath Away." He had dated them, October 9.
Three weeks after he'd left for the tour.

I've seen it all, see it now
and the answer is a breath away
from your lips
Had to fall, had to find out the hard way
all I want is this

And if you still got room
for another heart
tell me if you can
Or we could do away with talking
its just time to be your man
Its time to be your man

Been around, been alone
and its crazy what the miles and years can see
Bottom out, bottom line
is the diamond in the rough road back to me

And if you still got room
for a lonely heart
tell me if you can
Or we could do away with talking
its just time to be your man
Its time to be your man

Dreamed a dream, saw a sign
then its over, I remember what I see
Comes a time, come to find
that the only one who matters isn't me

So if you still got room
for a selfish heart

tell me if you can
Or we could do away with talking
its just time to be your man
Its time to be your man

Hold me like you want to
Hold me like your there
Touch me like you need to
Kiss me like you care
Love me like an ocean
Love me everywhere
Singing hey hey one more time
Ain't no where to draw no line
We're both one I understand
but its just time to be your man
Its time to be your man

And if you still got room
for another heart
catch me if you can
Or we could do away with running
its just time to be your man
Its time to be your man

I've seen it all, see it now
and the answer is a breath away

I went through half a box of tissues.

Then I went grocery shopping and came back and made him his favorite meal. Pot roast. Mashed potatoes. Sugar snap peas. Cheesecake. Well, I bought the cheesecake.

He came in the door excited, having smelled the roast all the way up the stairs. "Oh man, I was hoping that was my supper cooking!"

The smile. And kisses.

I felt shy, serving him. When I set his plate on the table he took my hand and tried to pull me onto his lap.

"No," I said. "We'll crush you."

"I don't think so." He tugged till I sat on him and shifted his legs so that not even my toes were touching the floor. Then he tried to get me to look at him. I set my forehead on his shoulder.

"What's up?"

"Nothing."

"Are you sure?"

"I listened to the song," I said into his neck.

"Oh."

"I'm sorry I didn't listen when you sent it," I continued in a small, muffled voice. "I'm an idiot."

"As I've said before, gigantic brain and dumb as a bucket of hair."

I rubbed my cheek against his. It was scratchy.

He kissed me, in lots of places. My cheek, my eyelids. Behind my earlobe (shiver). On the knob of my collarbone. Between my breasts. My breasts. Under my breasts. In the bend of my elbow.

In the palm of my hand.

nesting

We shifted into impending-baby mode. Ty scheduled his life around me, around us. Accelerated childbirth classes. Parenting classes. Weekly doctor visits. The requisite baby shower at the office, with blue crepe streamers and yellow balloons and paper plates adorned with little blue giraffes.

Lakshmi gave me a dozen onesies, a tiny New York Yankees uniform, and a toddler-size lunghi, the traditional wraparound skirt worn by Indian men.

Lavelle gave me a rubber ducky and other tub toys, tiny blue jeans and T-shirts, and a pair of tiny red Converse.

"Hey, look," Lavelle said. "Between Lakshmi and me, he's got a full wardrobe."

We had a relatively new office secretary, a girl from Queens named Jess. She gave me an enormous stuffed dog. Completely impractical for a New York apartment, but she was only nineteen and hadn't started thinking practically yet.

"I know, it's huge! I'll help you carry it home," she said.

"No worries, my husband is coming to help. I love it!"

Lakshmi made a big blue-and-white-iced chocolate cake in the shape of a baby rattle. I knew she lived all the way up in Inwood.

"How on earth did you get this here?" I asked.

"The subway. In pieces," she said grimly. "Over the last two days."

"You assembled it here?" It seemed impossible. Our "kitchen" consisted of a mini-refrigerator with a microwave sitting on top in the corner of the room.

"I iced it on Lavelle's desk."

At four o'clock sharp the air in the room changed. I knew before I looked up that Ty was standing just inside the door. People turned around to see who I was waving at, and conversation stopped. Three silent seconds passed. Then everyone snapped out of it and looked at me expectantly. Except Jess—she was still staring at him, open-mouthed.

"Everybody, this is my husband, Ty."

"Girl, we know who he is." Mykesha worked down the hall at Actors' Equity and was even drier than Lakshmi. "You got that song on YouTube."

Ty smiled and turned on his public personality.

"What's that song?" Mykesha asked.

He told her.

"That's it. Lord, if I have to hear that song one more time! My daughter thinks you're 'cute.'"

"Hey, look at what everyone gave us." I drew him over to the pile of loot on my desk. He only got a quick look before my colleagues swarmed him. I took the opportunity to slip out to the bathroom. The Bump lived on my bladder, these days.

Jess followed me into the hall.

"Grace!" she said, wide-eyed. "What the fuck?"

"Yes," I said agreeably. "Yep."

"That's Tyler Wilkie!"

"Mm-hmm." I headed on down the hall. She followed.

"This means . . . you've had sex with him!"

I paused at the ladies' room door, hoping my straining Kegel muscles could hold up for just another half-minute or so.

"Oh my God, I'm sorry! That was so rude."

"It's okay."

"Yeah, you of all people understand, right? Oh my God, wait till I tell Amber! She has a Facebook page all about him! She wanted to kill herself when she read he got married!"

"Well, I'm just going to go in here for a minute. . . ."

"Oh, sorry! Go ahead. Do you want me to wait?"

"No, no. I'll manage."

She was already halfway back to the office.

I had so little time left to be utterly selfish. I went to the Cloisters, alone. I didn't tell Ty.

I sat in the sun on a bench in the Bonnefont Cloister and watched white butterflies skim lavender buds and boats float down the Hudson. It was one of those balmy, blue-sky, gorgeous spring days that could make a questioning person believe in Goodness. In God, or Peg's Goddess. Like maybe She's right there with you, in your pocket.

When I felt quiet enough, brave enough, I leaned over and extracted Ed and Boris's wedding gift, *The Prophet,* from my bag. I opened it and found "On Love." I skimmed through all the stuff about love threshing and baking you, until I came to the dreaded passage.

> *But if you love and must needs have desires, let these be your desires:*
> *To melt and be like a running brook that sings its melody to the night.*
> *To know the pain of too much tenderness.*

To be wounded by your own understanding of love;
And to bleed willingly and joyfully.

I read and reread and let myself meet, head-on, the pain of too much tenderness. I could not pretend I did not understand. And it wounded me. It hurt, as Ty might say, like a motherfucker.

One day—let it be a long, long time from now—one of us would die.

It was the cruelest thing I had ever experienced. What if he died first, and left me here without him? How would I endure it? And in the meantime, how did I accept the idea and go ahead and love, willingly and joyfully?

It seemed like this might be the biggest reason I'd been afraid to love him.

I rubbed my belly, for comfort. The Bump was quiet, just when I could have really used some distracting internal upheaval.

The garden curator, a pretty young woman with dirt on her face, got up from weeding a nearby plant bed and came over. She sat beside me and pulled a small packet of tissues from her pocket and handed it to me.

"Thank you," I said, and blew my nose.

"Can I do anything for you?" she asked gently.

I shook my head. "I wish. Thank you."

She patted my shoulder and went back to her verbena and Saint-John's-wort.

I picked up *The Prophet* and read "On Love" again, all of it, slowly. There was a part that seemed kind of helpful.

But if in your fear you would seek only love's peace and love's pleasure,
Then it is better for you that you cover your nakedness and pass out of
     love's threshing-floor,
Into the seasonless world where you shall laugh, but not all of your
     laughter, and weep, but not all of your tears.

Okay.

So maybe I'd keep working on being less fearful, even about this, and just go ahead and love.

Because I really wanted to laugh all of my laughter. And I imagined I had a few more tears to shed, too.

You think?

Three days before my due date, the baby still hadn't dropped. Dr. Goldstein thought I might go another week, which I found unacceptable. I needed to be the only person in my body, and now. I put on my sneakers. The way people stared, you'd think they'd never seen a full-term pregnant lady jogging before. Ty came home from rehearsal and caught me, mid-block.

"Stop!" He scowled. "This can't be good. Come inside."

After we ate supper I sat on the bed and watched him put together the crib. He was underneath it, on his back, tightening the hardware. It seemed like a good time to talk about names.

We went over the obvious choices. Ty eliminated Tyler. He felt kind of okay about Graham, his middle name, as a middle name for The Bump. We looked at Daniel or Nathan, for our dads. Grandfathers' and other relatives' names. We nixed them all.

I suggested Nicholas.

"Where'd you get that?"

"My favorite actor, Nicholas Desmond."

Ty made a smirky face.

"What?"

"That skinny English guy in the movie about getting lost in Antarctica?"

I rolled my eyes. "Yes, that guy."

"He needs to eat a sandwich and get some sun."

"He's a *Sir*. He was knighted by the queen last year."

"Like I give a crap."

He always got like this about my movie star crushes. Ridiculous! "Well, what do you think of the name?"

"Too many letters."

I gave up. I lay down on the bed, exhausted. "Maybe we'll know the baby's name when we get a look at him," I muttered.

"Yeah, let's wait till we see him."

On my due date, Ty and I went for dinner at Dan's.

We ate spaghetti Bolognese that he made for us, and then the two of them spent a couple hours in Dan's studio, looking at his paintings and talking about art. I hung with them at first and then slipped away for a nap on the sofa.

On the way home in the cab Ty said, "Grace, I think I might like to try painting."

"Yep," I said. "Saw that coming."

After we got home Ty went to the bedroom to work on a song and I cleaned the kitchen and vacuumed the living room. I baked cookies and burned the bottoms. When I was scraping them into the trash can I found a scrap of paper with the words to a song. It was the one he'd started in bed on our wedding night; he played it a lot around the house.

loving late, think I got it right
shooting straight on a cloudy night
I'm on my way
watch which words your saying to me

marching through my civil war
see your eyes and I'm wanting more
I'm on my way
watch which words your saying to me
cause I might believe you

letting go my soul, my fear
feel you whisper in my ear
I'm on my way
what are these words your saying to me

bringing down the barricades
I'm in your arms now I've got it made
I'm on my way
what are those words your saying to me
I think I believe you

For the past month or so I had been having painless Braxton Hicks "practice" contractions for a couple of hours every day. That night, they woke me every few hours.

When I slept, I dreamed of rushing water.

Early morning, I sat up and tapped Ty on the shoulder. "I need to go to the waterfall."

He rolled over and looked at me with bleary eyes.

"The one by your house."

"Wha?"

"The waterfall. I need to go there today."

He rolled away and went back to sleep.

"Ty!"

He rubbed his face. "Grace. We are not traveling at this point."

"Yes, we are."

"There is no way you can do that hike. It's too steep."

"Is there another way to get to the water?"

He covered his eyes with his hand like I was giving him a headache.

"There is a way!" I crowed.

He sat up. "Grace! We are not leaving town! What if you go into labor?"

"We'll have plenty of time to get home." I kissed his hip and wrapped my arms around him. "Just for the day. One day. We drive there, go to the waterfall, and drive home. We'll be back here by late afternoon."

"And you need to do this why?"

"I don't know! I just do."

He sighed. "I'll reschedule my session."

water

Bogue lent us his car and Ty called Jean and Nathan and told them we were coming. They said they'd close the shop for an hour and meet us at the house for lunch.

They were in the garden, weeding, when we arrived. Nathan patted our backs and Jean gave us warm hugs and kisses. She rubbed my belly. "I'm ready to meet this child!"

We sat on the side porch and ate chicken salad sandwiches. Jean and I did most of the talking. Ty consumed his food in about a minute and then sat frowning at me.

"What?" I asked.

"Eat up."

"Did you tell her about castor oil?" Nathan asked Jean.

"Oh, yes—Grace—my friend Clarie is a midwife and she says if you drink a few tablespoons of castor oil it will start your labor."

"Really." I wasn't sure I was that desperate.

"She also says that if you two would . . . well . . . she says intimacy will help get things going, too."

I glanced at Ty. "Um, yeah, well, except with this baby," I said. "He's stubborn."

"But we'll keep trying, thanks, Ma." He looked at his dad and I could see they both wanted to laugh.

"Well, I'm just trying to help," Jean said. "My babies came early, so I don't know what to tell you. Now, where is it you're going?"

"I'm taking her to Jake's," Ty said shortly.

"Jake's! What for?"

"She wants to see the waterfall. Actually, we gotta go." Ty stood up and dropped his napkin on his plate.

I wasn't finished eating, but he was literally tapping his foot. I sipped some tea to wash things down and got up.

It was about twelve back-road minutes to Jake's Water World. I commented on the mostly empty parking lot.

"On the weekend it's packed," Ty said tersely. He was a man of few words today.

Jake's was a slightly seedy Poconos tourist trap. We went into the log-cabin gift shop and Ty purchased two seven-dollar tickets from a teenage girl attendant who blushed and fumbled giving him his change. She reminded him that she was his cousin Heather, daughter of his mom's niece, Beatrice.

"Oh yeah, hey, Heather!" He went around the counter and gave her a hug. Oh sure, I thought, soften up and be sweet to the little cousin and be grim and bossy with me.

"Is this your wife?" Heather asked shyly.

"Yeah, this is Grace."

I shook her hand.

"Looks like you're about to bust!" Heather said.

"Feels like it, too!"

"Well, we'll see you later." Ty marched me toward the exit.

When we got outside he grumbled something about paying money to enjoy nature.

We passed waterslides and carnival rides and concessions.

"Hey, can I get some kettle corn? I've never had it," I asked.

"It's nasty." He didn't even slow down.

I planted my feet. "What's nasty about it?"

He stopped and came back to me. "Grace, can we do this and go?"

"Why are you being so mean?"

He sighed and went over to the concession. I stood a few feet away and listened to his protracted conversation with the teenage boy running the stand. It seemed that they shared a high-school English teacher. Ty could not believe Mrs. Zawicki was still teaching, she was about ninety when he had her. He asked the boy if she still pulled people's hair if they looked at other people's test papers. She did.

"You cheated on your English tests?" I asked as he handed me the bag of corn.

"*Accidentally.* You can't help if you're looking around the room and you see something."

He marched on and I followed slowly, tasting the corn. It was weirdly sweet. I nibbled a couple of pieces before discreetly dropping the bag in a trash can along the walkway.

A staircase built into the hillside made our winding ascent and descent marvelously easy, even for an overly pregnant woman in a sundress and blue Keds.

At the top of the stairs I heard the water. Our water. We came down on the opposite side from where we had trespassed, but there it was, now thickly surrounded with vegetation, roaring from recent rains, and sparkling in the June sunlight.

Our rock, the rock I'd stood on, was on the other side. Over here I couldn't reach the fall to touch it, but I got close enough to feel the cool spray. I opened my hands to it and closed my eyes.

Bliss—the heat of the sun on my face, the mist, the breeze. I swayed a little and felt Ty take hold of my elbow.

"I'm all right," I said.

He squeezed my arm gently. "I know."

Something skimmed my face and I opened my eyes. A blue dragonfly—lacy, lazy, iridescent—hovered inches away. I laughed, and a warm river rushed down my bare legs. My shoes were soaked.

"Hey," I said to Ty, "I think my water just broke."

I have never seen his brow so furrowed.

"We have time! I haven't even had a contraction since before we left your mom and dad's."

Then I had a contraction. Considerably stronger than the ones I'd been having since last night. I grabbed Ty's arm, surprised and a little freaked out. "Oh! Ohhhhh."

He held on to me. When the contraction passed, he said, "Okay, let's go."

"Not yet."

"Grace."

"We have plenty of time. I want to stay here awhile. Is there a blanket in the car?"

"No!"

He walked me back through the park. Pretty much yelling at me the whole way, though the yelling was more in the content than in the actual volume of his voice. He couldn't believe he let me talk him into this, he couldn't believe I'd been having contractions and didn't tell him, was I expecting him to deliver this baby in the woods and gnaw through the umbilical cord like a wild animal, how could I be this irresponsible, and so on.

"You'd use your pocketknife, of course. Gnawing would be nasty and unnecessary."

He didn't smile even a little.

"I don't think this is *it*. I've been having contractions since we went to bed last night, but they're still really far apart."

"How far?"

"A half hour? Let's just start driving, I'll probably only have two or three more before we're back home."

He shook his head but did not slow down. "I can't believe you didn't tell me. Oh wait, maybe I can."

We had to stop in the parking lot for another contraction. It went on a long time, such a strong squeeze that I squatted and grabbed the bumper of a nearby car to try to take some of the pressure off my lower back. "Whoa. Wow. Ouch!"

"Shit!" Ty said. "That was less than five minutes since the last one! I'm taking you to the hospital in Stroudsburg."

We got to the car and he buckled me in. He sprayed gravel pulling out of the parking lot. "Ty," I said through gritted teeth. The squeeze was coming on again. "Take me to the house first, I have to use the bathroom."

"Hell no!"

"Ty, I have to go!"

I had two more heavy-duty contractions before we got there. It was quiet when we went inside. Jean and Nathan must have gone back to work. Ty helped me climb the stairs.

Turned out I didn't need to poop, it just felt like it. I stayed there on the toilet; it felt better than standing.

The bathroom window was open and the lace curtain moved

gently, stirred by warm, fresh country air. I breathed deeply, knowing somehow that it would strengthen me for the next round of intense pressure.

"Are you okay?" Ty asked from the hall.

"I think so."

He peeked in. "Can we go now?"

"No. Ohhhhh ohhh OH!" I could not suppress the escalating moan.

Ty came in and knelt in front of me. I leaned on him through the contraction. When it finally let up, he pushed my hair out of my face and looked me urgently in the eyes. "Grace, we need to get to the hospital."

I shook my head.

He stood and pulled me off the toilet. Tried to pull up my undies.

I shoved his hands away. "No. I want to have the baby here."

"Grace!" I thought the top of his head was going to blow.

"It will be okay, I know it will."

"No!"

"Yes! It's not that complicated. I've been reading about home birth. We can do it. It's a natural process."

"Oh, fuck," he moaned. "Fuck. You are going to kill me."

"Call your mom. Ask her to call her friend." Another squeeze was starting. I squatted and held on to the edge of the bathtub.

"What friend?"

"The midwife."

He went out to the hall. I heard him talking. He came back in, not looking so good, and sat on the edge of the tub. "She didn't pick up. I had to leave a message on her cell. My dad said she left the store a while ago, but he's gonna try to call Clarie, too."

"Okay, thank you."

"Shit, Grace! Shit! Why didn't I just keep driving?"

"Everything will be fine. Run me a bath."

While Ty was filling the tub, I got on my hands and knees and rocked. Anything, to try to shift the unbelievable pressure in my lower back. He helped me get naked and get in the bath, which felt amazing. Everything felt more manageable. What had been increasingly scary pain seemed to become simply a *force*, in the warm water.

Ty pulled off his T-shirt and knelt beside the tub. A nearly overwhelming squeeze made me grab his hands.

"Breathe, baby." He looked worried.

When the force finally passed, I kissed his hand. "It will be okay. I love you."

"I love you." He leaned in and kissed me, long and warm.

The next contraction made me yell. For once, I was louder than Ty! This huge, relentless *thing*, this energy taking over my body, made these big noises come out of me.

He urged me again to do the breathing. He puffed away, demonstrating. I tried. But instead I made this loud HO-HO-HO sound. It seemed to help.

I got on my hands and knees in the water and HO-HO-HO-ed through what seemed like endless cycles of waxing and waning intensity. The HO-HO-HO-ing also seemed to help Ty. The stark terror on his face gradually receded and he now looked guiltily, painfully amused.

"Go-HO ahead and laugh! I know-HO I sound funny!"

He completely lost it.

"HO! HO-HO-HO-HO-HO!"

He lay on the bathroom floor, eyes streaming. Seeing him laugh has always been contagious for me. I couldn't believe I was laughing in the middle of these incredibly intense sensations.

"I'm not laughing *at* you," he said, whooping it up.

"I know-HO! Oh! HO! HO! Oh. OH!" Something major was happening. "I need to—"

He reappeared on his knees at the side of the tub. "What?"

"PUSH!"

"Oh *fuck*! Are you sure it's time?"

"I HAVE TO!"

I braced my feet on either side of the faucet and Ty felt inside me. His eyes got wide. "Grace, I'm touching the top of his head!"

"Oh! Ho-HOOOOO!" I pushed, mightily. I reached down and

felt myself opening. The need to push subsided and I collapsed on my elbows. I tried to breathe and regroup.

Ty leaned in for a look. "Grace, I can see him," he said, in a shaky, awestruck voice. "He has *dark hair.*"

"Of course he does," I moaned.

I could feel the baby moving through me now, coming out of me, feel the insane, burning stretch. "Ty, I'm tearing!"

He was rubbing me, tugging, helping the crowning head squeeze through the tight band of flesh. "Grace, you're not. You're not. You're doing great."

"I can feel it!"

"You're not tearing, I swear."

There was nothing to do but hope it would end soon. I was certain I was going to be disfigured for life.

Ty cradled the baby's head as it came out. "Grace! Look at his face!"

Yeah, yeah, plenty of time for that later. I needed my vagina back. Now. I pushed.

"Hold on, stop! The cord—"

"What?"

Ty pulled the umbilical cord over the baby's head and out of the way, and then I didn't have to push anymore, he rotated on his own and rushed out of me.

He slipped through Ty's hands, and I will never forget him floating there for a moment, arms and legs spread-eagled, like a wrinkly, naked little astronaut still attached to the mother ship.

Jake's water world.

Ty scooped the baby up and he blinked, taking us in. Totally unimpressed.

"Jacob!" I gasped. "You're here!"

Ty was crying. He laid this strange, incredibly solid little person on my belly and I held him with both hands. His skin was so hot! And purplish white. The umbilical cord was pulsing. We felt it with our fingertips and looked at each other like *what a weird dream.*

Ty laid a towel over the baby and I tucked it around him and held him to my breast. He was so calm! He lay there blinking and we watched, fascinated, as he gradually noticed the nipple under his cheek. He rubbed his mouth over it thoughtfully, intrigued. He was clearly trying to figure out the situation, as if there was a vague memory lurking on the edge of his brain. Then the light suddenly came on—we saw it happen. He chomped down on me and noisily, ferociously sucked. The intense tugging made me gasp.

Ty laughed. "All right, that's my boy."

We watched him nurse and uncovered him and softly touched him and looked at all of his little moving parts.

"Ty?" Jean's voice, coming up the stairs.

"In the bathroom!"

She came to the doorway and saw me and Jake in the bath and Ty beside us, and she burst into tears and laughter. She came in and knelt and hugged Ty and kissed me and touched the baby's head. "Oh!" she said. "Look what you did! Look!" She crawled to the door. "Clarie, they're up here!"

Clarie, a smiling, quiet woman in khaki shorts and sandals, came in and opened up a bag of midwife things and totally took over. She clamped the umbilical cord and gave Ty a pair of scissors to cut it; then she wrapped Jake in a clean towel and Ty held him while she examined me.

"You didn't even tear," she said. "That's great!"

"Next time, you'll believe me," Ty said.

"Could we not talk about next time, just yet?"

Clarie massaged my belly. More contractions, and pretty soon the placenta popped right out. She held it up and examined it. It looked like a big, bloody, blobby brain. Very sci-fi.

"Damn," Ty said. "That makes me think of—what was that movie, where the little dude busted out of the guy's stomach?"

"*Alien*," I said. Great minds.

Jean helped me clean up and get into one of Nathan's big, soft old T-shirts and into the bed in Ty's room. She had made it up with fresh, soft sheets and layered it with clean towels. It was heaven to lie down. I was sore, exhausted, emptied out.

"Hello?" Nathan, downstairs.

Ty and Jean took the baby down to him for a few minutes. Then my husband brought my son back to me and laid him in the crook of my arm, and we slept.

supercollider

While I was asleep Ty called Julia, Dan, Beck, and Bogue. He called Peg, in California, and left a message for Ed, who might still be in Croatia. He called Dave.

The baby dozed beside us while we had dinner in bed. Huge steaks with baked potatoes. Grilled veggies. Chocolate cake. I ate all my steak and large portions of everything else. On top of all that, since my milk hadn't come in yet and there was no chance of intoxicating the baby, I drank a beer.

It was a bit much after the day's exertion; I spent the hour after dinner burping. A lot. Fortunately, the guy I married thinks that kind of thing is funny, especially coming out of a girl. Turns out it was a major form of entertainment and competition when he was a kid. The baby slept on, unperturbed.

Jean came and took away our dinner trays and Ty settled in next to me. He handed me a small, familiar box. "Think you might wear these now?"

I lifted the lid. The pink diamond earrings. "I remember these!"

"When you wouldn't take them I left them here with my mom for safekeeping. Remember, our wedding night I told you I had something for you?"

"I'd rather have them now."

He helped me put them on. "You did so good, Gracie. I think I was more scared than you were."

"Yeah, I think so, too."

"Usually it's the other way around."

"I know."

"What happened?"

"I stopped thinking. I think."

"It was awesome. And funny!"

"Hilarious! Certainly the most I've ever laughed while pushing a football-sized person out of my vagina."

He looked a little concerned, but patted my hip. "Hey, don't worry about that, you know they say that everything will tighten back up."

"I know you hope so."

"Fun as it was, next time, for my mental health, we will have some sort of professional there with us."

"Again, can we talk about next time a little later?"

We uncovered our sleeping child. How to describe the newborn wonder of him?

He had thick, fine, angel-soft auburn hair that stood straight up from his head in the most touchingly comical way. We cupped his warm little tummy with the palms of our hands, encircled his arms with our fingers, kissed his tiny toes. We watched him breathe. He had a rosebud mouth that screwed up in the funniest way in his sleep. He was miniature, living perfection.

Ty looked at me. "Jacob?"

"Jacob Graham Wilkie."

"Jake." He smiled. "Yeah."

How strange, at first, waking to a fussing baby every couple of hours. He was in the bed between us, and the first few times we both sat up and Ty helped me figure out the best way to hold him. I wondered how long it would be until my milk came in and Jake would get fed. Soon, probably, given his ferociously determined sucking.

At the 4:29 wake-up I said to Ty, who had groaned but not yet mobilized, "I'm going to try this lying down." I turned on my side and pulled Jake close and gave him the bed-side boob. It worked great, except that my nipples were starting to feel just a wee bit abused.

I fell back asleep and woke in daylight to find Beck leaning over me, studying my sleeping baby. Actually watching him like a hawk.

"Hey," Beck said quietly, when she saw that I was awake. "Did it hurt?"

"Um, yes. But I don't know if I'd call it pain, exactly."

She sat beside me on the edge of the bed. "What then?"

"It was more like . . . an undertow. Did you ever get caught in one, in the ocean?"

"Yeah, down the shore a couple years ago."

"You can't fight it, you know? It's too big."

"Mom said you named him Jake."

"Jacob Graham Wilkie."

"Jacob." She reached across me and cupped his head gently. "Sweet little Jakey. No one is *ever* going to fuck with you while I'm around."

Nathan and Jean went out and bought diapers, clothes, a stroller, and a car seat for Jake, and that morning we drove back to the city, straight to our pediatrician's office. She looked him over thoroughly and confirmed what we already knew: Our son was in perfect newborn health.

When we got home, I called and made an appointment with my doctor for the next day. Then, for the fifth time since dawn, I nursed my son. He fell asleep, and Ty took him from me carefully and put him in his crib in the bedroom. I waddled to the bathroom and had a long, warm soak. Sitting on my sore bum in the car for two hours had been brutal.

After the bath I pulled on one of my now-baggy sundresses and reclined on the couch with bags of frozen peas on my breasts.

In the books and magazines, they warn you that nursing a baby is going to take a little getting used to. They say it will make you sore for a couple of weeks. They don't tell you that you will feel like someone has been industriously scrubbing your nipples with heavy-grade sandpaper and then spritzing them with salty lemon juice.

And that you will wish for morphine. Or heroin. Or coma.

Ty sat down in the armchair and picked up his guitar and contentedly strummed a little ditty. His nipples were not aflame.

"Ty."

He stopped playing.

"Would you go down to the drugstore and get me some nipple cream?"

He made a mildly cringey face. "Couldn't I buy you some tampons, instead?"

I started to cry.

He put the guitar down and stood up. "Grace! I'm going! What brand do you want?"

"How the hell do I know?" I bawled. "Buy everything!"

While he was out I called my mom and filled her in on all the minutiae and gruesome details that Ty had left out. She was fascinated and amazed that we had birthed him at home, by ourselves, and no one was deformed by the experience. We agreed that tomorrow morning she would come and stay with us a few days.

I called Dan and gave him the whole story, too. He asked if he could come right over. I said yes, of course. Didn't even hesitate.

Other people began to arrive uninvited. First Bogue and Allison rang the buzzer, waking Jake. They brought champagne and diapers. Then Dave showed up carrying a little stuffed lamb. Ty's drummer Kyle, who lived a few blocks over, came with flowers for me and a box of cigars for Ty. This was the point at which I realized we were having a party and picked up the phone and ordered food.

Dan slipped in and quietly sat beside Jake and me on the couch before I even knew he had arrived.

"Oh, hi!" I said.

My father was looking at my son. I pulled back the blanket and showed off all of Jake's special features. The bright eyes and increasingly alert expression. The neat little toes, lined up like tiny pink peas in a just-opened pod. The downy, gravity-defying hair. The shriveling stub of umbilical cord.

You'd think I'd have wept a little in this moment, but no. My father did. I'd never seen such a thing. Dan was always all calm, smiling, quiet composure. He took Jake from me and held him and his face didn't change, he still smiled and talked to me and Jake. But tears streamed down his cheeks.

So maybe that's where I got the crying gene. Ty came over and sat beside Dan and gave him a napkin to wipe his face.

"Thank you for my grandson," Dan said.

I showed Dan the wedding pictures Beck had taken. Then I excused myself and went to the bathroom, closed the door, and just sat there for a while. I was not exactly in party mode. There were too many sore parts on my body, and I'd had so little sleep. I was still bleeding. I also felt a little blue.

I came out and went to the bedroom, thinking no one would mind if I just lay down for a few minutes before the next feeding.

Ty was changing Jake's diaper on the bed. "Your mom called, she and José just came through the Holland Tunnel. They'll be here in ten minutes."

"What? Oh. Ha ha. Funny."

He gave me a bemused look. "I'm not kidding."

"Yes, you are. You are."

"Uh-uh."

I clutched my chest. "Oh *God*."

Ty gripped my arm "Baby, what is it?

"It's *Dan*!" I hissed. "What do you think it is? Oh *shit!* What do I do? Do I ask him to leave?"

Ty scowled. "No. You don't."

I got down on all fours and started looking for shoes. "I'm going out for a while. Say I went to the store."

"Grace."

I came up from under the bed with a pair of flip-flops, but Ty took them from me.

"You're going to be here when your mom sees Jake."

"Ty, you do not understand. It will be awful. Apocalyptic. Earth-swallowing black holes may form."

"So let them." He tossed the flip-flops back under the bed.

"You are really bugging me."

"You don't have to fix this. It's their shit. Let them deal with it."

I clutched my stomach. "Do we have any Tums?"

Though he was being completely insensitive, Ty could not force me to witness the initial moment of confrontation. He took the baby to the living room and I stayed in the bedroom and listened.

Sounds of entry. Julia and José, saying hello to everyone. I recognized the convivial rise and fall of my mother's voice. She was in social-queen mode. I waited for dead silence to follow when she spotted Dan. It never happened. People just chatted away.

I crept down the hall and took a peek. There they were, the two of them, on the couch. Dan still in his spot, Julia now sitting beside him, holding Jake. Ty was standing in front of them, smiling at something one of them said. I walked over and stood beside Ty. I felt shaky, so I slid my hand into his and leaned against him. He was so solid. I wanted to hide my face against his shoulder, but I resolved to be brave.

Dan looked uncharacteristically pensive, but he smiled at me and winked.

Julia was touching Jake's face with light fingers. She looked up and saw me. "Oh, my darling." Still cradling him, she stood and hugged me, one-armed. "He is so wonderful."

"Isn't he? Look." I showed her the strawberry birthmark on the back of his head.

"Just like you had," she smiled. She smoothed my hair. "You look exhausted. Sit down."

Ty squeezed my hand and let go. I sat gingerly on the couch between my mother and father. We were all focused on the baby, so no one had to say much.

After a few minutes, Julia stood up and announced loudly that everyone had to leave, that I needed to rest.

"No, really, I'm fine!" No one listened. They all vanished, except Dan. Even José gave me a quick hug and left. Julia was staying.

Ty went to the kitchen and started cleaning up all the takeout.

So, there we were. The four of us.

"Julia, you look wonderful," Dan said.

"I do look good," Julia said.

Dan smiled. "José seems like a terrific guy. What does he do?"

"He's a detective in Trenton."

Dan nodded.

We all looked at the baby.

"How's your work going?" Julia asked.

"Fine. I just sold some paintings to a collector in Japan."

Julia nodded.

"I love the wedding cake you chose for Grace and Ty."

"Oh, did you see the pictures?"

"Grace just showed them to me. Thanks so much for doing that."

"Oh, of course." She waved a nonchalant hand but snuck a mild smirk at me.

"Well." Dan got up. He touched Jake's toes. "Good-bye," he said, to Jake and Julia. I got up and walked him to the door, and as he left he patted my face. "See?" he whispered. "Everything is fine."

I went back and sat beside Julia and breathed, long and deep. That hadn't been anything like I feared. No blood. No battle. Julia looked so natural, the way she held Jake asleep on her shoulder. Way more confident and relaxed than I felt holding him. I guess practiced moms don't forget, even if it's been a long, long time. I was glad she was going to stay for a few days and help me get the hang of it.

She had a small, strange smile on her face.

"What?"

"Well, nothing. It's just that he's become so old. And so serious!"

"Dan?"

"Yes! I thought he'd be a charming, maddening boy forever."

I was up at five a.m., nursing Jake. If you wanted to call it that. More like having my nipples chewed to pieces while simultaneously starving my baby. He was getting angry at me, and who could blame him? He was doing an awful lot of energetic sucking and not getting much for his trouble. He fussed and then fell back asleep. I thought about tucking him in next to his dad, but worried that Ty might accidentally flatten him. I put him in his crib and sat at the computer and e-mailed some pictures to Peg.

I got in the shower, and while the hot water streamed over me my milk came in. It was the most bizarre tingling, filling, stretching sensation. I watched my breasts inflate and rise up like twin Macy's Thanksgiving Day Parade balloons. Suddenly they had doubled in size and were rock-hard and threatening to burst. I got out of the shower, threw on my robe, and ran to the bedroom.

"Ty!"

He jerked awake, rolled over, and squinted at me.

I pulled open my robe.

He sat up, wide-eyed. "Dayum!"

I got Jake out of the crib and brought him to the bed. Ty piled pillows up behind me. Jake latched on and his first tug unleashed a crazy, pressurized squirt of milk that sprayed all three of us. It was like someone had poked a hole in a water balloon. Jake reattached and gulped away heroically, like the semi-starved baby he was.

"Oh, my poor boy," I said. "You're so hungry."

"Holy cow!" Ty said. He had droplets of milk on his face.

I frowned. "Don't say *cow*."

He wiped his face and licked his fingers. "Mm. It's sweet." He touched my other breast. "Looks like there's plenty for me, too."

"Eh," I said. Maybe intrigued. Maybe creeped out.

He saw my conflicted face and laughed. "I'm just sayin'."

the weird summer

My life had become so strange.

I wasn't working. There was this small, utterly dependent human appended to me at all times. My body was tired, and soft, and trying to get back to normal on very little sleep.

All that crazy auburn hair of Jake's? It fell out. He became fashionably bald. My mom assured me it would grow back, eventually.

Ty was gone long hours every day, working on his record, or in meetings, or on the phone with producers and lawyers and publicists and all kinds of business people I didn't know. Doing radio and magazine interviews.

Even when he was physically home he was frequently absent. We'd be in the middle of a conversation and I'd realize he was actually no longer hearing me; the music in his head was taking over. It helped that he brought home tracks for me to listen to.

With two weeks of maternity leave left, I took Jake to visit Lavelle and Lakshmi and everybody at SASS. They were so sweet to Jake. Everyone wanted to hold him.

I told Lavelle that I had decided not to return to work, at least not during Jake's first year. I apologized for the short notice. She was wonderful about it. She asked me if I might like to do some writing from home. Grant proposals, brochures, training manuals.

I said yes, please! Anything, to stave off brain atrophy.

I also enrolled in an online memoir-writing workshop called "Telling Your Truths Without Making Everyone Hate You."

I've always thought I might like to try writing something one day. So why not start with a memoir? Just for practice, of course, and personal reflection. And I honestly thought I'd write about me and my dad. But I sat down to write the first page, and it amused me to type the words *How Tyler Wilkie Wrecked My Life*. It actually gave me a little chuckle. And then my fingers became possessed. That movie *The Red Shoes*? Where the ballerina puts the shoes on and can't stop dancing? She dances, and dances, and dances? She's crying and starving and desperate for sleep, and still dancing? It's been like that, only typing. I write with one hand while breastfeeding Jake. When I should be napping because he's napping. I take the laptop to the bathroom with me.

In spite of all his music and business distractions, Ty noticed.

"What are you writing?" he asked.

"A story."

"It's long, huh?"

"Epic."

"Can I read it?"

"I think so. When I'm finished."

"What's it about?"

"This confused person who becomes less confused."

"Autobiography?"

"Of course."

Jean and Nathan, Beck, Bogue, my dad, my mom, and José came for brunch for Ty and Beck's birthday in July.

Midafternoon, after cake, everyone but Beck left. I was in the living room feeding Jake. She and Ty were in the kitchen, cleaning up and negotiating. It started with low murmurs, but the volume rapidly escalated.

Beck: *(something unintelligible)* plans.

Ty: I never ask you for anything.

Beck: Just put him down for a nap.

> *(voices get low till Ty's rises again, exasperated)*

Ty: Take him to the park in the stroller! Come back in two
>   hours.

> *(long silence)*

Beck: What's that?

Ty: What does it fucking look like?

Beck: Add a zero.

Ty: Five hundred? No fucking way.

Beck: Right. No fucking.

> *(another long silence)*

Beck: All right. But make it one-fifty.

Ty: Seventy-five an hour. For babysitting.

Beck: Fine. See ya.

Ty: All right! Don't come back till five.

Beck: We said two hours. It could be earlier. You know he'll
>   get hungry.

Oh boy. I knew what this was about. Yesterday I had gotten the all-clear from Dr. Goldstein to have sex again.

Beck came in and took Jake from me carefully and quietly. He was asleep. "Ty wants me to take him to the park so you two can get it on."

"We can just put him in his crib."

"That's what I said. But he said you're gonna make noise."

"Me? I'm going to make noise?"

She smiled.

The indignity! "Oh, did he! Well, believe me, he—"

"Grace," she said, "please don't tell me anything sexual about my brother. I don't want to puke."

The minute she walked out the door he pulled me to the bedroom. I asked for and was allowed two minutes alone in the bathroom first, but was reminded that we had a limited time frame.

I worried that it was going to hurt. It turned out it did a little, at first, so we slowed down.

Oh, to be so close to him again. Skin-on-skin, eye-to-eye, so much of us touching the other all at once. No big belly between us. I realized that it was our first time being together like this, so unencumbered, since our long, fertile weekend last September. We were still so new to each other! But it also felt like coming home to him, finally. We were able to be together without caution or complication. With trust and excitement.

the fourth autumn

Late summer, Peg came home from San Francisco. We moved into Ty's apartment when the sublease ended. It's small for the three of us, but okay for now.

On my birthday Jake rolled over, completely over, on our bed, looking very pleased with himself. Ty pulled him back to the center and he rolled over again. And again. He was unstoppable. We laughed, and he looked at us and laughed, too, out loud. Two firsts, in one minute!

I found these words this morning on a coffee-stained piece of notebook paper.

I want to make your whole world better
I want to be your favorite song
I want to dance with you forever
and ever
til we're gone
I want to watch you while your sleeping
I want to win you when you wake
I want to be the warmest rain and
endless sunset
on your face

this is the finest moment
this is the only dream for me
and I want you
and this is the only
love
there is

this is the finest moment
this is the only dream for me
and I need you
and this is the only
love
there is
for
me

Today I printed out this memoir about us and gave it to Ty. It took him four hours, but he read it straight through.

"What do you think?" I asked. "Did I tell it right?"

"You made me look way too good. Damn, I'm sexy. I'm in love with me, after reading that."

"You were in love with you already."

"Well, now I love me even more."

He didn't say much else. After reading the whole thing. All the turmoil! All the Sturm und Drang! All the weeping! All the thwarted love!

I put Jake in his bouncy seat and followed Ty to the piano, determined to tease more out of him. "What else?"

He noodled around on the keys, quietly humming. "Your mom is like, 'Grace, be practical!' and your dad is like, 'Grace, give your heart away!'"

"Yeah."

"And you're like both of them."

"So it seems. Anything else?"

"I liked the sex."

"Oh, you did?"

"You're a good writer, babe. You should think about writing a real story next, instead of just a bunch of stuff that happened to us."

"Yeah, I'm already thinking about that."

"Awesome. Meanwhile, you may thank me."

"For?"

"Wrecking your life."

I looked at him, horrified. "Ty! I was *joking*. That was a joke!"

"I don't know," he said. "I think it might be true."

"Then it needed wrecking."

"Come here," he said.

I sat next to him on the piano bench.

"Breathe," he said.

I kissed him. And breathed.

He smiled. "Yes, Gracie. *Yes*."

author's note

The ridiculous publishing scenarios in this story are all based on real situations I either heard of from my editor friends or read about in Diane Ravitch's fascinating, infuriating book about the textbook industry, *The Language Police: How Pressure Groups Restrict What Students Learn.*

Ty's songs for Grace

"This Sign"
"Calling"
"Her"
"Something Sacred"
"Tonight"
"A Breath Away"
"Believe"
"The Finest Moment"

To learn more about the *Grace Grows* sound track of original songs written and recorded by Lee Morgan, including a bonus track from Ty, "The Bottom Line," go to www.shellesumners.com/grace-grows-book/original-songs.

Grace and Ty's playlist

"River"	Joni Mitchell
"Bell Bottom Blues"	Derek & the Dominos
"That's the Way of the World"	Earth, Wind & Fire
"Change"	Blind Melon
"Take Me to the River"	Al Green
"Maybe I'm Amazed"	Paul McCartney & Wings
"Feel It"	Kate Bush
"Janie's Got a Gun"	Aerosmith
"More Than This"	Roxy Music
"Romeo & Juliet"	Dire Straits
"Right Down the Line"	Gerry Rafferty
"Mona Lisas and Mad Hatters"	Elton John
"Have a Cigar"	Pink Floyd
"A Rock 'n' Roll Fantasy"	The Kinks
"Blue Eyes Crying in the Rain"	Willie Nelson
"Fly Me to the Moon"	Frank Sinatra
"Moon River"	Andy Williams
"I've Been Loving You Too Long"	Otis Redding

acknowledgments

Many people have helped me reach this place of wonderful fruition. I am deeply grateful to:

Tracey Post and Emily Townsend, who met me for breakfast twice a month and listened to the entire first draft of this story as I wrote it. They were wise and helpful and it meant so much that they were with me, caring about my girl Grace as she tried, and stumbled, and eventually got it right.

Jill Kearney, my beautifully gifted writer friend, who read one of my screenplays and suggested that I try writing a novel. Some years later, she read my *Grace Grows* manuscript and opened a life-changing door for me.

Ruth Pomerance, who has been steadfast in her belief in this book and its possibilities. I don't know what I would have done without her creativity, guidance, and extraordinary efforts on my behalf.

Laurie Liss, my phenomenal agent. She was willing to take a chance on a new author, guided me thoughtfully and patiently in preparing the manuscript for sale, and then sold it to my dream publisher in very tough bookselling times. Also, she has the most soothing telephone voice ever.

Brenda Copeland, my funny, dynamic editor, who brilliantly and gently eliminated everything unnecessary, rearranged scenes in clever ways, and inspired me to write additional material that made this book so much richer.

and

Laura Chasen, Brenda's shining assistant, who patiently answered my many questions and helped edit the manuscript with tremendous sensitivity and insight.

I must also thank my indispensible, expert research helpers and sources of wisdom about textbook publishing, pharmaceutical patents, natural childbirth, and shaky Spanish: Tobey Antao, Jewel Moulthrop, Kevin Townsend, Lynn Whitney, Anne Hohenberger, and Jorge Garcia Salas.

For their thoughtful reading and encouragement, I am grateful to Meg Cox, Brad Garton, Teresa Stevens, Sara Oderwald, Stephanie Cohen, Christina Chang, Karen Updike, Kearney McDonnell, Nora McDonnell, Mary Hull, Cindy Morgan, Leslie Morgan, Dr. Lee Morgan, Rachel Morgan, Florence Morgan, Julie Konigsmark, Carrie Sumners, Stacey Lynch, and my mom, Rose Hohenberger.

And finally,

Thank you to Lucy Rose Morgan, the most wonderful girl in the world, who is my inspiration in everything,

and

Lee Morgan, for sharing his life and his profound musical gifts, and for lending Ty his beautiful voice.

1. Is Grace's resistance to Ty understandable? Is it unreasonable?

2. What do you think Ty means when he urges Grace to "try to be real"?

3. What does Big Green symbolize for Grace? Why is she so traumatized when she leaves it on the train?

4. What are your thoughts about the complicated, intense relationship Grace has with her mother, Julia? Did learning of Julia's history with her own father and her marriage to Dan affect your opinion of her?

5. How was Grace affected by seeing Dan so infrequently in her childhood? How do you think this may have influenced the decisions about men that she makes as an adult?

6. The waterfall is a catalyst that helps Grace become "unstuck" at crucial times in the story. Why do you think that is?

7. Peg describes Ty as a "shaman." She tells Grace that he "entrances people," and "takes them out of themselves." Have you ever had a transcendent or deeply touching experience when listening to music, seeing a film, or reading a book? Do you believe it could be true that performers and artists provide humanity with something important and necessary?

8. How does Grace change by the end of the story? At the beginning, would she have been the kind of person who could follow her in-the-moment instinct to give birth to her baby at home?

9. Some readers might consider Grace and Ty to have opposite personalities. Grace is quiet, intellectual, and cautious, while Ty is more outgoing, elemental, and spontaneous. Why do you think they might be attracted to each other, given these differences? Who are you more like, Ty or Grace? In what ways?

10. The word *grace* has many possible meanings. Some think of it as a spiritual term meaning the intangible gifts we receive through the experience of profound, loving connection with other people, or perhaps through religious practice. Joy, forgiveness, peace, gratitude, awakening, blessing: these could all be aspects of the word grace. What does *grace* mean to you? How has grace grown in your life?

Discussion Questions

For more reading group suggestions, visit www.readinggroupgold.com.

St. Martin's Griffin